THE CAVALIER SPY

Yankee Doodle Spies series

S. W. O'CONNELL

Lanyard Press
Leesburg Virginia

The Cavalier Spy

Lanyard Press
Leesburg, Virginia 20176

ISBN: 9781737663652

Second Edition, July 2020

Cover art by Jennifer Gibson http://www.jennifergibson.ca/

Map by Bryon Line

Printed in the United States of America

For my Mother

And for the Few
Who inspired by love of country,
Marched, suffered and fought
When others slipped off
To seek comfort and safety
During the times that tried men's souls

Acknowledgments

Some talented people helped me develop this story: Paul Harpin, a former military history professor at the US Army Military Academy at West Point. Theresa Whitehead, former department head for Counterintelligence at the US Army Intelligence Center and School, provided valuable insights and thoughtful suggestions. Thanks also to Bryon Line, retired Army intelligence officer, whose map will help orient the reader to the setting. John Swift, former Director of Counterintelligence for the Department of the Army, brought his meticulous eye to the manuscript and provided invaluable commentary.

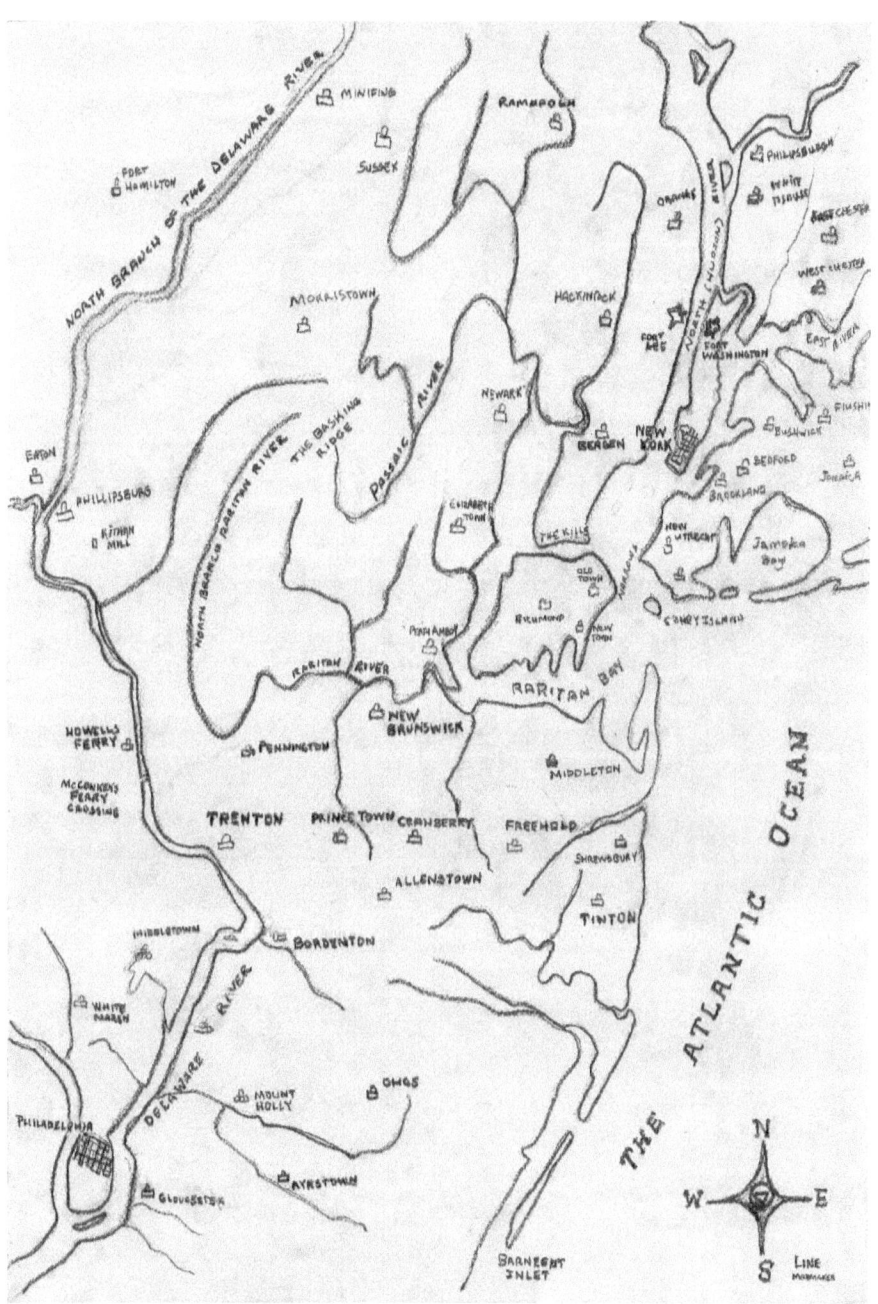

The Area of Operations September – December 1776

Letter to General George Washington's Second-in-Command, Major General Charles Lee:

Dear Sir: The Enemy are advancing, and have got as far as Woodbridge and Amboy, and from information not to be doubted, mean to push to Philadelphia. The force I have with me, is infinitely inferior in Number and such as cannot give or promise the least successful Opposition. It is greatly reduced by the departure of the Maryland flying Camp men and sundry other causes. I must entreat you to hasten your march, as much as possible, or your arrival may be too late to answer any valuable purpose. Your route nor the place to join me I cannot particularize. In these instances, you must be governed by Circumstances, and the Intelligence you receive, Let the former be secure. I hope to meet a considerable reinforcement of Pennsylvania Associators; it is said they seem spirited by this Occasion.

I am &c.

G. Washington
Brunswick, December 1, 1776

Source: The Writings of George Washington from the Original Manuscript Sources, 1745-1799.

John C. Fitzpatrick, Editor, University of Michigan Library, 1931.

...If you know the enemy and you know yourself...
Your victory will not be in doubt...
Sun Tzu

Prologue

Despite a narrow defeat at the Battle of Haarlem Heights on September 16th, 1776, Lord William Howe's army of British and German professionals solidified its grip on General George Washington's Continental Army, which was now firmly positioned on the high ground at the northern end of the Island of New York (Manhattan). As soon as the wind and tide in the treacherous *Hellegat* (Hell Gate) channel offered an opportunity, Howe, the British general in North America, initiated a series of amphibious landings along the coast of Westchester (today's Bronx). His aim was to threaten the American supply line from the Island of New York to New England.

An initial thrust at The Frog's (Throg's) Neck on October 12th was stopped by a few regiments of expertly positioned American riflemen. This forced the British to re-embark and land farther north, at a place called Pell's Point. Washington moved his forces a few miles north to block Howe. However, Howe's maneuver forced Washington to withdraw. He moved his army north along the Bronx River, positioning it in the central Westchester hills to protect his line of supply to New England and New Jersey.

On the 28th of October, Howe launched a surprise attack on the Americans, whom he caught before they could properly position themselves near the village of White Plains. He forced the Americans to withdraw, but Howe once again failed to exploit his success. Instead, he turned south and moved to assault Fort Washington, on a rocky promontory at the northern end of Manhattan.

Washington realized he needed to abandon the post before the British could trap the American defenders there. However, Brigadier General Nathanael Greene believed Fort Washington could still be held. Despite his doubts, Washington ultimately agreed to Greene's suggestion. He left the small garrison to defend itself and moved the rest of the army across the North River to the highlands of New Jersey.

Howe now held the initiative and all the benefits of eighteenth-century warfare: a well-equipped professional army; interior lines; control of the waters; and overwhelming force. Washington's strategy now was simply to avoid defeat, keep his army intact, and continue to threaten the British while maintaining communications between New England and the Middle Atlantic states. The erstwhile "war of posts" had also become a war of waiting, but waiting for what?

Chapter 1

Haarlem Heights, New York, September 1776

Lieutenant Jeremiah Creed tossed fitfully in the type of hazy sleep that comes when one is far past being overtired, and one's best efforts result in a certain numbness of both mind and body. He lay on a makeshift pile of pine needles with a piece of canvas tenting spread across them. The canopy of orange and red leaves from a tall oak tree protected him from the heat of the morning's warm Indian summer sun. Creed rested his head on his saddle, covered by a worn gray woolen blanket that formed his pillow. Not far away, his horse, a light brown gelding named Finn, nibbled at the sweet autumn grass sprouting along the gentle hillside.

While Creed slept, Privates Jonathan Beall and Elias Parker, Creed's companions and members of his command, were cooking up a batch of dough balls in a small pan of used bacon grease. The smell and crackle of the meager repast had the makings of a great feast. For the last three days, they had nothing to eat but hard tack biscuits and deer jerky purchased from one of the many sutlers that supplemented the Continental Army's woeful commissariat. During that time, Creed and his men had been constantly on patrol or in combat. Their ordeal ended with the burial of Lieutenant Colonel Thomas Knowlton, leader of the elite ranger unit to which they had been attached during the battle for Haarlem Heights.

After Knowlton's burial, a saddened Creed had a confrontation with Colonel Robert Fitzgerald, the commander-in-chief's intelligence advisor. Officially just another of Washington's many staff officers, Fitzgerald assisted Washington in one of the most critical of matters facing the army: figuring out what the British would do while also cloaking American actions from the British. This was no easy feat, as there was no American intelligence service to speak of. Washington took a personal interest in such things, both for reasons of security and practicality. However, the commander-in-chief had many other issues facing him and relied on his advisor to attend to all but the most sensitive matters. Fitzgerald worked tirelessly to establish a system of intelligence less dependent on leadership from the headquarters. But when young Lieutenant Jeremiah Creed asked to return to serve in his regiment, the First Maryland Continental Line, the outcome was never in doubt. Fitzgerald, over a strange combination of whiskey and chess, convinced Creed to become the first official intelligence officer in the Continental Army.

***

"So, Elias, do we have any salt left? We should try to add some flavor." Meager and humble as the concoction was, the smell of the dough balls crackling in the bacon fat was driving Beall wild.

Parker chuckled. "I added the last crumbs of burnt bacon to the mix so there will be flavor enough for the likes of you, but I will gladly take your portion if it is too bland for your mountain boy's taste!"

After weeks of campaigning and more than a few life-or-death experiences, the two were closer than brothers. But like brothers, they mercilessly chided each other when not covering each other's backs. Both men were in their mid-twenties and sturdily built. Beall came from a small farm town in the Maryland piedmont called Frederick, located at the edge of the lush Catoctin Mountains. Parker, partly of Indian descent, was a waterman from a fishing family in Maryland's tidewater region.

"Should we wake Lieutenant Creed yet?" Beall asked, although he already knew the answer.

"Seeing as every time we wake him it leads to a patrol or some other comfortless duty, I would say no," Parker retorted.

Unlike Beall, Parker was not an original member of Creed's former unit, the Light Company, First Maryland Continental Line. During the Battle for Long Island, First Maryland's acting commander, Major Mordecai Gist, transferred Parker from a line unit along with several other steadfast Marylanders. Since that day in August 1776, his life has been one of constant fatigue and danger. During the following weeks of patrolling and skirmishing, most of the original command of over thirty men had been killed or wounded. Parker and Beall were the only active members remaining, and they were now permanently reassigned from First Maryland to the commander-in-chief's Escort, also known as his Life Guard.

"Wonder when we'll get a chance to escort His Excellency now that we are escorts."

"I don't care where we serve, or what we do, so long as it helps end the war. I want to get home to my family. I miss my wife Marie and our newborn, little Meg." Parker held a small charcoal sketch his sister had drawn. "Have you seen anyone more beautiful?"

Marie, like Parker, was part Indian and little Meg showed it, as well.

Beall smiled. "Must take after her mama."

Parker sighed. "Sure does. My Marie has the same copper skin. And just look at that head of shiny dark hair. Hoped to have a miniature of them made before I departed with the regiment, but there was no time. Thank God this charcoal sketch came with my last letter before the fight on Long Island."

Despite the longing for home, Beall knew Parker was proud to be working with Creed and to be on "the Escort," as they sometimes referred to it. And they both were proud to be serving His Excellency. This was heady stuff for a humble farmer from the west and waterman from the shores of the Chesapeake Bay.

When Creed had returned from his last meeting with Colonel Robert Fitzgerald, he seemed a changed man. A new intensity had been added to his usual Irish good humor. And there was something odd in his comment to them before turning in to sleep.

"Well, boys, Colonel Fitzgerald has convinced me the only way to checkmate a king is to keep him in check until he has no options. And the best tool for that is the knight — in this case, a 'White Knight'."

The bacon grease sizzled, and a piece of burned bacon rind and dough splattered and seared.

Beall's wrist in one of those intense but fleeting burns. "Damn! Damnation!"

Beall had taken to swearing since he joined the army back in the spring. His exposure to toughs from the backwoods, Chesapeake watermen, Baltimore laborers, and Annapolis stevedores provided exposure to a wide assortment of expressions and habits — some good, but most bad. He had promised himself he would break this one habit before he returned home.

***

The sounds of the sizzling fat and Beall's loud expletive stirred Creed. He sat bolt upright and rubbed his eyes. The pain in his head and the rawness on his tongue were not strangers, but a just few cups of whisky had never had this effect before. Creed reckoned he was getting old. He was barely twenty-two.

Creed grinned despite the stiffness he felt in every joint and the dull pain in his head. "Cannot let a man sleep in peace for long, can ye? Just as well, but you will now pay the price and share those victuals with your victim." He stood up, pulled on his boots, and excused himself to perform his morning ablutions.

Creed's routine, whenever feasible, included a quick plunge into the nearest water and a shave. On this day, he took advantage of a nearby well in the garden of the Morris Mansion, which served as General Washington's headquarters. The garden, once a charming mix of flowers and fruit trees, was now part of the commander-in-chief's base, complete with tents and gear of his personal Life Guard, aides-de-camp, couriers, and a variety of cooks, servants, and visiting officers. He returned after fifteen minutes and sat down to his share of the meal: half a dozen "belly sinkers," a mug of black coffee, and a couple of large, freshly picked pears.

"Quite good stuff, lads."

"How is the coffee, sir?" Beall asked

"As you well know, I favor tea, but I have accustomed myself to the American and Dutch penchant for the Arabica bean. It often proves more bracing, if not more refreshing than tea."

Parker snickered. "Even after a third time boiling! I swear we live lower than field hands."

Creed smiled and nodded. "Too true, but often a necessity in this army of ever-dwindling supplies."

He helped himself to a second tin full of the bitter black brew. "Now, in a bit, lads, I shall have to meet again with the good colonel. Before I do, we must talk. When I am finished, I will ask you to either join me or return to First Maryland and forget our discussion and everything we have done in the past several weeks. Fair enough?"

Beall and Parker both nodded, almost mindlessly.

Creed looked intently at them as he spoke, "My discussions last evening with the good colonel were sobering, although they took place with no insignificant amount of whisky."

Creed's mouth formed a faint smile for a fleeting second, then disappeared as his eyes narrowed again. "We played a game of chess. Somewhere in my kit, I have a set. Does either of you lads play? Well, never mind now. The point is this: both he and I agree that this war will be long and difficult. We face a brutal and stubborn monarch who commands the greatest forces in the world and commands its commerce through a powerful navy. This king can march or sail his army at will, at least wherever there is sufficient water."

"That means the king has the advantage," Parker said.

Creed cocked his head. "Indeed, the initiative belongs to 'His Majesty.' General Washington cannot likely hope for a great victory to end this conflict quickly and to our advantage. So his strategy has to be to avoid defeat. Nibble away at the British until they are worn down and are forced to concede our freedom and independence. However, to do this, the Continental Army needs to survive, and it must present a threat to the British until... well..."

"Until what, sir?" Beall interrupted like a schoolboy.

Creed glanced left and right. "Well, there is considerable speculation that Congress can perhaps gain us allies to force the British hand. This is as much a political fight as a military one. In that sense, we have some advantages."

"Now what might those be, Lieutenant?" Parker asked. He was a shrewd and practical man in his own right. "Because I don't see any."

"Well, the cause itself, of course. And the people as well. Certainly, many Americans are loyal Tories, but most are not. Many are still undecided. However, so long as there remains a General Washington and a Continental Army, there remains hope. Where the British Army does not occupy, the patriot cause, the American cause, lives. We are closer to our people and their sentiments. And where we are not, strong measures need to be taken. We know the land and can draw people and sustenance from it. Many in England, Scotland, and Ireland are favorably disposed to the colonies and their grievances, so perhaps we shall have a political solution over the objections of King George. But there is one ingredient essential to the successful outcome of this enterprise."

"Good food and dry powder!" Parker said sarcastically.

"Well, no, what I meant was information. That is intelligence. This war will turn on that to a great deal. Colonel Fitzgerald has asked me to take part in that aspect of the enterprise. With no small amount of reluctance, I agreed. I'm not yet fully sure what that means, but I gather he wants to form a unit to collect information on the British and Loyalists, to assist General Washington."

"Are we to be spies?" Beall asked.

"In a manner of speaking, yes. And we must detect spies, too. The way the good colonel and His Excellency see it, failure to collect intelligence could lose a battle, but failure to detect a spy could lose the war, and thus the nation. So, if you follow me, when, not if, we are caught, it shall be a swift journey to the gallows if we are lucky. Do ye lads understand what I am saying?"

Beall and Parker looked at each other.

"Not everything, sir," said Parker. "But it makes no matter to us. You are our leader and we trust your judgment."

After a pause, Beall spoke, "Sir, I joined the regiment to support the cause and to be with

Simon. If he were here, he would stand with you, sir. So now I fight for two!"

Creed's heart pounded with admiration. He barely managed to hold back the tears welling in his eyes. "Good lads! You are most honorable. I am proud to be among you."

* * *

Fitzgerald offered Creed a glass of port, but Creed declined as he still felt some effects from the previous night. Fitzgerald pushed away stray strands of his hair, which he had tied back in a queue and, strangely enough, powdered white. His office in the Morris mansion was a clean, bright room. Not large, but with a nice bed and a big desk now cluttered with Fitzgerald's many papers and a map. In the corner, there was a small chest of drawers with a small white porcelain wash basin on top, elegant but not fancy. Creed noticed the room was decorated with fine wallpaper instead of paint.

"Well, Jeremiah, His Excellency needs your services once more. Your task is both complex and dangerous."

Creed smirked. "Not unlike previous engagements, sir."

"Worse, I'm afraid. He would like you to find our lost spy."

Creed thought he had misunderstood him. "Beg your pardon, sir?"

"Find our lost spy. As you know, we sent a young captain of the unfortunate Colonel Knowlton's battalion to spy behind British lines on Long Island. But now he may well be in New York. His name, I can finally reveal, is Nathan Hale —from Connecticut. A place called Coventry, I believe. Seems so many of our brave lads come from Connecticut."

"I'd like to think Marylanders are brave."

Fitzgerald ignored the retort. "Hale was to advance across Long Island and find the rear of the British Army. To obtain information on unit strength from patriots and unsuspecting Tories. Also, to report on their morale, supply, and if possible, British plans."

Creed winced. "Perhaps you should have asked him to capture General Howe as well."

Fitzgerald nodded. "I know. It seems foolish now, and it was, is. Truth be told, I advised against it. Nor am I in favor of sending you after him. But His Excellency insists we try. Still, I am adding to your troubles with a secondary mission, though between us, it is your main mission."

Creed cocked his head slightly and placed his index finger against his cheek. "My God, sir, just two missions behind British lines? 'Tis hardly worth the trip, I'd say."

"Please refrain from sarcasm, my dear boy. These are desperate times. The curtain is closing on the City of New York, and perhaps the entire island. We may not have another opportunity to infiltrate someone there for many months. Once the British consolidate their gains and establish forces loyal to them, access to the city may well be hopeless, and it most certainly will be dangerous. What I want is for you to contact one of the men given up to our late departed British spy, Jan Braaf."

Jan Braaf, a lawyer and active Whig politician in Brooklyn, had spied for the British and betrayed the American army, contributing to its defeat on Long Island. He died from a wound received while attempting to reach New York under Creed's protection. Before dying, he confessed his treason to Creed and Fitzgerald, who retrieved the valise supplied by his British spymaster, Major Sandy Drummond. The valise contained "spy paraphernalia," including codes, chemicals for secret writing, and the names of contacts, one of whom had access to a bank account for Braaf. Posing as an escaped murderer of British soldiers, Braaf was supposed to secure a civilian post near or with the rebel army and report on its activities.

"We were fortunate Braaf took a bullet on the boat ride with you, Jeremiah. And a British bullet at that."

"I daresay, sir, we were more fortunate he had some semblance of a conscience and confessed his sins before he died."

"I believe it was more from good questioning and his eternal connivance. I believe he wanted to keep his family out of future trouble. Well, it worked to our advantage, but now we must follow up."

Creed frowned. "What do you mean, sir?"

Fitzgerald swirled the remaining port in his glass. Its ruby color reflected the sunlight that radiated through the open window. They were on the second floor, so nobody could eavesdrop, at least not very easily.

"I mean, the 'spy Braaf' must try to contact the British, of course. Since you deftly hid his body, there is no *corpus delecti*, so we can assume they do not suspect his demise. But they must surely expect contact from him."

"So soon?"

"Of course, young man, we are at war. But the contact will be perfunctory. Just enough so they know he is active and has successfully placed himself near the American camp. By doing so, I hope to buy us some time until I decide how best to pursue this case. And in any event, we may delay them from sending another in his place."

"And I suppose I should find this Captain Hale while I am at it?"

Fitzgerald grinned complacently. "That is correct. His Excellency would be most pleased with the return of his spy. Captain Hale, by all accounts, seemed a very decent and honorable officer, not spy material at all."

Creed once again ignored the barb. With a coy wink, Fitzgerald downed the last drop of port and smacked the glass on the desk. He then removed some papers from the "treasure trove" of codes and contacts taken from Braaf. It provided the names of two men established by the British as Braaf's contacts in the city.

The older officer pulled another wisp of his white hair away from his pale Irish face and looked intently at Creed. "Now, here is what I propose..."

* * *

When Creed returned from his meeting with Colonel Fitzgerald, the concern on his face was obvious. He removed his cocked hat and ran his fingers through his dark hair. He then took a deep breath and sat under one of the pines.

"Why so glum, sir?" Beall asked.

"Not glum, Jonathan, concerned. We have a hard task ahead... get through British lines, find a lost spy, and convince the British that our friend Braaf is alive and well. Oh yes, and return alive of course."

Creed went over the plan in detail. When he finished, his men questioned him. "Do we rehearse this one, Lieutenant?" Parker asked.

"Not this time, much as it disturbs me to say. We have no time. We depart immediately."

"Right now?" Beall asked.

Creed nodded. "We must gain entry to the city before the British restore order and tighten security."

Parker looked incredulous. "You mean they haven't, sir?"

"Not fully. I hope to exploit the chaos that always ensues when one army supplants another in an area of occupation. Many Whigs and patriots have already fled the Island of New York."

"So, most of the Americans who stayed in New York will be hostile to the patriot cause," Beall said.

Creed nodded. "Or neutral and indifferent. We shall have to rely on our guile and the occupation's initial confusion to get through."

"Sir, we have done more than this before. You seem disturbed by something. Something more than this.

Creed lowered his head. "Our orders, the part that disturbs me, are stark. Should one of Braaf's contacts become suspicious, I am to kill him."

Beall's eyes widened. "Just like that?"

Creed nodded. "His Excellency was staking much on deceiving the British, and Fitzgerald wants nothing to frustrate the effort. We are also authorized to reveal the existence of the other spy, Hale, to help establish Braaf's credibility, proof of his validity as an agent."

Parker interjected. "Now, let me get this straight, sir. We are to save this spy, Captain... Hale? While using knowledge of his existence to convince the British that Braaf operates in the American camp. Makes no sense at all, sir!"

"Precisely my initial thought." Creed grinned and scratched himself on the lobe of his ear.

Parker's dark eyes narrowed. "Then why..."

"However, after some reflection, I realized there is a devilish madness to this."

His Excellency wants his man back, but he also wants to use Braaf against the British. He sees this war now as an intelligence struggle as much as a military struggle. And he may well be correct. Our forces need time to bring themselves up to a point where they can face the British on equal terms. That day will come, he is convinced, but until then, he must preserve the army and keep the British off balance. Intelligence will be indispensable to the success of this strategy. We are merely pawns in all this."

Beall corrected him, "You mean knights, sir, do you not? White Knights, to be exact."

Creed laughed and grabbed Beall firmly by the shoulder. "Yes indeed, Private Beall. Thank you so much for remembering that for me. "'Tis the White Knights we are now."

Chapter 2

Haarlem Heights, New York, September 1776

Everything was ready by nightfall. Creed remembered the cowboys he and his men had encountered while trying to escape the British invaders and reach safety along the Heights of Haarlem. He now decided that posing as Loyalist cowboys would provide a useful way to cloak their mission. Since the outbreak of the struggle for independence, armed bands from both sides, variously called "cowboys," "skinners," and sometimes "pirates," roamed between both armies in a struggle for control of the no man's land. Skinners were patriot irregulars. Cowboys were Loyalist irregulars. However, many worked for both sides and had little difficulty switching allegiance as the situation dictated. They were mere plunderers, brigands, and thieves. As with the other rogue gangs, Creed and his men carried no papers. It was a simple matter to declare themselves if caught by either side. As cowboys, Creed's men could carry weapons without attracting too much attention. Usually, brigands were hanged on sight, but in the chaos of the British occupation, Creed reckoned that mere thieves would be a lower priority with the authorities than Whigs, patriots, or spies.

* * *

The darkening twilight enabled them to slip past the sentries. After a half-mile of riding through the dark brush, they reached a glade faintly brushed by the last rays of light. They could see a dozen or more mounds strewn carelessly across the sloping field – corpses left after the battle. They had been stripped of all belongings, and, strangely, the animals had not yet fed on them, which were dark, bloated, and stiff.

Beall nearly choked on the smell.

Parker chortled, "Not your first sight of corpses, farm boy. Brace up. We've just begun."

Creed signaled silence and slid from Finn. He crouched behind a boulder and scanned the glade. Then he swiftly sprang back into the saddle and spoke softly to his companions, "The Enemy must be nearby. Otherwise, the creatures of the night would have left us bare bones by now. We'll need a guide. Let's see if our young friend Thomas is available."

Parker shot Creed a skeptical look. "I am sure Thomas has long moved on, sir. Might have even stayed on with Miss Emily."

Creed's heart skipped a beat at the mention of Emily Stanley's name, but he kept a blank face and simply stared straight down the darkening trail. Their sturdy mounts carried them along a path that led east from Haarlem Heights. Creed was familiar with the route since he had led a patrol in the area shortly before the battle there. Although it was only three days ago, it felt more like three years to Creed and his men.

Beall chimed in, almost gushing, "Yes, surely he remained with Miss Emily."

Creed's thoughts drifted to the beautiful young woman of nineteen who had captured his heart. Emily Stanley managed the Stanley boarding house for her father, Dr. Reginald Stanley, a staunch Tory serving with the British Army. Her father had come to America with the British to fight the French about twenty years earlier and had remained in America since. Emily's mother died during her birth. She was raised by a series of "aunts," the last of whom left when Emily was sixteen, supposedly after a falling out with her father.

But these "aunts" were nothing more than mistresses who showed little interest or sympathy for her or her upbringing. Instead, they spent their time attending social events, such as soirees, dinners, and balls. She told Creed she had several excellent tutors and also learned more from the servants of the house. They brought her a sense of reality, the need for hard work, and the harshness of life. By sixteen, she was very adept at running the boarding house and stable. But unknown to her father, Emily also secretly read many of the political treatises of the day and, in silent opposition to his Tory and Royalist sentiments, became a Whig. In the brief time he spent there, Creed and Emily became very close. At great personal risk, she helped him evacuate the mortally wounded spy, Jan Braaf, to the Heights of Haarlem.

Creed and his men had stayed at the Stanley House during the American occupation of New York. It was just north of the city, making it several miles to the south of their current location, with thousands of redcoats between them.

Creed was both distraught and relieved when Emily suddenly returned home. Although unsure that he would, or could have said the right things to her, the thought he might somehow see her again sent a chill down his spine. It was a two-edged thrill: that of a young man's dreams of a beautiful girl and the dread that his return might harm her.

Creed snapped a gruff, out-of-character response, "We shall check the post house in Yorkville first."

Creed nudged Finn into a canter, and soon they were whipping through the dark, the only sound the clumping of hooves on the loamy soil and the snap of branches against leather and the occasional face. After a silent ride, they halted.

"Fortune favored us, for along the way they thought we'd ride an hour without encountering any British," Creed whispered.

Parker let out a low whistle, "Not even a patrol or sentry."

***

Situated just off the main Post Road near the northern end of the island, the post house held a strategic position. It sat back from the Post Road and offered a vantage point to observe the comings and goings of traffic on the main artery connecting New York to Westchester and New England.

Inside the post house, a captain of infantry had just finished an evening meal of mutton and potatoes. His two subalterns were settling in to begin their meals, as they had just dispatched the last patrol.

"Don't rush your meal, gentlemen. We'll have no further business until the patrol returns at midnight," the captain said.

The patrol consisted of eighteen veteran infantrymen, almost half of the company. It would be gone for nearly four hours. Another nineteen men were already sound asleep in tents quickly set up behind the stable.

The captain swigged a second glass of Madeira. "When you're done, you may check on our little black friend. I want our steeds well turned out for tomorrow."

The subalterns laughed. In the stable, the officers' horses were now under the care of the young black groom, whom they had found to be the post house's sole occupant. The groom called himself Thomas Jeffries and claimed to be a freeman.

Well, all these dark rogues claimed to be free, thought the officer. He would now serve his rightful king, regardless of his status. "When you see him, don't let on that he will be leaving this place to join us as our valet and groom. Spoils of war, eh?"

The subalterns laughed at the captain's remark, and they all lifted their glasses in celebration of their find.

***

Creed dropped his reins onto his saddle. "We'll finish on foot. If the British have patrols out, they'll use the paths and trails to avoid breaking new ground through the thick underbrush."

They led their horses through the thick woods just north of the post-house, avoiding any of the many deer trails that covered the woods and forests in the area.

Creed's precaution was justified. To their left, they heard the shuffle of a squad of men heading north. Sentries are a bit late in getting out tonight, Creed thought. Well, even the most professional enemy made mistakes. The trick is to recognize those mistakes and exploit them. Creed hoped to do just that. They could now make out the silhouette of the post house highlighted against the night sky, with dull candlelight cascading from its windows.

Suddenly, they heard the jabbering of British voices in the dark woods. Creed placed two fingers over his lips and whispered, "Patrols sent out, the British commander and his staff are probably settling in for a night of drinking. Perhaps they would like some company."

Creed gathered his men in closer so as not to alert the British, and then quickly explained his plan of action, "Thomas, if still here, is likely in the stable. Elias, utilize your Indian heritage to good effect. Go to the stable and retrieve our young man. Jonathan and I will cover you in case the British have a stray sentry or two. "

"Easy enough to do, Lieutenant, but supposing he refuses to come? Not everyone enjoys skulking behind enemy lines for little pay and less food."

"If the lad declines to join us, you may thank him for his previous efforts on our behalf and wish him well. We shall then make our way south without his assistance."

***

Thomas thought he heard faint footsteps. Before he could turn, a large figure appeared in the doorway and stepped into the stable. When he realized it was Parker, his eyes widened with a mix of disbelief, fear, and confusion. Thomas had been torn and conflicted when he escorted Emily Stanley back across the no man's land between the British and American forces. He had intended to stay with Creed after helping him find Emily and Parker and rescue them from a band of cowboy thugs. But when Emily decided to return home, he offered to guide her back to the Stanley boarding house. Unfortunately, once there, it was too dangerous to attempt another trip through the British lines. So, Thomas returned to the only home he had ever known, the lonely Yorkville post house.

"Mister Parker! How'd you get in here? You join the British?" Thomas blurted when he saw Parker emerge from the shadows.

"We need a guide, Thomas, and Lieutenant Creed prefers experience."

The young man's eyes widened, and his face broke into a wide grin. "Lieutenant Creed? He's here, too?"

"Not far. Where are the rest of the British? And why haven't they posted sentries?"

"Not sure. They was up all day and night. Maybe they're just too tired. They ordered me to clean all the officers' tack, boots, and weapons. Suppose they got big work tomorrow. The way it looks, I will be up all night doing this."

Parker cut him off with a wave of his hand. "Not if you come with us, right now. Lieutenant Creed promises us great hardship, greater danger, little pay, and no guarantee of a return. You interested?"

"Yes, sir!" Thomas could not believe his luck.

"Then get your gear and pick out and ready the best horse for yourself. I shall work on their tack and weapons." Parker drew a long, serrated fisherman's knife from his belt and began to cut the leather straps of the officer's tack just enough so that, though unnoticeable to a casual observer, they would likely rip at the worst possible moment. When he finished, he took their pistols. Each officer had two. They were high quality and might be useful later. He then snapped their saber blades in half.

By the time all this was done, Thomas had the best post relay horse saddled and bridled, and had his few belongings tied fore and aft of the saddle. This included a long leather whip, with which he was an expert from years of driving horses. Parker had bundled the pistols in a gunnysack and placed them on the horse. Noiselessly, they led the horse from the stable.

An English voice called out a challenge from the wood line, "Where are you going with that fine horse, lad?"

A British corporal had decided to relieve himself and was stepping out of the outhouse. "And who is that with you? Are you selling one of His Majesty's horses to this rogue?"

Thomas responded coolly, "This gentleman just arrived here from headquarters looking for the captain."

The corporal, dressed only in breeches and a white shirt, approached Thomas, his eyes straining to make out the visitor's uniform and rank. "Now, I say, why would headquarters send a civilian here to see the captain? State your business, sir!"

Before either could answer that very logical question, Parker's knife was in the corporal's chest. Inside twelve feet, he rarely missed. Parker sprang on him in an instant, but as he twisted the blade from the dying man's breastbone, the corporal let out a loud and final death rattle; loud enough to alert the British. In the dim moonlight, they saw a band of soldiers running out of the trees behind the stable. Parker wiped his blade on the unfortunate corporal's shirt, sheathed it, and then led Thomas to Creed and Beall.

By the time they reached Creed's position, shouts and cries from the British echoed through the dark forest. A soldier had found their dead corporal, whose white shirt was now stained a dark red that looked especially frightening in the moonlight.

A panicked British voice bellowed for help, "Murder! Murder! To arms! To arms!"

Soon, the cries for revenge reached a fever pitch as angry redcoats scrambled to find the killer. A scattering of shots tore through the woods, but Creed and his band were already moving south along a little-known trail that ran parallel to the Post Road.

* * *

City of New York, September 1776

With Thomas as their guide, they managed to ride most of the way along a rarely traveled trail that ran parallel to and eventually crossed the Post Road just north of Kip's Bay. The young post rider knew nearly every back trail and road on the eastern half of the island. Creed recognized Kip's Bay as they passed it. The shallow inlet was where the British landed on the island of New York a few days earlier, and Creed had played a significant role in saving the commander-in-chief from capture.

Several times during the trip, they had to bolt into a wood, orchard, or farmer's field to avoid detection. Despite the early morning hour, Howe's forces were indeed imposing their will up and down the island, and patrols seemed to be everywhere.

After a close call, Creed whispered to his men, "'Tis indeed a wonder there are any forces to face our lads, as so many of these redcoats seem to enjoy occupation duty."

"Well, sir, that just adds another complaint against them and their oppression," Beall replied.

During the trip south, Creed briefly explained to Thomas the importance of their work and their need for his skills to navigate through the British lines. Thomas promised to do his best but pointed out that while he was an expert on the roads and byways along the Post Road and the upper parts of the island, he knew little about the area around the city.

They made camp in a small potato field shortly before dawn. The field was bordered by the type of stone fence so often seen in the northeast. The low stone walls, or fences, were less than a mile apart in some areas. Creed's men sat resting with their backs against one such wall. "Now remember, Thomas, we are not in uniform. To anyone we meet, we are Loyalist cowboys, just like the rascals we tangled with a few days ago."

Creed affected his version of an American back-woods accent—somewhat grating to the ear, but surprisingly passable. "If anyone asks, my name is Roland Scruggs, but I go by Burns, Root Hog Burns. Private Beall will go by Hammer Head, and Private Parker is Fish Belly."

Thomas broke into a wide grin. His white teeth were bright and impressive. "So, who am I?" the sixteen-year-old asked impishly.

Parker chimed in, "Little Colt."

Creed smiled. "'Tis sure is an apt name."

"Where'd you learn to talk like that, sir?" Beall asked.

"A skill I learned at school but perfected later. But it's not important now. We must all try to play our roles or we risk discovery." Creed looked at Parker, who was nodding and grinning. It was settled. They went from White Knights to cowboys that quickly.

They reached the northern edge of the city just as the sun started to rise, casting a faint glow from Long Island. Creed had not planned to go near the Stanley House, mainly because he was worried about Emily's safety. However, his three companions convinced him that finding a place to stay there was sensible, even for cowboys. The Stanley House was close to a key junction on the Post Road. It made sense to leave the horses there and walk into town for business. Creed set aside his doubts and reluctantly agreed.

* * *

Emily Stanley was alarmed to see a most frightening gang of ruffians enter her premises. Their leader wore a beaver-skin hat with three tails hanging down the back, a shirt, and trousers of dun-colored homespun. He walked with a familiar step, although his scruffy appearance marked him as a backwoodsman from somewhere west or north. His companions were similarly dressed in various shades of brown with old wool blankets slung across their shoulders. The man she failed to recognize as Parker wore an old broad-brimmed cap, although the face beneath it had a familiar look. Their faces were blackened with stubble, soot, and road dust.

Emily saw their weapons and rugged cowboy clothes and realized the troublemakers were more than just wandering refugees—they were something worse. Thousands of people were now coming and going around New York during the chaos of the occupation. Most were Loyalists fleeing the Continental Army or trying to get help from the reestablished Royal government. Others were Whigs trying to escape Loyalist revenge or British oppression.

The former Royal Governor of New York, William Tryon, was back, along with the hated William Cunningham, the loyalist Provost Marshal. Cunningham, a notorious figure even among Tories, despised Whigs and patriots more than they hated him, if that was possible. Tormented by Whig mobs in 1775, Cunningham fled the city with the British, but he vowed revenge and returned determined to get it.

Keeping her composure, Emily spoke to the vagabonds in a polite tone, "I believe you gentlemen are looking for one of the ordinary houses. They are in the city, near the docks, although there are a few on Broadway."

Their leader spoke with a strange back-country American accent, "Well, Miss, we ain't your fine Britishers but we be loyal fighters for King Georgie and can pay well as any men, I reckon."

She became alarmed. *These men actually intend to stay at the boarding house.* If they could pay, she suspected they must be thieves, brigands such as those who kidnapped her near

Haarlem Heights. She replied with great trepidation, "I'm sure that is true, gentlemen. But you see, these rooms are reserved for..."

Her turquoise-green eyes suddenly widened as if she had seen a ghost. "Jeremiah?"

The ruffian before her broke into a wide grin, and she threw herself into his arms and hugged him as she covered his face with kisses. Her affection was obvious, as his. They held each other longer than would normally be appropriate. She finally broke free from his embrace and warmly grasped the hands of each of his three companions.

She led them into the barn behind the house, where they could talk privately and be unseen from the lane. She couldn't hold back anymore. "What on earth are you doing here? Why those clothes? Have you left the cause?"

"I can only admit to being on unfinished business for Colonel Fitzgerald."

Emily arched her eyes and gently scolded him, "Jeremiah Creed, I am as guilty of treason to His Majesty as any of you, perhaps more so. If there is anything I can do to assist your efforts, you know I will... I must."

She knew she was right. And she knew he knew. Her assistance with the dying spy, Jan Braaf, had been invaluable. At first, unaware that he was a spy, she knew there was some nefarious business that had General Washington's interest. He father was a Loyalist, but she was not. She just prudently withheld her political leanings from him, which were decidedly pro-patriot.

Emily Stanley was, in fact, a spy—more so in some ways than Creed. Recognizing a potential British occupation of New York, she volunteered her services to Colonel Fitzgerald shortly after the Continental Army arrived in Manhattan. Fitzgerald assigned her a cover name—"Mister Smythe." As Mister Smythe, Emily began transmitting information to Fitzgerald via another spy, whose identity she did not know, but whom Fitzgerald called "Mister Jons."

The Stanley House boarders, now, for the most part, British officers, provided her a trove of knowledge, all of which she carefully noted each night when she worked on her diary. In an even greater twist, she delivered the packets of information under the escort of the young and not-so-young officers she would invite for a picnic along the river. Most of her drop-off points were in the thick bushes along the various coves and inlets around New York. Emily correctly surmised Mister Jons had some connection to the water.

Creed rubbed his stubbled face. "Very well, I can tell you we are searching for two men. One is an American officer sent behind the lines by His Excellency to report on British activities. Since New York is now in British hands, his services in that enterprise have ended. As for the other gentleman, I must merely pass on a message to him. The latter business is the more urgent and compelling."

"Who is this man?" she asked breathlessly, while wondering just how many spies Fitzgerald had engaged on the island. "As you are aware, I know most of the distinguished society of New York."

"A Mister Neeley. He is one of two men Braaf intended to meet in New York. That is all I can, all I should say." Creed was gazing intently into her green eyes.

"Well, I suspect I know the rest." She grimaced and unconsciously placed her slender arms across her breasts. Creed looked enthralled at the sight of her. Yet she wore only a bright housedress and had her hair tied up in the back, with curls the color of dark honey at her temples.

Creed smiled. "Let's hope not, Emily."

She frowned and closed one eye impishly. She loved his humor but tried not to let on too much. "There is a Neeley Apothecary near the docks by Whitehall Slip. Father does some business with him, but I have never met the man."

"Then I must meet him. This very evening. Until then, my band of cowboys needs a place to sleep."

"I can make up some rooms, Jeremiah and..."

"Emily, so long as we are here behind redcoat lines, call me Root Hog, and no, the barn is more fitting to our station. I suspect I shall need to return here in the future. The barn is also more convenient to our comings and goings … and more secure."

She thrust her delicate hands into his. "I will bring food at two this afternoon, Jeremi–uh, Root Hog."

Chapter 3

British Headquarters, New York, September 1776

That afternoon, a subaltern knocked on the door of the ornate drawing room at Beekman House, serving as headquarters for General William Howe. Howe smiled at the red-faced officer. "What do you have for me?"

The subaltern waved a letter. "Sir, you have received an urgent communication."

"From whom?"

"Major James Drummond, sir. A sergeant named Digby delivered it. He's waiting in the ante-room."

Howe had placed Major James "Sandy" Drummond in charge of security on Long Island. A dragoon officer, Drummond had distinguished himself with an aggressive reconnaissance against the Americans, which led to the nearly bloodless capture of Brooklyn and the American defense works. But what now esteemed Drummond most to Howe was that he also excelled in the recruitment of informants — that is, spies, and in so doing had already advanced the British cause.

Howe snatched the letter from the subaltern's hand and motioned for him to leave. The officer snapped to attention and hastily bowed before he stepped out of the room. Once alone, the British commander-in-chief furtively opened the letter.

Brooklyn, September 20th, 1776

My Lord,

I have the pleasure to inform you that through a most fortuitous set of Circumstances, we have captured a Rebel Agent, who entered behind our lines, in civilian clothing, with the obvious intent to spy upon His Majesty's Forces. One of my trusted Agents identified a solitary person landing on the shore of the Long Island Sound, near a Village called Huntington in the early morning hours of the 17th. Acting on the tip from said Agent, our own Major Robert Rogers and his Loyalist band from the Queen's American Rangers, pursued the individual and, by no unimpressive bit of Skullduggery, obtained his full Admission of his Crimes.

The Spy purports of course to be an American officer, a Captain Nathan Hale –
of Connecticut.

Naturally, we refuse to recognize the privileges of his Status — neither as an Officer nor as a Combatant.

With your Lordship's kind permission, I am sending this Rogue to you forthwith and request you pronounce the Sentence appropriate to a nefarious Spy.

I Remain, As Ever -

Your Most Humble and Obedient Servant
S. Drummond

Howe scribbled a short response in his own hand approving Drummond's proposed action. He summoned Digby in and handed him the letter. "Take this to your officer, sergeant."

"As you say, sir."

Howe was elated not only at catching a spy but at Americans catching Americans, precisely as he viewed this as the key to the conflict. Drummond was one of the few officers who agreed with Howe's view that more Americans were for the king than against, and that the whole mess could be resolved as a family quarrel rather than as a mortal struggle between the crown and its subjects.

** *

Creed woke up just before noon. His men were still sleeping soundly, so he decided to let them rest for another hour. They would need it. Carefully, to avoid waking them, he gently pushed open the barn door and slipped out quietly. He left most of his weapons and gear behind, only taking a tomahawk and one of the British pistols for protection. Creed planned to take a short walk around the city, hoping to overhear rumors of the American spy and gather any useful information. Along the way, he aimed to learn the layout of the lanes and back alleys between the Stanley House and the city proper.

The smell of the midday meal wafted across the yard from the Stanley kitchen. Creed paused a moment to enjoy the aroma of the chicken dinner being prepared. Emily was certainly happy to see them, he thought to himself with a warm smile.

As he slipped by the side of the Stanley House, he glanced through the open kitchen window and saw Emily directing the activity of three servants. He resisted the temptation to get her attention and steal a moment with her. His mission was difficult enough without the added complication of affairs of the heart. He sighed, then squared his shoulders and casually stepped toward the main road.

Once in the city, Creed had to work his way through the crowds of refugees, soldiers, and other debris of an army in flux. He began with a brief check of some taverns and coffee houses near the East River. He considered it the most likely place for Hale to appear if the spy made it over from Long Island. Fitzgerald's description of Hale was straightforward: tall, very handsome, and with piercing eyes. Fitzgerald also revealed Hale's cover—an itinerant schoolmaster. As Root Hog, he told folks the teacher owed him money, and he needed to find him before heading north to help the British finish off the rebels.

No one on the docks or in the various establishments admitted knowing of any such teacher. Nor had he seen anyone matching Hale's description. Most laughed when Root Hog told them a "teacher-man" had dunned him of money.

One fat tavern keeper had belly-laughed at the idea of it. "So, Root Hog, this teacher borrowed a goodly sum from ye and bolted? Did ye not take any collateral? Not even a Latin book?" The rest of the patrons in the dark, smoky room laughed along.

Creed feigned embarrassment and not a little annoyance. "Well, see now, he looked real honest-like and such. Well, a teacher now, who would think him a crook, ya see?" Better to play the ruffian and rube to keep their suspicions away.

A wiry patron joined in the fun. "Say, mountain man, did you walk into town or ride in on a turnip wagon?"

And so it went until he gave up and made his way north. There was no chance of finding this lost spy in a city thrown into the turmoil that war-torn New York was experiencing. Tories were on the rampage. Refugees choked the streets. Troops marched through the thoroughfares in columns and swarmed the back streets when off duty. Supply wagons, barges, and pack horses all moved north and south as supplies and food followed the march of the British Army.

When he arrived back at the Stanley House, Creed found Emily waiting pensively at the front gate. When she saw him, her face went from a mild grimace to a gracious smile that warmed his heart and set his blood a-boil.

"Mister Root Hog, I have saved you some food." Emily accompanied him into the barn, where his men were finishing eating.

"It's just fried chicken and bread. But I made sure they had saved you a princely portion."

"Smells wonderful. And after a few hours pounding the lanes of the city, it shall not last long." When Creed finished the meal, he revealed his plans for the evening. "Lads, the city is in chaos. Swarms of people coming and going. The Tories are already organizing citizen groups. If there are any patriots left, they dare not reveal themselves for fear of reprisal."

Beall wiped grease from his mouth with his sleeve. "Reprisal sir? Reprisal for what?"

Emily, who had spent the entire time watching Creed eat, provided a gentle response to his naïve question, "Why, Jonathan, this poor city has seen nothing but atrocity and reprisal for over a year. The Tories and Whigs vied for power and treated each other mercilessly with beatings, burnings, tarring, and feathering. It was awful to see such wanton violence. When they controlled the city before, the Loyalists rampaged against the Whigs. After they left and the Continental Army occupied the city, the Whigs went rampant. I am sure the Tories will now take their vengeance."

"This is a test of will, then, as much as of arms, is it not?" Parker said.

Creed nodded. "Indeed." It pleased him that his men took an interest in the politics of their cause. He looked over at Thomas, who was at work grooming the horses.

"As for tonight, we shall go into town. I pray this Neeley is our man, or at least has a kinsman or two he can point out to us."

Beall responded with a sly smile, "We shall rely on your good Irish luck to assist us, sir."

Creed gazed at Emily, who lowered her eyes. "Yes, we shall indeed. But call me

Root Hog!"

The barn erupted in laughter.

When Emily excused herself, Creed turned to the mission at hand. "The less Miss Stanley knows of our mission, the safer she shall be. We will depart at six sharp. Now here's what we must do..."

After he went over the plan, Creed left his men to rest. He wanted to reacquaint himself with the area around the Stanley House, the site of their first bivouac in New York. Nobody noticed him dart through the garden and make his way across the sunken lane to the orchard. He decided to pick a handful of apples for himself and his men to munch. As he picked the fruit, he took note of the travelers along the road. Most traffic headed south into the city, although a few wagons rolled north to supply the British lines. An occasional file of green-jacketed Loyalists marched north to some appointed mission or another.

Creed suddenly saw someone among the trees moving towards him at a casual, almost languid pace. The trim figure of Emily soon reached him. They embraced without exchanging a word. He kissed her fervently and stroked her face. Her arms circled his back, and her soft hands seemed to probe every muscle. After what seemed both an eternity and an instant, they paused. For a moment, they just absorbed each other, as if nothing else mattered, and for that brief moment, nothing else did.

Finally, Emily spoke in a soft rasping voice, "My most ardent wish has been granted. I thought I should never see you again."

Creed stroked her hair. "It would likely be better for us all if you didn't. By Jesus, I am glad I came this way. But I won't do it again. I fear I have put you at grave risk already."

"I would risk a hundred scaffolds to see you, Jeremiah. Besides, this place attracts many strange people. It is a suitable lair for you and your men." Emily kissed him eagerly, and he returned the ardor.

Sighing, she placed her head on his chest and whispered, "We have an hour before I need to be back. Let me show you the rest of the orchard."

Chapter 4

New York, September 21st, 1776

General Howe watched the sun dip over the North River from New York's Old Battery. Its gentle rays caressed the Jersey Highlands behind the Sandy Hook. He could already tell it would be another steamy New York evening. How different all this looked when he compared it to the harbor on the Thames River back in London, completely crammed with stone and half-timbered buildings, large warehouses, dockyards, and the denizens of the world's largest and greatest city. New York was just a poor provincial city in comparison.

Howe's powerful black horse stomped the ground and swooshed its tail to evade the swarm of flies swirling around its legs and hindquarters.

Howe exhaled. "I love America, but do detest its extremes of weather, especially the summer humidity and its attendant mosquitoes, flies, and whatnot."

"The extremes are part of its charm, Milord," replied Major General Charles Cornwallis. "Of greater concern is that New York remains in chaos."

"I have dispersed soldiers throughout the lower half of the island to ensure the city's safety and security; at least until more local Loyalist units can be organized."

"News from Long Island is good. Sandy Drummond has organized the locals."

Howe nodded. "Drummond's steady hand is now required on the Island of New York, as well."

"But what of Cunningham?"

"William Cunningham is doing fine work as Provost Marshal, but I want the assurance brought by a solid British officer at my side."

"But you are famously a Whig. A friend to loyal Americans."

"Indeed, I am, Milord. And overall, New York is loyal to the Crown and I intend to keep it that way. I am heading back. Join me, Charles?"

"No, Milord, I have a mind to double-check the garrison here."

Howe touched his hat in farewell, turned his horse about, and headed north at a canter, the dust swirling up behind him like a whirling dervish before dissipating into the evening sky. If he hurried, he could arrive at the

Beekman House and change in time for his evening assignation: his tryst with Mrs. Elizabeth Loring. The stunning beauty, who was the wife of a Loyalist office seeker, had settled in nicely as his mistress. Howe's affection for the Americans had its carnal as well as its political side.

* * *

By nightfall, Root Hog and his three companions had entered their fifth tavern in less than three hours. Ironically, this one bore a patriotic name—Liberty Arms. Creed recognized the place, having eaten there just before his regiment, the First Maryland, was deployed to Long Island. Located at the end of Princess Street, Liberty Arms was a two-story wooden building freshly painted white with bright blue shutters. The proprietor was a notorious Whig and patriot.

The previous venues Creed and his men had visited were Tory through and through. Creed thought he would see what the atmosphere was like in a patriot establishment. The Tories and Loyalists would soon start their purge of all things patriotic, and such places would soon be closed or renamed.

Creed's plan seemed to be working well. He had located Neeley's Apothecary in the late afternoon and convinced the clerk that he needed to meet the owner that evening. The clerk, a tall, thin man in his early thirties, was well dressed, with fine long fingers and an almost girlish way of moving.

He spoke in a low voice and made it obvious Root Hog revolted him, "Mister Neeley will be here at nine this evening. But I am sure he will have no time for the likes of you, sir." The clerk rolled his eyes as he spoke.

Creed ignored the insult and stayed in character. "Well, you be sure and tell him Root Hog Burns has money for him. More'n that, tell him, he has information. Information from a friend. A friend in high places. He's been told. He knows."

"How should he know whether you are lying or not?" the clerk stammered.

"Well, if he doesn't know, he'll soon know. Root Hog ain't no liar."

The clerk drummed his long fingers on the countertop. "Certainly, Mister Neeley would have little or no interest in your... information and..."

Creed grabbed the clerk by his frilled silk cravat, pulled his head an inch from his own, and glared into the man's eyes. He stroked the clerk's powdered hair, which was tied back in a fashionable queue. He tugged gently, then firmly on the queue to the point where the clerk whined from the pain.

"Now you hear me well, fancy city-boy. If you look down, you'll see a tomahawk tucked in my belt. 'Side that's a pistol. You tell your boss-man. Root Hog's been sent here by a friend who's risking his neck for the king. This friend – he needs to get a message to Neeley. So, you have him here or you will be a traitor to the king, and I reckon it's open season on them."

Creed's boot lashed out, striking the clerk in the groin. Then a powerful arm pushed him so hard that he slammed into a shelf full of jars containing various types of liquid chemicals. The jars fell forward, raining glass and chemicals on the hapless man. As they departed, they could hear him crying. Creed grew sick to his stomach at the brutal charade. Killing men in combat was one thing, but hurting men, brutalizing them, to achieve even a just cause, he found much more difficult. But he realized the stakes were now too high to do otherwise.

***

The Liberty Arms was almost deserted except for a group of sailors waiting to ship out that evening. They were well into their cups. Then Creed noticed a pair of well-dressed gentlemen in the corner, quietly finishing a meal.

The tavern keeper, a cynical-looking man named Stone, viewed Creed and his men with justifiable suspicion. Just the name of his tavern meant his time under British occupation was at risk. He placed one ham fist into another and cracked his big knuckles as Root Hog and his cowboys entered. The evening wind had begun to pick up from the south, blowing the door wide open and almost extinguishing a candle near the entrance.

"I will ask you to close the door, gentlemen. Quickly, please!"

Stone's tone was unpleasant and waspy. Creed realized he had years of experience with all kinds of riff-raff, and to a patriot, cowboys were trouble.

"Beggin' your pardon, barman," Creed responded politely, but not too politely. "Bring us each a tankard of ale."

"My name is Jonas Stone, not barman."

"Then here ya go, Jonas." Creed slapped a coin onto the bar, and the tavern-keeper swept it into his apron sleeve with a flourish, not taking his eyes off the cowboy leader. Then Stone poured the drafts. As he did, Creed changed his manner, though he continued to play the ruffian. He had sized up the tavern keeper as a hard-boiled proprietor who would react better to a kinder line of discussion. The tavern keeper wiped the top of each gray pewter tankard with a large, flat knife, clearing the foamy head and spilling the froth down the tankards' sides.

Creed suspected the knife was a warning to the cowboys to behave rather than an attempt at hospitality. "We will be on our way in no time, sure 'nuff. But we don't like the look of your placard out front, 'cause we stand for king and country."

Stone replied in a voice surly but even, and just polite enough, "That will change in good time. The placard, that is."

Creed looked at him critically. Stone wanted to avoid giving Loyalist thugs a reason to steal from him or destroy his property. Rumors of Loyalist revenge were already spreading across the island. On Long Island, there was little rape, theft, or destruction when the British arrived. But the Island of New York was a tinderbox of chaos. Angry and bitter Loyalists had resurfaced, beginning to reclaim what was once lost to the rebels.

Creed's face broke into a devilish smile. "That's a good thing, pardner. Tomorrow, if we come back, we want to see a more royal-sounding name. Somethin' we can all be proud of, you know?"

Stone chortled, "Well, as a matter of fact, I have already painted a new placard. Drying out back. "

"Come tomorrow, we shall be the 'Royal Luck.' How does that suit you?"

Creed grinned again, his angular jaw made more distinctive by the darkness from his stubble and the coal rubbings. "Not me, you have to suit, Jonas. We are Loyalists but not politicos. Watch out for them Tory boys, though, they're hell-bent for trouble."

Stone cast him an amused look. "You cowboys, not political?"

Creed slammed his hand on the bar. "We are loyal! But we're here on business. Money makin' business, not political. Looking to get a contract to buy horses up north and bring them down south. For the army, now. King pays hard currency, we hear. Root Hog Burns and his cowboys are businessmen, and that's all."

Creed spoke loudly so that the businessmen and sailors could hear. He wanted to establish who they were and why they were in the city. The businessmen snickered at each other and quickly turned away from the unruly crowd at the bar. The sailors, in their drunken state, barely noticed.

After an hour of banter, the cowboys left the tavern. They had only one mug of ale each, but to the tavern keeper, it looked like a wild celebration. They made a lot of noise and boasted about foolish exploits against Indians, patriots, and other rival gangs.

* * *

Darkness had enveloped occupied New York. There was no moonlight, and a thin layer of clouds moved swiftly across the low sky. A strong wind was blowing north from the lower New York harbor. People of all kinds still filled the streets and alleyways. Refugees had poured into the city from the north. Some came to gain advantage or seek revenge; others simply sought safety with the British. Some were trying to leave the city, sometimes with only the clothes on their backs.

A few sailors and merchant seamen wandered the streets and alleys in search of drink and prostitutes. British soldiers and German mercenaries patrolled the streets looking for rebels and patriots. Others had taken leave, official or unofficial, in pursuit of the city's lowest pleasures, most of which were centered near the Holy Ground, the city's notorious red-light district north of Saint Paul's Church and close to King's College.

Root Hog and his band of cowboys blended right in with the mass of distressed and confused humanity that always seemed to show itself during times of crisis, disaster or war. The city of New York now faced all three of these calamities at once.

They pushed through the throng, trying to look like so many other refugees and displaced people. Beall whispered to Creed, "Do you think your friend from the apothecary carried the message, Lieutenant, uh, I mean, Root Hog?"

"Good question, Hammer Head. Suppose we'll soon have the answer."

Parker tried to play his role. "Could be a simple case of mistaken identity, Root Hog."

"Could be, Fish Head, but I am bettin' not. Only hand to play right now."

They made their way up Broad Street until they reached the narrow east-west lane called Wall Street. A small British regimental band was playing in the square. The music was intended to impress the locals with the strength of the British Army. For the most part, it succeeded. A small crowd had gathered around the band, which played an energetic tune. People clapped along and stomped their feet to the music. They turned west onto Wall Street, leaving the disturbing yet enchanting music to fade in the cacophony of the New York evening. It was completely dark when they arrived at the apothecary. The moon had not yet risen, and in the confusion of the day's events, the night-watch had not made their usual rounds to light the street lanterns. A few homes and businesses emitted faint light from their shuttered windows. Other than that, all was shrouded in darkness.

Creed whispered, "Fish Belly, you and Little Colt best walk around the building and make sure we have no unwanted visitors. Then cover the entrance here. Hammer Head and I will go in and wait for our man, Neeley."

An hour later, Creed and Beall heard a key work furtively at the tumbler, finally unlocking the door of the apothecary shop. A figure, obscured by the room's darkness, moved with an instinctive knowledge of its layout. He re-locked the door, then moved swiftly across the room and lit first one, then a second, and then a third lamp. As the third went from spark to glow to light, Neeley looked up to see the menacing visage of Root Hog Burns.

Creed confronted the man with a grimace he hoped would awe the man to better control of the situation. Control was key. "You Neeley?"

"Who wants to know?" Neeley's answer was cold, unimpassioned, and completely unimpressed by the strange figure confronting him.

Creed was expecting a fat, soft burgher-type, but Neeley, although short, was muscular and robust, with a barrel chest and thick arms and legs. He wore a simple dark green coat with dun-colored breeches stained with various colors. *Obviously works without a smock or apron.*

"Well, you ain't King George. You're too short. And I'm Root Hog, Root Hog Burns, sent here by someone who moved from Brooklyn to this island."

Neeley seemed interested. "Why didn't he come see me himself, then?"

"'Cause he's stranded some miles north of here. He can't get through rebel lines, so he asked me to come instead. Said you would know. Said you'd pay us too."

"He did, eh? How much does he have in mind?" Neeley asked, his face twisted in a suspicious glare.

"Needs five guineas," Creed replied calmly.

"Five guineas? Where the bloody hell does he get off demanding five guineas? Furthermore, I have no guarantee who he is or who you are."

"You callin' me a liar? I could get five guineas a lot easier than riskin' my neck this way. He said to tell you his friend was staying put. They like things where they are, least so far."

Creed had no idea what Washington's plans were, but he thought it likely he would move the army soon. His subterfuge, although risky and unauthorized, seemed reasonable.

Neeley changed his demeanor. "So you say?" His face shook back and forth while his eyes narrowed to dark little slits. Then his voice softened just a bit.

Creed knew he had him. "Just did. Like I said, Root Hog's no liar."

"What else did he say? Your... friend? Does he still have the book? Is anyone suspecting of this?"

Neeley's mouth closed. His demeanor showed he realized his questions were already revealing more than they needed to know.

"He said I should give ya this." Creed handed him a sealed envelope. It was opaque and had no addressee. Creed had no idea what was in the note Fitzgerald provided him. They mutually agreed he should know only as much as Root Hog needed, in the event of capture and interrogation by the British or the Tories.

Neeley glowered, the shadow on his face giving him a menacing look. "Very well. Wait here."

He exited through a door into a small back office. It was dark. He lit a candle, then a second. Creed could not see much but a small table, stacks of papers, and shelves with more chemicals, both liquid and powder.

He saw Neeley fumble through his pockets and remove a key. He unlocked the table's small drawer and removed a notebook. He cut open the envelope with trembling hands. Despite his bravado, it was obvious he was new at this business and nervous. Slowly and deliberately, he translated the five-line coded message. In response, he wrote a short-coded note, carefully choosing his words as he transposed from the simple codebook. It was almost half an hour before he finished.

Neeley finally merged with two opaque envelopes. He cocked his head and squinted with one eye. "This should do it. Deliver both if you know what is good for you, Mister Root Hog. Five guineas is a handy sum in these troubled times."

* * *

They took a winding route back. Creed wanted to ensure Neeley didn't have them followed. The encounter with the clerk might have made him concerned. Creed walked with Beall, who stayed to Creed's left. They tried not to seem too hurried or nervous, just confident enough. The city's people were wary of everyone, especially strangers. As cowboys, they were feared. So, most folks, even Tories, kept their distance from them.

The streets seemed more crowded than earlier although they heard rumors of a curfew. The main streets were flush with many soldiers and sailors looking for whisky and women. Most of the taverns and coffee houses were alive with customers, and the tumult of anxious and riotous chatter cut the windy night air.

After much thought, Creed decided on their route back. "All right, boys, let's make our way through the Holy Ground."

"Jorns used to speak of that," Parker said. "Do you know where it is, Root Hog?"

"Believe it's just north of Trinity Church. This way..."

Beall's eyes widened, and his mouth bent in dismay. "Are you sure, Root Hog?"

Creed laughed. "Hammer Head, this Holy Ground is a good place for us, at least tonight. Anyone following us will have a rough time there. And most folks there are Loyalists." He winked mischievously. "Why, we'll fit right in."

The Holy Ground was almost a city unto itself, bustling with activity, with its alleys, taverns, and brothels densely packed with doxies working their trade to sailors, businessmen, itinerants, and the occasional student from King's College. In a city that was largely Loyalist, the residents of the Holy Ground were loyal. Music and laughter filled the air. Men's and women's curses, along with many bawdy, mostly off-key songs, clashed with the night wind.

Parker and Thomas kept them in sight, some thirty paces to their rear and on the opposite side of the street from Creed and Beall. In the event of an ambush, they would rush to Creed's aid or, in the worst case, escape and continue the mission. Parker's other task was to make sure they were not followed.

As they strode, Creed spoke softly to Beall, "Once we double back and come 'round, we'll head north, just past the church. If anyone is following us, we're sure to lose them in the Holy Ground."

The patter of anxious feet alerted them. Creed reached for his weapons.

Thomas stepped up from behind them and tugged urgently at Creed's elbow. "Root Hog, we're being followed."

Creed's eyes narrowed as he kept moving while looking straight ahead. "How many?"

"Least six men, m – maybe more," Thomas stammered.

"Don't look back, Hammer Head." Creed kept walking forward with his eyes ahead. "How long?"

Thomas stammered, "Pa – past five minutes. Thought they were just folks, at first. But they turned with us two times already."

Creed saw the fear in Thomas's eyes. These people would hang a young black man just for sport and hang the rest of them for business. He steadied Thomas with a clap of the forearm. "Not to worry, Little Colt, the advantage is ours."

Beall's eyes widened. "It is?"

Creed smiled grimly. "Yep, 'cause they don't know our next move."

In fact, Creed had no idea what he would do next. He decided to improvise. They kept moving along the street, trying to act casual as the group of men closed on them. Thomas remained with Creed.

"Where's Fish Belly?"

"He dropped back as soon as he saw us being followed. Ducked into a dark doorway, till they passed him."

"I'm sure he's following our pursuers discreetly," Beall said.

Creed nodded his head. "Good man, that Fish Belly. We'll turn here and head west, toward the North River. Maybe we can lose them among the warehouses and docks. If they confront us, Fish Belly's presence in their rear will add to their discomfort."

They turned west onto Stone Street, then north onto Lumber Street. Sure enough, the group, a bit noisy now, had closed the gap to about twenty-five paces. Dropping any pretense of discretion, they tramped their feet in unison, creating an eerie sound that sent a chill through Thomas and Beall. But Creed knew the tramping was meant to boost the stalkers' bravado as much as to frighten the quarry.

"In here," Creed whispered, and he and his two companions suddenly darted left into an alley on Lumber. The alley was just a bit wider than a man's shoulders, and its darkness offered the three of them little comfort.

The alley led to a courtyard, a small gravel-covered quadrangle shared by several warehouses. The darkness numbed their senses. Creed and his companions moved along the wall to their left, their hands guiding them through the inky darkness in hopes of finding a door or window. As they felt their way, they could hear the sound of their pursuers' hob-nailed shoes scraping along the gravel.

Creed tried the first two doors, but they were bolted tight. He checked a window, but it was nailed shut from the inside. Finally, he found a third door, also locked. Desperate for a way out, he shoulder-checked it. The old lock snapped open with a screech.

He staggered forward clutching the broken latch and nearly fell flat on his face. Thomas and Beall pushed behind him in a frantic rush. Beall tried to close the door quietly, but he ended up slamming it, with the sound echoing through the dark alley like a thunderclap.

Creed muttered a desperate command, "If they confront us, we'll meet them here. Empty your pistols first, then we take them with the tomahawk."

Light suddenly painted the quadrangle. They could see their pursuers now standing in a gaggle. Several brandished torches, and some had muskets slung across their backs. Their dark, flat shadows reached the top of the warehouse walls and danced erratically in the torchlight. There were six of them, but the silhouettes along the quadrangle wall made them appear like an army of ghouls.

He peered through a dirt-encrusted window. "They're in some sort of uniform, but as far as I can tell, they're not British or German."

The figures fanned out across the quadrangle, checking doors, windows, and other escape routes. Creed strained his eyes for a way out of the warehouse, knowing they would be found in seconds.

"Root Hog, this place is full of wooden barrels that contain some sort of liquid," Beall whispered.

Creed smelled the aroma, a distinct and potentially deadly aroma—stacks and rows of tar, turpentine spirits, and other naval stores.

"Stay away from the barrels. Check your flints. Once we fire, get at them quickly. This warehouse is full of spirits, very explosive. One spark will blow us all to heaven…or hell."

His men each carried a pistol taken earlier from the British officers. Generally inaccurate at long range, flintlock pistols were deadly at ten paces. The heavy wooden door swung open, flooding the room with light. Several men entered, each holding a torch. Creed and his men kept their pistols steady as the six spread out along the wall, less than ten paces away.

Creed challenged them in a gravelly voice, "You boys been followin' us for some time now, pardner. Who are you?"

A tall, thin man with hair tied back in a queue stepped forward. "Provisional New York Constabulary Militia, Mister Root Hog. You, sir, are under arrest."

"On what charge? We've done nothin'!" Creed knew these so-called provisional constabulary were little more than Loyalist vigilantes, no better than a gang.

They were a city version of the skinners and cowboys who plied their trade between the armies. Just like their patriot counterparts, these were violent zealots. Most were hell-bent on vengeance and would just as soon kill any suspected patriots. In the torchlight, Creed could make out the man's face standing next to the leader. He was short and squat, with a thick neck, broad shoulders, and a broken nose.

Beall whispered, "Root Hog, that fat one is one of the businessmen from the Liberty Arms."

Creed nodded. "The tavern's name's a ruse to draw patriots and Whigs so they could be identified and marked for reprisal."

"But we gave them no cause," Beall whispered.

"Don't matter. Strangers like us make an easy mark for those seeking the king's gold. This man is paid a bounty for victims, and few questions are asked. I should have guessed as much."

Creed realized this was happening throughout the city and across the island of New York. The presence of the British Army provided such Loyalists the cover they needed to exact their brutal reprisals, settle old scores, or turn a profit.

The squat informer spoke before the group's leader could respond to Creed, "The charge is treason, of course."

"Now pardner, why would you think we's patriots? We's loyal subjects of King George. Who sez otherwise?"

The squat, ugly man chimed in again for the leader, "We care not a whit for your declarations, Root Hog. Nor your politics."

"Well, good then, we'll jus skeedadle back to..."

The tall leader cried out in a voice as deep and cold as an ice tunnel, "Enough! Around here, the crown's men deal only with us. We control everything between King Street and the docks. Now, give up your weapons."

Creed realized the men had no idea about his mission. They were nothing more than rogues and criminals. They were not unlike the thugs in Frederick, Maryland, whose brutal assault had drawn him into this war. Their hate-filled and greed-driven minds couldn't comprehend such things. They were destined to be killed and handed over to the British as bounty. Creed felt some relief knowing that the mission, and more importantly Emily, was not in danger.

"Root Hog recognizes no authority here but the king. Come back with a warrant, a magistrate, or his men."

There was laughter from along the wall. Creed could see more torches lighting the quadrangle.

There were more of the bastards, he thought.

"We need no warrant, and we need no king's men. We have men enough to take all three of you!"

Creed realized they were unaware of Parker lurking behind them. *Well, this bounty, if collected, would be hard-earned.* "Fire, now, boys!"

The sound of flints striking firing pans, followed by the sizzle of sparks, and finally a muffled *whoosh* and *bang*, echoed through the warehouse and into the quadrangle. Three balls of lead tore through the line of men. The leader went down first, clutching his chest, sinking to his knees, and staring at the blood staining his vest. The businessman with the broken nose was shot in the eye by Beall's pistol. Thomas's shot missed its target but hit a third man in the hand, causing him to drop his torch, which ignited the sawdust on the floor. The flames erupted along the floor and gradually moved toward the barrels.

The other three stood along the wall, momentarily stunned as Creed and his men leaped over the barrels and cut into them with their tomahawks. Creed's blow split one man's skull down the middle. His dying eyes stared blankly.

The remaining two bolted toward the door as more militia members forced their way inside. The crowd of men now wrestled with each other. Creed, along with Beall and Thomas, swung their tomahawks at them. Two more men fell, shoulders torn from their bodies. The last four thugs ran out into the quadrangle and struggled to unsling their muskets.

Creed and his men burst out the door and rushed them. They dropped their torches and frantically pulled at the leather slings while grabbing the hammerlocks to fire the muskets. Creed and his men needed ten paces to reach them before they could shoot. Meanwhile, the flames from the militia torches began spreading along the wooden walls surrounding the quadrangle.

A militiaman cried shrilly and bowled forward, his musket clattering to the ground. A second twisted and fell backward, landing at Creed's feet and nearly tripping him. A third fired his musket, but the shot went high as he stumbled forward. He hit the ground with a hollow thud, his lungs gurgling up a pool of warm blood that went unnoticed in the chaos and the darkness.

The last militiaman dropped his musket and tried to flee, but the last thing the thug saw was the grim face of Elias Parker wiping his blood from a large knife. In less than twenty seconds, the stalwart Marylander had dispatched the last four of their assailants. Taking them from the rear was not noble warfare, but necessary to their mission and their survival.

Creed whispered hoarsely as he pulled himself up from the ground, "Elias?"

"I was trailing them all the way, Lieutenant. I just knew they were scoundrels out to get us."

Parker's face was masked in the shadows, but Creed could hear his panting. Killing four men with cold steel took strength and nerves few possessed. *No one could have done this as quickly and efficiently as Elias Parker.*

Creed recovered his composure. "Good work, Fish Belly. Now let's go. Each of you grab one of their muskets with some powder and ball. We might need 'em."

Creed barely finished his sentence when a muffled explosion rocked the warehouse. They turned to see a fireball burst, then envelop the old building, engulfing it in flames that spread to the dried-out wooden walls of the other warehouses near the docks.

"Fire mixed with spirits and dry wood. This is just the beginning, I fear. Tonight's wind and these wooden shanties will combine to make this an awful fire."

As Creed spoke, the heat of the fireball reached them, and they could see the white-hot flames licking their way rapidly along the roofs of the warehouses like some primeval dragon's tongue. In a few minutes, the quadrangle would be engulfed.

They hurried back up the alley toward the street just as the secondary explosions of turpentine and pitch began hurling flaming pieces of barrels, wood planking, crates, and roofing skyward like a volcano. They paused briefly and looked back in awe. None of them had ever seen such a fire. For a moment, they stood mesmerized by the ever-expanding flames spreading rapidly across the roofs of the other buildings in the quadrangle.

In the glow of the flames, Creed's men saw a wry smile cross his face.

"Lads, it seems we have a nice diversion for our enterprise. No one should question our motives now, as we are escaping the flames of hell from a man-made Vesuvius before they engulf the entire city..."

They turned east, away from the raging firestorm, then headed north. To their surprise, the flames seemed to follow them, leaping across narrow streets and burning through row after row of buildings. From buildings and alleyways, crowds of refugees rushed frantically to escape the living hell that had descended on them. Drums beat and bells rang as the British began to rally soldiers from their billets and sailors from the ships to fight the fire.

"Halt!" a sergeant shouted to them, "All able-bodied men must assist."

"Not tonight, pardner. We've other business to attend."

"What? Arsonists! Seize them!"

A file of sleepy infantry surrounded Creed and his men.

"No, sir, we saw your arsonists, though. They wuz drinking and ran back to the Liberty Arms."

The British sergeant hesitated as he considered Creed's story.

But Creed did not hesitate. He and his men formed a V and bludgeoned their way through the file of soldiers and made their way up Broadway, disappearing into the smoke. They did not get far before they saw a band of Loyalists in a rage. About thirty strong, they had tied up six patriots and began to toss their bound bodies into the flames.

"No! Please, no!"

The first patriot disappeared in a curtain of fire. The crowd jeered and cheered. His screams grew shrill, but soon the intense crackling of the flames silenced him as they scorched him to death.

Someone shouted, "Damn rebels! Feed the fire you started!"

The crowd echoed the sentiment, "Evil rebel bastards! Meet the devil while you live!" The next two were tossed, struggling desperately while shrieking and screaming.

"Sir, we must stop this!" Beall exclaimed.

Creed hesitated. Then one of the victims emerged from the flames, burning like a torch, like a human torch. They could hear his skin crackling and smell the body fat melting. "Check your flints. Present, fire!"

Creed and his men unleashed a volley into the Loyalist crowd. Men dropped screaming and clutching as musket balls tore through flesh and bone.

"At them with the tomahawk!" Creed ordered. In minutes, the band had dispersed, leaving three men dead and dying.

Parker's sharp blade cut the remaining patriots free of their bonds. "Get out of here. Get your families out of this city if you value your lives." The men needed no encouragement.

"Sir, we need to move the wounded Loyalists before the flames get to them," Beall said as a tongue of fire licked at them.

Suddenly, a dull pop, pop pierced the darkness. Several musket balls splattered near them.

"Stop! Arsonist!" a British voice exclaimed.

Creed looked at the bodies struggling in the flames and turned away. "Nothing we can do for them now. The lobsters are organizing." Footsteps and a line of British soldiers running up Broadway confirmed Creed's fears. "We need to keep moving or we'll be caught with the rest." They hurried north and west as fast as they could.

Fanned by blustery winds from the expansive bay to the south, the great New York fire spread quickly northward from Whitehall Slip through the docks and warehouses along the North River.

It took with it a large portion of the city west of Broadway. The flames engulfed hundreds of homes and shops, completely scorching the Holy Ground. Trinity was not spared the holocaust, but by some miracle, Saint Paul's Church was. The fire proved itself to be an enemy more devastating than the rebel army waiting expectantly on the Heights of Haarlem.

Tory vigilante groups, in their thirst for vengeance, rounded up anyone deemed suspicious. Many were hanged on the spot. In most cases, these were looters. Some, however, were political opponents, and in some instances, simply men in the wrong place and at the wrong time.

Patriots and Whigs blamed the British occupiers for starting the fire, while the British and the Tories pointed at the Whigs or the agents of Mr. Washington. The fire gave both sides useful propaganda to rally their followers.

Finally, they made their way north of the city and reached the quiet, safe Stanley Boarding House. It was already past three. After making sure no one was around to see them, they entered the stable, collapsing onto the straw piles in complete exhaustion.

Chapter 5

New York, September 22nd, 1776

Emily pushed open the freshly painted white door and stepped into the stable carrying warm bread and tea. The afternoon sunlight illuminated the stable, rousing Creed and his men from a restless sleep.

Even in his dreams, Creed had struggled with the night's events. The meeting with the suspicious British agent, a bloody encounter with a rogue Tory group, and the explosive and deadly fire combined to make the night as close to a visit to Hades as one could make.

Hot embers surrounded them, and sparks swirled north in a plume that seemed to stretch forever. Buildings burned as men, women, and children ran to escape the curtain of fire and waves of smoke that blinded and choked their victims. Loyalist constables began forcing stragglers to help douse the flames, while cries of desperation and random musket fire clashed with the roaring wind and flames.

"It's just bread and tea, gentlemen, but the bread is fresh and the tea hot and strong. And I have some fresh butter as well." After their night in hell, Emily's voice seemed sweeter than a choir of angels and did much to soothe their demons.

Emily served Creed last. She lowered her eyes demurely as he grabbed the enamel mug and the half loaf. He held her hand a second longer than he should have, long enough to signal his feelings for her as well as his thankfulness. While the men ate silently, she found a seat on a small sack of oats. She wore a rough-looking but still attractive farm dress of dark green. She clasped her hands to her knees and then looked at Creed pensively. "Jeremiah, I may have some bad news. I do not know the extent or importance of it, nor if it impacts you in any way…"

"And that would be?" He continued to sip the tea. It was hot, just as he liked it.

She briefly flicked her tongue at him, then narrowed her eyes and became serious. "Well, to begin with, a terrible fire has destroyed much of New York. Many people are dead. More are missing. Hundreds of homes and our great churches are in ruins. They say looters and arsonists of all sorts were caught, and the British and their supporters have made great sport with them. Of course, the provost and the governor are blaming rebel sympathizers. They will use this to press for even more repressive measures."

Creed looked at his men. "A fire! Well, it seems we left the city in the nick of time, lads."

Nobody spoke, suppressing what they felt so Emily would not be connected to their activities.

Emily eyed them suspiciously. They had fine white dust covering them–ash from the flames. But she knew not to inquire and changed the subject. "A gentleman came to the boarding house this morning around nine. He took a room."

"Then business is doing well, even in these most trying of times!" Creed quipped.

His men chuckled along.

"Hear me out, please. His name is Thomas Roche and…"

"Ah, a foin Irishman like me self, no doubt. Why I…"

"Please, Jeremiah!" Her tone doused his effusiveness.

"I have heard my father speak of him. He is one of William Cunningham's closest henchmen."

"Cunningham? Another Irishman? So two Irishmen working together, that is a good thing, I should say…"

"Not these two gentlemen," she responded abruptly, clenching her small white hands together in a ball, imploring Creed, who finally understood and let her finish.

"They are notorious supporters of the king's authority. Even among the Tories, they are considered somewhat, shall we say, rabid."

Creed swigged down the last drop of tea and placed the cup on the dirt floor. "I am sorry, Emily, please go on."

"Cunningham emigrated around the time my father did. He is red-haired and mad as a bull most of the time. He had a business breaking horses. I know, Jeremiah, another fine Irish trait." She smiled at him weakly, although she seemed proud. She beat him to his own punch line.

"Well, in April last year, Cunningham was beaten and dragged through the streets by a radical Whig mob – the Sons of Liberty. He escaped to Boston, where General Gage made him provost marshal. Now it seems he is back and out to exact revenge against the Whigs and patriots for the fires – and all their other perceived transgressions. What is worse, he has already drawn first blood."

"How so?" Creed asked.

She turned down her eyes to hide the tears swelling from within. "According to Mister Roche, who calls himself Captain Roche, it happened this morning, shortly after eleven. He hanged a rebel spy General Howe had condemned to death."

Creed's face turned white with fear. "A spy? Did this Captain Roche say who the spy was?"

"Yes, a captain named Nathan Hale. A handsome young man, around your age, Jeremiah. Is he the American you were hoping to find?"

Even as she spoke the words, she knew the answer from Creed's ashen face. Creed swallowed involuntarily. "Where did they hang him?"

"Not far from the Beekman House, which is about a mile or so north of here. General Gage has his headquarters near there. They hanged him in a small meadow near the British artillery park."

An hour later, Creed had his men packed up and ready to leave. "As soon as I have said our farewell to Miss Emily, we'll be off. I'll return the cups and pot to her. Meanwhile, check your powder and flints, and see to the horses."

Creed stole across the garden and entered the kitchen. He nearly tripped over Nancy, who was on her knees, scrubbing the floor. He placed the cups and teapot on the table. "May I pass, Nancy?"

Nancy looked up. "She is in the doctor's study, sir. Gives her more privacy with all the guests about."

She smiled as Creed tiptoed past, having seen through his disguise. However, it did not surprise her that dashing young Jeremiah Creed would risk his neck to visit Miss Emily. Creed slipped around the doorway and past the parlor where two boarders sat reading. He headed to Doctor Stanley's study, where he found Emily sitting at a desk, writing.

He slipped in silently and placed his hand on her shoulder. "Writing to a secret admirer, no doubt."

Emily startled and spilled the ink well, covering the letter. "Jer – Root Hog! You should never sneak up on a…"

"I know, on a beautiful woman."

He bent and kissed her tenderly. She responded with a fervor that bordered on passion. In the end, it was he who pulled away. They looked at each other for a moment.

She arched her eyes towards the parlor. "You should not have risked coming in here. Those men are…"

"Most fortunate. For they must not leave the one they love, perhaps forever, to the mercies of an occupying army with its camp followers and Loyalist toadies."

Emily blushed. "My father will soon return from active service. His connections and status will protect us, and besides, to all New York, I am the most fervent Loyalist."

He lightly stroked her chin. "I have an extra pack horse. You could come with us now."

She lowered her eyes to hide her tears. "I cannot. Father would die. And I have my obligations to…"

"To what? To whom, if not I? If not us?" He smiled, but the thought of shared affection discomforted him. In over a score of dalliances, trysts, and assignations, he had never felt this way. He could not imagine her real meaning.

"Father is getting older and not in the best of health. Nancy and the other servants rely on my guidance, and this house requires a firm hand. So, you see, you have obligations – and so do I."

Emily breathed a silent sigh of relief – she had almost said too much. He could never know the truth. That she also had obligations to the cause and, more importantly, as "Mister Smythe" to the commander-in-chief as his spy in the enemy's bosom.

Creed thought of his uncle's poor health when he left France and his mother's sudden downturn. "I understand, Emily. You are correct. I shall be back. I just don't know when."

"Even were this war to last one hundred years, I'd still be waiting here, Jeremiah."

They embraced, kissing tenderly for what were mere moments, but might have been an eternity as passionate thoughts and feelings flashed through them.

* * *

Washington's Headquarters, Haarlem Heights, September 23rd, 1776

Creed arrived at an army headquarters bathed in a gentle pre-dawn twilight. In his hurry to report the results of his mission to Fitzgerald, he was roughly shaven but wore his blue uniform with the familiar three-cornered hat. The uniform he and his men had hidden in an abandoned shed alongside one of the unguarded trails near the American lines. Creed knew there would be more such missions and did not want to risk a British spy seeing Root Hog and his band of cowboys sneaking through British lines.

The Life Guard on duty presented arms. Creed nodded and clambered up the stairs to Fitzgerald's room. He gently rapped on the door. When summoned to enter, he was surprised to see Fitzgerald sitting at his desk in the company of the commander-in-chief.

The colonel's uniform was rumpled, and his hair was whiter and longer than Creed remembered seeing it last. Washington, as always, looked sharp, even at this early hour. He wore his dark blue uniform with buff facings and breeches. Each button shone like a gem, despite getting up before dawn to inspect the lines and the fortifications along the heights.

Fitzgerald wagged a finger. "Ah, Jeremiah, your return is most fortuitous. We are anxious to learn of your exploits. There are reports of a chaotic fire in the city. Many patriot refugees from the city report that the fire has burned a great part of the city to the ground. We are already combating rumors that His Excellency ordered it."

Both men waited expectantly for Creed's response. It suddenly occurred to him that he might be the cause of some great embarrassment to the commander-in-chief. "Well, sir, I should like to report on my mission from the beginning and let you and His Excellency judge my actions and the outcome."

Washington and Fitzgerald looked puzzled. But Washington smiled and pointed to a chair. "By all means, young man. Take your seat at the table. I'll order coffee. We still have two hours till the morning staff meeting."

When Creed finished his report, Fitzgerald glanced knowingly at Washington. He then turned to Creed. "So, you are convinced this young lady, Emily, remains undiscovered by the British or Tories?"

Fitzgerald was aware of Emily, who she was, and her devotion to the cause. The discovery of the British spy Braaf came about in no small part due to her efforts, and Fitzgerald knew it because he was there.

"Indeed, sir. Her da' is a well-connected Loyalist if ever there was one. She, on the other hand, favors our cause. Our success was in no small part due to her support. Of course, her da' is unaware of her true loyalties."

Fitzgerald looked archly at Creed. "Personal affections play no role in this assessment?"

Creed blushed.

General Washington, not inexperienced himself in affairs of the heart, smiled and interrupted his intelligence advisor, "Robert, we must assume young Creed is providing us his professional assessment and nothing further."

An orderly returned at this time with a fresh pot of coffee. The soldier poured each a cup. Creed noted the cups were fine porcelain.

Washington smiled. "One of the benefits of establishing headquarters in a fine mansion."

The orderly was a tall man dressed in the sharp-looking blue uniform of the commander-in-chief's escort. He carried a large artillery pistol in a tan leather holster, and he also served as a bodyguard for the general due to the many rumors of plots to capture or kill him.

Creed placed the cup in its delicate-looking saucer and gave a knowing grin. "Affections play a role in everything, has been my experience, sir."

"Very good, young man," replied Washington.

Fitzgerald prodded him. "The man described as Neeley. Did he survive the fire? Is he convinced you represent our late spy, Jan Braaf? Did he communicate this to the British?"

"I have no way of knowing for sure, sir. I must admit, I hinted to him that Braaf had revealed the army was staying put. I needed to establish my, as you say, sir, bona fides, as he seemed doubtful. Not knowing the content of the letter, I could do little else."

"Excellent!" exclaimed Washington.

Creed was astonished. He feared his ploy had backfired. *More Irish luck.*

"You see, young Creed, that is precisely what the letter stated and what we, for now, intend. His Excellency has hopes of drawing the British into a major battle here on the heights, between our breastworks and Fort Washington. If the British think we are moving out, they may try to either outmaneuver us with a sally across the river to New Jersey or up into Westchester. We hope to avoid that and achieve a grander victory than the first battle on the heights. Something more akin to Breed's Hill, you understand."

Creed understood. A major battle outside of Boston the previous year, Breed's Hill, was not a decisive victory but marked the first real success for the Americans in the war. American defenders held their ground behind strong defenses and inflicted heavy casualties on the British. This set off a chain of events that eventually led to the British abandoning Boston.

"Now, this fire presents an interesting problem. His Excellency and, indeed, the staff had mixed feelings about the subject. General Greene and many others, including me, favored torching the city. There were pros and cons to this, of course, although His Excellency was ambivalent."

"Decidedly ambivalent," Washington interjected. He and Fitzgerald laughed at the quip.

"But the Congress ordered me not to burn the city, under any circumstances. That decided the matter for me until fate stepped in, in the form of your hazardous escape from a pack of Tory scoundrels. With one-third of the city burned and the chaos of the occupation, Howe may just hazard another frontal assault against our works, giving us the victory we need to secure the cause."

Washington and Fitzgerald glanced at each other with knowing looks. Creed correctly assumed he had received their approval.

Creed's eyes narrowed. *So, my mistake and its horrible consequence may play into their plans.*

Fitzgerald poured them another cup. "Now tell us what you learned of Captain Nathan Hale and his mission. That is the sad news in this entire affair."

Fitzgerald stole an "I told you so" glance at Washington, whose face now turned deadly serious. Fitzgerald's warning not to send an inexperienced and untrained spy behind enemy lines had been overridden by Washington himself. Sheer desperation to learn of British plans and intentions for once outweighed good judgment.

Creed explained how he and his cowboys had taken their leave of the Stanley stable in the evening. Surprisingly, they were able to negotiate the mile or so north along the Post Road without attracting too much attention. The city was in an uproar. Under military rule, all civilians were considered suspects, subject to searches and seizures. Despite the heightened security, Creed was able to talk his way past one patrol and two different sentries to make their way toward Howe's headquarters.

Creed spoke in a quiet and respectful tone, "We arrived at the Beekman Mansion around seven in the evening, sir. It was still daylight, although the sun was low off the western horizon. To the southwest, you could still see smoke rising from the city in a series of dark gray columns. It was as if an ancient Greek temple were rising from the lower part of the island. Using my Root Hog persona, I was able to bribe an ignorant young sentry, who informed us the unfortunate prisoner was taken to the army's artillery park for execution that morning, where they hanged him. The artillery park was near the Dove Tavern, located another mile up the Post Road. This time I risked discovery, and we all four mounted our horses and proceeded at a fast trot, arriving there at dusk."

"You were not challenged along the way?" Washington asked.

"Just once. We rode with determination. We saw few soldiers and pushed past any Tory checkpoints. Most accepted our affirmation that we were cowboys out to track down skinners suspected of arson."

Fitzgerald looked unconvinced. "You said most."

"I suppose most of the British were dealing with the aftermath of the fire or getting ready to head north. One stubborn group of Tories refused our passage, but we sent them packing with a flurry of tomahawk blades. Anyway, we found the execution site. A small crowd still watched the body, which hung from a tree limb. Hale was dressed in a white gown and cap. His eyes were closed, and he seemed at peace. I had a small flask of rum and used it to talk to some of the locals who saw the spectacle that morning. According to one, he died bravely and spoke with dignity to the crowd."

Washington hung on every word. "Told them what, Lieutenant?"

Creed's eyes welled with tears. "That every man should be willing to die for his commander-in-chief and for his country."

Washington maintained his composure. However, Fitzgerald's face darkened, and he started to dismiss Creed.

But Washington raised a hand. "It's quite all right, Robert. If I'm to send men on missions of mortal consequence, I ought to face the consequences myself, even if only in absentia."

The sentiment Washington evinced impressed Creed. Although the commander-in-chief was willing and able to order masses of men to combat and probable death, the life of even one soldier was still a concern for him.

Washington bowed his head in silence for a moment. He seemed to be in prayer. Then he spoke, "So he is gone. At least for him, the war is over, brave, noble fellow."

Chapter 6

Fort Lee, New Jersey, November 1776

The sky darkened as a cold November wind turned the light rain into an icy curtain that stung Finn's face with each of his powerful strides, but Creed pushed through it during the two hours of tough riding needed to reach headquarters by the scheduled time.

The rain had scattered into mere spray by early evening, and the wind had settled into a mild breeze by the time he arrived at Fort Lee. Washington had moved his headquarters and army across the North River after the defeat at White Plains and the stunning British assault on Fort Washington.

Fitzgerald had summoned him on behalf of General Washington. Creed came alone. Parker and Beall, as well as Thomas Jeffries, remained on station, observing movements of the British forces near Dobbs Ferry, located at one of the key North River crossing points.

He swung from the saddle and threw back the hood of his mantel. He handed Finn to an unhappy-looking orderly, who agreed to wipe Finn down and water him. A squad of Life Guards surrounded the large leather tent that served as Washington's headquarters. Since he was on paper an officer in this elite unit, the Life Guards greeted Creed with a sharp "present arms" as he entered.

Neither he nor his men spent time on normal Life Guard duties. They were totally preoccupied with special tasks for the commander-in-chief and his senior staff assistant, Colonel Robert Fitzgerald. The Life Guard members did not know the true nature of Fitzgerald's staff assistance, nor Creed's real work. As cover for Creed's activities, his declared duties included executive courier work, issuing special instructions to the selected regiments. This rationalized the comings and goings of Creed and his men, who needed freedom of action for their wide-ranging activities.

Creed met Lieutenant Abner Scovel, one of Washington's aides de camp, who flipped open the tent's flap as Creed was entering.

"Mister Creed," Scovel said perfunctorily. There was much happening, and Scovel had several hours' work ahead of him writing dispatches to the field commanders under the supervision of Tench Tilghman, a senior aide to Washington.

Creed was not at all surprised to see Fitzgerald and Washington poring over a map. Three heavy brass candelabras lit the tent, but enough wind slipped through the corner folds to cause a constant flickering that Creed found annoying. Creed unfastened his dark blue cloak and took a seat at the table. Fitzgerald poured coffee. Creed would have preferred tea, even without cream and sugar, but the hot, bitter liquid helped quench his thirst and chase away the chill from the long ride.

Fitzgerald nodded politely. "Well, Jeremiah, we are pleased you were able to make it here tonight. With the weather so inclement."

Creed took a second sip, then smiled across his cup. "Well, sir, I had little to do with my timely arrival. Finn is a good, sure-footed creature. 'Twas all his doing. You see, after the past few weeks, he seems to know all the roads here along the North River."

Washington, an avid horseman, smiled knowingly. "Yes, indeed, the horse makes the man, not the other way about."

Fitzgerald looked anxious to get to business. He had markings on the map that Creed could easily read, even in the dim candlelight. "Any change in conditions up north?"

"No, sir. Private Parker crossed over the North River, where he met couriers from Generals Lee and Heath. General Heath continues to hold the area around Peekskill. There is little British activity there right now, so he spends most of his time tracking down Tories, Loyalist militia, and of course, cowboys."

They all chuckled as Creed now often operated in disguise as a cowboy.

"General Lee sits at New Castle. Perhaps he is hoping to re-fight White Plains to his liking. But he is bound to be disappointed by the British."

Washington took this sensitive statement in stride. The British had outperformed him in what became a close fight at White Plains, the key town in Westchester. During that battle, Lee had identified ground more suitable for the army, but General Howe launched a sudden attack before Washington could move his forces to the better position. The battle was intense, but Washington eventually retreated under heavy pressure from the bayonet-wielding British and Hessians. However, the usually predictable Howe surprised him by shifting his army south toward Fort Washington, the large and seemingly impregnable stronghold on the upper heights of New York. It sat opposite the North River from its counterpart, Fort Lee, a less imposing fort named after General Charles Lee.

Fearing being cut off from Congress and his western supply route, Washington moved most of his army to New Jersey to block a sudden British attack on the nation's capital in Philadelphia. On Brigadier General Nathanael Greene's recommendation, he left a garrison at Fort Washington to keep a foothold on the Island of New York.

But he failed to place sufficient forces to defend it properly. The British and Hessians launched a three-pronged land and water assault that brought a quick capitulation before Washington could order an evacuation. This error consigned almost 3,000 irreplaceable men to the watchful bayonets of the Hessian brigades under General Knyphausen and the relentless Colonel Johann Rall.

Washington seemed to be thinking aloud as he recounted the event. "Although the post commander, Colonel Magaw, and General Greene both assured me the fort could hold till December, its capture was my responsibility alone. Now the forces of Lee and Heath, holding in the mountains north of Westchester, protect our northern flank – our link to New England. But if Fort Lee falls, that might be jeopardized."

Dissatisfied with the direction of the conversation, Fitzgerald spoke, "Sir, the lack of British activity in the Hudson Highlands makes it near certain they will soon attempt a coup d' main here against Fort Lee."

"Have we word from Mister Smythe?"

Fitzgerald glanced at Creed and replied, "No, Your Excellency. Mister Jons has not moved a boat in more than a fortnight. Next drop off is days away, assuming he can negotiate his way around or through the Royal Navy."

Washington leaned back and placed a large fist under his chin, immersing himself in thought. Fitzgerald eyed Creed knowingly. "Perhaps Root Hog could cross over to New York and ascertain this?"

Creed was not surprised Fitzgerald would suggest another forlorn hope mission. However, he was more surprised at Washington's reaction.

"No, ensure we double the sentries and alert the commanders to the likelihood of a British thrust. Although I would like to stop them right here, Fort Lee's real value lies in its proximity to Fort Washington. With that gone, we must plan for the worst: a British move on Philadelphia. I shall need General Lee to move across and join us, as our 3,000 effectives cannot do more than shadow and screen a British army of more than 20,000."

Fitzgerald rubbed his chin. "Even Lee's forces leave us outnumbered, by more than three to one."

Washington arched his brows. "Yes, but with proper use of local militia and terrain, we can fight delaying actions and tie him up in New Jersey. General Greene has a plan, but I digress."

Washington leaned toward Creed in a conspiratorial way. "I have requested Congress authorize the establishment of several more Continental Line regiments, two of which will be dragoons. I am going to nominate you for a position in one of the companies, a very special company."

Creed was stunned. His dream came true—assignment back to a line unit, a combat unit, a fighting command. And dragoons! *But my White Knights, Fitzgerald's special unit, so quickly disbanded?*

Fitzgerald cleared his throat. "Ah, I know what you are thinking, young man. Are my White Knights to go the way of their namesakes? Alas, for you, it is not to be so. The first company of the Second Dragoons will perform special missions just as you and your lads have performed for us. But unlike a Life Guard unit, we can justify dragoons being anywhere His Excellency requires them. Whether scouting, screening, performing special combat missions, or acting as couriers. You get the idea?"

Creed grimaced. He was disappointed but not surprised. "I am afraid I do, sir."

"You must be available to play out our ruse as Braaf's intermediary, should we require it. However, we need your ingenuity and skill to help us refine our intelligence system. To that end, you shall be under the command of an officer especially selected by His Excellency to command the company and oversee all its day-to-day intelligence activities."

Washington spoke in a quiet but firm voice, "I sense your concern, Lieutenant Creed. But your talents are needed for a variety of missions, and not merely the follow-up to the Braaf affair. That's why I did not select you for the overall command. For that, we have chosen an officer of good New England stock, someone with an education of some note, yet with combat and command experience of significance."

Creed did not know whether to be angry or glad. He wanted to command troops in combat. But he could already see commanding such a company would have many administrative burdens, which did not appeal to him. Yet he felt slighted.

Fitzgerald nervously rapped his fingers against his coffee cup as Washington spoke. Finally, he interrupted his commander-in-chief. "You see, Jeremiah, the politics of the day require such commands to go to officers who are politically connected. It helps cement the army in many ways, you understand. And besides, you are not really a..." Fitzgerald paused, already regretting his choice of words.

"Not really what?" Creed demanded. The pique he felt at the insinuation surprised even him.

"You know, my boy, from here. From the colonies — America."

Creed could barely control himself. "Surely, you're joking, sir! This army has more than its share of recent arrivals, immigrants, as well as freed slaves, and the occasional Indian. Why, even our esteemed second-in-command, Charles Lee, is English, a former British officer."

Fitzgerald backpedaled, unconvincingly. "Of course, we know all that, and you have our complete trust and confidence, but..."

"But what, sir?" Creed spoke to Fitzgerald but looked right at Washington.

"It is not where you came from, Jeremiah," Washington said. "It is how you came from there. Colonel Fitzgerald took the liberty of writing to some connections in Ireland. You see, we must inquire about even our most trusted officers as we enter this new business. You were, in fact, my first choice for command of the company. But I have to submit nominations to Congress now, as the regiments will begin forming perhaps as early as December or January. Appointing you second-in-command and placing you at the head of one of its two detachments was the best we could do under the exigencies we faced."

Creed glared. "So, what did you learn about me?" A shade of guilt, or perhaps even discomfort, crossed his face. His usual Irish good nature drained from him.

Eyeing him carefully, Fitzgerald answered, "Very little. That is the dilemma. Your family is well known, of course, no problem there. Nevertheless, it seems you disappeared for several years, and no one seems to want to discuss what they know, or whether they know anything at all. We were hoping you could provide the details that we lack, Jeremiah. Nothing you tell us will be held against you in any way. You have proven yourself on the field of honor. We need to know — for the record. Congress requires it."

Creed knew Fitzgerald was not being completely candid. They knew something, enough to cause them concern. He also knew everything *would* be held against him, depending on the circumstances. It seemed to him he had entered a new phase of his life. He could not refuse his commander-in-chief, the man who had placed a sacred trust in him before and who had responsibility for the fate of his adopted land.

"Where shall I begin?" Creed was, in actuality, asking himself.

Chapter 7

Officers' Mess, Regiment Berwick, Paris, July 1770

Lieutenant Colonel Maurice Creed dropped his knife and fork onto the empty plate and rubbed a fine linen napkin across his mouth, finishing the third course of a planned seven-course dinner. The roasted duckling with a cherry glaze, stuffed with chestnuts and basil, tasted better than usual. The cherry glaze left its traces on his fingers, which he hurriedly dipped into a small finger bowl. After he wiped them with a cloth, he rang a small bell to his right. He smiled at his guests, the regimental adjutant, Major Adrian O'Donnell, and four of his company commanders, Captains Kevin McCahill, Michel Fitzhugh, Reilly Dundan, and Joachim O'Higgins.

They were gathered on the eve of the anniversary of Patrick Sarsfield's death, a significant event celebrated each July 22d by this proud Irish regiment, which now served the King of France. Since the regiment's normal garrison was at Strasbourg, the regimental commander, Colonel Charles de Fitzjames, rarely spent time with it. He joined his regiment only when it deployed in full-field maneuvers, large parades, and occasionally, for battle. All three of the Irish Brigade's regiments: Berwick, Dillon, and Lacy had assembled in Paris for the event. Colonel Fitzjames would join the Berwick regiment on parade the next day. Until then, as usual, his Lieutenant Colonel, Maurice Creed, held command.

"The next course is on the way," Creed announced. "A glass of champagne to clear the palate, gentlemen? Let's fill the time with a toast. A toast to Patrick Sarsfield and The Brigade."

Chairs scraped and elbows jostled as they stood and raised their glasses high. Maurice Creed cleared his throat and began a history everyone knew by heart but heard told with enthusiasm each year: "Patrick Sarsfield, Earl of Lucan, led the Jacobite Irish resistance to King William's suppression of Ireland in the late 17th century. Following the Jacobite capitulation at Limerick in October of 1691, Sarsfield took a part of his army into exile in France."

"To Sarsfield!" Creed exclaimed.

"To Sarsfield!" heads flew back and glasses were downed and then charged once more.

Creed and his officers served in one of several distinguished regiments formed from Sarsfield's original army, whom lore and legend called the "Wild Geese." The Wild Geese were mainly infantry, meaning foot soldiers who acted as "shock troops" for the French armies.

Initially, there was one dragoon regiment, Regiment Fitzjames. But when the French disbanded the regiment seven years ago, its remaining troopers joined the Berwick regiment to fight on foot like their comrades. The Regiment Berwick had eight companies, each with just over fifty sturdy men, making it less than five hundred strong. Smaller than most French regiments, it compensated with spirit and bravery.

He continued, "Since that time, our brigade, *Le Brigade Irlandais*, has faithfully and gallantly served the kings of France in their wars.

"Hear, hear!" went around the table as chests expanded and the officers stood like proud peacocks.

The lads are energized, good.

"To the Wild Geese!" Creed exclaimed.

"To the Wild Geese!" they chanted in unison.

The glasses were refilled as Creed continued in a serious tone, "More notably, the Wild Geese inspired the Irish both at home and abroad. Although the brigade's famous infantry charge at Fontenoy in 1745 was our greatest achievement, its regiments have earned numerous honors in countless skirmishes, sieges, and battles from Flanders to Italy."

Creed lifted his glass and looked over the eager faces hanging on his every word. "To Fontenoy!"

"To Fontenoy!" came the response from throats hoarse with liquor and excitement.

Creed continued his soliloquy amidst the sound of wine pouring, "Because of its distinguished record, the brigade has attracted some of the more notable and aggressive types, as both officers and as soldiers."

Several officers murmured, "Hear, hear…"

Creed ignored them and continued, "This often has led some of our members to the most rambunctious and audacious behavior on the parade field, in the taverns, on the battlefield, and whenever possible, in the brothels."

A chorus of raucous laughs erupted, but Creed continued, "So, lads, the regiment has earned praise comparable to its brave counterparts, Dillon and Lacy. In numerous campaigns against the English and their allies, our cherished Irish Brigade has brought honor to itself and the French king, even though it has done little to advance Ireland's cause. Still, as is often the case with Ireland, hope remains alive. And, although generations have passed since our ancestors fled with Sarsfield, the Brigade Irlandais remains the best fighting force on the continent."

"*Sante! Slainte!*" Creed downed his drink.

The others did the same. The evening progressed. Maurice Creed's officers bantered back and forth with jokes and tall tales. They engaged in gossip, mostly fabricated lest any of them spark a duel, as dueling constituted a very real means of settling matters of honor among the officer corps. In that sense, these Irishmen differed little from their French counterparts.

The festivities droned on as the night grew old. Major Adrian O'Donnell played with the soufflé course and frowned into his dish as though it were a coarse gruel. Earlier, Creed had noticed he had hardly touched his wine. Several glasses stood more than three-quarters filled. O'Donnell appeared melancholy while the others were flushed with exquisite food, superb wine, and grand humor.

Creed decided to get to the problem. "Your row of claret stands like the British line at Fontenoy, Adrian. Is there something bothering ye tonight, on the eve of our grand tattoo?"

O'Donnell waved a hand nonchalantly, but his face reddened. "'Tis nothing, sir. 'Tis nothing at all."

Heads cocked. Everyone listening knew that meant anything but what O'Donnell declared.

Creed tried to stay light-hearted. "Nonsense! I know ye, and this is not normal. And 'tis disturbing the lads."

Creed glanced around at the others, who nodded in agreement.

"Come on now, lad, out with it," Creed demanded.

"Very well, sir. This time each year, I ponder the sensibility of all this pomp and circumstance over the late Lord Lucan. For sure, he was indeed a noble warrior. But with all said and done, he never returned home to finish the business. I believe he referred to us as 'an Ireland in France'. And here we now, some seventy-odd years later, still celebrate this glorious symbol of our impotence."

Dead silence filled the room. Had O'Donnell cursed the pope like a dark heathen protestant, he could not have stunned them more. The officers of the regiment always marveled at O'Donnell's intelligence and penchant for over-analysis. But they never realized to what dark depths it had brought him. The captains looked at Maurice Creed for a response. Creed knew none of them dared challenge or even question the adjutant. Besides being their superior, he had successfully fought over twelve duels, four of which resulted in his opponent's death. He was the best horseman, marksman, and swordsman in the regiment. In the case of the latter, he evinced accomplishments in both senses of the word.

Creed held his temper. He understood the words of his adjutant, stinging as they were. O'Donnell, at times, was like a prize stallion, powerful and determined, but skittish and in need of special care.

He tried to be conciliatory. "You make a point, Adrian, up to a point. However, impotence did not rout the allies at Fontenoy, nor foes on threescore battlefields from Ramillies to Genoa. And although Ireland yet remains in bondage and good Irishmen are relegated to serving a foreign king instead of their own, there is still hope. In the future, it may well be, but it lives on nevertheless, with the blood of each fallen Irishman as a down payment on the nation's future. So, I believe in what we do, and therefore, I serve."

Creed stood upright, grabbed his wine glass, and thrust it high crying, "*Vive le Roi! Vive Irlande Libre!*"

The entire table, including O'Donnell, rose and repeated the toast several, "*Vive le Roi! Vive Irlande Libre!*"

Then Creed broke into a chorus of "Farewell O Patrick Sarsfield," and they all chimed in, their usually passable voices now dried and scratched from too much drink.

Farewell, O Patrick Sarsfield! May luck be on your path!

Your camp is broken up – your work is marred for years – But you go to kindle into flame the King of France's wrath, Though you leave sick Eire in tears.

Och! Ochrone!

The poem, adopted and set to music by the Wild Geese as their anthem, never failed to inspire, and Creed could see that O'Donnell had shaken off his melodrama and chimed in with equal fervor.

Another lost sheep led back to the pasture, mused Creed, and his best one at that. By the time the officers finished the final course, it was past eleven. They passed around brandy and pipes, and the ribaldry continued until the clock struck twelve, when the celebration abruptly ended, and the officers lined up ceremoniously to shake their lieutenant colonel's hand.

As they did, each in turn softly intoned, "*Semper et Ubique Fidelis*" — "Always and Everywhere Faithful." This, the motto of the Irish Brigade, reflected their eternal and universal loyalty to Ireland, to their adopted sovereign, and each other. Indeed, they belonged to a brotherhood that stretched across time and space, in service to a lost cause. Sadly, though, in many ways, they were now more French than Irish, yet they would never quite be either.

* * *

Maurice Creed threw his tired body onto a divan near the large stone fireplace and took off his shiny boots. He was a sturdy man of average height with salt-and-pepper hair that he kept neatly brushed and styled. At forty-four, he had more than twenty-five years of tough campaigning behind him, and his weathered face and rheumatic joints showed it.

He gazed into the hearth. The embers still glowed, but the fire had consumed itself, and he felt too tired and groggy to start another one. Creed often ended a night of celebration with a period of maudlin remembrance of things now gone: his family, his country, and his late wife.

Suddenly, the double-framed doors flew open, and the chamberlain announced a visitor. Creed snapped out of his mood while pulling on his boots. "A visitor? At this hour? And who would that be?"

The chamberlain bowed and smiled. "He claims to be a relative of yours, sir — your nephew."

Creed's face went pale — no mean feat after all the wine and brandy consumed that evening. "What? My nephew? Robert? How the…"

Creed's mind raced. His brother's oldest son had a commission in the British army from whence he would return and eventually manage the family estate in Cork. *Why? How? Could he be here in Paris?*

The chamberlain bowed his head slightly, then shook it. "No sir, I believe the gentleman said his name was Jeremiah. Jeremiah Creed."

Creed's eyes widened. "Jeremiah? Here? Impossible! He is at the seminary in Saint…"

A young man suddenly stepped into the room, a boy really, of sixteen. He was just under six feet, above average height, and broad-shouldered with dark hair and eyes.

The last time Maurice saw his nephew was… well, never. It then occurred to him that he had not been to Ireland in nearly twenty years. The last time he visited was for Robert's baptism. It was a fine event, but was spoiled by a terrible argument with his older brother Robert, whom he had accused of treason to Ireland because of his dealings with the authorities. Robert was a trained surgeon and maintained the family property and status by converting to the state church. His wife, Kathleen, remained a devoted Catholic, causing much tension in the family, but that was not unusual in a land still torn between conflicting loyalties, both religious and political.

The young man crossed the room in a bound and grasped the colonel's wrists, looking deeply into his eyes. "Uncle Maurice, 'tis I, your very nephew-Jeremiah."

The older man briefly looked at his nephew before pulling him into a tight embrace. They held each other warmly. After a flood of tears of happiness, Maurice composed himself and told the chamberlain to bring his nephew some food and open another bottle of claret. They had much to talk about.

Maurice let his young visitor eat before he began the barrage of questions. Fortunately, the youth was a quick eater and in less than fifteen minutes, a half chicken and a loaf of bread were gone. The young man then sipped at his claret while his uncle questioned him.

"What a surprise this is, Jeremiah. I have not heard from your mother in some time. I would have thought she would send me a letter to inform me of your impending visit."

Creed's visage darkened. "Mother is dead, sir."

His uncle's face drained white, and his eyes began to well up with tears. "What did ye say? Dear Kathleen… dead? When? How?"

"Little more than a fortnight ago, sir. I am still not over the shock of it…"

Jeremiah burst into tears, and so did his uncle.

When the two finally exhausted their sorrow, the older man spoke, "She was the finest woman I had ever known, and that includes my own dear departed wife. Just a fine woman, too good for me, brother."

Maurice's face darkened. "Just what happened, lad?"

Jeremiah slowly shook his head and stared blankly at the floor. "She was caught in a sudden thunderstorm while out in the fields. They say she was bringing food to some of the workers, but I don't know for sure. Mother caught a cold, which turned into chills and a fever. Father called a colleague who was more experienced with fevers. They bled her multiple times and did other things, but 'twas to no avail. It soon turned to quinsy, infecting her throat, and then settled into her lungs. Gone in three days, they say."

"Not unlike me own Marie, dear heart. Despite the inner strength women have, I do believe they are at the heart of things, frail creatures…"

His nephew cut him off, to his surprise, "No, sir! Mother was strong—stronger than most men."

"Ah, correct ye are, Jeremiah. I am sorry, the grief and wine have gotten a hold of me and befuddled me brain. I have been in France too long. 'Tis indeed the ladies of Ireland that form the backbone of the Irish family and the very nation itself. Now, what brings ye here from the seminary? You know it was her fondest wish that you entered the priesthood. I suppose it was to counterbalance my own brother's apostasy in such matters."

"'Twas indeed her wish, uncle. The seminary was a fine place in so many ways: devout and pious priests and seminarians, loyal to Our Holy Father and Holy Mother Church. But also devoted to Ireland. I learned mathematics there, Latin of course, and some French, history to a fault, and some music. I liked singing with the choir, you know. Provided relief from the routine and isolation of the place."

The older man nodded. "That is all well and good, but then they gave you leave to stay on and bereave your dear mother after her funeral?"

Creed hesitatingly looked up at his uncle. "No, sir, I was to return to seminary the day after her burial. I never told them, but... I shall never return to the seminary."

Maurice Creed was scandalized. Despite the many sinful lapses they committed, they were, to a man, loyal to the Roman Church and tried to adhere to its tenets and practices as much as possible. In France, as in Ireland, you could be a great sinner yet be a good catholic. A people without a country hold their institutions dearly—the Regiment, the Brigade, the Church.

Maurice spoke anxiously, "You must return to the seminary, Jeremiah. It is your place, the place your mother wished you to be. She thought you would make a good priest, perhaps a monsignor or even a bishop."

His nephew's voice turned icy, "No, sir. After much reflection and prayer, I have decided it is not the place I am meant to be. I am not fit to take Holy Orders. I remained there only to please my mother. With her death, I no longer have that obligation. When I returned home for her funeral, I decided to make the break. I plan to write to the Rector and explain. As many drop out as remain, you know."

Maurice Creed nodded, although he did not know. "And what did your father say of this?"

The younger Creed stared at the table with a blank expression.

Maurice's tone became conciliatory, "Well, I suppose he was glad. Perhaps he will make you a protestant like your brother?"

Robert Creed and his wife Kathleen had an arrangement. She agreed to let him raise their older son, Robert, in the state church on the condition that she could raise any others as Catholic. Since Robert's only goal was to be his father's heir, and primogeniture granted the estate solely to the oldest son, this met his needs.

"No point in that, is there, uncle? Robert inherits the estate. 'Tis all he cares about. Besides, although not suited for the priesthood, I am and shall always remain catholic. 'Tis who I am. Who my mother was, what her beloved soul is. That will never change. *Per omnia saecula saeculorum.*"

The Cavalier Spy

"*Amen*," responded Maurice. "Well said, like the good Irish lad ye are, Jeremiah. Still, he might have bought you a commission in the British Army."

The young man waved his hand and shook his head. "'Twas in fact my fear. And that is why I am here. If I am to fight, it will never be for those who have enslaved my country. If my destiny is to be a soldier, I prefer it to be for Ireland rather than against her. I had hoped, sir, to join your regiment and serve here instead."

Maurice Creed felt a quick jolt of pride and then frowned. "A commission, even in the King of France's service, requires money, just as in English service. Despite our fussing over it, all these monarchs are the same. Still, I can make you an ensign, an officer cadet, for nothing. Once you have served a year or two, I can have enough saved to buy you a lieutenancy."

"That would be an honor, sir. You are very kind. But when it comes time to buy my commission, I prefer to pay for it myself."

The older man smiled. "Jeremiah, an ensign earns but five sous a day, while a lieutenancy costs well over fifty Louis d'Or."

"I have enough money. One of my saddlebags contains gold, Uncle."

"What in the name of Jesu—did you rob your father? Do not tell me that! Or worse, did you rob the church? Don't tell me you robbed the church!"

Creed smiled faintly. "In a manner of speaking, sir, I did both. When I entered the seminary, my mother instructed me that if anything happened to her, I was to go see the Abbot at St. Francis's chapel, Father Boyle. She had provided him with money years ago, money withheld from her dowry by her parents. Insurance it was, as they were not hopeful of a successful outcome to her marriage. The money was to help me rise through the church ranks. She did indeed want me to be a bishop, I believe. I saw Father Boyle and told him of my plans."

Maurice's heart was beating. "And just what did the good Father say?"

"He said Ireland had enough priests and bishops, but not enough men fighting for her liberty."

Maurice Creed laughed at the thought of it. "Bravo for the Abbot! And how much was it?"

"A little over two thousand pounds in gold coin, sir. Plus, half that in silver."

The older man choked, then whistled. "Now, that is enough to make a cardinal, even in France.

Or a colonelcy in the *Garde du Roi*! Very well, we must get this money into a safe place. I know a banker here in Paris, Irish he is, too. It will be safe with him, and you will earn interest." He winked at his nephew, "Better that folks think you a penurious ensign. This country is full of devious and larcenous men...and women."

They both laughed, and the older man hugged his nephew as if he were the son he never had. They talked until the embers in the fireplace had gone completely cold, draining the room of its last vestige of light.

"Enough now, we must get you to bed. Reveille is at six sharp. Tomorrow, you shall watch the *Brigade Irlandais* parade in full regalia before the king of France. After that, you will no longer be a spectator, but one of a sacred band of brothers, Lord Lucan's own, Wild Geese."

Chapter 8

Souffelenheim, Alsace, France, July 1772

Major Adrian O'Donnell snapped his telescope shut and returned it to his saddlebag. "I fear the reports are true, Jeremiah. Smoke is rising to the east. The Prussians may well be behind this, or it could be the Austrians. No matter, the King's peace is once more violated, and we Irish must now avenge him."

"Should we ride forward towards the smoke?"

"Yes, but not today."

"Then when? Why else are we here?"

"To learn who they are and what they want. Then we'll return to the garrison. Your uncle will send riders to the other regiments. Once we have a full brigade in hand, we'll come back."

Creed watched the rising smoke for a moment. "My instinct is to ride to trouble, sir."

O'Donnell looked at his young protégé and smiled. "I'm here to check that instinct. Until your instincts are mature enough for you to lead men."

Since Jeremiah Creed had enlisted in the regiment, he had taken the young ensign under his wing and made it his duty to teach the young man everything he would need to be the regiment's best officer. O'Donnell's loyalty and devotion to the regiment were deep and powerful, trumped only by his loyalty and friendship with his mentor, Lieutenant Colonel Maurice Creed. The two officers agreed that O'Donnell, not the uncle, would be the better mentor for the young man. O'Donnell was closer to Creed in age and could relate better to the boy, and his martial skills were unsurpassed in the brigade. In addition, they decided on it partly to avoid talk of nepotism, even though nepotism and cronyism were rampant in the brigade. In that sense, too, the Irish had become like their French hosts.

In the almost two years Jeremiah had served as an ensign, O'Donnell taught him the use of the sword, foil, and saber, as well as the use of firearms. He also gave him hours of instruction in military drill and tactics, as well as in map use. For his part, Jeremiah's uncle paid for a tutor so the young man could polish his French, improve on his mathematics, and read the classics. In addition, the uncle insisted his nephew take dancing lessons. The young man resisted the latter but eventually became a reasonable practitioner, convincing himself that it helped him with the footwork necessary for successful fencing.

Maurice had explained to his nephew that dancing was considered an indispensable skill for officers, equal to anything military-related, because when in garrison, much of an officer's life, even an Irish officer, centered on grand balls, fetes, concerts, and other social events.

It was Adrian who told him that such activities were encouraged by the French to provide foreign officers with the necessary political and social interaction to integrate into French society rather than remain isolated as foreign guests. Subaltern Creed later learned that the social agenda also had the additional purpose of providing bachelor officers with the opportunity to meet prospective brides and develop social graces. This also helped avoid the heavy drinking and senseless dueling earlier generations of Irish had so heavily engaged in, and which still occasionally occurred.

Adrian O'Donnell had neither siblings nor children. His wife, Olive, the daughter of a sergeant from Mayo, had died in childbirth along with their baby, and he never remarried. Creed's arrival enabled him to fill the void of the brothers and sons he never had. A strong bond grew between them. When not in training, on parade, or at maneuvers, O'Donnell and Creed read and discussed politics, played chess, and hunted. The forests of Alsace teemed with game, and the two took in no small amount of boar, stag, roebuck, and fowl. Both were expert riders and spent hours in the saddle, challenging one another's equestrian talents: jumping walls, fences, hedges, and streams at breakneck speed.

***

Their first such challenge between O'Donnell and his young charge took place in Creed's second week with the regiment. After the Paris review, the Berwick Regiment began a long and tedious march back to Strasbourg. The men faced many days of marching, which they ameliorated with lusty jokes, Irish ballads, and good-humored banter. Sometimes the regimental band departed hours before dawn to station itself along the route of march. It entertained the companies with stirring music as they marched along the dusty highways of France.

However, the men mostly enjoyed the competition. If a suitable meadow or field lay along the line of march, several of the officers, primarily the young bloods, would stage races. Two riders would gallop across an open field to cheers of the infantrymen, who could only watch. While strictly forbidden, many units still placed bets.

Although the second most senior officer in the regiment, O'Donnell participated in these races from time to time and, without exception, emerged victorious. On the first day of the journey, O'Donnell went head-to-head with one of the more arrogant officers of the regiment, a lieutenant named Tabard. Tabard had married into a family of French nobility and annoyed his fellow officers as he began to take on the airs of the aristocracy. For reasons nobody remembered, Tabard challenged O'Donnell to a race.

"My new horse, Rouen, is the most powerful charger in the army. I bought him for ten Louis d'Or from a cavalry captain in Paris. He was bred in Normandy," Tabard pronounced.

O'Donnell smirked. "Seems a fine nag, Tabard. But the rider has something to do with the steed's achievements. You should have saved your gold and bought a mule."

The nearby officers laughed at the remark. It was pure O'Donnell. Tabard maintained his composure like the French aristocrat he aspired to be.

"So you say, *Monsieur*. But you must oblige me to prove your case."

O'Donnell, with the entire regiment watching, beat Tabard in a quarter-mile dash.

"He's a fine horse, Tabard. You need to learn how to get the best of him, is all."

Tabard lowered his head and cursed silently.

The entertainment complete, the regiment renewed the march amid great merriment. Hours later, Creed was tramping along the hot, dusty road with his company, still marveling at O'Donnell's prowess. To his surprise, the adjutant suddenly rode up and slowed his mount to a walk.

Creed saluted smartly. "'Twas a foin race ya put on yesterday, sir. Lieutenant Tabard's horse was a grand sight stronger than yours, but you bested him anyway."

"Yer uncle tells me you were raised among horses, *Monsieur* Creed," O'Donnell replied.

"'Tis true, I loved caring for them almost as much as I loved riding them. But now I am in the infantry. And glad of it, I might add, sir."

O'Donnell smiled. "A good infantry officer can best any cavalryman when it comes to a real ride."

"I've heard as much said, sir. But by infantrymen, of course."

The men within earshot all laughed at the remark.

"Well then, what do you say about trying your hand at a race?" O'Donnell asked with a grin.

"A race, sir? I haven't sat on a horse in over a year." Creed looked down between his legs. "And beggin' yer pardon, sir, I don't seem to have a horse under me arse at the moment."

Laughter erupted down the line.

Caught between amusement and embarrassment, O'Donnell threw down the challenge. "Very well, *Monsieur* Creed. About four hours into tomorrow's march, we'll cross a large open plain near Reims. There is a meadow one league in length. It is bisected by a stone wall followed by a rivulet about two-thirds along the course. We shall race there. You shall ride Desiree! Fitzhugh's mare. She is the gamest creature we have."

"*Merde!*" exclaimed Captain O'Higgins, who rode next to O'Donnell. "Fitzhugh will have a fit, letting someone ride his Desiree."

"I have heard rumors of his jealousy. He should keep as close an eye on his wife as he does his horse," O'Donnell retorted.

Laughter broke out from the men marching along the road.

***

The next day, O'Donnell, O'Higgins, and Fitzhugh rode up to Creed's place in the column. He was marching with the First Company.

O'Donnell commanded the column to halt and take a rest period. "This is the place, *Monsieur* Creed." He pointed at bay with firm flanks and long, powerful legs. "This is the horse, Desiree."

Scowling, Fitzhugh dismounted and handed the reins to Creed. "She is a good girl. But keep her tightly controlled at the start, then give her the whip."

Creed leaped into the saddle as if he were born to it. "I have never taken the whip to a horse, sir."

He patted Desiree's long neck and talked to her soothingly, "Ye have good lines, Desiree. A good filly, ye are."

"Enough of this, Adrian! Have your little race," Fitzhugh said. Already, the men along the road were throwing coins, tobacco plugs, and anything else valuable in an orgy of bets.

"No wager, Fitzhugh?" O'Higgins asked slyly. "I will give you two to one on our good major."

"Ha, you are the fool. Desiree is the better horse," Fitzhugh retorted.

"Yes, but sly Major O'Donnell knows this field. And he knows Desiree is fast on the flat but not a powerful jumper like his Nicol. He's fixing to teach the parvenu a lesson."

"Then make it three to one," Fitzhugh sighed. "*Merde…* he better not kill my horse."

Not long after, the riders pulled up at the designated point.

Fitzhugh pointed. "Look there! That's O'Higgins waving his hat. That's the endpoint."

Creed squinted. The morning sun was to the east and pierced his eyes. "I can barely make it out. 'Tis over a league distant. The stone wall obstructs my view. Oh, very well. I see him now."

O'Donnell chuckled. "Let's begin. I can barely keep Nicol steady. He's anxious for laurels."

Fitzhugh pulled his pistol from his belt, cocked it, and pointed it skyward. "On my shot, gentlemen. One, two…"

The pistol emitted a dull crack, sending sparks and powder into the air. The horses bolted forward at the gallop. O'Donnell gave spurs and whip to Nicol, but Desiree jumped ahead. Creed had no spurs, so his infantry brogans, firm knees, and a commanding voice were all he used to guide her forward.

Crack, crack. O'Donnell drove his horse with the whip, trying to stay within a length of the faster mare. He had full confidence she'd break or slow down at the first obstacle, and likely never attempt the second. The joke was on his young ward. He had promised Maurice his mentorship would not spare hard lessons for the lad, and this was one of the first—Do not get talked into situations you have no control over.

They were half a league through, and the stone fence lay fifty meters ahead. O'Donnell watched, waiting to give a final spur to Nicol as Desiree began to slow and balk at the jump. But to his amazement, the mare maintained her gait and cleared the fence without any hesitation. O'Donnell and Nicol followed, but he could see the effect on the gelding. Nicol had never trailed another horse across an obstacle. Now Nicol's spirit sagged.

"We'll carry this as they tumble, my friend!" O'Donnell cried. He gave whip and spur to Nicol once again. The gelding lurched forward in a burst of effort and cleared the rivulet. But Creed had already guided Desiree gently over the obstacle, and along the flat, she sped towards O'Higgins, who stood in disbelief at his miscalculation. Creed passed him standing in the saddle and plucked the feather from O'Higgins' hat as he rode by. He slowed Desiree's pace and guided her to a walk.

Creed patted the mare. "Good girl! I knew you could do it. That's all you needed."

"The laurels are yours— this time, *Monsieur* Creed." O'Donnell doffed his hat as he brought Nicol about and walked him alongside Creed.

They finally ended up in front of O'Higgins. Creed returned the feather. From over a mile off, they could still hear the cheers and shouts of the column where men were sitting on shoulders and hanging from tree limbs to get a glimpse of the event. The cheers of the few who won big almost drowned out the boos of the many who lost. But few would bet against young Ensign Creed after that day.

When they got back to the column, Creed dismounted Desiree and handed the reins to her master. "You have a fine filly there, Captain Fitzhugh. She can do anything for ye. But I'll give you this advice. Spare the whip."

"*Merde*! Pure luck she made that jump," Fitzhugh replied.

O'Higgins pushed back his hat and scratched his head. "Creed is right. You should listen to the young man's advice, Fitzhugh. Why, Ensign Creed is a regular cavalier!" A chorus of laughs came from the soldiers nearby.

O'Donnell grinned broadly. "'Tis true, O'Higgins. From now on, Jeremiah Creed will be our cavalier. The cavalier ensign! A fitting appellation."

* * *

Although O'Donnell's mentorship of Creed quickly made him a fine officer, it was the political discourse that had the most significant effect on the young man. O'Donnell, despite his strong and passionate Irish nationalism, read many of the political and philosophical works of the current French and English writers and encouraged young Creed to do the same.

The two spent many a long ride or rain-soaked afternoon discussing the nature of God and the church, their relationship to government, and the sources of authority. O'Donnell accepted the French society he lived in but loathed it. If Ireland were ever free, he explained to Creed, it should not have a monarch, other than perhaps a figurehead. Its connection to the church should be spiritual, not temporal, its relationship to God spiritual and moral, not dogmatic. He also felt that Ireland should have a representative government that respects individual rights and affords men a reasonable means to redress grievances.

They often talked of the American colonies. There, transplanted Englishmen had begun to develop their own governance, like O'Donnell's ideas for Ireland. The Americans had even begun to show resistance to the British crown and the British Parliament. They protested, pushing back against a string of oppressive tax measures, governance edicts, and trade controls.

Creed agreed with O'Donnell's idea that perhaps the troubles in the colonies might help Ireland's cause in some way. He obtained as many pamphlets and newspapers on the subject as were obtainable in France at the time and even managed to find some of the works of Thomas Paine and Benjamin Franklin. O'Donnell often hinted to Creed that he would like to go to America when he finally left the army.

One day, Creed said to his uncle, "If I leave the army, I shall return to Ireland and fight for her freedom."

"You have been spending perhaps too much time with O'Donnell. Sadly, the hope is worn from our brave land, Jeremiah. 'Twill be some time before she can stand up to the tyranny that has beset her."

"When she is ready, we shall be there for her, then."

For almost two years, Jeremiah Creed served as an ensign in the Berwick regiment, bearing the regimental standard for the colonel and assisting the adjutant as his aide. The "ensign cavalier" enjoyed the honor of carrying the standard, a red and white cross on a red field with the Latin inscription "*In Hoc Signo Vinces*."

From his study of classical and church history, Creed knew this motto harkened back to the Roman emperor Constantine the Great, who saw those words and the cross in a vision just before the battle of the Milvian Bridge, which gave him sole possession of the purple. Its translation, "In this sign, you shall conquer," connected the regiment to its Catholic roots that went deep into the earliest days of Christendom and reflected the strong faith of these often-wayward men.

In time, O'Donnell had turned Creed into a true soldier, officer, and gentleman. "The Cavalier", as many now called Creed, excelled with the saber, pistol, and musket. He rode, of course, like the wind. More importantly, he understood how to maneuver men and fight on horse or foot. And most importantly, unlike most of his peers, Jeremiah Creed could use a map.

However, it was his sense of humor, fair play, and relative modesty that most impressed the officers and men of the regiment. But Creed had an artful side as well. He read plays. And he often put together plays of his own, adapting the script and schooling several officers as actors. Creed himself acted in them and developed an uncanny ability to change his persona, in more than one language.

Yet he had a pious side that was evident to all. Although no saint by any means, Creed was devoted to the church. He never forgot the lessons of the seminary nor his mother's desire for him to serve God. He often led his men and fellow officers in prayer, and he made sure they attended mass on Sundays and most important feast days.

* * *

Souffelenheim, Alsace, France, October 1772

The long line of men clad in red stretched along the road north for several miles. The dry road gave up a cloud of dust with each tramp of a brogan and every drum of horse hooves. Two months earlier, Maurice Creed had finally secured a king's commission for his nephew. Now, a freshly commissioned lieutenant of the Berwick Regiment, Jeremiah Creed, at the young age of eighteen, commanded a detachment of handpicked men. His twenty-five mounted infantry led the pursuit of a hostile force that had crossed the Rhine in one of the many incursions committed by both sides.

Alsace sat along the eastern border of France, just over the Rhine from Germany. At the time, Germany was not a country, but an intricate amalgamation of independent duchies, states, bishoprics, and principalities that constituted most of the German-speaking world.

Earlier in the year, the ruler of one of the larger principalities, the Elector of Palatine, had sent a force of almost 2,000 men on a raid south through the town of Rheinstetten, a pleasant city that guarded the west bank of the Rhine. From there, they marched south along the west bank of the great river. The dangerous mix of German and Dutch mercenaries sacked any town or village with allegiance to the French king. If they faced resistance, they murdered the men, ravaged women of all ages, and seized anything of value. Despite the military overtones, this was primarily a venture aimed at plundering and intimidation.

Lieutenant Jeremiah Creed led the vanguard of the king's reaction force, commanded by Major O'Donnell. O'Donnell had marched his command the twenty miles north from Strasbourg as quickly as he could. It included six companies from the Berwick Regiment and four companies from the Royal Alsace Regiment. Since being posted to Strasbourg a year earlier, the Berwick Regiment had fought a series of small actions, both offensive and defensive, to protect the Rhine crossings near the city. But this incursion was different. The king feared the enemy intended to stay awhile. It was a challenge that could not go without reprisal.

Creed's mounted command was his idea. Once the regiment returned to Alsace, it did not take long for Creed's youthful imagination to recognize the need to react quickly to foreign incursions. He soon argued with O'Donnell, then his uncle, that a half-company of men should be mounted, not as cavalry but as mounted infantry, dragoons. Creed offered to fund the purchase of horses if the regiment paid for their upkeep. Creed's reputation as the cavalier and his natural leadership abilities were indisputable.

After some debate, the elder Creed agreed. The two older men gave the new lieutenant command of the unit. Creed approached the job of selecting both horses and men with relish and efficiency. Creed's unit, an unofficial troop of dragoons, enabled them to react quickly to incursions and to perform reconnaissance that was more effective over longer distances.

O'Donnell gave his instructions, "Your mission is simple, Jeremiah. Find a suitable place to begin a defense and hold there until I arrive with the rest of the column."

"But if there is an opportunity to attack? If I catch the *Allemandes* in their depredations? Should I not do something?" Creed asked eagerly.

"No. Find us a suitable place to stop them. Mass volleys work best from a defensive position. Never lose sight of that. I plan to lure the *Allemandes* into us and mow them down."

Creed led his force forward at the trot. He headed in the direction of the smoke. The way was often blocked by a flood of refugees whose numbers increased with each league. *We should have done this back in July.*

Creed had to slow down the column more than once to allow the peasants to continue their flight without risking his horses' massive hooves. He had selected the powerful and hardy Ardennes draught horses to carry his men. Descendants of the powerful battle horses that confronted Caesar, the Ardennes horses proved compliant and willing to learn. O'Donnell once joked that Creed's horses complemented his men's characters perfectly. Each dragoon carried a brace of pistols, a musket, and a heavy saber. Although forbidden by French army regulations to drill as cavalry or even "charge home," Creed wanted the ability to face cavalry without dismounting. So, he had drilled them in both mounted and dismounted combat.

The Irish soldiers quickly grew fond of the young officer and gently referred to him as *Le Chevalier*. *Chevalier* was a rank of knighthood that could only be bestowed by the king himself. Their use of the title showed that their loyalty went to him first, the king second.

As they proceeded farther north, Creed saw fresh smoke plumes billowing from over the tree line to their front. The newly minted lieutenant turned to Sergeant McElroy, a second-generation legionnaire from Clare. "Sergeant, *Les Teutons* are just over the rise and somewhere beyond that forest. Send a man back to report this to Major O'Donnell. Rather than try to defend here, I hope to interrupt their work."

"But I thought ye had orders otherwise, sir. The major will have your skin," McElroy said.

"They don't call me Le Chevalier for naught. Pick someone, please."

McElroy saluted briskly and selected his best rider, a private named Swan, for the task. With most of the lads new at this riding business, Creed's new command had few who could proceed at more than a trot for very long. Swan, a third-generation member of the brigade, had grown up on his grandfather's small horse farm in Normandy. Normally, such a young man would be bound for the French cavalry, the most prestigious arm of the Royal Army. But Swan never considered any other calling than the Irish Brigade, preferring to serve as an Irish foot soldier rather than a French cavalryman.

Creed drew his saber and pointed up the road. "In two files, forward!"

At that, the small troop went from a single file to two abreast. They took off at a fast trot to catch their officer, who was already over the rise and out of sight. In minutes, they were trotting up the dark forest road, deeper into the dense, dark woods. To Creed, the forest seemed like a large tent, and even at mid-morning, somewhat eerie.

The Alsatian forests were mostly coniferous with a sprinkling of oak and other deciduous hardwoods. Rays of sunlight illuminated the forest like light from a cathedral's windows. The Alsatian foresters maintained their woods in pristine, almost park-like condition. As a result, visibility could stretch for fifty yards or more, even though foliage. And small groups of men could pass through them with ease.

Creed suddenly saw dark figures ahead. *Another group of peasants fleeing south?* A second look revealed horsemen, moving down the road at a surprisingly casual pace. *I suppose this stretch of forest road is as good a place as any.*

Just before them, the road dropped into a steep slope, then rose and leveled off. He glanced to the side. Several large trees, narrow and scrawny poplars, each almost thirty feet long, lay in a neat pile. Conveniently, the foresters had also pruned them of their branches. Creed decided to take advantage of what Providence and the foresters provided him.

"Sergeant McElroy, have those trees pulled across the road. Stack them as best you can right here. Then form the men three deep and prepare to receive cavalry. We shall begin our defense here and now."

"I thought our orders were simply to find a defensive point, sir?"

"Indeed, Sergeant. We have," Creed answered with a laugh. "And now I intend to use it!"

McElroy's ruddy face broke into a wide grin. "By Jesus, the lads are ready for one!"

In minutes, the powerful horses had dragged six poplars across the road at the top of the slope. The hasty pile of trees was just enough to stop a pell-mell charge along a narrow and sloping forest road. The men knew their drill well and formed three ranks of six, enough to cover the road. The remaining men held the horses at ready, twenty yards to the rear.

Creed stood behind the poplars with McElroy and peered down the road.

"Those horsemen move at the walk. Why the slow advance?"

"They're in no rush. The main body is likely finishing its rapine of whatever village lies beyond. Let's take our positions with the lads."

Creed moved to the right of his little command. McElroy moved to the rear. Creed looked down the dressed ranks to check their alignment one last time. The shadows and sunbeams mixed under the forested canopy in a compelling spectacle. The detachment stood motionless in three neat rows: tall men in bright red coats with black leather collars and cuffs, white belting, and off-white breeches and stockings. Brass buckles and steel musket barrels glistened, as did the bayonets hanging from their belts. Each man's black cocked hat had a simple brass plate with the Irish harp superimposed over a cross with the Latin words "*In Hoc Signo Vinces.*" A simple green cockade completed the work.

Creed spoke firmly, "We shall fire by rank, lads. Volley fire to commence at forty yards, just before they proceed down the slope. I need three volleys each. Fix bayonets before the third volley. Those who are not willing to lay down their lives here and now can go. But no invader shall pass here whilst any of us remain alive."

He spoke with confidence and authority as O'Donnell had instructed him, but Creed's legs felt wobbly and his throat was dry. A sickening feeling coursed through him. What did he know of combat? He was a teenager, leading men, yet they followed his every command as if he were O'Donnell or the colonel himself. *Why in the name of Christ did they do it?*

"The lads would like a prayer, sir," McElroy said from the rear. "We always pray before battle."

Creed felt embarrassed at not thinking of God at that moment. "Very well. The Lord will excuse us not kneeling, however. You may lead the men, sergeant."

McElroy looked to the canopy above. "Hail Mary, full…"

The men chimed in unison with the prayer that had seen the Irish through trial and tribulation since the time of the Vikings. When they finished, Creed cried out his own prayer, "St. Michael the Archangel—defend us in battle…"

The men responded, "St. Michael the Archangel-defend us in battle!" Then they broke into a bevy of cries, curses, and oaths, in French and Gaelic. Suddenly, all went silent.

***

The German hussar captain squinted at the pile of trees blocking the road some hundred yards ahead. "*Wass solle dass… die verdaemte Foerster haben nicht gut gearbeitet…die Elsasicher Schweine…*What can that…the damned foresters did not do their work well…Alsatian swine…"

The captain's scowling face highlighted a wicked saber scar—a long and deep wound received in some long-forgotten skirmish that gave him the appearance of a demon.

As he muttered insults at the quality of the Alsatian foresters, he failed to notice the line of men standing silently behind the trunks and boughs. Their blooded horses continued the slow thump of hooves on the soft forest trail. Sunbeams glistened off the silver buttons that adorned the dark blue hussar dolmans and the fur-trimmed pelisses, the trademark hussar jacket worn jauntily over the shoulder.

The hussars rode closer. The captain's trained eye scanned the logs blocking the road eighty paces ahead. He thought he saw something shining as a sunbeam doused it in light. He instinctively knew they had walked into a trap!

"*Die Franzosen! Halt!* The French! Stop!" He called out in desperation as he reined his horse.

***

A nervous but determined Lieutenant Jeremiah Creed took a deep breath. *They're at the defile. Now's our time.* "Fire!"

As one, each rank belched smoke and fire, sending a cascade of lead balls zinging into the horsemen just across the defile. The hussar commander died in the saddle, with two rounds hitting him squarely, one in the chest and the other in his head.

The concentrated volley was devastating. Around him, six more men dropped, as did several horses. The rest of the horses shrieked with fear and began to rear and turned in disarray. But a second volley and then the third slammed into them. Before the troop of hussars broke and fled headlong back, they left over a dozen men and as many horses dead or dying on the road.

Creed's men began a rousing cheer, a strange mix of English, Gaelic, and French. He could hardly see the end of the ranks. The smoke from the muskets hung so heavily in the warm morning air. Creed had trouble breathing for a few seconds. Finally, he ordered his men to mount. They would take cold steel to these rascals. Minutes later, the troop cantered down the road, the heavy hooves of their horses breaking and crushing many of the wounded and dying hussars.

* * *

Garrison Irlandais, Strasbourg, November 1772

The usual evening din had died down in the Irish garrison. After two weeks of hard marching punctuated with several swift but deadly skirmishes, the Elector's designs on Alsace abated. The invasion force swarmed across the Rhine, content to lick its wounds and prepare for its next incursion. Despite the cost in money and men, the many wars of Louis XIV had done little to stabilize France's frontiers. Since his demise, France continued to fight pointless sieges, skirmishes, and the occasional battle, sometimes as the aggressor, sometimes as the aggrieved.

Lieutenant Colonel Maurice Creed presided over an officer's mess, elated by its success but too tired to celebrate in the usual fashion of heavy drinking and loud song. Instead, a half dozen sheep provided mutton and chops fit for a king, washed down with Alsatian wine of the finest quality. When the meal ended, their commander lit his pipe, and the captains and lieutenants all lit theirs in anticipation of the brandy they knew would soon arrive. Creed did not smoke, nor did O'Donnell, but they each sipped a crisp Riesling wine as they discussed the campaign.

"Jeremiah, your audacity at the commencement of the campaign set the tone. When their hussars broke, all the fight went out of the Germans. To be expected, after all."

"Expected?"

"Jeremiah, they are paid mercenaries, merely fighting for loot and rape. Let that be a lesson to ye. Men who fight for a cause shall always triumph over hirelings."

"You may be right, sir, but only if the men fighting for the cause are properly trained and equipped. Our lads knew what they needed to do and had the means to do it."

"Indeed, men require faith in themselves, but also in their leader. They had faith in you, me laddie."

"And their God."

"Always back to God, eh?" O'Donnell chided.

"Where else, sir?" Creed responded incredulously.

"Reason and mankind would be a start."

"Belief in God requires as much reason as faith."

"Your mother and the seminary have ye brainwashed!" O'Donnell gave him a friendly punch.

"Of course, sir. 'Tis the Irish way…the only way."

"I wish I had your faith, young man. But back to the battle… if only our esteemed Colonel-Proprietor had seen it. By the time he arrived at Strasbourg, we were returning victorious. Now, rather than staying here to congratulate the regiment, he hurries back to Versailles to report his victory to the king. That is what we Irish have become, Jeremiah, lap-dogs for effete monarchs."

Creed took a sip of his wine, slightly sweet, slightly tart. "Surely he will tell the king of my uncle's shrewd planning, or how you led the brigade forward to victory or the bravery of the men."

O'Donnell waved his hand dismissively. "Nonsense, lad. He will claim the victory, from planning to completion, as if it were his own. You see, Jeremiah, to men like Charles Fitzjames, it was his victory. He is the Colonel-Proprietor. In his mind, and under French law, he owns the regiment and can take full credit for its achievements, while he can blame your uncle for its failures. That is how these French noblemen, how noblemen everywhere, are."

Creed bristled just a bit. "But he is an Irishman, sir. He ought to know better."

O'Donnell smiled ruefully. "He is no longer an Irishman in anything but name. His grandfather and father have intermarried with French nobility to secure their sinecure. What's more, it worked. When the Fitzjames dragoons merged with our regiment some years past, his family succeeded to the colonelcy. They beat out gallant DeLacey, and that is no small feat. No, he and his family are now more French than Irish."

Jeremiah Creed took in O'Donnell's words and reflected on the world he had recently entered. "'Twould be a grand thing to fight under a great general and free Ireland. That is my dream, to live in freedom in me own land, to earn that freedom on the battlefield."

O'Donnell nodded in sympathy. "Aye, 'twould be a fine thing, Jeremiah. Not very likely, though. Now, if it is freedom you want to fight for, fix your eyes across the ocean, lad."

"The Atlantic?"

"Yes, the Atlantic, of course. There might be a fight brewing between England and her colonies. Since the parliamentary Stamp Act back in sixty-five, the politics there have become quite heated. I daresay that within five years they will be in open rebellion."

Creed's eyes widened. "And how do you know that, sir?"

O'Donnell grinned a wry grin. "Common sense. You read some of the pamphlets and papers I gave you, did you not? The colonies are too distant and too disparate, even for the reach of the English king. More importantly, the American colonists are a people who have faced savages, the wilderness, and the ocean. They are self-reliant. And, they have lawyers."

"Lawyers? What in the name of Christ do lawyers have to do with anything?"

O'Donnell slugged back the last drop of Riesling and laughed. "They have everything to do with it, me lad – everything. Trust me."

Chapter 9

La Rochelle, France, July 1775

A sickly gray pall of tobacco smoke filled the tavern, darkening the room and cloaking its patrons, most of whom preferred it that way. The rancid mix of smells — stale hops, over-spiced food, and the unwashed bodies of merchant seamen, shady businessmen, and the prostitutes hustling them. was overwhelming to the senses. Yet Jeremiah Creed hardly noticed. He had another four hours before his ship sailed with the evening tide.

He and his companion would finish at least one more bottle of wine before then. Creed drank too much these past days. Recent events had overwhelmed him. He vowed to reduce his drinking once aboard the ship. He would need a clear head when he arrived in America, a land he now aimed to make his third and last home.

The two men had a piece of paper spread on their small table. Under the weak light from a dying candle, he penned farewell letters: one to his uncle, Lieutenant Colonel Maurice Creed, and the second to the royal prosecutor in Paris. By the time each received their missives, he would be halfway across the Atlantic, destination the West Indies. From there, he would find passage north and begin his new life.

Creed scribbled clumsily and took little time to ensure that his French grammar met the standards of its intended recipient, or that the English prose adequately expressed his feelings. He knew he likely would never see his uncle again. This disturbed Creed more than he thought it would. In the past five years, his uncle had become the father he never really had, and Adrian O'Donnell the brother he wished he had, instead of his cruel and arrogant older sibling. Creed hardened his heart to the loss. This was not, after all, his greatest heartache.

Major Adrian O'Donnell talked while Creed wrote. He spoke English in case police informants loitered nearby. As with any port city, La Rochelle had many non-Frenchmen, especially near the docks. There, one could encounter seafarers from Germany, Holland, Spain, and Portugal, as well as the occasional *Anglais*. France and England were enjoying a brief respite from the wars they had fought over the last hundred years. During that period, they expanded their trading efforts and commerce between the two nations.

O'Donnell sipped at his wine, his eyes flitting around the tavern for signs of trouble. "Try not to spill any more ink than you can, Jeremiah. It must last you some time. I don't think such quality ink exists in the colonies. I understand they distill the blood of *Les Sauvages*."

O'Donnell chuckled at his little jest but then grew sullen. He regretted he could not depart France and the Old World as well. In some sense, he would live that fantasy through his young protégé. O'Donnell needed to return to the regiment where he faced court-martial and dismissal.

Creed looked up from his work and smiled. "Major, I shall save every drop of this fine liquid. Apropos that, may I please have another glass?"

O'Donnell reached for the bottle. "Indeed, but pace yourself, lad. Who knows what servants of the crown we'll encounter before you depart?"

* * *

Creed and O'Donnell had already survived several near encounters with the gendarmerie and local constables since their flight from Paris a month earlier. Creed, imprisoned for two months in the Bastille, escaped disguised as a prison chaplain. O'Donnell had bribed sufficient guards and officers to smuggle in a priest's cassock and frock, which Creed used to great and dramatic effect. The former seminarian insisted on hearing confessions and performing other services as he worked his way out of the labyrinthine prison. This ploy allayed any suspicions the jailers might have had. Creed's escape was greased by some of the small fortune Creed had been amassing over the past five years, which had reached a sum of nearly 75,000 Livres. In British money, this came to a little over 5,000 pounds sterling.

Using some of that money, O'Donnell had purchased a wagon and commissioned it to deliver Creed's possessions to La Rochelle, where he planned to arrange passage for the young fugitive. The escape gave Creed an eight-hour head start on the authorities. He did not return to the regiment, but met O'Donnell on the outskirts of Paris, in the Jewish quarter, *Le Ville Juive*. O'Donnell chose to meet in the Jewish quarter because crime was nearly nonexistent there. No *Prévôt des Maréchaux*, or constables, patrolled it.

Thus, more than a fortnight of clandestine travel across the country began. Because the crown wanted Creed for the commission of a high crime, the murder of a nobleman, the authorities had immediately sent word of his escape to all the major cities in the kingdom. Fortunately for Creed and O'Donnell, the local police's efficiency varied.

In most of the towns and villages through which they passed, they went completely unnoticed. However, in three jurisdictions, authorities had established elaborate informant networks among the populace and posted a reward for his capture. This resulted in their near capture twice. Both times, they eluded the police through guile, bribery, or just fast riding. In another instance, however, the constables of a village on the outskirts of Orleans discovered them and made a major effort to bring them in.

The night this occurred, O'Donnell had found them a comfortable pair of rooms at a chateau named Le Haute Orleans, which an impoverished nobleman had turned into a high-class bordello for local gentry and nobility grown bored with their wives and mistresses. Hard riding had fatigued them both, and O'Donnell, in a rare lapse of judgment, opted for comfort over caution. After a small but elegant supper, both men took baths and then retired to their rooms, where Creed hoped to get a good night's rest for the first time in a long time.

However, at ten that evening, Creed's slumber was broken by the sweet smell of perfume and the rustle of petticoats. Despite the shadows, he saw his visitor, a young woman, had deftly inserted herself between his sheets, applying gentle caresses in not so subtle places. The seminarian in Creed was appalled. However, the rake in him won out in the battle of will.

As the young woman, a fiery redhead who called herself Monique, was in the final throes of her passion, the door to the room burst open. Before he could extract himself from this compromising position, four menacing policemen surrounded the bed.

"We arrest you in the name of the king!" the captain among them declared.

Creed threw the covers over Monique. "*Monsieur*! This is a mistake, I assure you. Have you no decency? See here, I have a lady…"

"We see plain enough, *Monsieur.* "

"Am I not allowed to dress?"

The captain chuckled. "Of course, *Monsieur*. It would be inappropriate to enter the gaol as a newborn. But be quick about it."

Creed eyed the manacles dangling in the hands of a fat policeman. He then eyed the window. As he pulled up his pants and stuffed his shirt in, his would-be jailers took time to eye Monique, who now lay across Creed's bed, her lithe figure pushing through the silk sheet and exposing her seductively.

Creed scanned the room for a possible escape. "You gentlemen have made a mistake. This is a case of mistaken identity."

"Are you not the fugitive Irishman, Jeremiah Creed?" the captain asked.

"I am not he! I assure you."

"So, you are not a fugitive?"

Creed saw the small seed of doubt had confused them just enough for him to act, and act he did. "I never said that, *Messieurs*!" As he fastened the final buckle on his bootstraps, Creed leaped out the window onto a ledge and made his way down a drainpipe.

One of the officers, a corpulent man of middle age, attempted to climb down after him but lost his footing and fell two stories to the stone patio below with a sickening thud. Another discharged his pistol at Creed, but it misfired, and sparks caught his eye, temporarily blinding him. The remaining officers decided not to chase and went to find the other visitor at the chateau, O'Donnell.

However, the shot had alerted O'Donnell, who grabbed his belongings and scrambled down the hall before they could find him. At the rendezvous point in a nearby stable, they readied their horses and gold-laden saddlebags, hidden under a pile of hay and dung. In minutes, they were galloping in the night air. Each carried a brace of pistols plus a saber.

Looking back at the chateau Haute Orleans, Creed could see it fully lit against the dark sky. Silhouettes moving furtively in every room as the police roused the other patrons, whether bourgeoisie, gentry, or nobility, who submitted indignantly to a search by the inept and frustrated team of officers.

O'Donnell turned his head and hollered at Creed as their horses pounded down the gravel highway. "Thank God they were locals and not *Prévôt des Maréchaux*."

Prévôt des Maréchaux was the title once awarded to the noblemen charged with policing the King's Highways. Now, although no longer noblemen, their men, mounted and well-armed, provided the backbone of the yet vestigial national police system.

"Do not thank the Lord too soon," exclaimed Creed. "Look ahead!"

O'Donnell looked up and immediately understood Creed's concern. A half dozen mounted horsemen blocked the road. Because they carried so much gold, O'Donnell was not sanguine that they could outrun their pursuers and decided to try a different tactic.

"Slow down to a trot, and then a walk. I will talk to them long enough for our horses to regain their wind. If they do not believe my story, we shall fight our way through them, by God."

As they came to a walk, they checked their pistols and sabers, positioning the weapons for immediate use. They halted nonchalantly in front of the *Prévôt*, who wore a dark blue jacket, white breeches, and a belt. They carried sabers, but only the sergeant had a pistol. The others had muskets slung diagonally across their backs that were most likely not loaded. *A grave mistake, Messieurs.*

The *Prévôt* sergeant, an older man with a droopy mustache long gone out of fashion, raised his arm and challenged them. "Halt, *Messieurs*, in the king's name. What business have you on this highway at so late an hour?"

O'Donnell spoke with authority, "I am Gerard Pierre Pardue, *Comte* du Rondac. This is my nephew Etienne. I had taken the lad here to partake of the pleasures of the chateau. He has a mind to join the priesthood, and I am doing everything in my power to dissuade him. His father died in the wars, and Etienne is his sole male heir."

The *Prévôts* laughed at the idea of the boy tasting the charms of the chateau's high-class prostitutes before deciding on the cloth.

The sergeant did not look amused, however, and tugged at a whisker, eyeing O'Donnell suspiciously. "Our troop searches for a fugitive from the Bastille, a murderer, and his accomplice. He escaped dressed as a priest. Coincidence, *eh bien*?"

O'Donnell nodded patronizingly. "Your officer at the chateau seemed to think so. He let us depart so the young man would not be caught *en flagrante* and perhaps be rejected by the clergy, not to mention the embarrassment to his family. Now, we must be on our way, *Monsieur*."

The sergeant twisted his head as he pondered the dilemma, then decided to act. "Very well, but first we will inspect your saddlebags. While we do so, I will send a rider back to the chateau to verify everything. You understand, of course, *Monsieur*?"

O'Donnell smiled and nodded politely. "But of course, *Monsieur*."

The sergeant never heard the shot that killed him. At eight feet, even on a dark road and firing from the saddle, it was a shot O'Donnell could never miss. The body fell from the horse and tumbled onto the road with a thud.

Stunned by the shot, the others watched in astonishment, the smoke clouding their vision and assaulting their nostrils. O'Donnell emptied his second pistol into the face of another *Prévôt*, who fell twisting in his horse's stirrups as it took off down the road.

Creed immediately emptied his two pistols into the two nearest *Prévôt*. One died instantly. The other suffered a shoulder wound but had sufficient strength to reach for his saber. As he did, Creed rode through him and delivered a backhand blow that nearly decapitated him.

He then wheeled his horse and joined O'Donnell, who was engaged in a saber duel with the two remaining officers of the king. Creed ran one through the back, the man's eyes widening as blood spurted from his mouth.

Sufficiently terrified, the last trooper tried to break contact with O'Donnell and flee, but Creed's horse blocked his passage. He dropped his saber in a desperate plea for mercy. O'Donnell raised his saber to finish their work and move on, but Creed interceded by placing his horse between them. Instead, he made the *Prévôt* dismount and remove his flint from his musket. Creed slapped his saber on the *Prévôt's* horse's hindquarters. The startled animal took off at a gallop across the dark fields. The man's eyes widened as Creed stood in his spurs, towering over him.

Creed waved his saber. "A fine horse like that won't stop until he is halfway to Paris, I reckon."

Expecting the worst, the man's eyes widened and he bowed his head. But instead of sending him to join his comrades, Creed flipped a large gold coin at him, more than a year's pay for a lieutenant of *Prévôt des Maréchaux*.

"This will pay for your horse should he not return, and provide care for your comrades' families. I am truly sorry it came to this, *Monsieur. Adieu!*"

As Creed tried to make amends with the remaining officer, O'Donnell collected the remaining *Prévôts'* horses. Then, without speaking a word, the two galloped down the road. They traversed central and western France, in constant watch for *Prévôt des Maréchaux* and local police, who seemed to turn up in the most inconvenient times.

* * *

Creed finished his two notes and sealed each in a brown opaque envelope. He handed them to O'Donnell, who carefully tucked them in his vest pocket. Unbeknownst to him, they were not just Creed's final words to his beloved uncle, but also his full admission to the killing of a highly connected nobleman, and a complete exoneration of O'Donnell in any part of the affair. Creed had hoped O'Donnell would flee the continent with him, but the older officer insisted on returning to ensure the reputation of the regiment. How he could do this and avoid the scaffold, he never explained to Creed.

The waiter, a short, stout, and extremely ugly man with a bulbous nose and two days' growth of beard, brought a final bottle of wine to the table. He uncorked it without a word and left, jingling a pile of copper into his apron sleeve. When he was gone, the two men made a quiet toast to the future as well as to the past.

"Had I no obligations here in France, Jeremiah, I would go with you without hesitation. The New World is where men can be men and men can be free. The troubles with England and her colonies are growing. I assure you the day will soon come when they must be cut free or they will do it themselves."

Creed nodded. "Most of the pamphlets you showed me said as much. I will perhaps be part of it. When the time is right."

"Well, first you must get there. And you must be sure *Le Roi's* justice does not follow you. The ship you take tonight is Dutch-registered. It arrived last week from Africa with a load of ivory and spices. It will take you to the Dutch Antilles, that is, to an island called Sint Eustatius. There, you can deposit your gold in a bank and draw upon it as you need, once in America. You should have no problem booking passage to North America from there. The island is a frequent port of call for vessels from the Carolinas, Maryland, and New York."

"Just how did you arrange all of this, sir?"

O'Donnell smiled. "I was wondering when you would get around to asking that question. It took long enough."

Creed shot him a puzzled look. "Forgive me, sir, but I have had other things on my mind, such as avoiding the guillotine. But now it appears my immediate arrest and execution are diminishing in probability. I should like to inquire into things of less immediate interest."

O'Donnell shrugged. "Over the years of service to the French king, several generations of the brigade retired or otherwise left the king's service to pursue more genteel professions. Thus, throughout the realm, a network of Irishmen has evolved, bound to each other by faith, blood, and dedication. There are surgeons, teachers, shopkeepers, tradesmen, and the like. Even a few priests..." O'Donnell grinned widely at the last revelation.

"So that is how..."

"Yes. Now, concerning our current circumstances, a fellow named Colm O'Brien, formerly Sergeant Colm O'Brien, served with me several years ago. Injured on maneuvers, he retired with a small stipend and used it to build a modest but profitable trading house here in La Rochelle. Colm mostly ships wines to England, Ireland, and the Americas, but he has been known to smuggle contraband items from time to time, mostly unfortunates on the run, such as you. Tonight, at nine, you will board his ship, the *Nutmeg*."

"An interesting name."

"An interesting ship," replied O'Donnell without the blink of an eye. "A former slaver turned pirate ship, captured by the French navy a few years back. O'Brien won her cheaply when she was put to auction after the authorities hanged her crew-the guillotine was deemed too easy a death for the likes of them. Her master now is a certain Henricus Gault, a Flemish Jew. I envy you that, too, Jeremiah, you are entering an exotic world few of us even dream of."

Creed took another sip of his wine. "But why Dutch-flagged?"

O'Donnell shrugged and smiled innocently. "I am but a soldier and not privy to the nuances of international trade. I suppose there is some legal advantage to it. You know, the work of lawyers."

Chapter 10

Sint Eustatius, the Dutch Antilles, September 1775

The *Nutmeg* rocked gently as it lay at anchor in *Sint* Eustatias's wide natural harbor, her lines creaking in rhythm with each move and her flag snapping whimsically in the light breeze. The *Nutmeg* had dropped anchor in *Sint* Eustatias's harbor at midnight. The brig's Master, Henricus Gault, told Creed it could be a day or two before she cleared customs and could begin off-loading cargo. Until then, passengers and crew had to remain on board.

Creed stood on the quarterdeck watching the stretch of land that formed the bay, his gateway to a new world and a new life. The light, balmy breeze caressed his face, and the smells wafting across the bay from shore provided a welcome respite from the long voyage across the dark Atlantic. The aromas of the island, a mix of food cooking, body odors, spices, animal dung, and exotic plants, overwhelmed his senses. After almost eight weeks of the stagnant stench below deck and the raw salt sea air up top, he felt as if he were in paradise. He gazed across the bay and marveled at how much life teemed within the saddle between the two rocky promontories that dominated the small island.

Gault approached Creed with a satisfied look. He removed his pipe from his mouth and waved it expansively at the panorama before them. "Almost five thousand people live on less than eight square miles, *Heer* Creed. More than ten percent of them are Jews."

"Jews in the West Indies? I had no idea." Creed did not know what else to say.

With a look of pride, Gault pointed out the large stone and brick building along the shore. "That's the Honen-Dalim Synagogue. Built over thirty years ago. You seem surprised? Don't be. As in so many other places in Europe, the Jewish populace provides much of the oil that drives the machine of commerce. We are merchants, bankers, importers, exporters, and the like."

Creed smiled. "And sometimes ship's masters?"

"*Ja*, sometimes," Gault replied with a wink.

Creed nodded and continued to gaze at the shoreline. His first real look at this new world impressed him beyond anything his imagination could have conjured.

Soon after, a longboat approached the *Nutmeg*. After exchanging appropriate salutes and formalities, the crew hoisted several large barrels aboard. They maneuvered the boom and winch with a dexterity that impressed Creed. He would soon learn the reason. The barrels contained urgently needed drinking water and even more urgently awaited rum.

Not wanting to waste his days on board the ship, Creed had spent as much time as reasonable for a passenger studying the ways of the sea. His efforts enabled him to learn quite a bit about navigation and steerage. He tried his best to be part of the crew and occasionally pulled shifts when crew members were ill. Because of this, the entire crew came to like and respect him. Besides all that, on one occasion, he saved the ship and their lives.

As Gault predicted, the customs office scheduled the *Nutmeg's* clearance inspection for the next morning. The master invited Creed to dinner with the other officers that evening. He had dinner with the captain most nights, but this would be a special farewell dinner. As the evening got underway, Gault raised his wine glass and stood. The officers joined in.

"A toast to the *Staatshalter*!" Gault said ceremoniously.

There were six in all, including the First Mate, Frideric Goosen, another *Flamande* from Antwerp.

They all echoed their captain, "To the *Staatshalter*!"

Although only a third of the crew was from the Netherlands, the officers saluted the ruler of the nation that flew the ship's flag. The Netherlands did not have a king. Instead, it was governed by a quasi-oligarchy of propertied men whose leader was called the *Staatshalter*, a curious mix of a president, prime minister, and monarch.

As the dinner proceeded, they toasted the ship, the crew, the master, the commander of Sint Eustatius, Johannes de Graff, and finally, Jeremiah Creed.

Creed's face turned crimson, and he stood with a glass in his hand, now more than a little in his cups. "God Bless you all, gentlemen. God bless this ship. God bless this new world, which I hope brings me a new life. And may God bless Ireland."

With that, they all stood and reprised, "God bless Ireland!"

None of them had ever been there, but Creed had often described his homeland as an incredible green paradise that suffered the blight of English oppression.

When the last piece of bread scooped up the last bit of gravy, the officers staggered to their berths. But Creed decided to go up on deck to clear his head. The watchman, a Portuguese of indeterminate age, greeted him with a quiet nod and a heavily accented, "Good evening, *Senor*."

Leaning up against the gunwale on the quarterdeck, Creed looked out across the harbor at the island he would soon visit. Light from several score buildings glowed faintly against the dark shoreline, giving the appearance of cats' eyes in a cave. The warm night air smelled exotic, and the wind's feather-like breeze pleasantly caressed his face.

Despite the obvious sensuality in the air, a sudden feeling of spirituality came over him. He decided to pray for God's help in this new land. Creed began to fumble through his pockets for his rosary. A gift from his mother upon entering the seminary, the rosary was his most prized possession. Imported from Spain, it had a cross and a chain of heavy silver, with beads of semi-precious stones. He knew it had great monetary value, but it had spiritual and sentimental value unsurpassed by anything Creed owned or could own.

Sometime later, Gault appeared on deck. "May I join you, *Mijnheer*?"

Creed put his rosary away and bowed politely at the master. "Of course, sir. Or should I say, *Mijnheer*?"

Gault chuckled. He pulled out his pipe and lit it. "I never asked, do you smoke? I'll have one of the men fetch you a pipe from below."

Creed raised his hands. "Thank you, but no. I already have enough vices for one life, *Heer* Gault." His mouth was dry from all the wine, and his head throbbed, but mixed with the fresh sea air on deck, Gault's pipe smelled pleasant.

Gault stared across the dark bay as he puffed. "So, Jeremiah, tomorrow begins the next phase of your journey, eh?"

"Not quite yet. I have some banking to attend, letters to write, and other arrangements to make. I hope to make passage on a ship to the mainland by the end of summer."

The master took another long puff on his pipe. "Why not stay in the islands? The economy here is much more lucrative. There is much money to be made and plenty of exotic and beautiful women, especially on the Spanish Main and Cuba."

As Gault stared out over the water, Creed supposed he was reminiscing on his numerous sexual conquests, all made through guile or gold. At fifty, he claimed he still had the libido of a man of twenty-five.

Creed shook his head. "I do not fancy learning Spanish. And the climate brings fevers. No, I prefer a more temperate place. I understand the English colonies are much more like Europe, and in some places, not unlike Ireland. I should like to find good horse country. Horses are what I want to raise. Perhaps I will go to Virginia or the Carolinas."

"Why horses? Someone like you can make a large fortune in trade. There are so many opportunities beyond shoveling manure."

"I grew up in a family torn by passion, religion, and politics. I took consolation in reading, prayer, and horses. The reading opened my mind to the world. Prayer to God. The horses to my humanity. Noble creatures, they are."

Gault puffed and waved an arm expansively. "Why not then go to Maryland?"

"Maryland?"

"Ja. It is fine horse country, they say, and already many of you Catholics have settled there."

Creed's face brightened. "Why, I never thought of Maryland. Perhaps I shall, sir. Perhaps I shall…"

The next afternoon, Gault and Goosen waved farewell to Creed as a longboat rowed him ashore.

Goosen talked as he waved, "He is a fine young man, is he not, captain?"

"Ja, but there is something dark and serious beneath that friendly and modest exterior."

Goosen's mouth widened in surprise. "Dark? Serious?"

"And mysterious. He has untapped talents I fear may be wasted raising horses. Despite his piety, I see a bit of the pirate in him. I suspect he could have made a fortune in these waters."

Goosen nodded, then turned and waved once more at Creed. Then Goosen turned back to Gault. "Well, he is resourceful and courageous. His quick mind and flair for decisive action saved us all."

The two went on to speak of Creed's gallant action during the voyage. For several days, a mysterious ship trailed *Nutmeg,* and during a storm-filled night, it closed on them. The boat, a Spanish privateer, was a modest schooner, but it carried four small-caliber carronades on each side. It launched a sudden broadside loaded with grapeshot that cleared several crew members from the deck.

With fierce battle cries in a mix of tongues, a score of fierce sea-brigands clambered over the side with grappling hooks and halberds. Their captain, a one-eyed Spaniard named Rocca, known as the scourge of the Leeward Islands, led the attack. The boarding party, a mélange of deserters of all races from several navies, expected the usual quick surrender.

But submission would not happen that day. Instead, Creed, who was armed and on deck before the broadside struck home, rallied the crew's survivors and led them in a counter-charge. Creed personally killed three of the brigands and made his way straight to Rocca.

The pirate chieftain waved a large cutlass in his right hand as if it were a feather fan. In his left, he brandished a large musketoon as if it were a pistol. He wore no hat, only a red scarf tied around his head like a gypsy. Two large gold earrings jangled off his left ear. His one good eye was bloodshot from a night of drinking. His bad eye carried no patch. Instead, a large ruby-like jewel filled the gap. A Flemish sailor lay at his feet, begging for mercy.

"Leave the sailor and face me!" Creed called out over the clang of swords and screams of men.

Rocca turned and grinned at Creed. He casually discharged the musketoon into the sailor's chest. He then threw the heavy firelock at Creed and charged him, waving the cutlass in both hands. Both their bodies slammed together in a heavy thump. Each staggered back and then forward. They uttered no curses, no war cry, no threats. The only sounds were heavy breathing, wrenching muscles, and rasping steel.

Creed managed to turn sideways before Rocca's cutlass struck home. Its brass hilt caught his elbow with a glancing blow that sent a raw tingle up his arm. Creed ignored the pain and bent into a forward crouch. Rocca stood over him and brought the heavy cutlass down in a powerful two-handed stroke. But Creed struck quicker. His blade entered Rocca's chest just under the breastbone. Creed's body followed the thrust, and both men tumbled to the deck. Creed's blade plunged into the wood planking, fixing Rocca's still struggling torso to the deck. Creed quickly struggled to his feet and picked up Rocca's powerful weapon. He held it at the ready, turning slowly to ward off the circle of pirates that now surrounded him.

Stunned to see the fiercest pirate of the Caribbean so easily killed by a youth, Rocca's men were only too happy to drag his body back to the mother ship and avoid further loss. To be profitable, piracy required prey that offered little resistance. Enough such ships sailed the seas for them to allow *Nutmeg's* escape.

Gault nodded grimly as his mate finished reminiscing. "Precisely my point, Frideric. A Maryland horse farmer! Such a waste."

* * *

Six weeks later, Creed was ready to leave Sint Eustatius. He had deposited half his money in an account with a bank Gault had recommended, a respectable mid-sized institution with correspondents in Amsterdam, Ghent, and, fortuitously, Baltimore. The remainder he kept in specie and cash, using Dutch *gulden*.

During his time on the island, Creed learned much about trade and commerce in the West Indies, as well as the politics behind them. France, Spain, the Netherlands, and Great Britain all vied for control of key islands and ports. Sugar, spice, molasses, hemp, and slaves provided the engine— commodities that intertwined in a complex system of trade that yielded tremendous profit. Ships from all the ports of Europe sailed through the islands carrying goods of all sorts back and forth. Britain's economic gain from its North American colonies, although not inconsiderable and growing, paled in comparison.

The bank on Sint Eustatius would lend out Creed's deposit at a fixed interest rate and pay Creed a dividend each year. This guaranteed a steady income without the risk of directly investing in commerce that could sink to the bottom of the ocean or fall into the hands of privateers or pirates.

Moses Briscoe finished signing the contract and presented Creed with a copy. "Well, *mijnheer*, you shall be quite the *Landhalter*, I should say. We will miss you here, though."

"I have found this island pleasant enough. But I long for fertile fields and hills. How much will I draw from this arrangement, *Mijnheer*?"

"Your expected income will be about five hundred pounds sterling per year. Enough to live very comfortably in the new world, and *ja*, in fact, the old."

Creed nodded as if he understood, but he was still unused to finance. "What do you plan to do with the balance, *mijnheer*?"

"I shall use it to purchase some land, hire help, and buy horses, *Heer* Briscoe. There are feed and seed to obtain, plus tools and equipment to build a farm."

"You have enough cash to build a farm as large as *Sint* Eustatius, *mijnheer*."

"That's precisely what I plan to do, *Heer* Briscoe."

They both laughed.

During his time on *Sint* Eustatius, Creed had met many of the island's important people and quickly became part of their society, such as it was. He became acquainted with the island's governor, Peter De Graaf. De Graaf was a harsh but efficient governor. He took a liking to Creed. Creed's poor opinion of the kings of England and France did much to endear the young man to him. But the tales of Creed's brave action against the dreaded Spanish pirates endeared him most to the governor.

"Henricus told me of your gallantry against the *verdammt* Spanish. Rocca has terrorized our shipping for years. Why not remain here? I could use a man such as you,

Heer Creed. The *Staatshalter* gave me the authority to commission privateers to take the offensive against the Spanish. Henricus says he can underwrite a ship and recruit a crew. You would be rich beyond your wildest dreams in just a few voyages."

"*Bedankt, mijnheer*. But the line between a letter of marque and piracy is thin. And I seek lush fields and streams, not vistas of ocean."

De Graaf shrugged. "You are quite an Irish dreamer, *Heer* Creed. But as you wish."

Creed also met many of the wealthier Dutch inhabitants and was of considerable interest to the few eligible young ladies on the island. That interest typically faded when they learned of his religious beliefs. Although Creed did not flaunt his faith, he never denied it when the topic came up. Worldly though they were, the Dutch did not favor connections to the papacy.

More endearing to him was the island's Jewish population. They had varying degrees of wealth but seemed warmer and friendlier than the Dutch. Yet he knew from the start he could never be accepted into their circle, at least not without a ceremony that was uninteresting to him on both religious and aesthetic grounds.

"*Heer* Briscoe, I have every intention of becoming quite the *Landhalter*, as you say. And I promise in a few years I will present you with the gift of a fine horse, if only there were a place to run the creature on this island. You may have to move to the mainland."

Both men laughed. One could walk around *Sint* Eustatius' shores in less than a day.

"So, Heer Creed, when do you leave?"

"There is a small schooner leaving for Charleston in the Carolinas on Saturday morning. I have booked passage on her. From there, I will find a ship sailing north to Baltimore."

"Then come to my house on Thursday for supper. We eat at eight. Arrive at seven, and we can toast your farewell."

Creed smiled graciously. "Nothing could please me more, *mijnheer*."

* * *

Fells Point, Maryland, August 1775

The schooner slowly slid against the quay at Fells Point, a small port just east of Baltimore on the Patapsco River. Excited voices filled the air as the crew tossed coils of rope and tied the craft securely against the wharf. After the long and dangerous Atlantic crossing, the voyage from Sint Eustatius to Charleston and northward proved uneventful. Creed spent only two days in Charleston, being fortunate enough to catch passage on the schooner the night after his arrival.

Creed instinctively liked Fells Point. The deep harbor allowed his ship to dock along a fine quay that led to a waterfront as fine as any he had seen in Europe. Neat houses, shops, and warehouses lined Thames Street as he walked off his sea legs. Creed had no difficulty finding a suitable boarding house for the night. The next day he engaged a wagon to move his belongings and money to the larger town of Baltimore, where he found the bank that corresponded with Moses Briscoe's bank on Sint Eustatius. Not surprisingly, the owner was a distant relative of Briscoe.

Creed stayed very busy in Baltimore. He hired an attorney to arrange his legal situation. Through an agent, John Walters, he began reviewing property in various parts of the colony.

"So, Mister Creed, have you decided on where to settle?" Walters asked.

"I have assessed values of available land on the eastern and western shores along the Patuxent River and the Chesapeake Bay, as well as along the Potomac and north and west of Baltimore. But I have decided on a piece of land along the Monocacy River."

"Why, that's over seventy-five miles west of here. Are you sure you want to be so far from civilization?"

"I do, Mister Walters. And besides, the land there is more reasonably priced."

"But you'll have to contend with frontier ruffians. Perhaps even Indians. You can certainly afford something closer to the coast."

Creed shook his head. "I liked the idea of its proximity to the western frontier. Besides, this property lies just outside the town of Frederick. So, I'll be near some of the amenities of civilization. The nearby Catoctin Mountains might afford interesting hunting and other diversions."

"That's my point, Mister Creed. It is too far into the wilds for a fine gentleman such as you. Very rugged. Frederick is small and offers little to a man like you. Besides, better land can be found between here and Annapolis. Or to the north."

"But the prospectus says the land east of Frederick is rolling with excellent water sources and quality natural grass. That's perfect horse country." Creed smiled. "I plan to go there at once."

Creed leaned forward in the saddle and let his new three-year-old gelding, Finn, stretch his powerful legs. The roads between Baltimore and Frederick made the journey pleasant, and it took only a few days. Creed immediately fell in love with the property and the area, which indeed had everything to offer for raising fine horses. He found the perfect stretch of land and returned to Baltimore to close a deal. Working with Walters and his Baltimore attorney, Silas Groat, Esq., Creed made an offer on the property.

A few weeks later, the offer was accepted and Creed began the arduous work of ordering equipment and tools, seed and supplies, and hiring a couple of hands to work for him. In the latter case, he found two recently arrived Irishmen from his own County Cork. They were happy to get work that did not entail going to sea or hauling goods along the Baltimore wharf. Moving west might offer them the opportunity to get land of their own, instead of wasting their time on menial work gangs and their money on waterfront taverns.

By the end of September, Creed was ready to head to Frederick. He had his goods loaded on two sturdy wagons, each pulled by a pair of oxen. He had several quality-bred horses in tow as well.

After finalizing affairs with his bank and with Grout, an elated Jeremiah Creed stepped into one of Finn's stirrups and effortlessly hauled himself into the saddle. He wore a green riding jacket and white breeches. His knee-high riding boots gleamed in the morning light. A late summer wind blew lightly. Small puffs of white clouds drifting against the horizon only enhanced the deep blue sky. Ready for this new land and a new life, Jeremiah Creed gently spurred Finn and, with a wave of his hat, led his small party westward. A peaceful and prosperous future awaited him.

Chapter 11

Fort Lee, New Jersey, November 1776

Creed stepped out of the tent and tightened his mantel. The cold autumn rain had lifted, leaving a gray chill behind. He felt uneasy, emotionally drained, but also strangely relieved. Since departing the old world for the new, he had been determined to keep his past secret to protect his uncle Maurice, as well as Adrian O'Donnell. His unease also stemmed from a deep fear that the French king's justice might reach him in America. It was not his character to talk of his past or the people in his life. So, the relief he felt from this purging of past secrets surprised him.

Creed felt neither guilt nor remorse at the course his life had taken before coming to America, just the need to put it behind him. He had spent over three hours with Washington and Fitzgerald. The two men listened attentively to his story, occasionally interrupting him with a question or asking for clarification of some obscure point. Throughout, Fitzgerald took notes, recording the names of people and places mentioned.

At one point, Fitzgerald made a brief aside to Washington, mentioning the name Silas Deane, the American representative in Paris. *Does Colonel Fitzgerald maintain a correspondence with him?*

Creed returned to the stable. Although he had been truthful with his mentor and his commander-in-chief, he had not been completely forthcoming. There were still certain details he omitted, such as the name of the man he struck down in that fateful duel and the reason for it. They understood only that it was an affair of honor, the term often used by gentlemen to rationalize a blood grudge that often led to murder.

* * *

When Creed left, Washington sat back in his chair and stared into the candle. Although he and Fitzgerald trusted Jeremiah Creed, their plans for him required them to exhaust every measure in examining his past.

After a moment, he raised his eyes and looked hard at Fitzgerald. "What do you think, Robert?"

Fitzgerald glanced down at his notes. "I, um, think that trust in him is well placed, Your Excellency. But I shall have Deane attempt to discreetly check some of the facts and events Creed revealed in his declaration."

"Well placed? He has admitted to murdering officers of the law, consorting with wanton women, dueling, escaping royal justice, stealing a small fortune in gold, and evading his commitment to the clergy. Need I continue?"

"But he maintains an admirable devotion to his mother and his native land. He is skilled and experienced in battle. He only evaded a French king's justice and killed only when no other course presented itself. The young man is resourceful and courageous beyond what we previously imagined. I firmly believe he is completely committed to the cause, for where else can he turn?"

Washington nodded, "I agree with your assessment. Pray that we are correct, Robert, for before this war is over, its result and our future may well depend on the devotion and loyalty of Jeremiah Creed."

* * *

Sneden's Landing, New Jersey, November 1776

The sky cleared to a pale blue caressed by a late autumn sun just as Creed arrived at the observation point south of Sneden's Landing, an important North River crossing point directly across from Dobbs Ferry. It was midday, and Creed had brought his men some bread with fresh butter he had purchased in the hamlet of Palisades, located along the Albany Road. For days, they had nothing to eat but hardtack biscuits. Elias Parker desperately wanted to bring in a catch from the river below them. But the British had observers too, watching carefully from the other side.

Creed's men had one small advantage to help them in their duties as strategic observers. While manning the defenses near Long Island's Wallabout Bay back in August, they had received a pair of spyglasses to observe the British outside the American defenses. Somehow, both survived the intense action of the past few months. With them, Creed's men could distinguish uniform markings on the soldiers located almost one mile distant. So far, over the past three days, his men noted at least six different regiments.

Creed slipped Finn's reins over a branch and made his way through the pine thicket to join young Thomas Jeffries on watch at the overlook. They had chosen a stand of boulders forty feet up the bluff from the river. It had a good trail leading through the dense woods to the clearing that served as the men's camp. Creed dropped to his knees, crawled the last few yards, and pulled up beside Thomas. He looked out across the North River, which was still narrow at this point but widened just north of them into a large lake-like body the Dutch settlers had named the Tappan Zee.

The Tappan Zee (Zee means sea or lake in Dutch) was formed like an inland lake, stretching two miles across and more than twelve miles from north to south. The British Navy controlled it, as it was large enough to sail the smaller warships and transports with ease.

North of the Tappan Zee, the river narrowed again, to less than a mile, affording the Americans opportunities to slip small boats back and forth. Thus, Washington kept communications with some 5,000 men under General Charles Lee, his second-in-command. Lee's forces were positioned to block British movement northwards, while Washington remained near the fort named after the same subordinate, watching for a British thrust across the river.

Creed took the spyglass from Thomas and handed him a half-loaf of bread. "Have we anything interesting to observe, Thomas?"

Thomas began gnawing the bread as he spoke. "Yes, suh. In the cove yonder. A small, two-masted boat."

"That would be a brig, Thomas," Creed responded tartly.

"Yes, suh, a brig."

"Anything of note on the brig? Such as cannon, horses, equipment?"

"No suh...just folks."

"What kind of people, Thomas?" Creed asked patiently. Creed had learned this question-and-answer technique at the seminary. In France, he had used it to teach his Irish soldiers, and now he taught his American soldiers the same way.

He continued to prompt the young man, "Anything unusual about them?"

Thomas nodded. "The ship, the uh brig, sailed back and forth up the river but seemed to spend a long time on this side. They were looking for something. And then the ship turned and crossed back."

"What do you mean?"

"It turned south and made for the cove."

"How many aboard?"

"Eight of them. They wore dark clothes. Brown and maybe gray. Oh, and they carried muskets. Exept'n one. He carried a paddle, an' some rope."

"Paddle? Do you mean an oar?"

Thomas shook his head and then nodded. "Maybe. It was long enough. An' I forgot to mention the longboat. Two of them seemed very interested in something in a longboat that sat on the deck with a cover on top of it. Oh, and the longboat had lanterns front and back."

"You mean fore and aft. Very well, Thomas."

Creed scratched his chin and stared out across the water toward the cove just south of them. Suddenly, he slammed the spyglass shut and handed it back to Thomas. "We may have visitors this evening. Let us get back to the camp and have a small discussion with the lads."

Creed and Thomas crawled back from the bluff and returned to the camp. They found Beall still nibbling at the fresh bread, while Parker slept in a barely comfortable lean-to built from pine branches and boughs. Beall woke Parker so he could be aware of Creed's plans.

Creed took a stick and sketched a crude map on the soft, loamy soil. "In military planning terms, the army's position is precarious."

"That a good thing?" Thomas asked.

Creed smiled wanly as he made a rough circle on the ground. "No. The British now hold interior lines. They can move against our forces. We are now spread thinly in an arc from central Jersey to Connecticut."

"So why are we sitting here on our duffs?" Parker asked.

"Our orders are to maintain this observation point and provide information on British shipping in the Tappan Zee, to report on British Army movements across the river, and to prepare for his next mission."

"What is the next mission, sir?" Beall asked.

"What that mission might be, Colonel Fitzgerald has yet to inform me."

"What have you for me tonight, Lieutenant?" Parker asked wearily.

Beall handed him a mug of coffee to revive his spirits.

"Based on what Thomas observed, we can expect some mischief, I fear."

Parker glanced at Thomas, "What kind of mischief, sir?"

Creed rubbed his chin. "Typically, British naval vessels travel during daylight. This part of the river is tidal but has numerous areas where shoals and rocks pose a navigation hazard. When they sail at night, they carry lanterns or follow the longboat that serves as a pilot. I suspect the longboat Thomas spied on the British brig will land tonight. To what end we can only speculate."

"What do you want me to do, sir?" Parker asked.

"Hopefully, merely to observe the landing. Then follow whoever disembarks."

"To do what, sir?" Beall asked.

Creed grimaced. "'Tis a question whose answer I lack."

***

The only sounds Parker's sharp ears heard were the cut of the northerly wind sweeping down the river and the rhythmic rippling of waves along the shore. Parker always stood watch during darkness. He had excellent night vision. This night, he sat patiently at his watch post for almost four hours.

Suddenly, he heard a soft splash that only an accomplished sailor could discern. His eyes narrowed on the shore below, where a long, dark hulk seemed to glide like a shadow onto the shore. He squinted but could barely make it out. The British had painted the hull black, and a canvas tarpaulin, also painted black, covered the crew. The rowers expertly pulled in their oars and silently beached the boat along a narrow strip of sand and rock. Parker sprang to his feet and ran back to the camp.

***

Creed wasted little time giving orders. "Thomas, you remain with the horses. Elias, you lead us down the bluff to the British boat. We shall see what mischief is about this night. They are bound to leave a guard force."

"What weapons shall we use?" Beall asked.

"Take pistols and long arms with bayonets fixed. Bring your tomahawks as well."

Since they began their operations on the New Jersey side of the North River, Creed and his men had assembled a diverse array of weapons and clothing. In addition, Thomas had an eight-foot leather lash he used with considerable skill. Creed and Beall also had short Jaeger rifles with long sword-bayonets taken from a pair of Hessian Jaegers on Long Island.

Their outfits ranged from dark blue Continentals—formal line uniforms—to a variety of hunting and riding attire. Creed and his men needed to pose variously as soldiers, militia, Loyalists, or neutrals, and they donned whatever it took to travel across the lines established by the two warring parties. This night, they wore dark civilian clothing, not unlike that of their quarry.

Parker moved quickly through the brush and led Creed and Beall down the trail at the top of the highland cliffs. They stepped carefully and slowly, so it took almost thirty minutes to descend to the riverbank below. Lower down, the trail flattened, and the bushes and trees became scarcer. Boulders provided cover from observation from the river and the narrow strand. The tide was low enough that the rock-strewn beach reached up to twenty feet across in some places, more than double its normal width.

They kept firelocks unloaded, so as not to risk accidentally discharging if one of them stumbled on the way down. But once safely below, they carefully ran powder and ball down the hungry barrels. Then each quietly slid a blade onto the end of the muzzle.

Creed crouched and circled slowly around one of the boulders. Twenty yards away was a long, flat rock that did not match the others along the shore in size or shape. He motioned for his men to follow him. They formed a small wedge and advanced slightly bent forward, trusting in the wind and the dark to provide cover as they darted from boulder to boulder. When they closed to within ten yards, they heard voices in the wind. When they cleared the last boulder, they could see several heads in the boat.

"Those oarsmen are hunkered down from the sting of the wind that cuts along the shore from the north," Creed whispered to Parker. "Cover Jonathan and me."

Creed and Beall reached the boat in two long bounds. They caught the crew by surprise. Creed ran one sailor through the chest and then twisted the blade from his body. He turned and drove the butt of his rifle into the chest of another. The sailor's breastbone crunched, and he fell backward. As he did, he tripped one of his mates, who held an oar high over Creed's head. Before the oar could end Creed's night, Beall plunged his sword-bayonet into the sailor's exposed side, piercing his heart and sending the oar tumbling harmlessly into the sand.

"Don't kill me! I surrender to you rebels!" the fourth exclaimed in a loud voice.

Creed realized the sailor's loud voice was a warning cry. The sailor suddenly lunged at Creed and lifted him off the ground. With a bear-like grip, he drove him against the boat with a sickening thud, but Creed rolled sideward and twisted free.

Creed's weapon lay a yard away. The sailor rammed his head at Creed like a bull, but Creed took several quick steps, avoided the blow, and drove the stronger man into the boat. Creed managed to pull his rifle from the mud. But as he turned, the sailor was on him again. Half bent over, Creed made the only move he could, a short blade thrust into the sailor's groin. His eyes widened, and he let out a scream more like an agonized gurgle. Creed pulled the blade from his groin. He sank to his knees and collapsed onto the muddy riverbank, staining it with a pool of blood.

But the dying sailor's warning had done its work. Another pair of sailors rushed from the bluff, brandishing cutlasses and boarding knives. A cutlass required a strong, skilled man to use effectively. Boarding knives were long-bladed daggers with a special hilt that served as brass knuckles—the tars to stab, slash, or smash an opponent at close quarters.

Creed had Parker stay back for just this situation.

The lead sailor fell dead before reaching the boat. Parker's tomahawk had caught him in the side, sending him twisting to the ground with an open rib cage. Parker stepped in front of the next sailor and parried his cutlass. The two locked in a fierce struggle. The sailor faked a lunge at Parker and then rammed his boarding knife's heavy brass-knuckle hilt into his stomach. Parker keeled over from the blow. Before the sailor could finish him with a blow across the neck, Beall let his tomahawk fly. The blade caught the man square in the face, splitting his head open like a melon. He fell forward, gushing brains, blood, and gore over Parker.

"Are you hurt, Elias?" Beall helped Parker to his feet. "Are you hurt?"

Gasping for air, Parker shook his head. "No. Aches like hell and I'm winded, but I'll live."

He took several deep breaths and rubbed his stomach while Creed and Beall searched around the area for more sailors. Then they began going over the dead sailors and the boat for clues.

Creed muttered, "Looks like they came here devoid of papers, very wise of them. Well planned."

Beall cut open the pockets of the last dead sailor. He was a burly, older man with a barrel chest, and his eyes were already glazing over in death. Strangely, it was the dead sailor's barrel chest that caused Beall to notice the lump along the side of his left breast.

"Find anything, Jonathan?"

"No papers at all, sir. But something better, I think."

"And what could trump intelligence on His Majesty's plans?"

Beall held up a leather pouch in triumph. "Silver coin, sir. Silver coin, twenty-five British pounds sterling. As it is, sir, we haven't received any pay in three months."

"Well then, are we taking the king's shilling now?"

Beall smiled and tossed him the leather. "I hope so, sir."

Creed caught it. "Let's look at this craft now."

Creed marveled at the modifications the British had made to the longboat. "Look, their carpenters trimmed down the gunwale to the port and starboard and lowered the oarlocks. And they added fasteners along the gunwale to secure the black tarpaulin tightly. They cut tight loops into the tarpaulin so the oarsmen could project their heads out when necessary."

When Parker recovered his wind, he joined them.

"What does our sailor think?" Creed asked.

"Interesting…this longboat has a lowered rudder assembly with the tarpaulin to obscure the helmsman's silhouette."

"They also shortened the oars," Beall said.

"To allow it to make its way through tight places along the shore, or to navigate on narrower rivers and streams. The paddles that Thomas saw earlier. It's devoid of heavy objects as well. Elias, go inside and look about."

Parker climbed in. "Sir, two lanterns with smoked glass to reduce visibility. Also, a blackened hemp rope, a small hook-like anchor, and a capstan—a winch."

"Looks like a turtle, sir," whispered Beall.

Creed nodded. "A miracle we could see it. Sentries would not have noticed this until it was too late, if at all."

Parker whistled softly under his breath. "A marvel, sir. But it's not good in rough weather or seas. She would surely roll and capsize."

Creed shook his head. "Well, in rough weather, visibility is less of a factor. Sentries and lookouts hunker down, and the elements often provide the cloak that this craft presents itself."

"True enough, sir. I shall see to it this craft makes but a one-way trip tonight."

At that, Parker's powerful arm swung into action, delivering several well-placed tomahawk blows that severed several ribs from the keel. Then he dragged the vessel out into the flow of the channel. With a push, he sent it on a slow drift that would carry it another hundred yards where it gradually sank to the bottom of the river.

Creed gazed up at the cliffs towering one hundred feet above them. He now had to figure out who the intruders were and what their mission was. "I think they landed someone. Someone sent to spy on us. Or perhaps meet a spy. Get these bodies up into the rocks so the river tide does not sweep them away. We must find whoever they brought here."

"Well, sir, we could wait here. The sailors were likely waiting for someone's return. We could do the same." Beall glanced up at the cliffs high above them. "Save some effort, too."

Creed smiled. "We need to stop whoever went up those cliffs. But first, we must pick up his trail." He looked at Parker. "Elias, how do you feel?"

"I'm fine now, sir."

"Good. Then go back up and fetch Thomas and the horses, along with our sabers."

Creed glanced up again. "Jonathan and I will follow the spoor of the intruder or intruders. All these paths up this cliff seem to intersect near the road running along the top of the ridge. We should reach the summit about one mile south of the camp. Elias, after you fetch Thomas, head south along that road. We'll meet at the intersection there."

* * *

By the time he reached the summit of the heights, the sailor's lungs burned and his legs ached. His chest pounded from the heavy beating of his heart, which now beat like a bellows. Although he enjoyed an incredible physical condition for a man of thirty, he had never encountered a climb such as this. Aboard ship, he maintained fitness by climbing the rigging. Onshore, he ran, boxed, and fenced. He rode too, but not very well. He was, after all, a nautical man.

They selected him for this mission because he had experience climbing the lofty cliffs near Dover, not far from his hometown of Kent. But he had not been prepared for the height, the steepness of the path, and the ruggedness of the ground. Despite the cool November weather, sweat poured out of him. *Damn, I could drink a whole skin of water. Though gin would be better.*

He was only allowed to carry an oilskin pouch for the papers he needed to retrieve, a sharpened boarding knife, and a rope in case he had to lower himself down or pull himself up over a rocky overhang. He had wanted a boarding pistol as well, but they were too heavy, and his firearm might accidentally go off, jeopardizing the mission. His task, as the lieutenant said, was to climb the heights and retrieve some papers, the nature of which they refused, for security reasons, to reveal.

Able-Bodied Seaman Eldon Wright had no family. The Royal Navy took the place of the family he never had, and he gladly risked anything for it. His devotion and loyalty to king and country were unquestioned. For that reason, and because of his extraordinary strength and stamina, the lieutenant selected him for the "Black Boat" mission. It seemed like a simple task at the time. Now, he was not so sure.

Wright had no timepiece, so he had to estimate the time. The plan called for a local Loyalist contact to meet him within one hour of the ship's arrival, which was at ten. The wait did him good as it offered him a chance to rest. He needed to catch his breath for the trip back down the steep Palisades cliff.

Wright waited what seemed like a long time, but was in reality less than an hour. His perspiration turned cold in the chilly November air, and he began to shiver. England was a cool, damp country, but the Kent coast, where he was born and raised, stayed relatively temperate. *This America has a cold that doesn't just chill, it bites like the fangs of a weasel.* The fact that he had to keep quiet and still did not help. Soon, his limbs began to numb from the cold.

Suddenly, he saw a dark figure emerging from the woods on the opposite side of the road. Wright's grip tightened about the hilt of his boarding knife. The lieutenant had given him no security precautions, no password, no shibboleth to ascertain the true nature of the person he would meet. He knew local Loyalists had searched the west bank of the North River for a suitable landing for a planned British thrust. He also knew, from what the officers had said, it must be somewhere between the point opposite the Dobbs Ferry and Fort Lee itself.

He watched the shadow scurry across the road and looked in both directions before bolting. Wright stood up slowly, his body now numb from the cold and his muscles tingling. He grasped a tree limb and steadied himself. Then called out in a whisper, "Who goes there?"

"A... a friend," was the reply, equally unsure.

They stood six feet apart. Wright, an experienced sea fighter, could lunge and kill him before a musket or pistol shot could take him down.

The thought of it gave him confidence. "I have no friends in this rebellious land."

The other voice also grew more confident. "Well, then, a friend of the king."

Wright relaxed just a bit. "Then give me what you have and let us be gone."

He stepped away from the tree. The stranger seemed startled at his appearance. Wright wore sailors' garb, but it was all black trousers, shirt, and jacket. He wore no skipjack hat, but a black bandana wound tightly about his head. His pirate-like appearance menaced the stranger.

"What manner of British soldier are ye?"

Wright bristled. "A pox on soldiers! I am an able-bodied seaman in the Royal Navy."

He was, in fact, a member of a small group Admiral Richard Howe had trained at Staten Island for special actions along the coasts and rivers. A mix of sailors and Royal

Marines, he called them his "Scorpions". There were two teams of them. Another Scorpion team, mostly Royal Marines, trained back on Staten Island. Wright himself did not like Marines on board ship – unless they were young and compliant.

The stranger, a tall, rangy man of around thirty, though nervous, grew angry. "See here, I have traveled a long way on a cold night to help His Majesty. I have no time for questions and posturing. There are maps here identifying the best location to cross the river and a road to the rebel fort. Now, where's my money?"

Wright's voice deepened with anger. "Money, is it?" He knew nothing of money. The Loyalists supported the king because they were loyal Britons. Or so he had been told. Their petty officer, Billy Jones, never mentioned any money. Jonesy dealt with the lieutenant. *This Loyalist was a money-grubbing mercenary like all the rest of these Americans.*

The stranger grew angry. "Yes, twenty-five pounds sterling. Do not play games with me, or your army can spend the next ten years on the east side across the river, for all that I care."

Wright's voice grew loud. "They gave me no money. So you'll get no money. If you support the king, give me the sodding papers. Now!"

The Loyalist spy turned red. "Don't trifle with me, you damned British thief. Give me the money or stuff the papers!"

Wright exploded with anger. He lunged at the American. To him, they were all scum anyway, certainly not good Britons, regardless of their allegiance.

The Loyalist pulled the trigger of his handgun. At three feet, it was an easy shot. The jolt from Wright's grip pushed his hand down, and the pistol ball struck Wright's side, slicing flesh and bone across his ribs, burning its way through him. But the wound was not mortal.

The blast stopped Wright in his tracks. He stood for a moment, eyes wide open from the shock of the weapon's discharge. Then, realizing he still lived, he stepped into his assailant with a ferocious vengeance. His beefy left hand grabbed the Loyalist's throat. Wright squeezed tight and lifted the terrified Loyalist off the ground as his wicked boarding knife's blade plunged into the man's side, then his groin, and finally his throat.

The Loyalist dropped the pistol and struggled to scream, emitting only pathetic gurgles. Wright squeezed harder. Finally, splattered with blood, Wright dropped his limp body and stepped back. He needed those papers. His mission would fail without them. Then it would be back to a regular ship's crew. For him, that meant the rigging or the guns. Endless hours without sleep and little rum or food. *I need those soddin' papers.*

He dropped the knife and bent over his victim, who, surprisingly, still lived. Rummaging through his pockets, he found a canvas pouch. *Ah, me papers!*

Suddenly, two pairs of hands gripped Wright and pulled him from the hapless Loyalist. Wright reached for the boarding knife, but someone had already retrieved it from the ground and tucked it into his belt.

"Hold now, in the king's name. We shall make short work of this rebel," ordered one of his assailants, who looked to be the leader.

Another stood waving a brace of pistols at him. A third, larger figure picked the Loyalist up off the ground and held his forearm over the man's windpipe, ready to crush it if he uttered a word.

Wright stood up and dropped his head, desperately pondering his next move. He was confused. "Who are ye?"

"Friends of the king. This rebel purloined our papers, hoping to trade them for the king's shilling. We'll take care of him in good course. I am afraid he and his mob have done in your friends. We'll hang him, naturally, but we will let him bleed a bit more first."

"What? Killed me mates? It can't be!" Wright choked out the words.

"'Tis true enough," said the leader. "We went down the cliff to meet you, thinking the climb too steep for sailors. Found your crew dead and your boat gone. We must make haste as this bastard likely has rebel friends about."

"Christ's blood! If they ran the wind up me mates, there must be a hundred of them. We Scorpions are the best."

"Scorpions?" the leader asked.

"Special seaman, sailors mostly, a few marines. We do missions like this for the Admiral. For Black Dick. All handpicked men. Veterans, you know how it is, the best. Anyway, I got to get those papers back to the lieutenant. He'll flay me, otherwise."

"Have them, you shall. But first, let us make sure these are the right ones."

The leader picked the pouch up off the floor and looked at the notes and sketches. He smiled at Wright. "If General Howe makes haste, he can destroy the last of Washington's forces. Here is the place he should use."

He pointed to a marking on the crude map, a backwoods trail just five miles north of Fort Lee, near Closter. "Your craft is gone, however."

Wright grimaced. "Bollocks to that, I can swim it, even with this pain in me side. Once, I had a ship sink on me in the South Atlantic. Swam almost three miles in a rough ocean to another ship. This river ain't more than a half-mile, a mile at most."

"But the current is strong. When do you think we can expect help from His Majesty's forces? We are anxious to be rid of the rebels," the leader asked.

Wright smiled menacingly. "From what I saw, tomorrow night, next night at the latest. Those bleedin' soldiers will be sweatin' their way up these cliffs like I did. Ha! Serves 'em right."

"Indeed, it does," answered the leader. "You'd best head back at once. I am sorry for the loss of your mates. I am sure they were as brave and dedicated as you seem to be. But let that be a lesson, you cannot be too careful with damned Whigs and rebels."

Wright gasped. "You said the boat is gone?"

"Yes, but there is plenty of driftwood along the riverbank. Perhaps you can float across with that."

He handed Wright the pouch. With that in hand and nary a word of thanks or farewell, the burly sailor began the long trip down the cliff trail. He hoped to be across the river before dawn.

* * *

When Eldon Wright departed, Beall turned to Creed with a frown. "I don't understand, sir. You let him go with the information his masters sent him to obtain. Shouldn't have taken both in as spies?"

Creed smiled. "Some might have done just that, Jonathan. But as you should know, we play chess, not checkers. The British are determined to cross the river and take Fort Lee. Now we know where, and thanks to our good Scorpion, that is our seaman friend, we know when. We must get this information to the commander-in-chief. But first, we shall have a chat with our Loyalist friend here. Then we shall turn him over to our good colleagues in the local Detection Committee. They seem eager enough to deal with traitors and subversives."

***

Fort Lee, New Jersey, November 20th, 1776

General Cornwallis kicked over a steaming pot of brackish-looking soup some indigent rebels had prepared for their dinner. Mostly water with just a slice of rancid bacon, one old potato, and a handful of dried peas, spiced with herbs of indeterminate origin. It smelled even worse than it looked. The contents spilled onto the boots his lackey had spent most of the previous night shining. No matter. Now they would not need to present a smart appearance when the general accepted Fort Lee's surrender, as it had been abandoned without resistance. But the fort's capture without a fight was bittersweet.

"Rebels have scattered like rabbits before us, Milord," an eager subaltern said.

"We want a large buck standing his ground, Mister Wallace, not small game scattering before us. Bagging the rebel army was the objective, not these now-useless mounds of stone and earthworks."

The subaltern smiled like a schoolboy. "But the navy will be grateful, sir. We now command the North River. The rebels just beat us out by less than an hour."

"Precisely. In that sense, my surprise attack has failed. See to your men, Mister Wallace. Watch for stray rebels."

While the British column moved south from Closter and then east toward the fort, the rebels had just cleared out and hurried to the town of Hackensack and the river of that name. From there, they would eventually head southwest toward Newark and then New Brunswick.

Cornwallis glumly watched Lieutenant Wallace and his men round up rebel prisoners, all of them drunk on bad rum.

"We have found forty of the miscreants, sir," Wallace finally reported.

"That's all?" Cornwallis feigned surprise.

"That, plus the baggage and guns."

"How many guns? Are they useful?"

"Several, sir. But they have been spiked."

"Useless then," Cornwallis grunted.

There would be much marching now if they were to catch the rebels. However, he needed to rest his men before commencing the pursuit. The crossing of the river and the long climb up two-hundred-foot cliffs while manhandling guns and baggage had taken its toll. Still, he could not give them too much rest. Cornwallis intended to catch the fleeing rebels before Howe's arrival could slow him down.

Chapter 12

Hackensack, New Jersey

Washington finished his last dispatch of the morning and placed his quill in its holder. He paused a moment to reflect on the situation. Because of the work of Creed and his men, his army lived to fight again. Nathanael Greene had evacuated Fort Lee just hours before Cornwallis descended upon it at the head of a British force of more than 4,000. The British now outnumbered the Americans on the west bank of the North River. After a short pause at Fort Lee, Cornwallis's force pushed on, nearly beating Greene's men to the Hackensack River crossing at New Bridge, a small village just north of Hackensack.

There, defending from the town's stone houses, a small force of Americans held up the British advance guard. Accurate fire from the rebel defenders tore into the British ranks, keeping the attackers at bay until the militia could tear up the bridge's wooden planking. Washington himself galloped to the scene of action. He steadied his prancing charger beside Greene, who was directing some New Jersey militia.

"Tear up the planking, boys! Hessians cannot swim!" Greene cried.

Washington sat upright in the saddle, ignoring the musket rounds humming past them. He did not like the look of things. "General Greene, can you secure this place?"

"Indeed, sir. I believe we have."

"Question is, for how long?" Several more rounds passed, but Washington still did not budge. "I am returning to Hackensack to plan our next move. We need more troops to stem the flood of British soldiers now facing us."

"Where will we get them, sir?"

"I've summoned General Lee to hasten across the North River from New Castle and join with us in central Jersey."

Greene looked askance— he did not like or trust Charles Lee.

Washington held his gaze firmly. "I know. Despite your personal thoughts, he is, by order of Congress, my second-in-command."

Washington's decision to send for Lee was not without some complications. First, his staff did not trust Lee, and there certainly was much to distrust. Major General Charles Lee, the second-in-command of the Continental Army, openly vied with Washington for the affection of the senior officers and even many in the lower ranks. Even more suspect, he maintained a separate correspondence with key members of Congress. The staff speculated as to the nature of the discourse, but Washington refused to engage.

"I know your mind. However, we have bigger issues to concern ourselves with, General Greene. The supplies and equipment we desperately need now belong to the

British. And so long as our forces remain divided, we have a mere 3,000 to a British force of almost five thousand and growing."

Greene nodded. "But three thousand good men can stop them."

Washington slapped his saddle's pommel with a leather glove. "Many of the enlistments run out in December and January. Even our most stalwart boys can desert us legally in a few weeks."

"I'll do what I can with the boys who remain, Your Excellency," Greene pledged.

Washington's lips tightened into a grim smile. "That, I know to be the case. But we remain in desperate need of equipment, experienced men, and money to continue."

"At least now we have a chance, Your Excellency."

"Now the campaign becomes a foot race. The British will march across New Jersey to cut us off from Philadelphia."

"Is Congress aware of the danger, Your Excellency?"

Washington nodded. "I warned them of the events unfolding. They have provided little guidance and less material support."

"So you will…"

"Improvise, Nathanael, until the campaign is played out."

* * *

Creed finished checking his men's equipment and, more importantly, their horses. He usually checked on the horses himself before a long ride. Now, while his men rested, Creed went off to prepare for their next mission.

Thomas had scavenged some food, and he, Beall, and Parker ate cold porridge and sipped weak coffee. They sat in a makeshift lean-to in a small orchard just down from the Hackensack village green, the current site of Continental Army headquarters.

Parker waved a tin spoon at Thomas. "Did Lieutenant Creed find any problems with the horses?"

Thomas grinned. "He didn't. I checked them all first."

Parker nodded. "As it should be… Little Colt!"

"This seems a nice village. It reminds me much of Brooklyn," Beall said.

"Thinking of Miss Braaf, again?" Parker smirked.

Beall lowered his eyes. "I always do. Though I suppose I shall be in the grave before this army returns to Long Island. She has relatives here, though. I had hopes of finding one. Perhaps they could get a letter to her."

Krista Braaf was the beautiful young daughter of the erstwhile spy, Jan Braaf. In the short time Creed's men had been in Brooklyn, Krista and Jonathan became smitten with one another.

Parker shook his head. "Don't suppose we'll be here long. Lobsters are just a few miles away. Why don't you write a quick letter to her and leave it at the post office here in Hackensack? Maybe it will make its way to her."

Beall perked up. "That's a splendid idea."

Parker's brow furrowed. "Be scrupulous in your writing. Don't mention what we are doing or where we are. Concentrate on her beauty and your love for her."

Beall turned beet red. But Thomas burst into laughter.

***

While Creed's men rested, he went to see Fitzgerald. The army's retreat would take them through Newark, then New Brunswick, where they would turn west toward Princeton and finally the safety of the Delaware River and Pennsylvania.

By the time Creed arrived for his meeting, the headquarters was almost abandoned as aides and orderlies scrambled to load trunks and get the headquarters moving before the British came.

Fitzgerald looked up from his papers. "The British Scorpion, Eldon Wright, served your purposes well. The location of the British landing suggests he made it back across the North River and provided his superiors with the papers identifying the landing point."

"As I had hoped, sir. But unfortunately, the greedy Loyalist agent died before anyone could interrogate him. His body now feeds the carrion along the Palisades."

"I understand they couldn't identify him. A pity."

"Still, I have hope Wright's testimony will cast seeds of doubt among the British officers seeking spies among the Americans."

Fitzgerald nodded. "In this war, doubt is both a friend and an enemy."

"Indeed, sir."

Fitzgerald held some papers in his hands, waving them occasionally as he spoke in hushed tones, "His Excellency had toyed with sending you back into New York, to meet up with Golden Apple's contact, McNeeley."

"But why?"

"A desperate effort to influence British actions with false information. However, I succeeded in convincing him that the scheme offered too much risk for too little gain in a fast-moving military situation."

"Really?"

"He has made one such mistake already with poor Captain Hale. He would not do so again with Lieutenant Jeremiah Creed."

"I appreciate the sentiment, as do the lads."

"So, Jeremiah, instead of revisiting New York, I suggested you remain behind British lines as their forces advance through this great state. This may have its challenges, equally vexing."

Creed smirked at the understatement. "Indeed, sir. And what might those challenges be?"

Fitzgerald peered over his steel-rimmed glasses. "There are numerous armed groups scattered along the Hackensack Valley. Some are loyal, some are patriots, some are willing to be when it provides them with some advantage. You, Jeremiah, must determine a way to use all three to our advantage. No, small feat, I can assure you."

Creed's eyes widened. "Thank you for the assurance, sir. Do ye have anything specific in mind?"

The older man frowned and straightened his spectacles. "There is a faction under a man named Roy Harry operating near a hamlet not too distant, called Ridley. Ridley is rife with Tories. I know little about Harry, other than he's a notorious bandit of sorts. I sought Harry's services once before."

"You did?"

"He declined my kind offer, explaining that the time was not… ripe, was the word I believe he used."

Creed could only imagine how a bandit received Fitzgerald's offer. "So ye want me to recruit a skinner to be a cowboy or a cowboy to be a skinner?"

"Something like that, ah, yes."

"Looks to me like your man Roy Harry is motivated by profit. Not sure I like that, sir."

"Don't you think I'd prefer to know his true loyalties? Harry's camp is just north of Ridley, near the beginning of the great swamp. But he often stays at a place in town called the Blue House. Wherever he may be, find him and engage his services, if you can ascertain his loyalties."

"Why is recruiting this man so important, sir?"

"The area between Hackensack and Newark may constitute the heart of General Howe's supply line for some time. Roy Harry and his men, if they can be brought to our side, could prove useful in harassing those supplies and gaining intelligence."

"Would save the lads and me a lot of riding, to be sure," Creed mused.

"At some point, His Excellency expects our good General Lee to head south to join with us. I, as well as many others here, am not so sanguine. Still, His Excellency feels these men could prove invaluable in helping Lee's force avoid the British. So, as you can see, young man, you have no lack of challenges."

"Of course. How will I know him, this Roy Harry? How will he know me?"

Fitzgerald smiled like a schoolmaster whose student was beginning to understand the first declension of Latin. "I told him if I needed to solicit his services, I would send someone. He knows me as Mister Hadley. Use that name. See if he will now agree to work for us. If he will not, and certainly if he turns out to be a Loyalist cowboy after all…"

"What, sir?"

"His Excellency has authorized you to take measures to preclude him from supporting the British. You do understand what I mean?"

Creed's eyes narrowed and his lips tightened. "I do, sir. How long shall I engage in this enterprise?"

Fitzgerald cleared his throat. "I am not sure, Jeremiah. But once the army is safe across the Delaware, we'll send you word — if conditions allow."

"And if they don't allow?"

"We expect you to exercise good judgment and improvise. Establish a postal address in Hackensack. As Root Hog Burns, Loyalist, and cowboy."

"As you wish, sir."

Leaving the headquarters, Creed encountered Lieutenant Abner Scovel just returning from dispatch duties. Creed greeted him in a friendly manner, but he could tell Scovel did not match his enthusiasm. "Good day, Mister Scovel."

"So, off on another mission, Creed? Not that you may tell me."

Creed bowed his head politely. "Indeed, I may not."

"Well, as far as I can see, all this skullduggery has come to naught. This army has done nothing but retreat since Long Island. Soon, it will melt away as their enlistments end. Moreover, who can blame them? We lack the very basic necessities of life, not to mention those of war."

"Well now, Mister Scovel, just how do you think the British feel about all of this?"

"The British?"

"Yes. They hoped to destroy us for good just a few weeks ago on Long Island. Then they tried to bag us in New York. Overwhelm us at Haarlem Heights. We lured them to White Plains. And when they might have triumphed there, they failed to destroy us."

Scovel folded his arms across his chest. "And your point, Mister Creed?"

"My point, Mister Scovel, is that weakened though the army is, it is not yet destroyed. And winter is now upon us. I suspect King George will not be too pleased. These British and German hirelings cost him money."

Scovel's face reddened. "My God, Creed, you put a spin on things so nicely."

"Well, I have ranged back and forth between two armies. Let's say I have a different perspective. By the way, you may call me Jeremiah. Good day."

* * *

Ridley, New Jersey

The smell of roasting venison drifted through the small hamlet. Ridley served as a place for travelers to stay while they navigated the muddy bogs that acted as roads through the Hackensack wetlands. The swamp, as the locals called it, was a low-lying marsh fed by several large rivers and numerous creeks flowing down from the mountains and meeting the coastal estuaries.

The swamp bordered the Hackensack Valley, a prosperous stretch of farmland running north to south along the river of the same name. Its two main roads were the only way a farmer could move his goods without a long and circuitous detour inland. For that reason, Ridley, population fifty, was important. Many of the lawless bands that operated in this small but isolated wilderness clashed over control of Ridley, for he who controlled it controlled the swamp.

Their horses trotted along the dusty road into town as the sun dipped over the western horizon. They halted at a large frame house near the edge of town, the Brower House. Its owner, Abraham Brower, mined pig iron but made his profit from the boarding house he operated for travelers along the swamp road.

Brower answered the knock on his door with a look of puzzlement at the strangers. Dressed in a variety of homespun cloth, buckskin, and pelts, they looked like trappers from the mountains of the north and west.

Creed stood before him with a grin. "Howdy, friend. My name is Root Hog… Root Hog Burns. These are my boys. We wuz hopin' for a meal and a place to rest ourselves and our horses fer a few days."

Brower nodded. "Pay in advance, two pence each plus two for each horse."

"You charge as much for a horse as a man?" Beall asked.

"A good horse is worth more than a man," Brower replied.

"You're right about that," Creed said. "You got a deal,"

Creed and his men took a room in the rear of the Brower House. The main part of the house contained a great room, a parlor, and two bedrooms on the second floor. The stone fireplace in the great room also served as a kitchen.

Creed and Brower settled accounts in the great room. Brower handed Creed a mug of black coffee. "Rarely have guests paid three days in advance. You plan on staying here in Ridley, Mister Burns?"

"Call me Root Hog."   EDIT POINT

"Very well, Root Hog. That is a strange name. Were you born with it?" Brower smiled at his attempt with humor.

Creed grinned. "Practically. My pa gave it to me. Even as a boy, I was wandering hither and yon and bringing things home. You know, fresh trout, wild nuts, and berries, sometimes things purloined from a grumpy neighbor. Always rootin' about for things, like a root hog. Name stuck."

Brower sipped his coffee and eyed Creed suspiciously. "What are you rootin' for in Ridley, then?"

"A man named Roy Harry. Know where I can find him?"

Creed noted a faint hint of surprise on Brower's face.

"Hard to say. But I'd start with the Blue House. He spends a lot of time there. Might say it's his second home. It's a large stone and timber building just down the street."

***

Creed stepped into the Blue House, dressed in his cowboy backwoods homespun and leather, with a beaver hat. He carried a brace of pistols, his Hessian Jaeger rifle, and a sword bayonet. Several of Harry's men were bringing in a roasted side of venison into the great room. They began carving large chunks of the sizzling meat, which they ate with grinding teeth and smacking lips.

Creed immediately spotted Harry. Brower had provided a good description of—late twenties, of medium height, and with a thin frame. His wiry build belied the strength this former pig iron miner possessed. Harry, with his light brown hair, twinkly blue eyes, and clean-shaven face, looked surprisingly more like a choirboy than a brigand. To most folks, it was a terrible miscalculation.

Creed approached Harry just as he was pulling a strip of venison from the bone with a wicked-looking hunting knife. Two of Harry's men immediately stepped behind him.

 "Mister Hadley sent me here. Said I should speak to Roy Harry. You be him?"

Roy Harry bit the hunk of flesh from the knife and then wiped it on his thigh, the excess blood and grease staining his leather breeches.

He stared at Creed icily, his light eyes darkening as he narrowed them. "Come with me, Mister?"

Creed smiled. "Burns, Root Hog Burns, but you can call me Root Hog."

Harry nodded. "Then, come with me, Mister Root Hog Burns."

Creed followed him up a narrow wooden staircase onto a balustrade overlooking the tavern's main dining room. At the end of the walkway, he opened a door and led Creed into a small room.

Harry lit a candle, closed the door, and went right to the point. "So, what have you got for me, Root Hog? Another request for assistance? I hope with gold this time. That might get your old colonel some consideration."

Creed decided to push back. He stared hard at Harry and put on his best Root Hog voice. "Now listen up, good, Mister Harry. This army is on the run, but the fight ain't out of it yet, no siree. They will return, and when they do, you'd best be on the side of the good fellas. Those Englishmen don't care one bit for people like you or me. We just ain't their type. Besides, there's a lot more plunder in the British supply wagons than in Mister Washington's, if you get my drift."

Harry's eyes widened at the mention of plunder.

"Tell me more, Root Hog."

"Now, I know of one supply convoy."

Creed knew nothing of the sort, but he felt a bluff might work. Take Harry on a mission against British interests, and the rest would follow. There had to be a convoy of supply wagons following the British columns. In the meantime, he could use their time together to assess whether he could do business with Roy Harry.

* * *

The next morning, Creed and his men prepared for the foray. Creed asked Thomas to stay behind in Ridley to watch their packhorses, which had been purloined after they were found wandering after the great fire in New York. The animals were loaded with extra accouterments, uniforms, clothes, and weapons—plush Creed's gold.

Creed mounted Finn and turned to Thomas. "While we go on this foray, Thomas, try to mingle a bit and listen in on what Harry's other men have to say. Maybe you'll learn whether they are skinners or cowboys. The good colonel is not sure of them, nor am I. Until we are, we must be on our guard."

"They may well be playing on both sides, "Beall said.

"'Twould not surprise me the least," Creed replied.

Thomas nodded. "Yes, sir. But I'd rather come with you."

"Your time will come again, Thomas, of that you can be certain," Creed answered.

Parker had seen Harry depart for his camp just before dawn. He was to return mid-morning with four of his best men, who would join them in search of the British supply wagons.

Creed would use the interlude to check out the Blue House. But first, he spent some time pumping the tight-lipped Abraham Brower for more information. "Now tell me, pardner, that Blue House, why's it called that?"

"You've seen it yourself. It has bright blue shutters and trim. What else would you call it but the Blue House?"

"You called it Harry's second home. Does he own it?"

Brower laughed. "No, the owner is a young woman, and a handsome young woman at that."

"A woman, you say? Who is she?"

"Name's Ackerman. Jannetje Ackerman. She named it the Blue House. Before that, it was called Ridley Tavern."

"So, a young lady runs it? Mighty peculiar, ain't it?"

Brower shook his head. "Not really. We Dutch treat our women as persons, not property, like the English. *Mvrouw* Ackerman is wise and experienced beyond her years. She was a bride at eighteen and already a widow at twenty-two."

"What happened to her man?"

"Ach, poor Mathius. Her husband died two years ago while hunting in the swamp. He was forty."

"Accident?"

Brower spread his hands. "It's the swamp."

"So, the lady's a grieving widow at twenty-two, eh? Convenient, ain't it?"

Brower shrugged. "She mourned the required year but immediately took control of his business. She has better business sense than Mathius ever did. He gambled a lot. It was only a matter of time before he lost the place."

"That so? Maybe running a business is her way of grieving, ya think?"

Brower eyed him carefully. "Perhaps. Or perhaps something else."

"Like what?"

"I don't know."

"What's Roy Harry's connection to the place and to her?"

Brower shrugged. "There's talk. But I don't place stock in rumors, *Heer* Root Hog."

"I won't neither. I'll take a walk down to the place and see fer myself."

* * *

The Blue House had several long tables full of customers devouring breakfast of leftover venison with scrambled eggs and biscuits, along with plenty of coffee. Although busy with customers, *Mvrouw* Ackerman glanced inquisitively at Creed as he entered the tavern. *Did Harry mention me to the young widow?*

Creed took a seat at a table in a corner so he could observe the entrance. This habit began after an encounter he had with some Tory thugs back in Frederick, Maryland. That encounter seemed so long ago, although it had happened the previous spring. Creed had jumped into the fray when the local Tories attacked a recruiting officer from the First Maryland Continental Line. Creed killed the ringleader and wounded a couple of the others. In part to avoid the constable, Creed accepted the recruiter's offer to join the regiment.

Jannetje Ackerman had dark brown hair and light brown eyes, fine skin that tanned in summer, and maintained a healthy glow in winter. She stood a little over five feet tall and had a narrow waist, slightly wide hips, and, for her size, an ample bosom.

The rumors in Ridley had it that Roy Harry had made her his mistress shortly after she became a widow. But when he stayed at the Blue House, Harry's room lay at the opposite end of the tavern.

Jannetje sauntered past other customers to Creed's table to take his order herself. "Well, *Mijnheer*, I see you found the best place in Ridley for breakfast. "Can we start with a good cup of coffee?"

She smiled, but Creed could not tell if it was genuine. She dressed practically, in a simple brown dress with a crisp white apron.

"Well, *Mevrouw*…?"

"Ackerman. My name is Jannetje Ackerman. You may call me Jannetje. But please, don't call me *Mevrouw*. That's too old-fashioned."

"I thought you Dutch liked the old ways."

"Well, I am of Dutch descent, like most here in the valley. But *Mevrouw* seems so…"

Creed grinned at her mischievously. "Old? Or Dutch?"

She returned the smile, half closing her eyes seductively. "Yes, indeed. So, what is your pleasure, *Mijnheer*?"

Was her look an affectation or a flirtation? "I'll have black coffee, strong. Some of that venison and eggs, with a biscuit. That'll be a good start, miss. I can call you Miss?"

Her stunning eyes widened. "It is Missus. I'm a widow. But folks call me Jannetje."

She smiled pleasantly. Creed realized how pretty she was. "Could I get some fresh butter with those biscuits, Jannetje?"

Creed scanned the room. The murmur of the morning banter intrigued him. These men, seasoned travelers, talked of the war that surrounded them as though it were the weather. He learned that Hackensack was in British hands and that the main American force had headed south through Newark, with Cornwallis's forces hot on their heels.

The food came to the table, delivered by a middle-aged servant. Then Creed picked up the nugget he wanted. He overheard one of the men, an itinerant cobbler, tell his companions that the day before, he had seen British ships unloading wagons and horses near Fort Lee.

Creed reckoned it was a load of supplies for Cornwallis's column. With any luck, they would greet it before it reached Hackensack.

From his window, Creed watched Roy Harry and his men ride up. They reminded him of the types one found in seaports, burly-looking savages as happy to slit your throat as tip their hat to you. They had old-looking British muskets, relics of the last war with France.

Harry shot a grin clear across the room at Creed when he entered the tavern. He bounded past the other patrons and pulled up a chair next to him. "So, Root Hog, are we ready for this journey? The swamps are not a pleasant place to spend a day's outing, but the rewards can make the effort worthwhile."

Creed grinned at him. "Have ya eaten?" He saw Jannetje watching. "The little lady's lookin' at us. Think she hankers for ya."

"Maybe, more likely, she's thinking our two rough personalities could create some sparks. Sparks are something Jannetje likes, as long as she herself doesn't get burned."

"Like her husband got burned?"

Harry's eyes narrowed.

"I'm jess messin' with ya, Harry. Have some vittles."

Harry glanced at Jannetje. "Not too hungry right now. How about you? Have you eaten?"

Creed nodded. "Sure have, pardner. A nice meal right here at the tavern. Real nice lady that Jannetje. Good lookin' too. Swamp life hasn't hurt her much."

Harry looked at him harshly for a second and then broke into a forced laugh. "Aha! That's very funny, Root Hog. Well, we'll see how long you remain in the swamp, eh?"

Harry's men looked knowingly at their boss and laughed.

Harry went on, "See, the swamp had its way of driving men away or keeping them forever in its muddy embrace. We've seen that on more than one occasion. Tories and Whigs alike pay, sometimes handsomely, to make their opponents disappear. Staying neutral had its advantages if you knew how to play the game."

"Neutral or not, I think you'll agree the king's coin is up for the takin', right pardner?"

"What do you mean, Root Hog?"

"Found a nugget right here in the tavern. Time we used it."

Harry nodded and rose from the table. "Let's do it."

They went to the horses and mounted. Without another word, the eight riders headed up the sodden road into the swamp, their horse hooves splashing fistfuls of black mud on any passerby.

***

"How far before the mud ends?" Creed asked after a long hour.

Harry grinned. "Tired already? We'll take the road east and then south for several miles. There, the ground gets firmer and the road dries enough for the horses to move at more than a slow walk."

The sucking of the horses' hooves pulling out of the mud and the occasional rapping of a woodpecker or the honking of geese flocking south were the only sounds in the swamp's forest of scrub, tamarack, and oak.

Harry broke the silence. "Tell me, Root Hog, where do we go from here? Do we have an actual plan, or are you gambling we'll stumble into some hapless merchant?"

Creed put on his best Root Hog voice, "Now lookey here, Harry. While you was rounding up your fat boys from their beauty sleep, I took the time to listen to them rubes back in the tavern. Appears we got us a couple of English boats unloading wagons yesterday. Those wagons have to go somewhere. I figure we can skirt around and catch 'em from behind, or maybe the side."

Harry's face brightened. "Well now, Root Hog, I underestimated your industry. You have been busy! And all this time I thought you were chasing Jannetje's skirts in there."

Creed laughed. "What makes you think I wasn't, Harry? She is one fine lookin' woman."

As he said it, Creed eyed Harry to gauge his reaction, but the gang leader did not take the bait. It seemed business and pleasure stayed separate in the swamp.

By mid-afternoon, they halted at a broad highroad that stretched from the river to the east of them. Harry turned to Creed. "I'd say this is the only road the cargo could traverse. Let's take time to rest the horses and eat."

They turned off the road and set up camp in a small meadow a quarter-mile into the woods. Although the trees had no leaves left, the mix of conifers provided them with cover.

While Beall and Parker took care of the horses, Creed went back to scout the road on foot. He wanted to assess his next move while looking for a trace of the wagons. The sky was clear blue, and the November sun beat down on him, warming his bones and drying the last trace of the morning dampness from his clothing.

He reached the road, still about an inch deep in mud, which was clumped and rutted by travelers, both military and civilian. It ran westward but then turned, crossed the Hackensack River, and forked. The wider fork, the King's Highway, headed southwest toward Newark, while a narrower branch ran north toward Hackensack.

Any supply wagons should be turning south behind the British army. This would be as good a place as any to take them. He started to turn back to the camp when he heard the heavy pounding of hooves and the cries of a driver urging horses on.

He ran back to the edge of the woods. There, Creed saw the wagon. It was long, almost eighteen feet, an expensive-looking affair with European-style wheels that caused it to struggle as it made its way through the ruts and holes of the poor American road. The driver whipped and cussed the team, which was struggling to pull the load. At the back of the wagon sat two guards armed with carbine muskets.

The wagon carried no ordinary load. But it would be long gone before he could alert the others. *I need to try to bluff them into stopping.*

Before Creed could step out onto the road, a volley of shots rang out, and a gang of armed men swarmed over the wagon. Whether bushwhackers were cowboys or skinners, they had the same idea as Creed. There were eight of them, wearing bandanas over their faces and dressed in a curious amalgamation of uniform parts, civilian clothes, and frontier buckskin. They were armed with the latest French and British muskets.

The wagon's guards already lay dying in the mud-clogged road. The driver was slumped over, clutching a wound at his side. The bushwhackers ignored him as they tore through the wagon in search of plunder.

The driver was not seriously wounded. Creed watched him reach for a short fowling-piece at his feet. Suddenly, the fowling-piece boomed, spurted smoke, and belched hot lead. One of the bushwhackers collapsed in pain as a quarter ounce of birdshot tore into his leg. He screamed, cursing all the angels and saints, and then pulled at his blood-stained pants.

One of the thieves clambered from the rear of the wagon and stood over the driver, drove the butt of his musket into the man's chest. Then he saw the flash of a blade and heard a cry. The marauder brandished a long knife and yelled in a guttural language incomprehensible. He tore off the driver's hat and grabbed his hair in one hand, and began to slice into his scalp.

The sound of his victim's scream was the last thing the bushwhacker heard. The shot from Creed's rifle entered the side of his head, turning his brain to mush. Creed hated the very idea of scalping. Killing men in battle or a fair fight was one thing, barbaric mutilation another.

Now, other bushwhackers began pointing in his direction and hollering to one another. Creed stepped behind some trees. He poured powder down the barrel, hammered down his round, and primed the pan. He pulled the hammer back and stood against the side of the tree as he acquired his next target. He could take down one more, maybe two more, before they would be on him.

But in their rush for plunder, they forgot to reload. Now they frantically reloaded, several foolishly standing in the open. Creed's next mark was a big man, at least six feet tall with a barrel chest and huge arms, standing in the open and madly ramming a ball down the barrel of his musket. Then the bushwhacker scanned the tree line for the shooter.

The only thing he saw was a puff of smoke. Creed's second bullet drilled a hole through his chest. The large man fell onto the mud-rutted road.

Creed dropped to the ground as scattered shots sailed over him. He crawled into the brush, crouched against another tree, and began the reloading drill once more.

From his left, he heard a small volley erupt. The unexpected shots smacked into the bodies of three more bushwhackers. Creed turned and saw Roy Harry and the others emerging from the wood line, their legs pounding full-tilt toward the wagon.

The last of the bushwhackers scattered across the road like rabbits and melted into the woods on the far side.

Harry's men searched the dead and dying under Creed's watchful eye while Parker and Beall combed the wood line to make sure the bushwhackers had truly left. Satisfied they had not lingered, they returned to the wagon.

"Any sign of 'em?"

Parker answered with a laconic grin. "Root Hog, I believe they won't stop running 'til they reach Tappan."

Roy Harry interrupted. "Well, looks like these were neither skinners nor cowboys."

"Then who are they?" Beall asked.

"My guess is they're deserters," Harry said.

Creed frowned. "Deserters, eh? Question is, pardner, from which side?"

"Looks like both," Harry replied. "See this."

"The uniform jackets are a mix of red and blue. These are American cockades and British emblems," Beall said.

"And some of the bastards have papers from both armies," Harry said.

Creed frowned. "Seems we have common cause between rebels and red coats—plunder!"

Harry nodded. "I heard of such but didn't believe it. Root Hog, men such as these are very dangerous—they've nothing to lose, for whichever side finds them will surely hang them."

"Yessir. And facing hangin' focuses the mind real nice and leads to desperation. Can ya read, Harry? Get their papers. Might come in useful later. I am gonna check His Majesty's wagon and see whether the fuss was worth their effort."

Parker and one of Harry's men climbed onto the wagon while Beall removed the nearly mutilated corpse of the driver and laid it alongside the bushwhackers.

Parker called out in excitement, "Strong boxes, Root Hog. Four of them."

"Let's open 'em up and have a look," Creed said.

To their surprise, each box contained cash: small notes and silver coins amounting to almost 1,000 pounds sterling.

Harry sucked in his breath. "A payroll wagon. Looks like enough here to pay a couple of thousand men for months."

"Not so sure, pardner. A payroll wagon would have more guards. This wagon seems a little under-manned, just a driver and a pair of fools along for the ride. No, I reckon something else."

Harry's face showed annoyance. "What then? And why do we care, Root Hog? Regardless of the purpose, money is money."

"Not true. A payroll wagon, missing or hijacked, normally brings the king's revenge, and real quick! And if this driver and his pards stole or hijacked the wagon, by now someone would be on the trail. Probably comin' down this very road."

Harry cocked his head. "Then what is it?"

"Not sure, but I think this money's intended to buy the loyalty of people living here in the valley. What I reckon is a Loyalist band, organized like, was expecting this. Check the driver and search the wagon for a map or instructions."

Harry searched through the driver's pockets, shirt, breeches, vest, and jacket. All he came across was some coins, a jackknife, and beef jerky.

Creed smiled at his accomplice's obvious frustration. "Try his shoes, Harry."

Harry loosened the crude buckles, then pulled off the driver's shoes. The right one was empty, but in his left shoe, Harry found a piece of heavy parchment neatly folded twice.

"They always use the shoes, Harry." Creed took the paper from Harry and unfolded what turned out to be a clean, hand-drawn map of the area. It had several markings along the road, and then a special X marked just northeast of the village of River Edge. "Now, lookey here. We have something pretty interestin'."

Chapter 13

Oud Amsterdam Tavern, Hackensack, New Jersey, November 22nd, 1776

The door swung open, and a short, stocky man with a square jaw and barrel chest entered the tavern. He removed his black military hat, revealing dark brown hair tied back in a tight cue. Nearly twenty heads lifted from their cups and tankards, knowing they were about to get down to business. Despite his size, everyone knew Abraham Van Buskirk was no one to trifle with. He paused and took a deep breath. *The time all have awaited has arrived.*

Cornwallis's men had scarcely cleared the town of the rebel rear guard when the call went out to Tories up and down the Hackensack Valley. For weeks, Van Buskirk and other leaders of the Tory factions in New Jersey had maintained a secret correspondence with the British high command. Quickly establishing an indigenous loyal militia was essential to the success of the British invasion. So was the expansion of the Loyalist base, a scheme suggested by Major Sandy Drummond and approved by General Howe.

Van Buskirk's eyes scanned the room carefully, almost as if he were sizing up the men before he spoke. His gaze silenced the usually lively assembly of Loyalist farmers, laborers, and tradesmen. Finally, he asked, "Is everyone here?"

It was more of a command than a question. Van Buskirk's blunt opening surprised no one. He did not become the owner of one of the most successful estates in the area through small talk and banter. Still, to those who knew him — and few did — he seemed more intense than usual. They all knew well that he had a good reason. For nearly two years, he had been walking the tightrope of feigned neutrality, occasionally siding with either the Whigs or Tories as circumstances demanded.

When the British seized Staten Island that summer, Van Buskirk began a long game of secret negotiations with the British and the Royal Governor, William Franklin, estranged son of the famous writer, printer, inventor, politician, and now diplomat, Benjamin Franklin.

"Everyone we counted on, except Bram," replied Willi Sluyter, a small landholder from the English Neighborhood, a well-settled and extremely Loyalist area along the Jersey palisades.

Van Buskirk grimaced. "And where the *Deuvfel* is Bram? He knew of our plan for days. I had him in mind to command a company. No matter, the English are here now, and we must deal with what we have — the English hope to form at least four regiments, perhaps more. I shall command one, the 4th Battalion, New Jersey Volunteers. I nominated you, gentlemen, for leadership positions in the regiment and now have a letter from General Howe approving most of you."

Members of the Dutch communities in New York and New Jersey referred to the British as English to distinguish their nationality after Dutch New Amsterdam was taken from the Netherlands in 1664.

Van Buskirk began the arduous task of reading out the roll, beginning with the company commanders holding the rank of captain or lieutenant. This list included Bram De Groot, Daniel Isaac Brown, Peter Rutan, William Van Allen, Joost Earl, Samuel Ryerson, and James Servanier. He had assigned each captain two lieutenants and two sergeants, four corporals, and forty privates. Van Buskirk himself held the rank of lieutenant colonel, a fact that surprised a few of the more ardent Tories, who were unaware of his secret negotiations with, and support for, the English.

However, the British, not Van Buskirk, had selected Stephen Van Deman as adjutant of the 4th New Jersey Volunteers. Van Deman held the rank of major because he claimed to have served in Europe and brought almost eighty men with him from his hometown near Tappan. This did not please Van Buskirk, who hoped to place a distant cousin as his adjutant.

After some discussion of the overall military situation, Van Buskirk gave them their general orders. "Tonight, you will muster your men on the village green and receive uniforms and equipment. At dawn, the units will form up for two hours of drill, then breakfast. After breakfast, I shall issue each company a list containing the names of rebels to find and bring to the King's justice. Are there any questions?"

"*Ja*, Abraham, where do we take these prisoners?" Joost Earl asked.

Van Buskirk's face reddened with a bit of embarrassment as he, due to his lack of military experience, had neglected an important point. "Call me Colonel. I am your commander now."

"Very well, Colonel."

"The De Haring farm will be commandeered by our good adjutant, Major Van Deman. Each company will provide him four men, right after breakfast."

"Can we use force against the rebels?" asked Daniel Isaac Brown, a lawyer. The group laughed, amused that a lawyer should think up that question.

"*Ja*, but try to save as many for the King's justice as you can," Van Buskirk sneered.

Knowing looks went around the room at his comment.

"When do we get paid?" James Servanier asked the question that lay in the back of all their minds. Though Loyalists, they knew many of their men, especially the Scots-Irish laborers from the docks, farms, and iron works, had been promised cash for their loyalty to the crown.

"You speak of such things this night? The King's forces have crossed the mighty river and climbed the Palisades cliffs to take Fort Lee and come to our succor, and you speak of money? The Hessians chase Greene and his forces out of Hackensack and liberate our valley, and you speak of money? Anyone who demands money in such a manner can leave! For those who stay, when the time is right, you shall get your money, not before."

Van Deman spoke up for the first time, "Yes, but money was promised, and if we are to be professionals in service to His Majesty, we should be paid as professionals, not a rabble."

Van Buskirk's head pounded in anger, and his face reddened. His adjutant, the second-ranking officer in his command, just took sides against him in a public forum. He controlled the urge to scream at him and pound the man's lanky frame with his ham-like fists. Instead, he tried to defuse the situation without committing himself. "*Ja*, well, arrangements have been made. It will just take some time."

The group broke up shortly after. Van Buskirk knew the issue of money would come back to haunt him, but he had much to do and would consider that later. Besides, he alone knew the king's silver was already on the way.

** *

The next morning, Van Buskirk's careful gaze watched the Loyalist companies form for drill. They turned out in finely cut green coats with off-white breeches and black facings and belting. Their caps, a small, brimmed hat, gave them somewhat the appearance of village parsons.

The volunteers lacked musicians and flags, but one resourceful private found a couple of British flags in a nearby shop and took them for the regiment's use. By mid-morning, Van Buskirk watched the green columns march up the main street to their designated sectors. His men appeared excited. They all relished the chance for revenge against the Whigs and patriots, as they had treated Tories poorly. The rebellion, at least in the Hackensack Valley, had become nothing less than a civil war.

The English arrived around noon that day. As groups of British and Hessian soldiers marched through Hackensack, they displayed the full extent of British military strength in a deliberate show of royal authority. Women, children, and a few men lined the Post Road, waving kerchiefs, and a few British flags fluttered in front of various shops.

Van Buskirk watched the display with mixed feelings. Although Hackensack grew more comfortable with it, even the most loyal supporters of the cause felt a shudder as the Hessians marched past. Their reputation for severe brutality had gone before them, and no one could be sure how these large, fierce men would behave toward friends or enemies.

***

The best oarsmen in the Royal Navy heaved their oars as one, speeding the longboat across the gray waters. General Howe stared in awe as the cliffs on the west shore of the North River loomed larger with each pull of the oars. Next to him sat James Drummond. Drummond wore the scarlet jacket of a light dragoon along with his sand-brown leather breeches. The breeches earned him the nickname "Sandy".

Howe spoke in a low voice, "So, Sandy, at last, we can take this great land back from the rebels. I suspect Washington will ask for terms within the fortnight if we do not hunt him down first. My proclamation shall energize our loyal friends and cow the few rebels left into submission."

Drummond had read the proclamation that morning and was not so sanguine. Howe had accepted Drummond's strategy but did not fully understand the need for nuance, especially in political things. "Indeed, sir. Meanwhile, we have several good Loyalist regiments forming in this valley, some two thousand men in all. They may well prove crucial to the success of our plan. Their leaders are all true to the king, and unlike the rebel forces, they shall be paid with the king's coin."

The British commander-in-chief had fought that notion, but Drummond argued persuasively for funds to grease the machinery of Loyalist sympathy, recruit informants, and pay the Loyalists recruited into organized units.

"Well, make sure that none are overpaid. These men are not regulars, you know."

"I know that well, sir. Both officers and enlisted alike will receive half the pay of their counterparts in the Royal Army, minus deductions for uniforms, food, and the like. I sent the funds over yesterday. They should be at the appointed place by now. I shall meet with their regimental colonels, provide them with a pay schedule, and arrange for the funds to be disbursed. And some will be used to buy the loyalty of the uncommitted."

Howe chuckled. "Well, let's not spoil them too much. We have come to save them from the Whigs and rebels, after all."

* * *

Bram De Groot cursed silently. He cursed the darkness descending on him. He cursed the English. He cursed the Whigs. He cursed the Tories—the very Tories who awaited the success of his mission. But the chief object of his invective was none other than Abraham Van Buskirk.

Van Buskirk had sent De Groot on a very special and confidential errand, as he so delicately put it. When the British forces descended on the Hackensack Valley, De Groot was to secretly rendezvous with a wagon loaded with pay for the Tory volunteers there. That is, those taking up arms for the crown. Van Buskirk wanted the wagon secured by nightfall. Though loyal to the king, Van Buskirk's Tories expected payment from the crown. This would prove their status as paid regulars and offset the losses they incurred by leaving thriving farms and businesses.

Van Buskirk allowed only two men to accompany De Groot, and neither knew the wagon's contents. Still, they were good men and loyal Tories. Bram had received little instruction from Van Buskirk other than to position himself in the woods by the field outside of New Bridge. There, he would meet a wagon driven by a man named Tanek and return with the wagon, telling no one of it or its contents.

But now the wagon's arrival time had long passed, and the cold chill of a November night descended on them. De Groot puffed on his pipe and scanned the meadow on the other side of the road. The bare woods provided little overhead cover, so he could see the stars beginning to emerge. The birds had long gone, and the darkening twilight revealed only the occasional bat squealing overhead. Then he heard it, the faint drumming of hooves followed by the rumble of wheels. *The wagon!*

The wagon came around the bend and slowed as it approached the meadow. De Groot saw that the driver had just pulled the horses to a sudden halt, relaxed the reins, and set the brake. He then pulled out a firelock and checked the pan.

From what De Groot could make out in the dark, he was a large, strongly built man, around six feet tall. De Groot gave a low whistle and signaled his men to cover him. They had not yet received their English muskets, so they brandished fowling-pieces loaded with heavy shot. Experienced hunters along the extensive waters of the valley, they could cut a man down at twenty yards, even in the dark.

De Groot rose and strode quickly toward the wagon. Pressed now for time, he cut to the chase. "Are you Tanek?"

***

Creed cocked his weapon. "Before I respond to that question, who are you?"

De Groot bit down hard on his pipe stem, pointed his fowling piece at Creed's face, and sputtered, "I'm the man who will introduce you to God or the *Deuvel*!"

He could see the shadows of De Groot's men in the twilight. *No surprise*, he thought. But Roy, Harry, and Beall had already hidden in the woods on the opposite end of the meadow.

He raised a cocked pistol and pointed it at De Groot. "Then I shall enjoy your company, *Mijnheer*."

DeGroot lowered his weapon.

Now, his lordship gave me clear instructions. I need to know your name, but more importantly, the name of whoever sent you. If I return without those two pieces of information, the English will think I ran off with the wagon, and I will face their noose instead of your musket.

"You use the term English when referring to the British. Are you one of us? Yes, Van Buskirk would use one of us, but someone distant, for security. The man is shrewd, among other things." De Groot softened, just a little, and his teeth relaxed the grip on the pipe. "Very well, I am Bram De Groot, a captain in His Majesty's 4th New Jersey Volunteers. Colonel Abraham Van Buskirk, also of the 4th New Jersey Volunteers, directed me to meet this wagon and return quietly with the contents."

Creed now realized the money was a pay wagon to enlist Tories to fight for their king, to buy their loyalty, although the funds could be used for other shady purposes.

The wagon was unescorted to avoid attracting attention.

"*Bedankt, Mijnheer*." Creed learned some Dutch during his time on board ship and while on *Sint* Eustatius.

"So, you are Tanek?" DeGroot asked.

"I am Tanek. Would you like to inspect my wares?"

"Of course." De Groot stepped forward.

Creed pulled back the canvas cover and displayed a wagon bed full of boxes. He then looked at De Groot and pried one open for his inspection.

De Groot's eyes widened as he pulled his pipe from his mouth. "*Mijn Gott!*"

The box was full of small bills and coins, neatly stacked, all in British currency.

Chapter 14

Ridley, New Jersey

Creed wiped his mouth with the tablecloth. "Jannetje's ham with carrots and biscuits tasted as good as the finest French dinner."

"No doubt about that, Root Hog," Beall replied.

Creed, Beall, and Parker just finished a meal at the Blue House.

"How would you know anything about France, Hammer Head?" Parker said, fumbling to light up a pipe.

"I don't think I've seen you smoke before, Fish Belly." Creed gave Parker an amused smile.

"I just thought this would help me play the part." Parker coughed and his eyes widened.

"Not supposed to inhale those things, Fish Belly, just a puff every now and again is all."

Parker coughed again. "I suppose you're right, Root Hog."

Beall's eyes surveyed the room. "I see the Blue House has many patrons this evening, despite the late hour."

"Good point, Hammer Head," Creed said. "Apparently, the few men living in Ridley ain't committed to joining the British yet."

"But if they were Whigs, wouldn't they have fled like so many of the other New Jersey Whigs?" Beall asked.

"Like a wave, before the British advance across the Jerseys," Parker said.

Roy Harry did not join Creed at dinner. He had other business to attend. Shortly after their successful quest for British gold, Creed revealed he was, in fact, an intelligence officer of the Continental Army, but not his identity. Harry seemed unimpressed until Creed provided him with a sizeable sum from Howe's captured war chest. But only after Harry had finally committed to the patriot cause and agreed to recruit a small band of patriot fighters and to recruit local informants along the Hackensack River.

At the end of their meeting, Creed took a sheet of paper from his saddlebag and carefully wrote what became Harry's "warrant" to stand up this unit. It appointed Harry a provisional commander of what Creed glibly dubbed the "Bergen Swamp Rangers." They arranged to meet the next day at his camp, where, for the next fortnight, Creed and his men would train the Bergen Swamp Rangers in a variety of military skills they would need for encounters with Tory militias and British regulars.

* * *

Jannetje came from the kitchen carrying a jug. Several patrons turned to admire her hair, which she had pulled back into a soft plait. Her dress was fine-spun wool with a golden tint. Even in the candlelight, few could fail to notice her full figure pressing against the thin cloth.

She bent across Creed as she placed the jug and three glasses on the food-stained tablecloth. "Before Harry left, he asked me to provide you with some good Dutch spirits to warm against the night chill."

"What is it?' Beall asked.

She bent forward and smiled, revealing just the right amount of cleavage. "Dutch gin called Genever, almost as good as in the Netherlands, or so I have been told."

"Thoughtful of Mister Harry," Creed said. "One will sure 'nuff warm old Root Hog up really nice now."

She darted her tongue at him, smacked his thigh, and gave him a wink. Then, with a parting smile and swivel of the hips, she scurried across the room.

Creed noticed both of his men glaring intensely at him. He slipped out of his Root Hog speak and whispered, "Relax, lads. ''Twas just an act. My interest in our young lady is purely professional. Part of the Root Hog legend. Question is, was it one on her part as well?"

"Not that at all, sir… I mean, Root Hog. We just thought she was Mister Harry's girl, is all. As you have…" Beall hesitated and then lowered his eyes.

"I see." Creed was taken aback. He realized they were thinking of Emily. It comforted him that he had good men, but it discomforted him that they might doubt his motives.

Creed cocked his head with a mischievous look. "Maybe she is, and maybe she ain't. Now that we have Mister Harry on our side, we need to determine her loyalty. And that could prove a might harder."

They each tossed back a second drink. The Genever was cold. It tasted stronger than gin, although not as sweet. The clock struck eleven.

"Time to go."

They left the bottle on the table, pushed back their chairs, and got up to leave. Only three men remained in the room. They were glancing their way and talking in hushed tones.

Creed whispered, "Those men have been looking at us all night. There is something odd about them."

Parker's eyes narrowed in on them. "Sir, those men are wearing uniforms. Green uniforms. Almost like the Hessian light infantry."

Creed frowned. "Tory militia? Of course. I am a dunce, it would seem. I am going to talk with them. Otherwise, they might think us Whigs, or worse, rebel spies."

Parker glared at the men. "There are three muskets stacked against the wall behind them."

"Got it," Creed whispered. "Keep your hands on your pistols and cover poor old Root Hog."

Creed picked up the bottle of Genever and staggered across the room. He knew liquor easily distracted even the most professional soldiers, and these three bumpkins certainly were not professionals. He grinned impishly and feigned inebriation. "Pardon me, gents.

Could not help but notice your uniforms. Would ya share a toast to the king's health and the king's militia?"

They looked at Creed coldly. He then pulled up a chair and sat among them. They said nothing as he slowly poured the clear white lightning. After finishing their drinks, one of the men lifted his head and stared sharply at Creed.

Creed noticed his uniform, one single chevron on his dark green tunic sleeve. *A sergeant or corporal.*

The man scowled at Creed. "Militia indeed. We're not militia! We are regular soldiers of the 4th New Jersey Provincial Volunteers."

Creed poured each of them a shot of the potent liquor. "Do tell! I never heard of 'em. You sure you are not some of those Hessians? I heard they're as mean to us loyal subjects as to the damned rebels."

"I'm Corporal Matt Stettinus. We are with the Second Company — paid professionals in the service of the king, not militia rabble. We've orders to round up any Whigs and rebels we see. You're not from here, are you?"

"Who ain't these days?" Creed belched.

Stettinus tugged at his dark moustache. "Then what mischief brings the likes of you to Ridley and to our valley?" You are Whigs, aren't you?"

Creed chuckled. "Whigs? Why, no, sir. Name is Root Hog Burns. My boys and I serve the king's cause. That is, at least, whenever we can. When not, why… we find other work. Followed the English from New York, hopin' to find some work. Usually, there's work of some kind once they settle somewhere. Made more drinkin' money back in New York than I ever dreamed possible."

Stettinus's gaze grew more contemptuous. "So you are..."

"Loyalists, to the core. Some call us cowboys inasmuch as we occasionally like taking it to Whigs and all. Tomorrow we gonna ride into Hackensack and see what work we can find. Like I said, them English pay in hard currency."

One of the Volunteers grabbed Creed's arm. His breath reeked of liquor. "Why not go now? We'll escort you."

Stettinus pulled the man's hand from Creed. "That's fine, Rolf. Any Whig worth his salt has fled the area. Tomorrow we will have several hundred Volunteers on the hunt for them while the English chase the damned rebel army out of New Jersey."

Creed stared down Rolf and then glanced at Stettinus. "So, there's no English in Hackensack?"

Stettinus eyed him. "Just Hessians. The rest went with General Cornwallis. Once we clear the valley of the Whigs and get them to pay up their debts to us, the regiment will join the column. Hopefully, we will share in the glory when they bag Washington and his rebel pack."

Creed thought hard about the meaning of what Stettinus had just told him. Having heard what he wanted, he stood up. "So there just might be some work for us to help chase 'em to Philadelphia. Keep the bottle — a gift from Root Hog. But you keep away from little Jannetje, yah hear? Word is, she's spoken for."

Rolf threw his head back and laughed, "That is funny, Mister Root Hog. *Ja*, she has been spoken for, many times... *Heer* Root Hog."

* * *

Creed's eyes opened at five. He could hear the deep breathing of his men. *They're sound asleep.* He crept over to his gear and quietly packed it for travel. He slipped out the back door to check on Finn and the other horses.

That done, Creed trudged down the dark street to see if the cooks at the Blue House had started breakfast. The cold night air had stirred up a chilling morning wind that whipped across a hoar-frost coating everything in a white veneer—a light burned in Jannetje's second-story window. Creed smiled. Pretty women needed time to primp in the morning. Her unclad shadow suddenly appeared behind the curtain. Then his eye caught another shadow— a male figure. The two shadows merged and then seemed to swerve and sway. The dark forms then vanished into the recesses of the room.

At first, Creed was surprised to witness the early-morning assignation. Yet a good-looking young woman of means would have a lover, possibly several. *Perhaps the rumors of Jannetje and Roy Harry were not just rumors.* Harry might have left his camp and returned to Ridley for a last tryst.

Creed edged around to the back of the tavern to find the cooks. He badly needed a cup of tea. After a nice cup of tea, he would head to the well and begin his ablutions in the cold morning air.

A kitchen servant handed him a large ceramic mug steaming with tea. "Here's a piece of fresh, warm bread to go with that, sir."

"Much obliged, Miss." Creed gave her a grateful grin.

He munched on the bread quickly and went to the pump behind the tavern. With horrified servants watching, he stripped to the waist. In the cold, windy dawn, he ran a razor across his face and washed out his hair. He ran a cold, wet cloth across his upper torso and then dried himself with a small towel before pulling on his cotton shirt and homespun jacket.

The wind was bracing, so Creed stepped through the back door to warm himself by the kitchen stove, where he gratefully took a second mug of tea. As the last drop cleared his palate, he began making his way back to wake the lads. In the twilight, he saw a sudden movement. A dark figure slipped out of the side entrance of the Blue House. The figure moved too quickly to make out a face, but it was a man in some uniform—a dark green riding coat and calf-high riding boots.

Creed watched the figure disappear into the stable. Moments later, a large horse bolted through the doors. The horse then lurched forward and galloped furiously down the road toward Hackensack. It was too dark to make out the rider's face or even the markings on his horse. But Creed now became certain. Jannetje had more than a passing connection to a Loyalist in the valley. *But who?*

* * *

Roy Harry's Camp, near Ridley, New Jersey

The next few days at Roy Harry's camp brought long hours of training. Creed and his men taught Harry's boys the basics of skirmishing, firing in pairs, and moving from one position to another. Before long, the men could move silently through brush and woods, form pairs, and then form lines or columns as needed. Everyone could hit a twelve-inch disc at ninety paces. But their weapons left something to be desired: a mix of fowling pieces, old hunting rifles, and muskets from the French and Indian War. Their edged weapons were only slightly better, mostly hunting knives of varying quality.

"Your men are doing good, Harry," Creed said one evening. "But these antique toys of yours won't get you through a skirmish with regulars. We must find you better weapons."

"I was thinking that myself, Root Hog. There is a militia unit in Old Tappan — perhaps they can provide..."

Creed gave him a dismissive look. "No, Tappan is too far. I have a better idea. We'll let the Tories provide them!"

Harry gave him a puzzled look. "What do you mean?"

"Take weapons from the English."

"Now listen, Root Hog, we can't just..."

Creed grinned mischievously. "Nothing 'bout this work's simple, Harry. When your training's done, we can talk 'bout how to do it. Meantime, we need to talk 'bout our long-term plans."

The second part of their training centered on organizing a string of observation posts behind British lines.

Creed scratched the ground with a sharp stick to mark the posts on a stretch of loamy soil. "Harry, to cover the lookout points, you'll need to break up the Swamp Rangers into small groups. No more than six men in each. Spread 'em across the valley."

"Split them up?" Harry startled.

Creed nodded. "If the British take one, the others will continue operations."

"But let's suppose I need to make an attack or ambush a large formation?"

"That's different, but let's hope it don't come to anything big. Sometimes it's better to think small. Ambush couriers or a few Tories, from time to time. Steal dispatches. But when it comes to formations, best your boys stay hidden and just watch 'em." Creed stuck his stick into the earth. "Only fight in self-defense and only if you can't run away."

Harry looked puzzled. "Can we enter the towns and farms and try to gather more information?"

"Only approach known patriots but be careful 'cause they are likely being watched by the Loyalists."

Harry rubbed his chin. "What do I do with the information? How do I report it? Will you send a rider to me for my reports?"

"Not likely, least for a while. No, you will be between us and the Continental Army. You'll report your information to General William Heath. He has an outpost at Tappan."

"Heath? Never heard of him, Root Hog."

"He's commander of rebel forces in New York's upper highlands. Heath has regular correspondence with General Washington, so I've been told."

"We need to stay out of the dust-up that's brewing," Harry said. Just a few days after the British swept through the area, the cold war between Tories and Whigs spilled over into open conflict. And the Whigs received the worst of it.

Harry explained some of the politics of the Hackensack Valley to Creed, much of which derived more from the long-standing religious schism between the two factions of the Dutch.

Reformed Church: The *Conferentie* and *Coetus*. The former were adherents to the traditional Dutch Reformed Church. At the same time, the latter were part of the "Great Awakening," the religious revival of the mid-eighteenth century, and leaned toward a more zealous form of worship. They later became known as the so-called "True" Reformed Dutch Church.

Creed was astounded at the history of the conflict in the valley. "Now explain to me why these *Confreetie* are Tory and the *Cooties* Whig? Makes no sense."

Harry smiled. "That's the *Conferentie*. They are Tory while the *Coetus* lean Whig, Root Hog. I don't pretend to understand it much. I hardly am a God-fearing man."

Creed found this divide an ominous throwback to the great European religious conflicts of the sixteenth and seventeenth centuries. "What about your boys?"

Harry crossed his arms and stared at the ground. "Me and my men aren't religious, but we have no use for the English, the Hessians, or their sympathizers."

"I'm supposin' that's why you signed on, besides the money."

"We *were* neutral. But then we got word of things done in the valley by the British and their Hessian and Loyalist allies. While their columns pursued the rebels, some stopped to claim their share of the booty. Houses ransacked. Livestock taken. Some burned to the ground. Many of the boys' families were caught up in things. We heard some of the women…"

Harry hesitated for a moment. "We support you, Root Hog, based on our need for justice, not politics."

"But you took my money."

Harry grinned mischievously. "We thank you for that, Root Hog. Makes things all the better."

***

The last two days of training allowed them to practice raids and ambushes, as well as escaping and regrouping after being discovered or ambushed. By the end, the themes Creed taught echoed repeatedly in each man's mind. "Never get trapped into a fight. Slow 'em and confuse 'em. Wear 'em down. And never strike the same place twice."

They formed six-man units, which Creed called platoons. A sergeant selected by Harry led each. They would operate independently across the valley from Bergen Neck to Old Tappan. Each had a mounted courier to carry reports back to Harry, who in turn would then correspond with Heath.

"The night after the final training session, the two men held their final meeting. Harry broke out his best bottle of Genever.

Creed found he was beginning to enjoy the beverage, which, as Harry later admitted, was a gift from Jannetje. He downed his drink mountain-man fashion, then wiped his lips with his sleeve. "So, Harry, tomorrow my boys and I are gonna help you find some real weapons."

"And just how do you propose we do that, Root Hog?"

Creed lowered his voice. "Little Colt's been in Hackensack for the past few days, keeping his eyes and ears open. He overheard jabberin' 'bout some armory the English are fixin' to set up in some church."

Harry's eyes narrowed. He closed one eye and cocked his head. "What church, Root Hog? Around here, that makes a big difference."

"A Whig parson runs it. Believe named Romeyn, who conveniently 'nuf has disappeared. Not sure if he skedaddled or if the Tories got him. No matter to us though. I aim to find that place, and tomorrow night we will march in there and take them."

Harry's eyes widened. "So the war's come to this? I know of this pastor, Romeyn. He's a decent man. Well-liked by all."

"Harry, your boys are a tough bunch, but you're gonna need to be a sight tougher before this war is over. Now listen up. Assuming all this is true, we will have you some new weapons tomorrow."

When Creed finished explaining how they would do it, Harry chortled, "Just like that, Root Hog?"

"Yep, just like that, Harry."

Chapter 15

Hackensack, New Jersey, November 24th, 1776

The small sandstone church and parsonage sat at the end of a winding lane that crossed Kinderkamack Road. Soon after the British took control of Hackensack, a group of Hessians dressed in dark blue coats and with stern, intimidating faces marched into the parsonage.

They slapped irons on one of the valley's most well-known and respected figures, Reverend Domine Romeyn, and led him away. As an active leader of the Coetus church, their commander believed Romeyn's connections to Whig leaders in the valley could yield information about rebel sympathizers.

His daughter Karina watched in horror and was convinced she would never see him again. His wife, Julia, and son, Piet, begged her to have faith, but she could not shake the sense of dread. Her dread was well-founded. Romeyn proved resistant to all threats, so before long, more horrible figures, this time in dark green jackets, descended on the parsonage.

Karina knew at once why they were here to arrest her brother, the reverend's oldest son. *Not Piet, too!*

Piet was a Whig sympathizer, but not as active as his father.

The return of these barbarous mercenaries means danger for us all. Karina was not afraid of these men but feared for her brother, her mother, and their home. As they approached, she called out a desperate warning, "Pieeet! Maaaama! More soldiers! More German soldiers are coming! Hessians! Hessians! "

Mevrouw Julia Romeyn rushed out to look for herself. Julia Romeyn looked like an older version of her daughter but was much thicker around the waist and heavier in the breast. Her dark hair had a few silver streaks, but her skin maintained a fresh, youthful look. Julia's quivering lip betrayed the brave face put on to calm her daughter. "There is no reason to hide, Karina. They might be bringing us news about papa."

A sergeant and four stone-faced privates kicked in the heavy wooden gate. "*Wo ist Piet Romeyn!*" the angry sergeant bellowed.

Julia folded her arms across her bosom and stood her ground. "He is not here. And just what have you done with my husband?"

"*Herr Romeyn, komm jezt!*" the sergeant bellowed a second time, his voice rasping like a file on rusty iron.

"I told you... He is gone," stammered Julia.

"*Aus dem Weg, Frau!*" The sergeant roughly shoved her aside.

The Hessians burst through the arched doors and stormed into the church. They immediately began ransacking, tearing out the neat wooden benches, and throwing prayer books to the ground. These were fearsome Jaegers, roughhewn woodsmen, and hunters.

Karina and all the people in the valley feared the Hessians. *They will stop at nothing to get at Piet. He must run.*

Piet rushed from the parsonage into the church to stop them. "*Halt!* Stop!" he implored, placing himself between the ravagers and the wooden pulpit.

Two of the Jaegers pinned his arms back. Piet shook free and landed a powerful blow on one of them. He pivoted to grab the other's rifle. As he turned, his eyes widened as the Hessian sergeant ran him through the thigh with a short sword.

Piet slumped to the floor, his leg pumping squirts of blood onto the wooden planks. Julia pushed past the soldiers and tightened a sheet torn from a bed to stop the bleeding. His face already had a gray pallor. She tied the linen around his thigh and looked around for something to tighten it. It was then that another soldier appeared from the rear of the church.

"*Meen Gott!*" Julia gasped.

Dierk Van Buskirk, the nephew of Colonel Abraham Van Buskirk, stood alongside the Hessians, barely distinguishable in his dark green uniform of New Jersey Volunteers.

"And what has Dierk Van Buskirk to do with all this? Are you not one of us? Why don't you stop these beasts?" Julia asked.

Before he could answer, two of the Hessian soldiers pulled her from her son and dragged her, screaming and crying, into the parsonage, where they lifted her dress and petticoat and spread-eagled her across the kitchen table.

"Away from me, you *Deuvils*! Stop! Stop!" Julia shrieked. "Karina— run! Hide! Stop!"

But Julia's efforts to warn her daughter had the opposite effect. On hearing her mother's screams, instead of fleeing, the young girl seized a pitchfork from the garden and ran back to help. *These pigs must be stopped…*

Rather than becoming another object of the brutal lust of the invaders, she intended to become their foe. Her chest heaving with fear mixed with determination, Karina burst into the room like a protective she-lion.

Two of the Hessians surrounded her, laughing at the foolish Dutch girl who would offer an even better dalliance than the matron. They smirked and chuckled at the sport of jumping and weaving to avoid her wild and ineffective thrust with the fork. Then they laughed when she began to sob with fear and frustration.

"*Komm, Maedel – komm,*" they taunted her in German, arms outstretched.

Finally tired of the sport, one of the Hessians grabbed for the fork. A prong pierced the fat of his right thumb.

"Aaargh!" he howled with pain.

At the sight of his hand, impaled and bloodied on her pitchfork, Karina's eyes widened.

Enraged, the other Hessian pushed aside the shaft of the fork, clutched her throat, and squeezed. "*Du kleine Hexe…*little witch."

Dierk Van Buskirk stepped up and grabbed the Hessian's shoulder. "Don't do this… here. The stable is much better."

Karina's body tensed with fear and frustration. She tried to call her mother, but the soldier squeezed the air from her. Her head began to spin. She dropped the fork as he dragged her, choking out to the stable.

***

That evening, a group of local *Coetus* patriots went to their church to check on the reverend's family. Every window in the church was broken, and every bit of furniture and clothing was destroyed. The dark stain near the pulpit confirmed the worst.

"This is madness no one should witness," said the leader.

One of the men ran to the house and called out, "*Mijnheer!* Come quickly!"

When the leader stepped into the house, he found a shattered *Mvrouw* Romeyn ministering to her son's wound, muttering incomprehensively. Piet would live, but his mother's mad ranting showed no sign of abatement.

"They had a daughter, where is she?"

"I'll check the stable."

He found Karina in the stable. "In here, boss."

A dozen pairs of boots scrambled into the red barn. Stomachs flipped, and eyes turned from the horror. Even the most hardened of them never envisaged what the Hessians did to her both before and after they had killed her.

***

The next day, a company from Abraham Van Buskirk's newly uniformed 4th New Jersey Volunteer Infantry marched into the Romeyn parsonage. The stone building would be an excellent place for storing ammunition and weaponry for the American Loyalist forces in the area. Or so Captain Bram De Groot, the arsenal commander, was told.

Wagons rumbled up and down the lane all day long, each one delivering its load of muskets, edged weapons, powder, or shot. By nightfall, the once peaceful church had become the largest weapons cache in New Jersey, with nearly 2,000 muskets, one hundred hogsheads of powder, and several thousand cartridges and musket balls. Additionally, over 1,000 valuable bayonets and one hundred pistols and sabers completed the arsenal, which the Hessians called *Waffenlager*.

De Groot was told the weapons were taken from the Americans at Fort Washington or were abandoned at Fort Lee. But one-half the firearms were new British-made New Land muskets, the finest infantry long arm of the period that a later generation would dub Brown Bess.

De Groot still seethed. He had received this assignment as punishment for losing the British pay chest to the rebel militia. De Groot smiled when he recalled how he lied about the loss, claiming a company of rebel militia ambushed him, instead of the handful who bested him. He thought he made a good bargain, though, his life and some coin in exchange for confirming the treasure's destination.

Abraham Van Buskirk disbelieved his story but could not disprove it. For that reason, he did not have him removed from the regiment. Instead, the flinty Van Buskirk forced De Groot to take his nephew, Dierk Van Buskirk, as his deputy. Appalled by the savagery against the Romeyn family, Van Buskirk relegated his nephew to this minor security detail with the discredited Bram De Groot.

As commandant of his little garrison, Bram De Groot took the comfortable Romeyn bedroom for himself. The reverend's study became the company's orderly room.

De Groot had given simple instructions to his new lieutenant, "Dierk, place two guards on the road. Have two walks along the perimeter, and two more guard the church entrance. Secure the back and side doors. Change the guards at midnight and then every six hours. Men not on guard will sleep in the stable."

De Groot saw Dierk's face flush at the word 'stable'. *He's a pig.* He struck a long match, lit his pipe, and scowled. "And Van Buskirk, make sure one sergeant is awake for each shift."

Dierk frowned. "And what of me?"

De Groot eyed him with contempt. "You will be the officer on night watch until the rebels are driven from the area. I cannot afford another problem with your uncle." He eyed the younger man warily. "And neither can you. Remain in the orderly room. Inspect the guards once before and once after midnight, and supervise the shift change at midnight."

"*Mijn Gott*, when do I sleep?" Van Buskirk retorted.

De Groot pulled the pipe stem from his mouth. "Can one such as you ever sleep?"

* * *

The crack of the pistol butt sent the first sentry tumbling to the ground without a fight. After dragging his body off Kinderkamack Road, Thomas drove the wagon up the lane to the parsonage. Beall and Parker stayed hidden in the back, covered by a tarpaulin. Each held their tomahawk and hunting knives ready for action.

The sight of Thomas, even at such a late hour, aroused no suspicions among the sentries. Black men held many jobs in transportation throughout the Royal Colony of New Jersey. Perhaps another supply of munitions had arrived, although neither Dierk Van Buskirk nor the sergeants had ever mentioned one.

One of the sentries called out to Thomas, "Halt and identify yourself."

Thomas pulled back on the reins, and the wagon lurched to a halt. "Whoa."

The sentries approached him casually. They stood alongside the wagon with their muskets slung on their shoulders and their overcoats pulled up high to block the cold night wind from swirling down their necks.

"I'm Thomas Jeffries, sir. Have a load of boxes to deliver."

"More munitions? Why don't they send us more food?" one sentry said.

"Or rum?" the other quipped as he blew on his cold hands.

"Dunno, sir. They didn't say what's in 'em."

"Better you don't know, boy. Now, who sent you? We're supposed to alert the captain before your wagon can pass any..."

A pair of tomahawks slid through the dark air, slicing into the guards with a sickening crunch. Beall and Parker bounded from the wagon, hauled the bodies into the woods, and stripped them of their cloaks.

Parker sheathed his fisherman's knife and tomahawk. "We'll use these cloaks to make our way closer," he whispered. "Keep the wagon here, Thomas. Give us fifteen minutes, then move it down the lane, very slowly."

Parker picked up the Tory's musket and affixed its seventeen-inch bayonet to the muzzle with a click. "Lieutenant Creed wants only blade work tonight."

Beall did the same and then held his musket over his head. Some of Harry's men emerged from the shadows. They formed two files, one on each side of the road.

Beall spoke in a low voice, "Root Hog, Harry, and the others should have taken the other sentries by now. We'll move up along the side of the road. Root Hog says the rest of the guards are probably in the stable. When we rush it, make sure no one escapes. Any questions?"

"What's the watchword?" one of the Swamp Rangers asked.

"Brooklyn!" Beall replied.

***

Earlier that night, Creed had taken Harry, Beall, and Parker to check on the location of the sentries and buildings. Based on their reconnaissance, he had crafted a two-pronged plan of attack.

By the time Beall and Parker led their files along the trail to the church, Creed and Harry were already leading a band of four men, faces blackened to avoid glare and reduce their visibility in the moonlight.

When Harry gave the signal, Creed led his men toward the light coming from the parsonage while Harry's band approached the church where two sentries huddled against the frigid air.

Creed halted his men along the hedge fence surrounding the parsonage. When he saw the shadows of the men led by Beall and Parker, he rose and, with a circular wave of his sword, signaled towards the stable.

Beall and Parker's men burst into a run, pushed open the stable door, and without a word began to club and stab the shocked and groggy volunteers.

Creed kicked the parsonage door open and charged the sergeant on duty. His shoulder drove the sergeant off his chair, which he had pulled up near the warmth of the fireplace. Before he could stand, a Swamp Ranger stepped from behind Creed and brought his musket barrel down on the sergeant's head.

Awakened by the struggle, De Groot ran from the bedroom. He groped anxiously in the dark for his pistol but could not find it. Frantic, De Groot cried out for the officer on night watch, "Van Buskirk, what is the matter? Is there trouble? Dierk? Van Buskirk? What's going on?"

His last words went unanswered. Another of Harry's men drove an ancient yet deadly long knife into his chest. De Groot staggered back and collapsed. His brief but unremarkable service to the king had cost the Loyalist cause its payroll, its weapons, and a company of infantry. In less than ten minutes, De Groot's entire command was either dead, dying, or severely wounded. That is, all but one.

***

Dierk Van Buskirk had stomach cramps. He had raided the parsonage larder earlier in the evening and feasted on a meal of oysters and corn. Either the corn was too fresh or the oysters too old. By ten that night, he began to feel queasy, and by eleven, his bowels cramped and began the slow churn that was the bane of many a soldier.

Van Buskirk had just finished his second trip to the outhouse behind the parsonage when he saw the movement from the shadows. He knew immediately something was wrong. He had taken his pistol with him, but one shot would be of little use in the dark against so many men. *At least a battalion of rebels, I can't be of help.* That, in confusion and fear, was what Van Buskirk reckoned they faced. He buttoned his pants and carefully crouched in the stench and cold of the outhouse, whimpering and praying the rebels would not find him.

***

"When you have secured this place, Harry, prepare to torch it," Creed ordered.

"Thought you'd never ask, Root Hog!" Harry turned to one of his men. "Spread a few barrels of the gunpowder among the stacks of weapons and pour a trail of loose powder to act as a fuse."

Harry and his men dragged out the wounded Tories and loaded the wagon with the weapons. But only those selected by Creed's experienced eye.

Harry and a few of his men scrambled into the wagon. Thomas cracked the lines across the horses' backs, and they bolted forward, his steady hand guiding them back across the swamp and far from Hackensack and the expected Loyalist reaction.

Once they had a good head start, Creed struck a flint and lit the trail of gunpowder. The flame sputtered, then a line of fire ignited. Crackling and flashing in the darkness, the fire raced toward the hogsheads of powder stacked in the church. Creed and his men bolted for the tree line and dove for cover just as the hogsheads erupted.

Boom! The massive explosion shook Creed to the bones. A ball of fire erupted like a volcano, sending bursts of flame through windows and doors, collapsing the once-proud church in a smoking heap of rubble. All around him men were crying and trembling from a shock wave that broke eardrums and had men reeling in pain.

The expansive *boom* rolled across the valley for miles, waking Whig and Tory alike from their dark November sleep.

Chapter 16

Roy Harry's Camp, near Ridley, New Jersey

Creed felt pleased with the night's take. He walked down the line counting and inspecting each item. The main prize — fifty new British muskets with powder, shot, and bayonets, plus a dozen sabers and as many pistols with powder and shot.

Beall and Parker handed out each of Harry's men a musket with powder and ball, along with a bayonet. Platoon leaders also received a pistol and saber, as did the mounted couriers.

When they finished the inventory, Creed and Harry shared a breakfast of hard bread and bitter coffee. Creed bit into his biscuit and grimaced. "Least no weevils in this bread, just some cement, I suspect."

Harry smiled. "It will do, for now, Root Hog. But you know my men like meat."

Creed grimaced again and took a slug of the coffee. Then raised an eye over his cup. "Been meanin' to talk to you about that, Harry. Men at war like all kinds of meat, if you get my drift."

Harry looked back uncomprehendingly. "Just what are you getting at, Root Hog?"

"Jannetje. So that ya know, I saw someone leaving her room before we left Ridley. Believe now it was one of the New Jersey Volunteers. From the look of it, they were friendly. Ya know what I mean?"

Harry tried to appear indifferent, but Creed thought he caught the vague look of concern.

"Root Hog. I've known sweet Jannetje for some time. She has an easy approach to men. It's the talk of these parts. It was so even before her husband died. Jannetje's a strong-willed and passionate woman. I like that. Besides, I ain't no monk myself, Root Hog. If you know what I mean."

"I can see you ain't no monk, Harry. Just thought you needed to know, is all."

Creed understood what Harry meant. Jannetje's earthiness had certainly drawn him to her as well. And clearly, it drew others. *But whom*?

After a few moments of quiet, Harry asked, "Did you see who it was?"

"Not sure, but the rider wore a dark green coat. Tell the truth, Harry, I am more worried 'bout whether she's a patriot or a Loyalist. If the uniform was dark green, then our little widow is sleeping with at least one Loyalist. That might become one too many for us. You might want to stay away from Ridley."

Harry shook his head. "If I disappear entirely now, it might cause more suspicion. As for her Tory connection, this is New Jersey. For many around these parts, loyalty is relative and based mostly on who holds power. I prefer to keep an eye on her. There might be some advantage in staying close to her."

"I'm sure there is, pardner."

Harry shrugged. "Besides, many around here think I favor the Tories, and I'm not going to shed them of the notion."

Creed knew Harry's interest in staying close to Ridley had more to do with his paramour than he admitted. "I like the way you think, Harry. I got a feeling you are going to be really good at this new business."

They went on to discuss intelligence matters. Creed used a handy stick to sketch the plan in the dark soil. Most of Harry's men would deploy to locations on high ground near major road junctions. Creed provided each team with a list of information to report. Unless they spotted large British troop movements, the bands were to send the reports to Harry once a week, each on a different day. The difficult part of the plan was getting messages out of the valley.

"Now remember, you report routine information to General Heath. His army straddles the region between Old Tappan and Connecticut."

"I remember."

Creed stuck the sick into the ground. "Heath keeps regular contact with the main army. Anything urgent— send one of the boys directly to the Continental Army. If you can."

"Leave that to me, Root Hog. My men have slipped through patriot and Loyalist lines before. Never been spotted."

Creed grinned wickedly. "Not that you know of Harry. You best not add any more risk to this here plan."

Harry just stared silently into his cup and nodded.

The camp awoke just before twilight, and Harry assembled the sergeants in charge of each, as Creed now called them, "Observation Platoons."

Creed gave them their final instructions. Drilling them for hours, repeating the details until each man could recite the plan from memory. He was satisfied with their training. "Well, Harry, I do believe these men will be darned good spies. General Washington himself would be mighty pleased indeed."

Harry and his men all winced at the choice of words. "What do you mean, spies, Root Hog? We Swamp Rangers are scouts, not spies. Spies steal secrets, and what is more…spies can be hanged."

Creed shot them a knowing look. "What do you think those English are gonna do if they catch any of you boys skulking around behind their lines? Why, we're behind their lines now. You boys all take good care - or else."

Harry puffed his chest. "Root Hog, no Englishman and no damned Tory scare my boys. You tell General Washington he just hired the damned best scouts in his army."

"I certainly will, Harry. I certainly will. But you watch out now. You hear?"

* * *

British Headquarters, New Brunswick, Late November 1776

Drummond paced back and forth, the stiffness of his bad knee forcing him to sway his hip slightly with each step, to maintain his balance. The small house that served as his headquarters had one room on the ground floor, with a rough-plank oak floor and a stone fireplace. The fire burning in the hearth threw off enough heat to warm the first floor and the two small bedrooms above.

He sat at a small mahogany desk and gazed out the window at the dull gray sky. Every so often, he composed a new thought, and he would scribble it across the thin beige parchment spread before him. It pleased him that General Howe had called him from New York to help finish off Washington's dwindling army. Life as an intelligence officer in New York did not suit him as much as he had thought it would. He clashed with the newly appointed provost, William Cunningham, a petulant and ignorant fellow entirely too zealous for anyone's good. Cunningham's ragged police bands were little more than citified cowboys, mere ruffians who preyed upon Whigs and any Tory who crossed them.

Drummond finally completed the plan. He carefully placed his pen back in its holder and gently blew across the paper to dry the thick ink.

(Strictly Confidential) Plan Remus

~ Estblsh contact with the Tory Factions in New Jersey and Pennsylvania.
~ Ascrtn Washington's likely Destination.
~ Expnd Propaganda to rally Loyal Americans to the Crown.
~ Win support of Neutrals and Tories.
~ Rcrt Spies to follow Washington's Forces and reprt on Rebel actvty, Etc.
~ Re-contct Golden Apple (now assmd with the Rebel Force).
~ Arrnge meeting wth "X" to establish "Terms."
~ Explt "X" – method- in what manner to be determnd.

He looked it over once, then again. *Yes, that would do just nicely.*

Drummond reached into his vest and checked his timepiece. Time to spare before the scheduled meeting with Howe. He went to his special hip flask and downed a considerable swallow of the medicine the surgeon had prescribed for him. Although he no longer suffered from the sharp nagging knee pain, the elixir induced a numbing sensation that buoyed his spirits better than the strongest Scotch whisky.

* * *

General Howe removed his spectacles and pinched the bridge of his nose slightly. After a momentary hesitation, he looked up and smiled at Drummond. "An excellent plan, Sandy! I like simple things, to the point. With my proclamation demanding loyalty oaths, the Tory factions will certainly provide you with every consideration and cooperation. Still, it would have been easier if the special payroll had not disappeared."

Drummond cleared his throat. The loss of the secret payroll was certainly more than a minor complication. "Indeed, sir, a full investigation is underway. A rebel force of considerable strength also destroyed the weapons depot in Hackensack. I suspect the two events are connected."

Howe sighed. "Perhaps some of Heath's men came down from the highlands. "

Drummond nodded. "Perhaps, sir. I sent Sergeant Digby to Hackensack with strict instructions for Colonel Van Buskirk to secure the area. The Americans themselves best handle these things."

"I must disagree, Sandy." General Cornwallis's voice iced with impatience and anger. He had remained silent during Drummond's exchange with Howe. Now he spoke out.

"With what, Charles?" Howe came to Drummond's defense, albeit perhaps too quickly.

"Professional troops, whether British or Hessian, should be unleashed on these scoundrels. The loyalty oath is merely a palliative. We must destroy Washington's army and eliminate these local militias haranguing our flanks. And we are moving much too slowly against the rebels. Washington may deceive us and escape once again, as he did on Long Island, White Plains, and Fort Lee."

Howe pursed his lips, ignoring the blatant swipe at his policies of methodical advances and winning over the Americans. "No, Charles. A deliberate pace is a more prudent course. Letting the people see our army moving with confidence across the colony will draw more Americans out to swear loyalty to His Majesty. And it gives us time to enlist and train Tory volunteers. Unfortunately, there is now a bit less of the king's gold to pay them and bribe spies."

Drummond bowed his head. "For that, I am most sorry, sir."

Howe sniffed. "Our men must ever be vigilant. Although most Americans love their king, the rebels are nigh unto rabid with their chicanery."

"I have instructed Digby to investigate the payroll theft as well as the arsenal. He has instructions to request assistance from the loyalists under Van Buskirk."

Lord Cornwallis interjected with incredulity. "Van Buskirk? Is the king's business to be resolved by some… Dutchman?" With the accent on Dutch, Cornwallis's tone was clipped and truculent.

Drummond blanched but then composed himself. "I should like to remind Milord that Colonel Abraham Van Buskirk is a leader of the Tory loyalists in eastern New Jersey and a pillar of the community. He has helped raise a fine volunteer regiment whose men, despite the loss of payroll and the attack on their munitions, continue to serve admirably. Why, I have recruited four of his best men into my service."

Howe's face showed he was tired of the banter. "Enough of this talk, gentlemen. General Cornwallis will pursue the rebels at the pace I have set. Meanwhile, Sandy will try to contact his so-called Golden Apple. As much as I disdain such intrigue, his information might give us the best chance to end this campaign cleanly, without bloodshed. As for X—that is another matter which…"

Drummond interrupted. "I still have some questions about Golden Apple, but hope remains that his efforts will not be required."

Howe shot him an impatient look. "X is another matter which could prove useful to…"

Now Cornwallis cut him off. "General, with all due respect, this X business is most disturbing. Such things never come to any good. Divert us from our main objective, which is destroying the rebel army under Washington."

Howe raised his hand dismissively. "I once held your view, Charles. But I have changed my mind. Besides, such things led to the encircling of the rebels on Long Island. Don't you recall?"

"Indeed, they did, sir." Drummond beamed like a proud parent. He had recruited Golden Apple, the source of their success on Long Island.

"So, for now at least, my decision is firm. Let us hope Sandy's Golden Apple can be found… or he can reach out to us," Howe said.

"If he is indeed alive, and not hanging from a rebel gibbet," Cornwallis said.

Howe ignored the remark. "We shall explore our X options, of course. That is Major Drummond's business. Concern yourself with the advanced guard and our flanks, Milord. I do not want Heath and the rebels up north attacking our supplies as the weather worsens. Regardless, we shall soon be looking for suitable winter quarters."

"I am sure Washington is counting on it! Then by your leave, Milord." Cornwallis picked up his hat and strutted out the door.

Ever since he arrived in New Jersey, Howe had talked of preparing for winter quarters. The call of the luscious Mrs. Loring was the siren song that could yet bring this campaign to disaster.

When Cornwallis had gone, Howe closed the door and spread Drummond's plan on the table. "I have full confidence you will recruit efficient agents for our purposes. And that you'll re-contact Golden Apple."

Drummond nodded but would not admit to Howe that Cornwallis might be correct in his assessment of Golden Apple.

Howe removed a piece of paper from his valise and opened it. "Now let us discuss the X matter…"

The X matter bothered Drummond as much as it bothered Cornwallis. But Howe embraced the idea. It was Howe's small foray into skullduggery. Still, Drummond believed they could pull it off and mitigate any negative fallout. The plan appeared simple on the surface: identify a rebel leader of significant rank and stature willing to switch sides to the British. That might be straightforward, but Drummond thought such a gamble would be more effective if the officer could "come over" without defecting and thereby influence the war in their favor. Propaganda versus espionage made a very delicate decision.

Back at his office, Drummond examined a list of six senior officers in the rebel army whom Howe thought might make a suitable X. Drummond reviewed the names several times. After careful consideration, he eliminated three, as they were militia generals — locally important, perhaps even regionally, but not enough gravitas. Now he just had to persuade Howe to pick one.

"Well, what do you think of the list, Sandy?" Howe asked like a schoolboy presenting his homework.

Drummond chose his words carefully. "All make excellent choices, but I believe X should be a continental, and preferably, someone linked to Washington or Congress. "

Howe nodded. "I see. Perhaps you are right."

He pointed to three names on the list. "What of these three names? They are Continentals, are they not?"

"Yes, sir."

"All holding the considerable rank of major general."

"Indeed, sir." Drummond placed his chin in his hands and considered each.

"What are you thinking, Sandy?"

"These all have promise, sir."

"But what do you think of them, Sandy?"

"William Alexander, the self-styled 'Lord Stirling,' has a ferocious personality as shown by his heroism against our regulars on Long Island. Despite the battle being lost, Stirling led a forlorn hope attack by a brigade from Maryland and Delaware against our own Lord Cornwallis. But despite the heroics, he..."

Howe chuckled. "Was captured by Cornwallis's men. Although I hazard, he put a scare in Milord."

"He proved obstinate as a prisoner." Drummond reminded him.

"There is also the issue of the peerage," Howe said. "The House of Lords never validated Alexander's claim that he was the eldest heir to the first Lord Stirling. Such a title would grant him land over much of the New England and St. Lawrence coastal regions. No trivial matter and one that you could perhaps leverage to win him over."

"Certainly, if the rebels gain their independence, his claims would be invalid, and his title would hold no weight," said Drummond. "Yet Stirling refused even the simplest discussions while we held our prisoner. His stubbornness and unpredictable nature weigh heavily against him as a potential agent of influence. And now that he is exchanged and back in action with Washington, I fear he'll never give in.

Howe looked dejected. "What of Horatio Gates?"

Drummond cocked his head in thought. "Hmmm... Gates served in the Royal Army and attained the rank of lieutenant colonel, but financial difficulties forced him to sell his commission and accept a colonial commission. There are indications of his dissatisfaction. Reports are that he is insulted that the field command he was promised went instead to the wealthy, politically connected Phillip Schuyler. "

Howe beamed. "There you go! Gates certainly must seethe at the fact that he, a former British professional, now plays deputy to an inexperienced provincial. Reports..."

Drummond gave a skeptical shrug. "But reports from Tories, as well as prisoners and newspapers, paint Gates as lethargic, even unimaginative, a trait unwanted in someone who is to support the Loyalist cause secretly while maintaining his position among the rebels."

Howe sighed. "I thought my picks were all brilliant."

"Of the three, Charles Lee seems the most intriguing and promising."

Howe's face lightened, and he smiled. "He's a native Briton. And he held the rank of major in the Royal Army and later served several continental masters."

"Lee is a man of easy loyalty. Reports from knowledgeable Tories indicate he is avaricious, crude, and uneven. However, he is open about the fact that he had expected the colonials would name him commander-in-chief of the rebel army. And if Washington were replaced, many say Lee would assume command."

"So, he is no fan of Washington, I gather?"

"Indeed, sir. And I have recently intercepted correspondence hinting at Washington's dissatisfaction with Lee. Seems Lee is less than responsive to his commands. Washington is losing patience with him."

Howe played with his wig absentmindedly. "So, one could conclude that the feeling was mutual?"

"One could, sir. Lee feels he has received only begrudging recognition for his role in the victory over General Clinton at Charleston. He resents the whispering campaign that gave credit to the local Carolina militia commanders instead of him."

"What? Politics among the rebels?"

Drummond unfolded a small map and spread it on the table. "Charles Lee commands significant rebel forces on the North River."

"Not far from our lines, I see."

"That is the decisive factor. Charles Lee, a disgruntled senior general of the rebel forces, is in loco, making him the easiest to contact. He's your man."

To Drummond's delight, Howe approved the choice with surprisingly little discussion. "I know him, Sandy. I met him years ago when his battalion was brigaded with mine. Cannot say I was very impressed by the man, but withal, his flaws are what we must exploit. Conceit and avarice coupled with a paucity of loyalty may well provide us with our Mister X. How soon can you contact him?"

"I have taken the liberty of drafting a letter to him already. It is discreet, but also to the point. Strangely, the post still moves from Hackensack to Tappan and from there to points north. The missive will appear innocent enough. One of our Tory supporters will provide the return address, someone who knows the good general and has reason to communicate with him."

Howe's broke into a knowing grin. "A creditor?"

Drummond looked blankly at his commander-in-chief.

Howe broke into a wider grin. "Or a woman, perhaps?"

"Indeed. It seems our good General Lee, or should I say, Mister X, has had an understanding with a member of the fairer sex living in the Hackensack Valley. Unfortunately for him, but fortunately for us, she also shares her affections with a local Tory who is extremely loyal to the king—and the king's gold."

Howe nodded. "Say no more. I have much to attend to, Sandy. These matters, critical as they may be to our success, do strike me as somewhat tawdry. No reflection on you, understand, but you are so much more suited to these matters of subterfuge than I."

Drummond bristled. But he had scored points with his commander. "I understand perfectly, sir. That is precisely why I agreed to this line of work when my wound made field service impractical."

"I'm sorry. How is your leg, Sandy?"

Drummond grabbed his knee reflexively. "Tolerable, thank you, sir."

Howe laughed. "Well, make good use of brandy then. To drive away the pain."

Chapter 17

Washington's Headquarters, near Princeton, New Jersey, December 3rd, 1776

Colonel Robert Fitzgerald struggled to mount his horse. The constant riding to keep up with the army now caused him pain and stiffened his joints with rheumatism. But Fitzgerald was eager to meet Creed at an abandoned barn just south of the British lines near Brunswick. As his horse loped along the road, Fitzgerald's mind raced with thoughts and worries about the military situation.

Under constant pressure from Lord Cornwallis's advance guard of Hessians, grenadiers, and light infantry, Washington's forces had made a hasty withdrawal from Brunswick two days earlier. They now huddled behind a hasty line of defense near Princeton, but Washington had already sent parties to seize all the boats on the Delaware River. He hoped to ferry his army to safety and link his forces with those of Charles Lee, whom he had ordered to join him with his thirty-five hundred men.

Washington's army was weakened by months of campaigning, desertion, and disease. Worse, most of his regiments would soon disband as many enlistments expired in January. Many soldiers had already started leaving the army secretly at night. Fitzgerald knew it was only a matter of time before Cornwallis's forces pushed the rebels aside and entered Philadelphia. Washington's only hope was a union with Lee's forces. That alliance might give him enough men to stop Howe and boost American morale. But Washington worried the alliance might never happen.

The weather had warmed just enough to soften winter's early grip. Fitzgerald's horse moved north along the Brunswick Road. The rolling farmland looked washed-out, as if late autumn was giving way to early winter. Withered grass and bare trees dotted the landscape. Even nature seemed to need a break. *Why not the British? Indeed, why not the rebels?*

By early afternoon, he reached his turn-off point. Fitzgerald had scouted this location earlier and knew it well. He had notified Creed via a letter from Mister Hadley addressed simply to Root Hog Burns, Hackensack.

A short while later, his horse stopped in front of the barn. He looked quickly around for signs he was being followed. Seeing nothing suspicious, Fitzgerald dismounted and tied his horse to what was left of a once-strong fence. The barn belonged to a Tory owner, who had been driven out by local Whig gangs. Soon, the master would return and claim it. *There are reports of Tories across the Jerseys reclaiming their property and attacking their patriot neighbors in a vicious cycle of revenge and retaliation.*

Fitzgerald nervously pushed open the barn door and stepped in. *Empty!* He began to tingle anxiously. *Perhaps something had gone awry. Was their correspondence compromised? Was Creed uncovered?* The land was flush with spies and informers, and suspicions ran high. Fearing a trap, he began to step back slowly toward the barn entrance. As he did, he saw a vague shadow move from behind the door. Fitzgerald reached for his saber.

A familiar voice came from the shadows. "Lieutenant Jeremiah Creed, at your service, sir!" Creed stepped before him, grinning from ear to ear. "Or should I say, Root Hog Burns?"

Fitzgerald waved a finger. "It shall suffice to say that even the hazards of your mission give you no license to jest, Mister Creed, especially at my expense."

"Accept my heartfelt apology for discommoding you, sir."

"Not accepted, young man," Fitzgerald snapped. "Where are your men?"

"Covering the barn, sir. You were under the watchful eyes of the White Knights since you turned off the main road."

Fitzgerald sniffed. "Very well, Lieutenant Creed. You may call them in. I have some bacon and day-old bread in my saddlebag. And a small bottle of rum. Sorry, no whisky or tea to be found, or I would have brought some. Update me on your exploits, and then we can go over your instructions. I must return by dark. The army is likely to move at any time, making my return through our lines somewhat precarious."

Creed bowed politely. "I understand perfectly, sir. We have had our share of pickets to elude."

Now he felt guilty. "So right you are, my boy. My apologies."

Parker soon lit a small fire to cook their meager repast. He fried the bacon, then used the fat to fry the bread, which he cut into slices. He then mixed the rum with water and heated it over the fire, providing each a crude but potent hot toddy.

As they ate, Creed recounted his exploits of the past few weeks. A pleased Fitzgerald took notes and asked many questions. He was delighted by their capture of the secret British payroll and by their successful recruitment of Roy Harry and his band.

His Excellency will be pleased with your results. Spies reporting on British and Tory activities throughout northeastern New Jersey could be extremely valuable. This aligns perfectly with His Excellency's plans.

"As long as Harry stays out of Ridley. I fear this Ackerman woman is his weakness."

"A risk we shall have to accept, considering our situation. Besides, the capture and destruction of the weapons and powder stored at Hackensack were impressive. Your bold stroke aids Harry's spy network, weakens the British effort to arm local Loyalists, and sends a positive message to local Whigs."

By the time Creed finished his report, it was nearly four. His men went to check their horses and then enjoyed a few hours' sleep in the barn.

"When do you return?"

"We'll depart at ten tonight. British and Tory sentries will prove less observant, and more importantly, less supervised during the early morning hours."

"Yes, that's the optimum time for crossing lines, while the enemy has his guard at its lowest."

His note-taking finished, Fitzgerald licked his pencil tip before placing it, along with his papers, into his small leather satchel. "Fine work, Mister Creed. His Excellency will be most pleased. He hopes to hold the British here in New Jersey if our good General Lee can make juncture with the main army. Otherwise, I am afraid he must abandon this fine state to the British."

Creed shook his head. "Not totally abandon. There are patriots enough, and local militia, although that may change if Howe's amnesty plan works."

Fitzgerald winced. "What the devil do you mean?"

Creed removed a handbill from his vest. A simple propaganda piece printed on cheap paper with even cheaper ink.

New York
30 Nov. 1776
By authority of His Majesty, we are hereby offering Pardons to Americans willing to swear an oath of loyalty to the British crown. Pursuant to this, we demand all rebels, Whigs, and the multitude of undecided Americans, swear an Oath of Allegiance to the King as a precondition to any favorable Consideration and negotiation for Amnesty and restitution of Property.
By the Order of:
W. Howe, Maj. Gen.
R. Howe, Adm.

"Hmm, let us pray he has little luck with this."

Creed smirked. "'Tis paper useful only for the outhouse, sir."

Fitzgerald adjusted his glasses and peered at Creed. "Indeed! We shall see just how effective this effort proves to be. If only Lee's forces arrive."

"That should be any day now, I believe, sir."

Fitzgerald shook his head ruefully. "Lee's persistent dalliance flummoxes His Excellency. Lee should have arrived with his forces by now. General Washington gives this man every benefit of the doubt, excusing his slow progress as caution in the face of the enemy. The man is a scoundrel in my mind. At best a scoundrel and at worst a…"

Creed shrugged. "In his defense, sir, the British control all the main roads from Hackensack through Newark to Brunswick. The Tories are on the tear. He would be well advised to move through the mountains to the west, and I suppose the roads there, such as they are, are slow going."

Fitzgerald poured himself the last of the hot toddy. "I taught school in New Jersey shortly after the French War. I have made more than a handful of trips to villages there, and I assure you that, barring snow, the roads are as fine as any in the lowlands. No, there are other forces at work here. Lee has never shown His Excellency the respect due to the commander-in-chief. "

"Why is that, sir?"

"Because he feels he is the superior officer and is aggrieved that Congress did not select him for the job."

"Why, then, his ire should be with Congress, not General Washington,"

Fitzgerald shook his head. His white hair, tied in a loose queue, formed a silver halo against the evening campfire. His frown almost became a snarl. "One would think as much, but Lee believes the world centers on him. What's more troubling is his loyalty to the cause is purely opportunistic, in my mind."

Creed sputtered out his words. "You mean?"

Fitzgerald's eyes narrowed into slits. "I should not say. I have no proof. Oh, he is a sly devil. No spy, mind you, but the kind of person ready to make a deal with the British if it serves his purpose."

"What could his motivation be?"

"Selfishness, Jeremiah. The self-love of Narcissus. Lee has enough money and enough rank. I think he hopes to make His Excellency look bad in the not unreasonable hope Congress will sack him and Charles Lee will rise ascendant."

"But surely Congress has full confidence in General Washington! They proclaimed him commander-in-chief unanimously."

Fitzgerald tilted his head back and laughed. "Well, my boy, it grieves me to say, but Congress is as fickle as a spoiled young girl and as feckless as a rich young man. They hesitate to force the states to contribute troops of higher quality, like the Continental Line. They hesitate to vote for sufficient funds to feed and clothe the troops we have. They insist on appointing all his generals and organizing his forces for him. Yet they prove indecisive at every turn. And now some factions in Congress disapprove of His Excellency's handling of matters since Boston. There are even subtle hints at replacing him."

Creed's distress was so clear that Fitzgerald felt guilty. He might have shaken the young man's confidence in his commander. "But ultimately, the soundness of mind in Congress knows his appointment as commander-in-chief was the right choice. His Excellency needs to demonstrate that his strategy is working. However, to do that, he must keep the British right here in New Jersey. And he cannot do that without Lee's forces."

"So, sir, what has any of this high politics to do with the likes of me?"

Fitzgerald drained the last drop of the toddy and then placed the cup between his knees. "You must find General Lee and bring him to headquarters with all haste. With him here, his forces will follow quickly. Otherwise, I fear a div..." Fitzgerald cut himself short. He had already said too much.

Creed's eyes narrowed, wolf-like, as they bored into Fitzgerald. "Fear what, sir? I don't care to know myself, but my men must rest assured that I take on this endeavor with complete knowledge..."

Fitzgerald spoke in a slow, deliberate tone that displayed a menace Creed had not yet seen in him, "You know well enough, Jeremiah... having too much information poses grave risks should you or any of your men fall into British or Loyalist hands. This much I will say. I suspect, only suspect, that our dear general may try to affect communication with the British. He has suggested as much in some of his correspondence with certain members of the staff. However, His Excellency is unaware of it, nor of my suspicions. I am taking on this mission at my own risk, Jeremiah."

"As well as mine and the lads, sir," Creed replied.

Fitzgerald could not go to Washington without proof of Lee's possible perfidy. Despite Lee's stubbornness and insolence, Washington held his military skills and experience in some esteem.

He handed Creed an envelope. "You must find Lee's column and present this to Lee personally, and you must observe him read it. It is from me. It states that I have received a request from a group of Congressmen who plan to summon His Excellency to Philadelphia for consultations, once Lee is at headquarters. Lee is second-in-command of this army. In his blind conceit and ambition, he will naturally assume Washington is in danger of removal and that he is to be elevated to the supreme command."

"This is most risky and unorthodox, sir. Suppose he demurs?"

Fitzgerald smiled broadly. "Then it is an indicator he is either working for or otherwise in communication with the British."

"Sir, perhaps I should penetrate the British lines tonight and find Billy Howe, talk him into surrendering his army right this moment."

Fitzgerald ignored the barb from his junior officer and grinned sarcastically. "Now, Jeremiah, we must save some challenges for later."

Chapter 18

Haverstraw, New York

General Charles Lee examined the letter once more, then again, carefully studying each word. When he recognized the sender's address, he became quite excited. A wave of memories swept him back to his first visit to the Hackensack Valley. Shortly after taking command of American defenses at New York earlier that year, Lee had made several trips to the New Jersey side of the North River. He looked for militia to defend New York, inspected the batteries on the west side of the river, and collected provisions from the many fruitful farms in the area.

During his first trip, he decided to stay overnight in Ridley, at the place they called the Blue House. He enjoyed the rough-and-tumble patrons who frequented the tavern. The food was plentiful and satisfying, and the wines and liquors flowed freely. Most particularly, he delighted in the comely young widow who owned the establishment.

He had mixed success. The few local cannons could not prevent British ships from sailing north and thus cutting off New York. And only a few militia units were willing to cross over and help defend the city. But Lee did find the farm bounty abundant in New Jersey and procured enough to help feed the Continental Army when it arrived from Boston.

But Lee's infatuation with the young widow Jannetje Ackerman was something else entirely. It made him linger more with each of his four trips. The older Lee was immediately captivated by her sassy demeanor, her full décolleté, and her eager lovemaking. He had enjoyed a few enchanted weeks, but since then, her letters had decreased and finally stopped. He liked to believe that the chaos of war kept her from replying to his letters. Although he often sought comfort in available doxies, usually a willing camp follower or maybe the somewhat less willing wife of some unlucky sergeant, he still longed for her.

The worldly and cynical Lee found the letter's contents startling.

Ridley, New Jersey

My Dearest Charles,

I hope this Letter finds you in the best of Health and Vigor. Although it seems so long ago, only a few months have passed since we last enjoyed one another's Cumpany and I do miss you – especially your Vitality.

Since the arrival of the English, many once ardent Whigs and fervent Rebels have reconsidered their Veewpoint and taken the Oath to the King so genirously offered by Lord How. Even to the most rabid Patriots. Many of the Skinners have now transformed into Cowboys and their awful Depradations now refocused from the Loyalists and against what few Patriots are still left in the

Valley. On the pulpit, some of the most Whigish Dutch Reformed Church Leaders are beginning to preach Reconciliation and Peace. Rivington's Gazette recently speculated that Mister Washington seeks union with your Forces for a final Battle somewhere in the Jerseys.

I know nothing of grand Strategy or Politics, Charles, but I do know that I miss You.

If you do decide to march through New Jersey, I would be delighted to meet with

you either at the Blue House or at a Place of your choosing. Certain prominant Gentlemen who have stayed here at the Blue House have become aware of our mutual Affection. They have asked me to offer you the chance to meet and discuss your Future with the rebel forces and possible Role in avoiding more Conflict.

…Possibly even bringing a permanent settling of Differences to our mutuel Benefit.

Charles, I weary of the bloodshed and Strife this War has caused. An Accommodation with you as its principle Instrument could lead to a celebrated Life, something you so often whispered of.

Please consider this Charles and, in any event, please meet with me, as I do so miss you and need You, my dear Charles.

In breathless anticipation I Remain,

Your Most Ardent and Affectionate,

Jannetje

The letter excited and intrigued him. It immediately presented a rare chance to fulfill all his desires: fame, power, wealth, and the affections of a young widow.

Lee was unaware that, although Jannetje wrote and signed the letter, Major Sandy Drummond was responsible for its contents. One of his newest Tory recruits, Dierk Van Buskirk, had delivered it to her on a dark, wind-swept night. Van Buskirk also happened to be her current lover.

Despite his involvement in the damage at the Romeyn parsonage and his link to the destruction of the British arsenal there, Dierk faced little blame. Most Tories believed the influence of his uncle protected him from trial or even dismissal from the 4th New Jersey Volunteers. But his protection came from Major Sandy Drummond, who was now his true master.

* * *

Days before the British marched through Hackensack, one of Drummond's men, Sergeant Digby, visited Ridley, disguised as a New York businessman named Norton. He spent a few days in the area undercover, staying at the Blue House.

By the second day, Jannetje grew suspicious of his routine, which seemed mostly to involve drinking and walking around the green. Determined to learn more, she asked one of the servers, an older man named Woods, to discover who he was.

Woods placed a tall frothy tankard in front of Digby. "What business brings you here, mister?"

Digby cut him off. "Norton, Mister Norton. I see you and I are of like mind, sir."

Digby grabbed the tankard, took a long drink, wiped his mouth, and set the tankard down on the table.

"Like mind?" Woods asked.

"Yes, for instance, we both like to ask questions —like to know things." Digby placed a silver coin in Woods' bony hand.

"I don't… That's five— five shillings!" stammered Woods.

Digby placed his fingers to his lips. "Not too loud now. We both know your Missus sent you here. Does she always inquire into the business of her paying customers?"

Woods eyed the floor. "Well, sure, Mister Norton."

"I can tell a lie. But that's all right now. There will be five more shillings for your troubles."

"Troubles?"

"Yes. When the Missus goes to bed, you'll let me know. Also, you'll point out the gents here who are loyal and those who are not."

"And what are you?"

Digby's face stiffened. "I'm the bloke who'll cut your balls off if you ask me any more questions."

Woods blanched. In his day, he would have beaten someone like Norton for less.

Digby smiled and took another swig from the tankard. "There now. I was kidding. This is a business deal —information and discretion for silver."

"Well, Mister Norton, the problem with the swamp and folks in Ridley is…"

"Is what?"

Woods pocketed the coin. "They don't have any loyalty. None. They belong to the highest bidder."

Digby tossed back another gulp and belched into his sleeve. "I see… Then this is the kind of place I can do business in."

***

For the next few days and into the night, Digby kept up his routine. Through Woods, he quickly learned all about Jannetje and her methods. He also discovered details about her customers and how they operated. Before long, he had a list of potential suspects for Major Drummond's small network. However, he instinctively sensed that this was all too easy, and that these Ridley swamp folks might prove to be more trouble than they were worth.

Then, while returning to his chambers after one of his evening drinking bouts, he spotted Dierk Van Buskirk slipping out of Jannetje's room.

"Who was that leaving your Missus' room, Mister Woods?" Digby asked the next day.

"Why, nobody, Mister Norton."

"I find it quaint that you protect the Missus. I like that. But you'd do better telling me. I only want to meet the lucky devil, is all. Jannetje is a beautiful woman, and I am sure quite the pleasure giver."

"His name is Dirk Van Buskirk. A useless lout. A real sod. But part of the powerful Van Buskirk family. I think she fancies him because of his family. She's shrewd that way."

"You're sweet on her too, ain't you?" Digby asked slyly. "Been with her?"

Woods's face reddened. "Why no! Why, look at my age."

Although he suspected a lie, Digby winked. "I suspect the Widow Ackerman tolerates older men as much as she fancies younger ones. Introduce me to this Van Buskirk."

When Woods introduced them later, Digby befriended Van Buskirk with drinks. After ascertaining his strong Tory leanings and connections, Digby recruited him into the very small circle of Hackensack men Drummond had dispatched Digby to hire.

Digby concluded his recruitment with a stern warning, "You've chosen the right side, sir. Our good master will reward you with silver. On your part, loyalty and obedience must take precedence. You will be relieved of your regimental duties to make you available for other activities supporting His Majesty."

A drunk Van Buskirk closed one eye and tilted his head ever so slightly. "Such as?"

Digby rubbed his nose. "Delivering special messages, observing rebel movements, helping suppress the patriots in the valley, and reporting on the Tories…"

Van Buskirk gasped. "Tories? You want me to spy on my people, those who have stayed steadfast to the crown despite the indignities heaped on them by the Whigs? What exactly, who do you think I am?"

Digby tugged on his sleeve, cutting him off. "Now hear me well, sir. Do you not think the rebels have spies recruited among your, how do you Dutchies say it, Landsmen?"

He was proud of himself for coining that term. Digby appeared to be a simple dragoon, but he was quite shrewd and worldly. More important to his master, Sandy Drummond, he was both ruthless and opportunistic.

It did not take long before Dierk revealed Jannetje's brief but intense relationship with the would-be rebel leader, the former British officer Charles Lee. Digby's report to Drummond sparked a ruthless and cunning plot. Drummond's hope of ending the war with the Loyalists' help had taken a new turn.

* * *

Lee sat alone at his desk. A weak fire fueled by damp Faggots struggled in the large fireplace, with embers occasionally spitting out sparks with a soft crackle. Lee was an avid fox hunter and always traveled with a pack of hounds as spoiled and obnoxious as their master. One of them, a Pomeranian, let out a short, whiny whoof.

Lee smiled at her, his favorite. "Ah, my dear Mister Spado, you shall all eat soon enough."

He finished his reply to Jannetje. Suddenly, he felt a strong yearning in his loins, but also in his heart, the typical ache of an older man for a younger woman, the sense that her touch and her affection somehow made him younger.

Lee thought back to his earlier days in the British Army, how his considerable talents were never fully appreciated. He thought back again to the many European masters for whom he had long served and suffered.

He was rewarded, but he was neither appreciated nor accepted. Settling in America changed that. As a new Virginia planter, he was now part of a semi-aristocracy, and finally, with the start of the war, he had the chance to be the military leader he believed himself to be. Then politics and the rise of this man Washington blocked him. If the war ended favorably for the rebels with Washington still in charge, it would once again reduce him to a supporting role in the big event. But if the British won, he might face the rope. None of it seemed quite fair somehow.

Lee leaned back in his chair, his mind racing with possibilities. He saw a chance to return to Jannetje's arms and, through her, connect with those in the British and Tory camps who shared his views.

This offered him a unique opportunity to plan an exit if the war turned badly, which seemed likely while positioning himself as Washington's successor. Additionally, a relationship with the British could serve as leverage with Congress. Lee believed that they were growing tired of Washington. If Washington could not wage war effectively, perhaps Charles Lee could persuade them to make peace with the British on favorable terms.

He leaned forward and dipped his nib into the thick, black ink.

Haverstraw, New York

My Darling Jannetje,

I retrn your Ardor and your Love. Cirumstnces currently require my presnce with Frnds here, but as we depart on our Journey through your Neighborhood, I shall arrange for an Assignation. Then, we can discuss terms of our future Life together and Should time permit, I hope you can introduce me to your Frnds, who seem quite interesting.

Be prepared for a most amorous greeting from your Charles, as he has had little to satisfy him as comely as you, since we last reveled in Cupid's embrace.

I remain, as always,

Your most fervent and ardent Admirer,

Charles

Lee chuckled as he sealed the envelope and addressed it simply to:

Jannetje A.
Blue House
Ridley, New Jersey

He placed the envelope in a small leather briefcase. He dared not risk sending it through the military post. He would keep it secure until he could find a safe civilian way to get it along the route south through Jersey.

* * *

Washington's Headquarters, near Trenton, New Jersey, December 6th, 1776

The semi-thatched log home was much more welcoming inside than its exterior suggested. Four upper rooms offered airy and comfortable sleeping quarters, and one large ground-floor room, the so-called great room, served as the dining and living area, now occupied by the commanding general's staff.

General Washington's heavy boots wore out the carpet as he paced in front of the stone fireplace. Lieutenant Tench Tilghman, his top aide-de-camp, was feverishly scribbling orders to the few brigades remaining in the Continental Army.

Washington had summoned Colonel John Glover, commander of the Gloucester Regiment, the brave sailors and fishermen from Marblehead and points along the New England coast. Glover now stood before him, his greatcoat hanging loosely.

"Colonel Glover, have you secured the craft as I asked?"

"Indeed, Your Excellency, by the next morning, this army will possess every boat and raft for miles up and down the Delaware River. "

"Precisely how many?"

"Almost seventy craft, Your Excellency. And a few more possible by dawn. The boys are prepared for another desperate amphibious movement."

Washington's face showed a brief smile. "I would think no less. Their heroic efforts on the East River saved the army from certain annihilation on Long Island. Now I desperately need them to repeat their heroics on the Delaware."

"They're up to it, sir."

Washington stopped and faced the fire, clasping his hands behind his back. "We can only hope Cornwallis, intent on running us to ground, neglected to bring any boats overland."

"Aye, sir."

Washington turned and faced Glover. "Ensure your gallant men remove everything that floats to the Pennsylvania side for at least twenty miles up and down the river."

Glover thrust his thumbs under his lapels. "Aye, sir. If Cornwallis wants to follow this army, his men will have to swim."

"We have reports that the main body of British remains near Brunswick, inexplicably delaying their push south towards Princeton," Fitzgerald said from his corner chair.

Washington stared at the map before him as if it held some grand secret. "I think it is likely Cornwallis will move quickly and attempt to drive us into the Delaware."

"Why not face him here, sir?"

"I should like to, Colonel, but not before reuniting with General Lee. Yet time is running out. Although he has finally begun to move south, I had hoped to hear from him by now."

Tench Tilghman put down his quill and sighed. "Unfortunately, Your Excellency, dispatches from the north arrive only sporadically. The last one placed General Lee somewhere in the northern reaches of New Jersey. He is now moving, but slowly."

An orderly opened the door. "Sir, Lieutenant…"

Abner Scovel pushed past the soldier. From the look on Scovel's face, Washington knew immediately that something was a foot.

Scovel clicked his heels. "Sir, Lord Stirling's brigade is pulling back from Princeton with Cornwallis's advance guard in close pursuit."

Washington smiled reassuringly. "Well, yes, but our good General Howe is still in charge of the column. And he marches his army not ten miles in a single day. I have no reason to think he will change before tomorrow."

Fitzgerald chimed in. "Indeed, sir, but even the laconic Howe could make Trenton by tomorrow evening."

The commander-in-chief raised his head slightly. "We, however, shall be gone by then. Tench, are those orders ready for my signature?"

Tilghman nodded. "Almost, sir, in another half hour."

Washington's small group of aides, recruited from the finest young men the colonies had to offer, gave him some comfort during the difficult times he faced. Cheerful and self-sacrificing, every one of them worked tirelessly for the glorious cause.

Washington nodded at Glover and Scovel. "Carry on, gentlemen."

He tugged Fitzgerald by the arm and led him to his private study, which also served as his sleeping quarters. In a voice so quiet it was almost a whisper, Washington asked the question that had been bothering him all day, "Any news from Lieutenant Creed?"

Fitzgerald lowered his eyes. "No, sir. But we will hear from him soon."

Washington frowned. "Soon must be before we have this army across the river, Colonel. Tomorrow night at the latest."

"I daresay that if anyone can get through one hundred miles of British and Tories, cross a major river, and deliver, Jeremiah Creed can."

A day earlier, Fitzgerald finally told Washington that he had sent Creed to lure Lee to army headquarters. At first, Washington exploded over the secret plan. He gradually warmed to the idea, but not because Fitzgerald had done it without telling him. However, the former schoolteacher convinced Washington that the plan was in his, and the army's, best interest. "Your Excellency, you cannot be seen deceiving your second-ranking general or showing any suspicion in his direction. Leave that to me, and to others."

Washington rubbed his chin. "Very well, Robert. But unless we have incontrovertible proof of some perfidy, I shall take no adverse action against General Lee. Would that my entreaties not fall on his deaf ears."

Fitzgerald winced. "Deaf ears, sir? I think General Lee hears only what suits him. But then again, that is why Creed's mission provides an alternative to reliance on Lee's obedience to your orders."

* * *

Washington nervously pulled at his leather glove as he watched the Glover's Gloucester men rhythmically tugging at the oars, moving the last regiment across the Delaware River. The cold was numbing to the bone, but the sky was clear and sunny. Washington wondered how much longer he could depend on a few dedicated men while others deserted the army or, worse, were led astray by wayward commanders. He had become almost obsessed with Charles Lee, yet felt that without his forces, Philadelphia would surely fall to the British.

He murmured a silent prayer to Providence, which he felt surely guided him, then snapped into action. "Lieutenant Scovel, once the last company departs, I will conduct a final inspection of the camp. Ask Colonel Glover to leave just one boat. Please be so kind as to cross over now and take my horse. I'll perform my final inspection on foot."

Scovel began to protest, but Washington cut him off. "Don't worry, four of my Life Guard will accompany me."

Washington almost fell to the British at Kip's Bay in August and survived several plots. Since then, it has been standard for at least half a dozen men, four or five, to accompany him whenever he leaves the headquarters.

"As you wish, sir." Scovel took Washington's horse in hand and gently guided the magnificent white charger down to the riverbank. It struck Washington that Scovel, a New Englander, was just as devoted to his commander-in-chief as any of the Virginians on his staff. To think that men from different parts of the country could stay so steadfast in their loyalty. He turned for one last look at the abandoned buildings of Trenton.

Two of Washington's escorts had stationed themselves at the north end of Trenton, near Princeton Road. The town was now empty. Even the Loyalists feared the shortages caused by the Hessian troops, who, it was rumored, led General Cornwallis's advance guard. Washington saw little of the remnants of war that are often left behind by a retreating army: satchels, crates, trunks, stray pieces of canvas, and discarded weapons. Washington found this somewhat unsettling. *Have we become so skilled at retreating?*

The *pop* of muskets filled the air. He gazed in the direction of the Princeton Road. *The British!* Satisfied that the town was cleared of anything useful to the enemy, Washington shuffled down the riverbank to a longboat rocking in the icy water. The crew sat patiently, their oars raised skyward like a picket fence. These handpicked, hardened seamen would not let a few stray British musket shots affect their stoic demeanor.

The helmsman helped Washington clamber aboard and urged immediate departure. But their commander-in-chief stood patiently at the bow until all four of his escorts returned safely.

"Heave," the helmsman ordered.

A dozen oars lowered and began to push against the flowing current.

From the rocking boat, Washington could see a band of Hessian Jaegers moving down the main street toward the river. Their slouched bi-cornered hunting hats, dark-green jackets, and brass buttons stood out clearly in the bright afternoon sun. He counted about twenty. They spread out along the riverbank, but strangely, they held their fire.

Washington saw a half-dozen mounted men in red coats galloping towards the river like a fox hunt. In the lead was a senior officer – a general.

One of the Life Guards had his musket on his shoulder. "I have a bead on the fancy one, sir. Permission to fire, sir?"

"Not granted," Washington replied icily. "I believe it's Lord Cornwallis."

The British general, his frustration obvious, pulled up and circled his horse, first left, then right, damning both armies' commanders, Washington for his alacrity and Howe for his tardiness.

While the Gloucester men pulled at their oars in crisp snaps, and the Jersey shore faded from view, Washington's thoughts sped ahead to the many tasks awaiting him. His army, diminished by sickness and desertion to fewer than 2,000 effectives, needed to quickly set up defenses at the crucial Delaware River crossing points.

Gloucester had successfully seized or destroyed every available boat for seventy miles, giving them some time to prepare. Washington appreciated the small advantages gained from this retreat. He just hoped Lee would join him in time so they could stand firm and save Philadelphia, and perhaps the nation.

Chapter 19

Pompton, New Jersey, December 9th, 1776

Lee's men had been trudging through mud and cold for five long, tiring days. He decided to give them a rest for a day while he considered his next move. A cold December wind had picked up, blowing through his tent and cutting like the blade of a freshly sharpened razor. The ride would be even colder. Timing was everything. And if he timed things right, he could achieve his goals.

He had begun communicating with several other senior officers who he knew were less than impressed with Washington's handling of the war. Among them were Horatio Gates and Thomas Mifflin. Lee felt he could rely on their support. However, he needed to make his march through New Jersey appear like a victory to earn widespread praise from Congress and the army.

Lee reasoned that if he reached Washington before the British overwhelmed him, his additional forces and military expertise might provide Washington with the boost needed to defeat or at least slow down the British. Washington would then be seen as the savior of the cause.

However, if he failed to arrive on time, so be it. Likely, Washington would be dead, captured, or disgraced. In that case, Charles Lee would probably be appointed as his successor. If he could pull that off while maintaining some kind of connection to the British, he might be able to negotiate peace and be celebrated on both sides of the Atlantic.

The cold suddenly swirled around Lee as the tent flap opened and his aide, Captain William Bradford, entered. "Sir, your horse is saddled and ready. However, there is a complication."

Lee bristled. "A complication? What now?"

"Some men from General Washington's headquarters just arrived. Their officer wants to speak with you. He says it is urgent."

General Washington—the words slammed Lee in the stomach like the kick of a mule. *Another plea to make all haste, no doubt. And to what end? Another skedaddle? Another lost victory?*

Despite his string of defeats, Washington was exalted by most of the army, even by Lee's staff. Could they not see the man did not know how to fight British regulars? His mind raced through all the failed efforts against the king's professionals: Long Island a crushing defeat, Kip's Bay a rout, Haarlem a victory missed, White Plains a blunder, Fort Washington the loss of New York, and his namesake Fort Lee the loss of New Jersey. Since Fort Lee, Washington had done nothing but outrun the British, and barely at that.

The Cavalier Spy

Lee's 3,000 men, combined with Washington's force, were still half the strength of the British in New Jersey. Moreover, Lee felt the cause's greatest asset, his knowledge of the British Army and his experience on a dozen battlefields, would likely go unsolicited, or worse, ignored. No, Charles Lee would move at his own pace, lest his command become cannon fodder for another of His Excellency's fiascos.

Lee took his time putting on his overcoat and wrapping his neck with a woolen scarf. "Is my horse ready?"

"Yes, sir."

Lee smiled faintly. "Then tell them I have other plans, and I shall meet with them upon my return."

Grabbing one of his finely crafted hunting guns and a small satchel, Lee exited the tent, ignoring Creed and his men waiting patiently for him under a stand of pine trees just ten yards away.

Lee quickly put on his black jumper. Out of nowhere, a pack of about six speckled hounds circled around the horse's feet, yelping and growling. The excited dogs clearly knew they were headed for a hunt, and they loved it. Lee loved his dogs more than he loved any person, and he cared for them more than he cared for anyone else. Muttering something inaudible to his aide, Lee turned his horse around, struck its haunches with a crop, and galloped south down the road.

***

Creed squinted after the general. "You lads try to find some food around here and stay with the army."

"Where are you going, Root Hog, I mean Lieutenant? You wouldn't deprive us of another adventure, would you?" Parker asked sheepishly.

Creed ignored the tart tone. "After our fine General Lee. No telling what mischief he might get into without an escort. Your time for adventure shall come soon enough."

Beall stepped forward. "Let me come too, sir. You might need some help tracking him, and I have tracked all kinds of game in the Catoctins."

Creed pondered the idea for a second and then nodded. "Very well, Private Beall, gather Finn for me and wait while I chat with the good general's aide."

Captain Bradford was in Lee's tent, reorganizing the general's papers. Creed pulled back the flap and entered. Bradford was a small man, in his mid-thirties, who seemed earnest enough to Creed.

He decided that straightforward charm would work best with him. "Begging your pardon, sir, but where did the good general go? Did you not inform him that we come from the commander-in-chief?"

The aide rubbed his chin nervously and smiled. "Why… yes, I did… he went hunting, I think he said something about taking down a buck. I say, I didn't get your name."

"Creed, sir, Lieutenant Jeremiah Creed. And when will the general return from his hunt, sir?"

"Why, when he gets his buck, of course." Bradford smiled.

Creed nodded and smiled back. "Indeed, sir. And how long does the good general normally spend in such endeavors? General Washington's business is not often of a routine nature if you understand my line of discussion."

Bradford's face reddened. "See here, Lieutenant Creed. Charles Lee is the general commanding this division. He goes and comes at his will, not that of General..."

Creed squinted with one eye and cocked his head at him in a subtle warning.

The aide's eyes widened at his lack of discretion. "You do not mean that..."

Creed smiled wryly. "I'm not saying he is, and I'm not saying he is not."

"Well, he likes to take the hounds out every few days. Gets their blood up, you know. Afterward, they sometimes feast. He keeps them attached to him that way. Or so he has said. Sometimes he is back in hours, sometimes he returns in a day or two, often without visible signs of success."

Creed grinned broadly now. "Do you mean he hunts a different sort of game?"

Bradford lowered his eyes. "Perhaps."

"And just where do you suppose his hunting ground might be?"

"To the east, a half day's ride, maybe a bit more."

Creed was stunned. "How far east? As far as the valley?"

Bradford kept his head low. "I suspect he has an assignation."

"I see... just where might that be?"

"Ridley. I believe he said, Ridley. The general often hunted there in the spring, or so he said. I was not with the command just then."

Creed bowed. "Thank you, sir. We will await him with baited breath. Let's hope he doesn't bring any game home for us."

* * *

They followed Lee's trail just outside the camp. The muddy path was marked with hoof and paw prints. The day was cold but not freezing, though the wind chill was sharp. The sky was clear, but dark clouds moved in from the west. They rode in silence, with only the sound of hooves and occasional snorts breaking the quiet.

After a long time, Beall broke the silence. "Sir, how far do you intend to follow the general before we stop him and ask him to return with us?"

Creed leaned forward, his eyes scanning the road ahead. "Why, we'll follow him all the way, Jonathan. All the way."

They followed the tracks south for an hour through low mountains dotted with tiny villages. The trail then turned east through rolling hills that led to the Hackensack River. At one point, they heard Lee's dogs barking frantically. They stopped to avoid getting too close for Lee to see them or for the wind to carry their scent to the dogs.

Then the barking suddenly turned to baying, the sound worsened until it became shrill and almost demonic.

"My God, sir, what can they be doing?"

Creed stared ahead. "I suspect they found a fox or a young deer. Now our good general has allowed his beasts some sport. A type of sport I find particularly cruel but seems to thrill the English."

"Don't the Irish hunt?"

"Only when they become English," was Creed's gruff retort.

"Don't you like dogs?"

"Not in packs, Jonathan. They become more like wolves when in packs. And when the master is cruel, so go the dogs."

"Did you ever have a dog, sir?"

"Yes. A noble wolfhound named Seamus," Creed answered. His voice trailed off, and he hesitated uncharacteristically.

"What happened to him?"

"That's the sad part of it. He saved my brother from a pack of wolves but got mauled in the doing of it."

Creed fought back the tears that always accompanied the memory.

Beall hesitated. "I am sorry, sir. Did Seamus live?"

"Aye, but my brother put a bullet in his head. To relieve him of the pain, he told us. He never liked Seamus. I think he couldn't stand the thought of owing his life to my noble wolfhound. But enough. Let's change into cowboy garb."

They halted and led their mounts off the road, where they quickly changed into homespun and buckskin, then waited. Before long, they heard the din grow into a fierce crescendo of growls and then abruptly fade into the distance.

Beall whispered, "They're on the move, sir."

"Savagery done." Creed nodded back as he swung his leg into the stirrup. "For now, Jonathan, just for now."

Lee's trail took them to Ridley, just as Bradford said.

"While I conduct a walk about Ridley, you take the horses to Brower's stable. He's discreet, especially when paid in advance."

He handed Finn's reins to Beall. "I'll start at the Blue House. I suspect our good general is there or somewhere nearby. I will bring you back some food. Meanwhile, try to get some sleep."

He left his Jaeger rifle in its saddlebag but drew the sword-bayonet and a pistol. As Creed made his way to the tavern, he scanned the street for signs of British or Loyalist soldiers. He headed to the stable first. Peering inside, he saw the servant working on a large jumper, giving it a rubdown while the horse held its muzzle in a leather feedbag. From a dark corner, the growling and yapping of the hounds confirmed Lee's presence.

Creed backed off and then quietly made his way to the front of the tavern. Once on the main road, he looked for signs of surveillance or other suspicious activity. *Nothing unusual here.* He smiled. *Perhaps this was indeed merely an assignation.*

* * *

Lee had slipped into Ridley at dusk. The town had only a few residents, and on such a cold evening, any visitors would already be warming themselves at the Blue House, a place Lee knew well. He entered through the back alley, which kept him out of sight from the prying eyes on the main street. His hounds had quieted down, exhausted after a hard day of running. He led his horse to the stable where Woods took his jumper to be fed and watered. The hounds followed the horse, knowing food and water were on the way. It was their usual routine.

Lee ignored the noisy commotion from the taproom below and slipped up the back stairs to Jannetje's room. Drinking was something he could do comfortably enough in his headquarters. He had other plans tonight. The door swung open. Jannetje stood there in a loose shift, and before she could say a word, he was all over her, groping, fondling roughly, and whispering bawdy words into her ear as he smothered her with crudely placed kisses. She gave in to his advances willingly, but not enthusiastically.

***

Lee awoke the next morning with Jannetje standing over him. Her gown hung loosely, and he could see the slow movement of her décolleté. It stirred him again, but she held a tray with coffee and warm food, and he decided nourishment would come before refreshment.

She smiled a slightly forced smile. "I have eggs and ham for you, Charles. With biscuits and Dutch coffee. Your hounds have already been fed."

His face broke into a wide grin. "Thank you, my dear, on behalf of my hounds as well."

He pulled her to him with one hand while reaching under her gown. She returned his advances but not his passion and finally pulled away. He grinned lasciviously, then sat up and went right at the food. Jannetje found the sounds of him slurping and chewing at the food noxious. *To think I once embraced his wants.*

She straightened her shift. "I must change. You must meet a visitor here. Someone, I think you'll find interesting."

Lee dropped his knife and fork onto the platter. "Just who might that be?"

"You read my letter, Charles dear. It's a friend. Someone who will help you earn your rightful place in the army."

With that, she slipped out of the room but glanced back to see him chomping away at his food. Jannetje fought the shudder of revulsion she now felt. She hardly remembered that he once actually amused her. She entered her wardrobe and picked out her light brown day dress made of fine wool.

From the corner of the room, Dierk Van Buskirk eyed her with savage jealousy. "I'm not pleased by your antics with our guest."

"Do you believe it pleased me, my dear? But it served our purpose," she retorted.

"Our purpose does not have to please me," Dierk spat.

Jannetje frowned, then her eyes widened, and her face brightened. "You weren't pleased? Let's hope General Charles was pleased. That's all that matters now."

Van Buskirk's grew dark. "You said you no longer had feelings for the old man, that you would do this for king and country. But from the sound of things, you lied."

She lifted her dimpled chin haughtily. "Why, Dierk, you are jealous! Well, no need for all that now, my dear. Charles Lee means nothing to me. My assignation is complete. You'd best go down to the tavern and eat while we await our friend."

The Cavalier Spy

Jannetje regretted her affair with Van Buskirk. The entire community reviled him. His looks fell short of even the rugged homeliness of her late husband. And he was certainly not Roy Harry. His body was soft where Harry's was hard and muscular. He had no moral compass. But perhaps that was what attracted her to him the first time. And his connection to the British provided a sort of insurance. Or so she thought. One could not be sure which way the rebellion would turn. Therefore, Jannetje maintained her connection to Harry, whose nocturnal mutterings revealed latent sympathies for the rebels.

At times like these, she missed her husband. He would know what to do, to whom to turn. Suddenly, feelings of regret and remorse overwhelmed her.

Her ablutions finished, Jannetje quietly returned to Lee's room. His plate was now empty, and he had used her commode, oddly leaving it out from under the bed. The smell from his breath and body repulsed her. For a general, supposedly a gentleman, his hygiene seemed strangely lacking. She wondered how she ever managed to have an affair with him. She supposed his rank had impressed her. She shivered involuntarily.

Lee beckoned her with a wolf-like grin and a crooked finger that enticed and threatened. "Now, my darling, I want you again. Come here and let's have a kiss to start."

"Why, Charles, the tavern is busy. Breakfast customers are..."

He grabbed her roughly and pulled her to him with one hand, reaching under her dress with his other. His breath made her want to choke.

"Not one petticoat. So, you were prepared for me. You are a lovely and cooperative one, Jannetje."

"Really, Charles dear – not now." She struggled against his probes.

He whispered menacingly and entreatingly into her ear, "I rode long and hard to be with you, dear Jannetje, just as I am now."

With strength and urgency that surprised them both, she pushed herself away from him. "Charles! Control yourself! If our other business goes well, we'll have time for each other later, but not now."

Lee glared. "My, you are not the same Jannetje who could not get enough of me this spring. Very well, my dear, it seems the war has changed many things for many of us."

She lowered her eyes. "Yes, it has, Charles. It surely has. It's not you – it's just that..."

"Never mind that now, Jannetje. I'll meet your friend. But I shall take you up on your promise of later."

* * *

Lee drummed his fingers on a corner table in the smoke-filled main room of the Blue House. Over a dozen patrons already ate breakfast and sipped coffee, followed by shots of liquor to warm up. A pot of good Dutch coffee separated Lee from Dierk. Lee grew impatient with each passing minute.

Lee took a slurp from his cup and let it fall roughly on the white tablecloth. "Your friend, the businessman, is on the tardy side. I don't like to be kept waiting. "

From the moment Jannetje first introduced her two paramours, tension abounded. Lee sensed Dierk still resented Jannetje's assignation with him, even though he helped arrange it. Lee, for his part, immediately sensed Van Buskirk was more than her friend, which accounted for her newfound hesitancy. It could never bother Charles Lee that the object of his desire had another paramour. He just liked to know these things. And he might have enjoyed her telling him about it. Lee enjoyed ribald talk, especially from young women.

Van Buskirk wiped coffee from his lips and said, "So you see, when Jannetje invited you here, it wasn't just to meet you during your sojourn through this fine state but to introduce you to an important businessman from across the river."

Lee startled. "Across the river? The North River? New York?"

Van Buskirk smiled. "Why yes, sir, there's still much commerce from there. It just takes influence or money."

Lee eyed him suspiciously. "And pray tell, which did it take for our businessman to make this trip?"

Van Buskirk smiled again. "Frankly, it took both, sir. And that is what he shall discuss with us. Influence… and money."

Digby entered the tavern just as Van Buskirk finished speaking. The sergeant of His Majesty's 17th Light Dragoons looked impressive in civilian clothes: a dark burgundy jacket with a cream-colored vest and ruffles, white breeches, and calf-high riding boots. His slouch hat was adorned with a large black feather. Woods greeted him at the door and nodded toward the two.

As if on cue, he approached the table, doffed his hat, and bowed.

Van Buskirk made the introduction. "This is my dear friend, Mister Norton. He sells dry goods."

Lee gave an oily smile. "Ah, Mister Norton, I have been anxious to meet you."

Woods brought Digby a tankard of ale, but he declined. "No ale for me now, the coffee is excellent."

Once Woods left, Digby looked at Van Buskirk. "Why don't you leave us two so we can talk alone?"

Van Buskirk scowled, "What the…"

Norton's eyes narrowed. Van Buskirk hung his head sheepishly and slid from the table.

They started their conversation with some friendly small talk. Mister Norton mentioned he had fought in the French and Indian War but now aimed to profit from the current conflict. He gave a mischievous grin, showing a set of teeth surprisingly full for a seasoned soldier with many years of tough campaigning. "So much the better to profit from the tragedy of war, is it not, general?"

Lee was unimpressed. He had hoped to meet with a senior officer of Howe's command, not this obvious trickster who could barely disguise his lowly origins. Finally, tired of the charade, he decided to challenge the stranger. "So, Mister Norton, this is all about selling me dry goods? My men need food and clothing, and good shoes. Not dry goods. Surely you are aware of that? The press makes no secret of it, even the Whig press.

Nor should they. Mismanagement and poor leadership must be exposed and expunged, however possible."

Digby nodded and poured himself a second cup of the thick, strong brew. He doused it with a spoonful of brandy from his flask. "Nothing could be further from my mind, sir. I am, coincidentally, more concerned with your second point. The part about exposing, and what was the other word… expunge? Well, you see, sir, I represent some fine gentlemen who hold exactly your view. That is, they see the mismanagement of this war and hope to, what was that word? Ah, yes, expunge it."

Lee's pulse quickened at Digby's comment. He stared intently at him. "And just who are these… fine… gentlemen?"

Digby flashed his teeth. "Time enough for that later, sir. Let's say they wish to meet with you to discuss certain matters. They reckon your former ties to Britain, which is of course your commission in His Majesty's army, make you the only American general of any worth. Of any consequence, so to speak."

The blatant flattery had its desired effect, and Lee put aside his suspicions and thought a moment. He laced his fingers together and rested his chin on two upright forefingers as he pondered things. *Of course, this man is correct!*

Lee wished more in Congress thought so clearly. If they thought clearly, they would realize the ragtag forces of the rebellion could never stand against British regulars. Peace and liberty could only be won through negotiation. Lee felt the Army was merely a bargaining chip. *God save us from the politicians and Mister Washington!*

Lee nodded in agreement. "True enough, sir. What do you, that is, what do they have in mind, Mister Norton? Be advised, I must return to my command today. The charms of dear Jannetje notwithstanding, I do have my duty."

Digby slurped at his coffee. Then he poured another splash of whisky into it. "Indeed, you do, sir. Well, these… fine gentlemen… wish to know if you would be willing to meet with them to discuss the future. Your future."

Lee startled. "My future? Now just what exactly are you getting at, Mister Norton?"

Digby's eyes grew dull. "I can't say exactly, sir, because I don't know. What I can tell you is that, in their estimation, you should command the rebel army, flawed as it is."

"Indeed, I should command the army!" Lee blurted, louder than he should have under the circumstances.

He looked around, but none of the patrons seemed to notice. They continued to talk as the clank of utensils and cups and the bustle of the servants filled the room.

Digby threw down the whisky and drained his cup. "Now, sir, they feel, and this is only their opinion, sir, that with an officer of your quality in command, the war could be ended quickly. More importantly, sir, and mark my words, to the satisfaction of all parties."

Lee filled his coffee cup, nervously gulped down the entire contents, and loudly set the cup back in the saucer. He glared at this businessman, who was something far different than that.

Digby sighed and then slowly pulled a small silk purse from his vest, counting out a stack of five-pound notes. "Here are fifty guineas. Of course, sir, my friends understand that an officer of your stature's time is valuable. This is a small token of their appreciation for you taking time out from your cause to hear them out. There will surely be much more when you meet."

"Are you trying to bribe me, Mister Norton?"

"Not at all, sir. This is a business transaction."

After a long pause, Lee picked up the notes. "Very well, Mister Norton. Let us then get down to business."

After another thirty minutes of intense discussion, Digby stood up and, without so much as a glance around the room, departed. Lee peered through the window and watched Mister Norton slowly mount his horse and canter down the road towards Hackensack. He noted the man rode well, for a businessman, if he was one.

Lee rose from his chair and went upstairs to find the tavern's proprietress. He thought he had time for a quick adieu before gathering up his hounds for the ride back. Lee bounded up the stairs with the spring and the intent of a schoolboy. His ego had him at the top of his game. Both sides of this conflict viewed him as a pivotal figure, and this sensual young woman was sharing her charms with him, regardless of her other love interests.

Chapter 20

Norton and Lee failed to notice a occasional visitor to Ridley. Root Hog Burns had watched their entire meeting, sipping coffee and genever while looking over the latest edition of the New Jersey Gazette.

As soon as he saw Lee ascend the stairs, Creed headed back to the Brower stable with a sack full of biscuits and a tin of coffee for Beall. Beall had kept watch on the Blue House from the Brower's front portico.

His caution paid off. By unlucky coincidence, a gang of Loyalist cowboys wandered into Ridley to relax. As their boots and hobnails pounded through the mud, Beall counted five tough-looking troublemakers who were obviously up to no good. They ignored the boarding house, focused on reaching the Blue House just down the road.

Beall grew alarmed. In minutes, Creed would face the gang, and he wondered if more were coming, or worse, already in town. Beall needed to distract the men and lure them away, but before he could act, the sound of hounds baying echoed through the hamlet.

***

Lee had just finished his adieu to Jannetje when he heard the hounds. At first, he just grinned. This was not the first time the lads had gotten into mischief.

Van Buskirk, who had been jealously lurking outside the room, suddenly began pounding at the door. "*Mijnheer*, your dogs are loose." He inflected *Mijnheer* with sarcasm. To him, the former English officer was a pig.

Lee adjusted his breeches. "Let them have some fun, you blockheaded Dutchman."

Van Buskirk bristled, but he managed to control the rage he felt at playing the cuckold for king and country. He knew it would not go well with his English masters if something happened to this important gentleman. Then came the dull *pop* of a pistol shot.

One of the servants, sent to prepare Lee's horse, had left the stable door ajar. The hounds barked loudly as they broke free of their confines, and their instincts took hold. The smell of blood and offal was too much for them. Their noses led them towards the scent of the cowboys, whose unwashed bodies stank from weeks of killing and dressing wild game.

***

Once loose on the streets of Ridley, the blood-crazed hounds confronted the first person they encountered, Root Hog Burns.

They circled Creed, who talked softly to the hounds, even as he quietly slipped his sword-bayonet from its scabbard. Fortunately, the pack had a different scent in mind, and after circling Creed a few times, the lead dog turned his nose towards the cowboys, intending to feast on the aroma that permeated its nostrils. The rest of the pack scampered behind.

Barking madly, they circled the cowboys. At first, the cowboys thought it was all so much fun, but they soon realized their error. The lead dog hurled himself on the rankest-smelling cowboy, Slim Demarest, a butcher by trade, who had done the balance of the gang's skinning and gutting. Slim, who was five feet six and nearly two hundred pounds, had neglected to load his musket. So when the lead dog leaped at him, he brandished it like a club. Before he could bring it down, the dog tore into his thigh, toppling him to the ground in pain.

"Heah, aaargh!" Slim rolled, gripping his bloodied leg. The rest of the pack swarmed him as he kicked and screamed in panic.

His companions laughed in amusement until the lead cowboy, Bo Shupe, realized the dogs were tearing him apart piece by piece. "Hey! Quit laughing, boys! They're killing him. Stop 'em now!"

The cowboys began swinging their muskets at the dogs. One hound took a crack across its skull and died instantly. Spado and two others received angry kicks and musket barrels in the ribs and ran off towards the stable, whimpering. But the lead dog was a frenzied mad-eyed alpha and continued to chomp down on Slim, who now had chunks torn from his legs, arms, and torso.

A shot suddenly rang out. With a final yelp, the dog slumped to the road, its blood mixing with Slim's and darkening the cold mud.

Creed shoved the still-smoking pistol into his belt. "Once a dog like that gets a taste of human blood, there's only one way to stop it. Now, you best clean yer friend's wounds and hurry him to a doctor."

Two of the cowboys rushed to check on Slim, who screamed in agony from the exposed shards of fat and blood oozing from his body.

Bo Shupe eyed Creed with obvious suspicion. "Just who are you? Have you been in Ridley before?"

"Name's Root Hog, Root Hog Burns. Been here once or twice before... do I know you?"

"I'm Bo Shupe. Most folks in these parts know me well. These boys and me range the swamp and serve the king himself. Have a warrant and all."

Creed knew he was lying. He had heard the name. Bartholomew "Bo" Shupe led a small but violent gang of cowboys known as the Swamp Pirates. If they worked for the king, it was to plunder in his name and nothing more.

Creed decided to bluff his way past him. "Now, that is a strange coincidence, pardner. So do I. Now you show me your warrant. Then I'll show ya mine."

Creed spied Beall emerging from the boarding house stable yard with horses saddled and ready to go. He also had his Jaeger rifle primed and slung over his right shoulder, ready to bring it down and into action if need be.

"Bo, I've seen him before! He's a friend of Roy Harry!" one of the cowboys suddenly said.

Shupe spat out a wad of cheap tobacco juice. "He is? Then I'll show you the gate to hell first, Root Hog. Get him, boys."

The cowboys tried to circle around Creed, but he moved first and drew his sword bayonet. He took a sudden step toward Shupe, and before the burly ruffian could react, grabbed his musket by its barrel and placed the point of his blade at the cowboy's throat.

Creed rubbed it along his Adam's apple. "Now let me see the lock to that gate to hell, Bo. Better yet, you just come with me and we can talk this over with the constable in Hackensack, or better yet, an English provost. Tell these swamp rats to back off."

Shupe's eyes widened as the blade's point began to break the skin. "Do as he says, boys."

The men needed no more encouragement. Vicious as they were, they were foremost cowards. Creed spun around, holding Shupe between the men and himself. In the background, Slim's screams had subsided into slow moans as shock slowly set in.

Creed relieved Shupe of his musket and shoved him toward his men. "Get your man to a surgeon quick-like before he dies."

They stood watching while Creed slowly stepped back towards Beall. The two leaped to their saddles and spurred their horses up the road and out of Ridley before the cowboys could react.

* * *

General Lee's Headquarters, Pompton, New Jersey
The distant sound of barking dogs shattered the morning silence. Lee had returned. Beall and Creed had come back to Lee's camp at Pompton just before dark. He told Lee's aide they hadn't found the general and would wait for his return after all.

As the yelping grew louder, Creed rolled out of his blanket and stretched. The ground was covered with a thin layer of snow. He looked up at the morning sky. The low clouds indicated more snow was coming. During their ride back to Pompton the previous day, heavy clouds had started to gather. Now, the December weather was cold and damp, chilling him to the bone.

Thomas had risen before the others, fed the horses, and was now saddling them. Elias Parker had already prepared their morning meal, a kind of grueling paste made from flour, water, and whatever else was available. This morning, that meant bits of apple and raisins.

Creed spooned the paste into his mouth and grimaced as he swallowed. "'Tis not Irish oatmeal, but still quite good."

Parker took a spoonful. "It is hot, and it has some nutrition, sir. We eat better than most of the men."

Creed suddenly felt guilty. "You are quite right, Private Parker. Starvation and the cold, along with their inevitable companion, disease, will do more harm to this army than a dozen battalions of British grenadiers."

Creed's men had special access to rations because of the nature of their duties. General Washington had only a modest amount of funds that they could use for various "special" needs. But Creed had permission to use some of it to maintain and sustain his unit without coming to the attention of the commissariat or inquisitive staff officers.

Creed spent the rest of the morning preparing a note for Colonel Fitzgerald. Parker would carry it to army headquarters, now somewhere on the far side of the Delaware River. Creed selected Parker because he was a sailor and a fisherman in civilian life. His experience would help in crossing the river.

***

Charles Lee galloped up to his tent and jumped off his frothing jumper. He angrily handed the reins of his horse to an orderly. His pack, though now reduced to three hounds, seemed just as lively as when they had left a few days earlier. Lee's lead dog and two of his companions had died. Their loss was crushing. He strode into his tent and called for a fresh uniform.

His aide, William Bradford, entered the tent with a wide and engaging smile. "Sir, I assume you got your deer?"

Lee frowned, then turned his head and smirked. "Yes, William, twice, in fact."

The thought of Jannetje as his game pleased him. Lee fancied himself the predator in every way. But then he almost burst into tears. "However, I lost some of the lads... damn it! They were good English stock. I paid ten pounds sterling apiece for them, too. They will be hard to replace around here, sorry to say. At least Spado is okay."

"I am sorry to hear of your loss, sir. The lads are the pride of the division." Bradford appeared undisturbed. "Is there anything I can do, sir?"

"Send me some coffee and some brandy and tell the adjutant to prepare the division to move out at noon, sharp. We can make a few miles before dusk at least."

Bradford scratched his forehead. "Somewhat unusual, sir, to start a march at midday. Have you decided to heed the commander-in-chief's suggestion after all and hasten to join our forces?"

"What? Why... yes... something like that, William. Now get along, if we move out by noon, we can make almost seven miles before dark, almost halfway to Morristown."

"There is one more thing, sir. The messengers from His Excellency are still here. Their officer has a message he says must be delivered to you personally."

In all the excitement, Lee had forgotten one small matter, another urgent plea for him to head south, most likely. Well, now he would meet his purpose, although with a slightly different purpose. "Very well. Send him to me. After you fetch the brandy."

A short time later, Lieutenant Jeremiah Creed stood in front of Major General Charles Lee. Creed had changed back into his Continental Army's blue uniform with white facings and breeches.

Lee did not offer Creed a seat, a tactic intended to emphasize his authority and power. "So, Lieutenant... Creed, is it? I have only a few moments for this chat. The division moves out in less than two hours, and I have much to do."

A strong smell of the brandy came from the general's breath.

"Sir, I have orders to ensure you open and read this letter. Furthermore, I am to assist you in complying with its contents."

Lee's eyes widened at the impertinent comment. He assumed it was another letter from Washington urging him to make haste. "Indeed. Whatever this letter contains, I assure you, Lieutenant, I shall need no such assistance from you in complying… should I decide to comply."

Lee took a jackknife from his desk and slit the edge of the envelope. He clumsily placed a pair of spectacles on his nose and read the note with a show of disinterest. When he finished, he looked up at Creed casually. "You're still here? You may go, Lieutenant. I shall call on you if I need you."

Creed stood fast. "But sir, I believe the contents of that letter require us to repair with you to the main army and…"

Lee's face reddened. He stood up and placed a finger on Creed's chest. Although much shorter than Creed, he was used to directing and bullying larger men. "Now see here, Lieutenant, whether I repair to anywhere is my business. When I do, I shall take my own escort, but for now, my duty is here with my division. Now go, before I ask Captain Bradford to escort you out."

Chapter 21

Southwest of Morristown, New Jersey, December 11th, 1776

Worn shoes tramped for over eight hours, as exhausted men shivered under a sky that shifted between shades of gray and silver, then finally took on the dull appearance of darkened steel in early winter dusk. A damp, chilling cold forced the column to keep moving, but it reduced the number of stragglers and malingerers. All realized that those who fell out would likely die.

General Lee had promised hot food and shelter when they made camp. Bradford shook his head as he observed the companies, mere packs of tired, cold, and hungry scarecrows, filed off the road. *Unfortunately, the promise of warm food is an empty one.*

The men gathered wood for fires and makeshift shelters. The few who had managed to save their meager rations shared what they had with their comrades. Most would face a long, cold night of hunger. A dejected Bradford turned his horse and spurred it up the road to catch up with his general.

Lee didn't linger near the column. Instead, he hurried to the comfort of a small but thriving village in the central highlands of New Jersey. With a patchwork of tidy homes, shops, and a few grand mansions, Morristown felt cozy. While his men shivered, Lee dismounted in front of a ramshackle tavern called the Red Fox Inn. "This will do."

Bradford was surprised at Lee's choice. It was out of character. "But there are other, more convivial inns, as well as homes and mansions, all more appropriate quarters for a major general commanding a division, sir."

Even more surprising, Lee took a sparse room on the ground floor, telling his staff it afforded him easier access to the stable, his hounds, and the privy. Bradford thought it odd and out of character for Lee but gladly shared the better quarters on the second floor with Lieutenant James Wilkinson, Lee's other aide.

***

Sandy Drummond gazed at the ledger with the names of his growing network in the Jerseys. In just a few weeks, he and his men had set up an array of informants from among the Tory populace.

He carefully dipped his nib in the inkwell and scrawled a few notes next to a name:

Solomon Remington, Proprietor, Red Fox Inn.

Drummond's real prey was Mister X, and he now had him in his sights. Lee chose the Red Fox Inn because Digby (Mister Norton) had strongly recommended it. Digby advised Lee that certain patrons at the inn would be Loyalists sent there to protect him in case his activities drew suspicion.

Digby had misled Lee. The only informant at the inn was Remington, who had orders merely to observe Lee and report on him. This phase of Drummond's scheme was a ruse to test Mister X. *Would Lee comply with instructions, and as important, had anyone gained knowledge of his defection?*

Drummond feared the duplicitous Lee might betray his new friends and seize the Loyalist officers. Drummond was becoming more sophisticated in his intelligence work. His crude initial foray into espionage, coercing the hapless attorney Braaf, had yielded almost nothing. Drummond had received only one report from him, and it was very general and vague. *Had Golden Apple been swept along in the swift rebel flight across New Jersey?*

He went to the page in his ledger labeled 'Braaf'. He carefully penned a new comment: *Failure to maintain Contact.*

Fortunately, Drummond started getting useful information from the Loyalist Jersey Dutch and a few Scots-Irish on his payroll. The king's gold helped. Despite losing the wagonload of secret funds, Drummond managed to keep going by taking money from local Whigs who were foolish enough not to escape before the army's advance.

But Drummond instructed Digby to be parsimonious in the distribution of such money. Fortunately, many loyal subjects of the king seemed satisfied with just a few shillings in their pockets. Many were motivated more by loyalty to the crown or by revenge against the Whigs and rebels for grievances, both real and perceived. However, most just wanted to be on the winning side, as a British victory seemed ever more apparent. The civil war among the American factions was something Drummond was quickly learning to exploit.

* * *

Creed shuddered with each gust of cold wind that whistled through the tent flap. While waiting for Parker to return with instructions, he toyed with the idea of simply seizing Lee.

A short time later, the tent flap opened, and Beall squatted next to Creed. "No sign of Elias, sir. "

"Where's Thomas?"

"Loitering near the general's headquarters in case he bolts again. Perhaps we should act without further instruction."

Creed's lips tightened. "Just we three are not enough to overpower Lee's guard. We need to wait for events to unfold."

"Should we send for Mister Harry?"

"I considered that. A half dozen or so Swamp Rangers would do the trick, but we do not have time to wait for them. Yet…"

"Sir?"

Creed scratched his head. "We must think through the situation from Lee's perspective. Why did he delay in complying with His Excellency's request? Colonel Fitzgerald has grave suspicions about Lee's character and motivation. But what if he is wrong? And what will bringing Lee to army headquarters without his division accomplish?"

"Was the meeting in Ridley part of this?"

Creed pondered a moment. "General Lee was commander of American forces in New York before His Excellency arrived. He must certainly have maintained connections of various kinds in New York and New Jersey. Perhaps his own network of spies."

Beall nodded. "That could account for his strange ride to Ridley. "

Creed thought of Jannetje and her amorous and aggressively flirtatious ways. *Could she be his connection? Was this a mere affair of the heart, and Lee's meeting with the strange Briton a coincidence? Should Creed have confronted Jannetje instead of avoiding her?* Creed hoped Fitzgerald had more information to shed light on this.

"Well, Jonathan, I suppose for the time being we stay as close as possible to General Lee and pray Elias returns with word from Colonel Fitzgerald."

* * *

The cramped dining room at the Red Fox Inn smelled of a delightful blend of aromas. Lee and a few of his officers sat at a long plank table situated near the open-hearth fire. Remington had followed his instructions carefully and ensured the general received special treatment during dinner.

Remington personally served him. "For your dining pleasure, General Lee, I have a fine cut of specially selected roast beef cooked to near perfection and served with dark potatoes and some seasonal vegetables."

"Your choice of wine is excellent, Mister Remington. Do you stock many of these?"

"Why no, sir. I have no wine cellar. I cater to a clientele that prefers beer, ale, cider, and stout. However, to please your palate, I purchased several bottles of this Madeira from one of the more sophisticated establishments in town."

Lee took in the bouquet, then sipped it. "Quite passable. You are to be commended. But bring us something stronger to start with."

Remington nodded with a broad smile. "I had the cook prepare a special bread pudding strongly laced with raisins and rum and swimming in fresh heavy cream. I'll do something with the remaining rum."

He did not tell Lee that sated men with full bellies moved sluggishly and proved easier to keep watch on.

"Will General Sullivan join us?" an officer asked as he tore a piece of bread.

His second-in-command, Major General John Sullivan. Sullivan had just been released from British captivity, along with Lord Stirling, in exchange for several captured British officers.

"General Sullivan declined my invitation to dine. He decided to spend the afternoon with the column. I believe he is doing penance for getting captured on Long Island."

The table erupted in guffaws.

True to his word, Remington brought Lee's party a hot toddy to start the meal. Lee raised his cup and, with a mischievous grin, toasted his host. "Now, gentlemen, our good host has prepared us as fine a meal as can be expected in these trying times, or so he has promised..."

The tavern-keeper-turned-spy scowled at the rebel general's crude humor, but he held his composure. He had a job to do. The rum and wine had their effect, and Lee's humor became more offensive as the meal went on.

Remington noted the general's coarser comments were aimed at his commander-in-chief. He also noticed Lee eyeing the tavern's other patrons as the meal progressed, sometimes stretching awkwardly to get a look at each of them. *Is he fearful of his security?*

Every time Lee made a back-handed slur against Washington, he leered knowingly at the other patrons, ignoring his officers. Remington thought this very strange conduct indeed, all of which he planned to put in his report.

Throughout the meal, Lieutenant Wilkinson, whom Lee referred to as Wilkie, paid particularly sycophantic heed to his superior. The others, including the aide called Bradford, discoursed and even argued, albeit politely, with their general. But Wilkie assented to even the most asinine postulations by his superior. *He's got his nose all but up the general's arse,* Remington thought.

By the time the platters emptied, Lee and his staff were well into their cups. Remington listened to the ever-thickening tongues wag.

"Gentlemen, it is time to discuss certain matters. It seems that various individuals are showing a keen interest in my talents. I have received correspondence from the army headquarters requiring my presence there. The implication is that our commander-in-chief's competence has been questioned by some of the more astute members of Congress. To protect himself, His Excellency, as they foolishly call him, is seeking my presence and advice. Lee hiccupped, then took another sip of the Madeira. "My God, this is good."

His eyes shifted around the tavern. The room was empty of the other patrons, and Lee grew bolder. "Now it seems, and this is strictly confidential, gentlemen, certain other factions have also shown an interest in my counsel, perhaps to a purpose that could end this war on reasonable terms."

From behind a cracked door, Remington's heart pounded with excitement. *What subterfuge is this?*

Jaws dropped, and the officers grew silent. Lee gazed around the table. His eyes took on a wolfish look as he assessed his men for their reaction. The officers, caught up in the drink, the frustrations from three months of defeat, and the sheer inability to ponder their situation, began to nod, one by one, their assent.

"This is not what you may think, gentlemen. I plan to talk with these people merely to gauge their plans and thoughts. Perhaps they are ready to accede to our national aspirations or concede the rights we have fought so long and hard to secure. Still, they cannot be completely trusted, and we must prepare a second course of action."

Remington could not believe his ears. *They'll never believe my report.*

One of the colonels at the table, a stout planter from Virginia, an actual neighbor of Lee, bluntly asked the obvious question, "Sir, what exactly do you plan to do?"

Lee cast his eyes around the dining room. He bent his chin to his chest, and his dark, bushy eyebrows closed together in a conspiratorial tone. "First, I shall place the entire division into good defensive positions here in these very highlands. This army cannot face British regulars in the field. If they do not offer us terms I deem acceptable, we shall prepare a flank march and return north into winter quarters."

The officers looked at one another, each trying to gauge the appropriate reaction.

"And then?" his onetime neighbor asked.

"I shall parlay!"

Bradford made the sole dissenting comment, "But sir, we have, you have, written orders to move the division with all haste and join General Washington for the defense of Philadelphia…"

Behind the door, Remington bit his lip. *They reveal much in their cups.*

Lee's face turned purple with rage. "General Washington's orders be damned!"

Immediately realizing the impropriety of his outburst, even among his closest staff, Lee composed himself, looking around the room a few times to make sure nobody else heard him.

After a long pause, the one Lee called Wilkie spoke, "I dare say, sir, your plan is magnificent! The British will never allow such a threat to their communications. We could lure them into another Breed's Hill and save the cause... pure genius…"

The others mumbled their agreement, except for Bradford.

Lee shook his head with a sneaky grin. "We can never beat the professionals of the British Army. Our only hope is that they proceed slowly against us and then go to winter quarters. We can end the campaign pretending to have a victory in front of Congress and make up for the incompetence shown by Mister Washington since I turned over command to him at New York."

The eyes of all around the table bulged wide at the last comment. The British refused to recognize the new nation and its new army. Therefore, they referred to the commander-in-chief as "Mister Washington" rather than "General." Washington and his staff were very sensitive to the affront. Even his closest confidantes found Lee's comments to be very poor taste.

Solomon Remington had heard enough. He pushed open the door and stepped up to the table with another bottle of rum and a pot of coffee. "My compliments, general. I thought this would end your evening on a warm note and help drive out the chill in your bones."

***

By five, the staff had finished dinner and departed to attend to various duties. Lee retreated to his modest room to handle his correspondence. He penned letters to each brigade commander, his adjutant, and his quartermaster. Satisfied with his work, he pulled a map from his saddlebag and spread it out on the table. He glanced at the crude markings. American maps are nearly useless. He marked the spot where he thought the division was, then slowly ran his finger along the curving line marking his route. His finger stopped at a solid dot with the letters BR next to it.

A knock at the door interrupted his work. Lee hastily folded up the map and stowed it in his saddlebag. When he looked up, both of his aides stood in front of him.

"What is it?"

Bradford stammered, "General Sullivan wishes to discuss…"

Wilkinson cut him off brusquely. "Sullivan demands to see you immediately! I told him a meeting with you this evening was out of the question."

The sound of boots pounding on the stairs was followed by the door slamming open. Sullivan stormed into the room, shoved the two men aside, and shut the door behind him. Now, he and Lee were alone.

Lee grew indignant. "What is the meaning of this intrusion, General Sullivan?"

Sullivan, a man of a frequently violent temper, responded with a surprisingly subdued demeanor. "General Lee, while you sat here all afternoon, isolated from your men's discomfort, I've found enough provisions to keep the division viable for another day or two. I've gathered enough stragglers to form a regiment, and considering the weather, have done as much as possible to protect them from the elements."

Lee's face lit up. He realized that Sullivan's experience during the failed winter attack on Quebec in 1775 gave him skills he could use to his advantage this winter. He needed Sullivan to lift the men's spirits and keep the division together until his big meeting. Another march would bring him close enough to slip away to BR and possibly alter the course of North America.

A sense of power and a rush of adrenaline overwhelmed him. "You are quite right, General Sullivan, please forgive me. Now, tell me more about what we have accomplished…"

Chapter 22

Washington's Headquarters, Yardley, Pennsylvania, December 11th, 1776

Colonel Fitzgerald's face tightened, and his eyes shifted away from Creed's note. His clever plan to trap General Lee had fallen apart. Fitzgerald had to admit defeat in his attempt to lure Lee and his forces back to the army.

He looked up at Parker. "Well, it pleases me to learn that Lee's three thousand men had finally begun the march across New Jersey. The question now is whether we can achieve a junction in time to prevent a British move across the Delaware."

Congress had fled Philadelphia for the safety of Baltimore, leaving Washington with a mandate authorizing him to do "whatever he deemed necessary" to save the new nation in its hour of peril. They had given the commander-in-chief essentially dictatorial powers. But Washington needed supplies and men, not a mandate, to prevent final defeat.

Fitzgerald tapped his nib against the side of the desk and waved it over the dull flame of the candle to warm the ink enough to flow. The cold morning temperature affected more than the ink's viscosity; his hands numb easily. Fitzgerald had picked up a touch of frostbite during the march south. He chuckled to himself—even mundane paperwork had its hazards. When he finished the note, he folded it and sealed it in an opaque envelope for Parker to take back to Creed. "This must be delivered to Lieutenant Creed immediately."

"Yes, s-sir." Parker's teeth were chattering.

"Parker, you are wet and cold. What happened? As urgent as this is, you must warm and dry yourself and your horse before returning."

"I found no serviceable boats on the east bank of the Delaware. "

"General Washington had ordered every available craft seized and taken across to the west or destroyed. How did you cross?"

"I patched together a damaged skiff I found and poled across the river, my horse in tow. The water was flowing quickly, and there was ice. As we neared the far bank, however, the strong and erratic current caused the boat to spin. I soon lost control and the skiff shattered on some rocks."

"My God, Parker, how did you get over?"

"Had to swim the panicked horse the last twelve yards. He kicked wildly, but I managed to get us to shore safely."

A few hours later, Parker returned to Fitzgerald's room for the letter.

Fitzgerald pulled off his spectacles and peered at him. "Tell Lieutenant Creed his original orders have changed. With General Lee's division now moving to join us, Lee's presence is no longer required here. So long as he makes sufficient progress in our direction. In the meantime, His Excellency wants to take advantage of your time in New Jersey to bring him a report on British and Tory activity there. The specifics are contained herein."

Parker placed the letter in his vest pocket. "Yes, sir! With luck, I shall have the letter in Lieutenant Creed's hands by tonight."

Fitzgerald smiled grimly. "Indeed, Private Parker. Knowing Mister Creed, he could be anywhere between Trenton and New York."

* * *

The Cole House, north of Brunswick, New Jersey, December 12th, 1776

The clock on the mantel struck one a.m. Sandy Drummond sat in his night robe, a warm quilt wrapped around his shoulders and a featherbed comforter covering his legs. His bad knee ached more often and more deeply since the weather had turned cold. Sergeant Digby, now back in the red jacket of a British dragoon sergeant, stood patiently by the fireplace. When the British arrived at Brunswick, Drummond took over the small house as his command post. Its Whig owner had fled, making it conveniently available.

"Can we trust this… Remington's… report, Sergeant Digby?"

Digby smiled. "He's honest as a vicar if I can be so bold."

Drummond smiled wryly. "Hmmm, not much comfort there."

"Sir, I met personally with Remington, who reported on Mister X's activities at the Red Fox Inn. The innkeeper was paid well. He risked a hard and cold ride in the dark to render his report."

"When does Trooper Quaif return from New York? He was to bring General Howe's letter providing me the authority to request other forces to support the plan."

Digby frowned. "He should have been here this morning, sir. I suppose the weather has delayed him."

"Well, I suppose the plan must go forward with just you and Brent. Meanwhile, I'm meeting with Captain Baker early tomorrow. Did Remington confirm tomorrow's activity?"

"Yes, he did indeed, sir. Mister X will slip away from his division tomorrow, sometime before noon. He shall go to Basking Ridge and prepare for a meeting with the… distinguished gentlemen."

Drummond smiled. "Excellent! Excellent! I tell you, Digby, if I can recruit this officer to our cause, the possibilities are endless. The value of the information he could provide might seal the rebels' fate. Why, he could influence military decisions in our favor, if not by our direction. He could influence the politicians."

Drummond lowered his voice, "And then, if something were to happen to Mister Washington, we would control the fate of these hapless rebels."

They reviewed Drummond's plan once again, then Digby left to get a few hours of sleep. But Sandy Drummond couldn't sleep. His aching knee kept throbbing. He pulled himself across the bed and reached into the bag on a pine end table. He grabbed a small bottle and took two long swigs of the special elixir provided by the surgeons. He believed it helped him think more clearly and see things others couldn't. Slowly and easily, he drifted into a dream state, awaiting the next day.

* * *

Basking Ridge, New Jersey

The heavy hooves thudded along the half-frozen road that twisted through hills dotted with bare trees. Captain Sidney Baker raised a gloved fist and stopped his small band of Loyalist volunteers. "Basking Ridge is just up ahead. We'll walk the horses into town from here."

Drummond chose the thirty-year-old merchant from Liberty Pole, New Jersey, along with his Loyalist Provincials, to act as couriers and to identify or recruit potential informants among Tories and Whigs. They also helped in searching for spies and carried out other "special" duties. Baker was chosen because he knew people and the Jerseys well, having spent years traveling to buy and sell goods across the colony. Additionally, he had connections with both Tories and Whigs, which was another valuable trait.

The three hand-picked men, sergeants from the New Jersey Volunteers, rode with Baker. Baker left a fourth in Hackensack. Dierk Van Buskirk was never truly his choice. Baker hated him. But he was pressured by Colonel Abraham van Buskirk to choose his rebellious nephew for the special unit. Baker was aware that the elder Van Buskirk hoped his nephew's nefarious activities would stay hidden from the public.

Baker's orders were simple. Take his men to Basking Ridge and establish himself in the home of a friendly Loyalist sympathizer. From there, his men would keep watch on a "gentleman" of interest.

The early afternoon sun was shining weakly, its rays barely warming the day. Their horses moved slowly into Basking Ridge. Little neat homes, built from brick, stone, or wood, lined each side of the main road. The hamlet had two taverns and a couple of shops on the main green, which also featured a small, whitewashed Presbyterian church. From his business travels through the area, Baker knew several merchants in the town.

Their arrival went unnoticed. Many British and Loyalist patrols had already moved through over the past few days. Baker and his men pulled up in front of the appointed home where a friendly boy of fourteen greeted them.

"That place, the MacTavish house, young man?" Baker casually pointed down the road.

The boy squinted at them with myopic eyes, straining. "Why, yessir. Different name now, though—White's Tavern. You must be the men we wuz told of. My name is Dick. Been told to care for your horses. You can go right in. I expect Jammy has food-waitin'."

The green jackets swung out of their saddles. They slid their muskets over their shoulders and secured their sabers around their waists. Dick led the horses around back to the stables.

Jammy, an indentured servant from Scotland whose real name was Jemma, greeted them at the door. She curtseyed, holding the folds in her white apron. "Now, you gentlemen just come right in. Dinner is ready."

She led them into a large parlor that had a dining room table set for three. Exhausted, the men sat down without a word and feasted on baked chicken and sweet potatoes. Black coffee was the beverage of choice.

When they had finished, Baker gave his men their instructions. "We have orders to keep a watch on the place Dick called, White's Tavern. It's at the edge of town, less than a quarter-mile from here. I stayed there years ago. A two-story clapboard building painted off-white and framed with dark red trim and shutters. You'll take turns on watch. And call me if you see something unusual."

"What would be unusual, sir?" another of his men asked.

"Rebel soldiers," Baker replied tersely. He could not tell them the real reason.

"Rebels here?"

"Yes, the place is owned by the Widow White."

"She a Whig?"

Baker shook his head. "I don't know. But we are to watch her place. We are looking for a rebel officer. A senior officer. That's all I'll say right now."

Baker's men found a discreet observation point from which to observe the tavern's comings and goings.

Drummond's orders required Baker to await his arrival and to send a message if Mister X arrived early or was accompanied by his staff. Drummond planned to meet Mister X on the morning of the thirteenth. The message was to state the number accompanying him, the party's location, and how they were armed.

* * *

Lee's forces had struggled to walk even a few miles by dusk. His tired and hungry men shivered as they trudged along the now frozen road. With each passing day, winter's cold wrapped them tighter in its ever-tightening grip.

Lee did not ride with his command. Instead, he rode alone, accompanied by a small, mounted escort chosen for loyalty. His plan was ready to unfold. But now that his moment had arrived, his mind wavered and twisted with doubt. He had agreed to meet the distinguished men he believed were high-ranking British officers seeking talks.

One of his escorts, James Wilkinson, cunningly engaged his commander as they rode. "Sir, what is your plan? Do we engage or retreat?"

Lee confided in Wilkinson, who appeared interested in him. "I can only tell you this, Wilkie, while Washington wants our forces to save Philadelphia and earn accolades. I want our forces to save New Jersey. We'll earn our own laurels."

Wilkinson drew a breath. "We'll fight the British on our own, here in New Jersey?"

Lee laughed. "Not at all, my dear Wilkie. No American force could, under any circumstances, defeat the British in a pitched battle. Yet if I abandon the state, I might be held responsible for its permanent loss. Still, it is possible to make a stand without a full engagement."

"So, you plan a bluff of sorts, to throw them off their plans?"

"Of sorts. If I were only commanding the whole army…"

Wilkinson's eyes narrowed. "It is clear to most officers no one but you should command the…"

Ahead, they saw a rider coming at the trot. The man wore a blue coat and knee-length boots. A young captain from one of the lead regiments pulled up on the reins when he realized he had found the division commander.

The officer doffed his hat. "Sir, General Sullivan requests you ride forward and select the direction of march."

"Direction? What do you mean?"

"The road ahead divides. One branch turns towards Pluckemin. The other continues west towards Chester and Pennsylvania."

Lee hesitated. If he continued towards Pluckemin, he might eventually come across the British. He could not afford that before reaching an accommodation with the distinguished gentlemen. "Have scouts been down that road, Captain?"

Lee was stalling as he pondered his decision.

"Captain Tether, sir. No, sir…"

"Moving west towards Chester would bring us closer to General Washington, sir," Wilkinson whispered.

Lee tried to come up with the best response. He thought he might decide to return to where he came. Until he had his meeting with the distinguished gentlemen, he would not commit his army to a given direction.

"We shall use neither road this day, Captain Tether. Tell General Sullivan to establish camp near the fork. I'm moving with my staff to Basking Ridge to spend the night. We shall proceed sometime tomorrow. Until then, he must be prepared to move the column in any direction."

Dumbfounded, Tether turned his horse back towards the head of the column.

Bradford had sat patiently on his horse during the exchange. "Sir, this comes as somewhat of a surprise. I have not made plans to reconnoiter the town to find a suitable establishment."

Lee merely tugged at his jumper's reins, turning back toward Basking Ridge. "No need for that, William. There is a place at the edge of the town called White's Tavern. We will stay there tonight. "

"But that's miles from the division, sir."

"Yes, and the sooner we get there, the better. I have much correspondence to which to attend."

* * *

Creed sat astride Finn, beside Sullivan, studying a map.

"I'm pleased you've seconded yourself to me, Lieutenant Creed. Your map seems more accurate than mine."

The two had met briefly during the brutal fight with the Hessians on Long Island, where Sullivan had the unlucky task of holding the passes against the British thrust. But he neglected to defend the vital Jamaica Pass. The British encirclement soon cut off Sullivan's force, and the brave but tempestuous Sullivan was captured.

Creed placed a finger along the road towards Pluckemin. "The road south leads towards British outposts. They are no more than twelve miles distant. If General Lee attacks down this road now, he may well succeed in collapsing their supply line."

"Risk a fight with our forces divided? His Excellency would disapprove. He's counting on these men."

"'Tis but an option, not a recommendation. Surprise figures large in successful military campaigns."

Sullivan shook his head ruefully. "General Washington needs reinforcements. Let's hope General Lee orders the division to take the westerly road. It's the fastest route to Pennsylvania. Despite these conditions, the boys still fight within them. But we must join His Excellency and fight as a united force—not take on the British piecemeal."

Captain Tether pulled up beside them. His mount snorted, and a light vapor puffed from its nostrils. They could see from his face that the news from Lee was not what Sullivan wanted to hear.

When Tether relayed Lee's instructions, Sullivan glowered. Since rejoining the army, he had many occasions to hold his temper when it came to Lee's curious and mercurial actions.

Sullivan folded the map and handed it back to Creed. "Well, it is late. And, if we get an early start tomorrow, this may prove a reasonable decision."

Creed shook his head. "Sir, remaining here is the worst option. If the British decide to attack while we tarry, this force could be destroyed. Either move on their supply line or head west and join with the rest of the army."

Creed's boldness intrigued Sullivan. He knew nothing of Creed's special status or that he had Washington's trust. As far as Sullivan knew, Creed was a brave and talented young light infantry officer serving as a mounted courier.

He eyed Creed cautiously. "You seem to have a knack for grand strategy, Mister Creed. Maybe you should continue this discussion with the good General Lee. Basking Ridge is only seven miles away..."

"I don't think he would appreciate my advice, nor my presence, as much as you do, sir."

Sullivan threw back his head and laughed. "True enough! But once the regiments are in bivouac, I want you to guide a small detachment from the 11th New Jersey Militia a mile down the road toward Pluckemin."

Sullivan gestured west. "They will be our advance guard for the march, should that be General Lee's decision."

"And if his decision is not to march on Pluckemin?"

Sullivan's face darkened. "Doesn't matter what he says. That shall be our line of march."

* * *

Baker felt a gentle tug on his arm. The fire in the small hearth beside him had faded as the evening went on, and the room felt chilly. He opened his eyes and looked up into Jammy's large gray eyes.

"Captain, your soldier said I should come to wake you," Jammy whispered. "Rebel officers just rode into town. They went back to the…"

Baker smiled. "I know where they went. Thank you, Jammy. What time is it now?"

Baker had broken his timepiece and, in the exigencies of the campaign, had yet to have it repaired.

"Just after seven, sir. "

"When did they arrive?"

"Around six."

"Then I need to go." He needed to assess the situation and report back to Drummond. Baker hurriedly pulled on his boots and grabbed his saber. He headed towards the door.

"You might need this tonight, sir." Jammy stood holding his heavy cloak. "The temperature has dropped again, and it feels like it might snow."

"Thank you, Jammy."

She pulled the coat around his shoulders.

"Will you be back tonight?" she asked softly.

Without answering, he stepped out into the cold evening. The less she knew, the better.

Chapter 23

The Cole House, Midnight, December 13th, 1776

A roaring fire filled the room with heat as intensely as the cold outside. Drummond paced the room, dragging his game leg as he desperately considered his approach with Lord Cornwallis.

Trooper Quaif had finally returned with new orders from General Howe—bad news. Howe unexpectedly directed Drummond to call off the plan if there was the least chance the Americans knew of Lee's dialogue with them. But Drummond had invested too much in the Mister X plot. So now he had to convince Cornwallis, the senior officer in the Jerseys, to carry on, regardless of the risk.

He stopped and turned. "Now tell me again, Sidney, exactly how many men did you observe at White's Tavern?"

Baker gripped a hot toddy of rum mixed with warm water, butter, and brown sugar. He and one of his men had ridden more than three hours through the cold and dark to meet with his British spymaster. Baker hesitated, stirring the toddy with his finger. "Perhaps a dozen or so… several officers. Maybe a half dozen armed escorts. Because of the darkness, I cannot be too precise."

Drummond felt a sharp pain in his knee. The pacing did no good. "Of course, Sidney. How many sentries did they place? Did they act as though they were concerned with anything out of the ordinary?"

Baker's eyes widened. "Why, sir, they didn't even place one guard at the tavern door. Four or so of the men, I suppose now your Mister X and his staff, went into the tavern proper. The rest took shelter from the cold in the stables. It was too late to start a fire or pitch tents."

Drummond threw himself on a chair across from Baker and clasped his knee with both hands. "I am going to assume, for purposes of our planning, that Mister X has not betrayed us. That the rebels have no trap set for us."

Baker dabbed his finger in the toddy and then sucked on it. "Well, sir, your General Lee, rather, Mister X, is rather unpredictable, in my humble estimation. You should prepare for either eventuality."

The remark stirred Drummond's interest. He relaxed his grip on his knee and leaned forward attentively. "How so, Sidney?"

Baker stirred the toddy and then downed the drink in one swallow. He looked blandly at Drummond and smiled. "Seize him and seize the moment. Once he's in your custody, this plot can be made to unfold in any way you desire."

Drummond scowled – but then his face slowly broke into a devious smile. "I say, Sidney, you have a way of putting things quite to the point. Must be your business acumen, eh? Seize the day. Seize the general. Seal the deal. And quite to the point. General Howe wants little risk, and I want Mister X. As they say – a confluence of interest."

* * *

By eight in the morning, the regiments had risen and formed into lines for another day of tough, cold marching with little food. Creed's men were ready too. Their horses were saddled and packed. Creed and Beall had spent most of the night checking on the units on watch. Sullivan was worried about British patrols and wanted to get an early warning in case of a surprise attack.

At half-past nine, Captain Tether, greatcoat flapping in the wind, strode up to them. He looked exasperated. "Mister Creed, General Sullivan requests the courtesy of a word with you."

"Yes, sir, and that would be what word, sir?"

Tether's face darkened. "Marching orders from General Lee arrived an hour ago. The regiments are ready to move. General Sullivan would like you to carry a message to General Lee."

Creed drew his saber and a pistol. And at the last moment, his Jaeger rifle. "Thomas, take the pack horses and wait for us on the main road. Private Parker should return soon. Be on the watch for him."

Beall and Creed guided their horses along the trail to meet Sullivan. The road was already crowded with groups of men. Creed thought they looked prepared to march or fight, despite the hardships they've faced. For that, Lee had Sullivan to thank.

* * *

White's Tavern, Basking Ridge, New Jersey, December 13th, 1776

Ebenezer White's widow, Mary, ran a respectable establishment. Since her husband's death, it had become less profitable because she, unlike her husband, had little patience for the late-night carousing that often took place. Located at the southeast edge of town, travelers from Perth Amboy, Brunswick, and points south and east frequently stayed there. Strangely enough, there were no other guests when General Lee and his entourage arrived late the night before.

The general claimed the best room in the tavern for himself and his yelping hounds. He demanded a joint of ham, which he did not share with his fellow officers but kept some for his dogs. Lee was expecting the distinguished gentlemen to arrive mid-morning. He told his orderly to wake him early enough to prepare for the event.

Before he turned in, Wilkinson knocked on the door to his room. "You sent or me, sir?"

The door closed, and Lee gazed into the fireplace, gathering his thoughts. He then turned and smiled. "Wilkie, I asked you here to entrust you with our plans. Of all my staff, you show the most promise, my boy."

Wilkinson's lips pursed in an oily smile. "Thank you, sir. I would lay down my life for you and our cause with equal fervor."

Lee eyed him craftily. "Equal?"

Wilkinson flushed. "Well, sir, equal fervor but not equal devotion."

Lee smiled. "Of course, your loyalty is unquestioned, Wilkie. To the cause or me."

"Are they any different?"

"No, Wilkie, they are not."

"Then, what is your wish, sir?"

Lee nervously rubbed his hands together. "I have arranged a rendezvous with a pair of Tory spies who have news of the location of the British forces."

Wilkinson's face brightened. "So, your hunting trip…"

Wilkie believes me. Lee nodded with a devious smile. "Now, establish a cordon around the tavern at dawn. However, to ensure my visitors get through, they are to allow civilians to stop at the tavern. "

The stage was set. Now, Lee hoped Mister Norton and his friends would arrive on time.

Shortly after eight the next morning, Captain Bradford entered the general's room. He found the general still in his robe. "Sir, your instructions have been sent to General Sullivan. Should I make your horse ready for the march?"

"Not just yet, William. I am meeting with Tory informants, whom I expect to meet shortly. Meanwhile, I have more correspondence to finish. But do send up Widow White with another pot of coffee."

Lee could tell Bradford did not like the idea of a senior officer meeting with recalcitrant Tories or any other informers. The young officer, a lawyer from Pennsylvania, was a politically active idealist.

Bradford looked disapprovingly at Lee. "Very well, sir, but I must say we would better serve the division by marching with it now and corresponding later."

Lee ignored the rebuff. Bradford left the room, closing the door behind him.

Once alone, Lee removed a piece of paper from his portfolio and sat at the small table near the window. He dipped the nib of his pen into a small jar of black ink. He began to finish a letter to one of his intimate correspondents and fellow disparager of His Excellency, Major General Horatio Gates.

…The ingenious maneuver of Fort Washington has unhinged the goodly fabric we had been building. There was never so damned a stroke. Between us, a certain 'great man' is most damnably deficient. He has thrown me into a situation where I have my choice of difficulties: if I stay in this province, I risk myself and army, and if I do not stay, the province is lost forever… In short, unless something which I do not expect turns up, we are lost…

I Remain, as Always,
Your Humble and Obedient Servant

C. Lee

Lee sealed the letter and sent it off immediately with Gates' courier, who had arrived the previous day. A knock on the door interrupted his next letter, which Lee planned to send to Thomas Mifflin, another officer unhappy with Washington and a leader among the small group of officers who believed Lee should command the army.

Widow White's grating voice came through the door. "I have something for you, sir."

"Do come in, Widow White."

Widow White carried a tray with a pot of steaming coffee. "Ah, General, your young man requested this on your behalf. I added some scones, thinking you might still be hungry."

"Scones? How delightful! Well, thank you, mum."

She placed a cup on the table and poured the coffee with a forced smile. "Cream and sugar, sir?"

"No, black is fine, Mum."

"General, I overheard one of your officers say that you expect guests here. Is that true?"

Lee was not pleased that this woman had eavesdropped, but he smiled pleasantly. "Why yes, Mum."

"Would you like me to prepare a nice lunch for you and your guests then? You know, General, some forewarning would be nice when guests arrive here. I prefer to be prepared for such occasions."

Lee hid his annoyance and smiled patronizingly. "I'm sorry I didn't inform you in advance, Mum. Military matters have kept me quite busy, as you know. But no, a meal will not be necessary. We shall have a small business meeting and be on our way by noon if all goes well. But something for the lads might be nice."

The Widow White, duly chastised, glanced over at the hounds sleeping by the open fire. Then, tightly pursing her lips, she shuffled out the door.

* * *

The icy ground thundered with the sound of pounding hooves. Sandy Drummond and Sidney Baker led the column, followed by Sergeant Digby, with Troopers Trent and Quaif. Quaif finally returned from New York with Howe's guidance, which Drummond found ambiguous. Briefly, it advised him to do what he thought best but made it clear he was responsible for the consequences of the enterprise.

After reviewing the contents, Drummond met with Cornwallis and informed the general of his plan to capture Lee instead of attempting to recruit him and keep him in place as an agent for the British high command. "Lee is expecting to meet with his co-conspirators. Instead, he will face a court-martial for treason."

Cornwallis, a soldier and a man not inclined toward conspiracies and all that came with them, readily agreed. "Very well, Sandy. This is much sounder than the deception you initially considered. But I must insist Colonel Harcourt take overall command of the operation. You may accompany him and help."

This hurt Drummond. His disappointment and anger were obvious. Lieutenant Colonel William Harcourt led the 16th Light Dragoons, the other dragoon regiment in

North America. Before his knee injury, Drummond had once aimed to command it. In another twist of irony, Harcourt had briefly served under Lee in Portugal.

Cornwallis tried to make things easier for Drummond. "Of course, Sandy, once he is securely in our custody, you shall have control of the prisoner. Harcourt's cavalry will capture him and get him back to our lines."

Drummond's voice thickened, "Milord, I feel up to the task of leading such an enterprise, especially as I conceived and planned it!"

Cornwallis stiffened. "You are still an officer in the army, Sandy. Regardless of the special work you do for General Howe, you will follow orders. If this causes you trouble, I suggest you ride back to New York."

"But General Howe…"

"Is in New York, Sandy. I command here."

Harcourt and his troopers followed Drummond's men in a line of two abreast. The cold, gray dawn gradually gave way to a pale pink light. Surrounding them were bare trees and brown fields, but the countryside looked somehow picturesque with its rolling hills interrupted by frozen streams and crowned with the numerous woods of a piedmont that slowly embraced the low-lying mountains dividing New Jersey.

They rode first toward Morristown to hide their true destination from enemy spies. Along the way, they encountered two rebel soldiers, militiamen, trying to make their way home—deserters. It took little effort from Drummond's experienced troopers for the men to confirm that Lee's division was on the move. The question now was whether Mister X would still avail himself of the meeting with the "distinguished" gentlemen.

Drummond turned back to report the news to Harcourt, who rode at the head of his dragoons.

Harcourt let the reins drop across the saddle's pommel. "Excellent work, Sandy. The question now is whether your Mister X will still be at the meeting place. What is the name of it?"

"White's Tavern, sir."

Harcourt fumbled for his pipe. "Yes…White's Tavern. It seems such a tawdry place to dally."

Drummond realized Harcourt was unenthusiastic about the mission, which he believed was beneath his dignity as an officer and gentleman. This was Drummond's opportunity to claim control of what was rightfully his enterprise.

"Sir, I recommend we rest the men and horses here while scouts go forward to ascertain whether Mister X still awaits us."

Harcourt puffed at the pipe. "Who will you send?"

"Captain Baker knows the area, and more importantly, the location of White's Tavern."

Harcourt raised his stirrups and looked through a spyglass at the woods behind Drummond. "Very well, Sandy. But I'd like Lieutenant Tarleton to come along too. He's an up-and-coming young guy and eager to prove himself – get some action, so to speak."

S.W. O'Connell

Banastre Tarleton was a twenty-two-year-old lieutenant serving as brigade major, the staff coordinator of cavalry for the commanding general. The position gave him some prominence, considerable influence, and as much opportunity to see action as he desired. Though short, Tarleton, with his shock of red hair, had a lively presence that caused Harcourt to call on his services whenever special cavalry actions arose. Now he was assigned to the very important mission to seize Mister X.

Drummond concealed his disdain for Harcourt's affectation as well as the intrusion into his affairs. He nodded in agreement. Without further discussion, the Loyalist American and the British staff officer rode ahead to find the disloyal Briton who fancied himself the savior of both causes.

***

The pair of riders urged their horses over streams and fences, each vying for the lead. Steam was pouring from the noses of horses and men alike. The pounding of hooves and panting of the mounts were the only sounds as Baker finally edged into the lead. He soon led Tarleton to a small promontory that overlooked Basking Ridge, where they dismounted. Even without spyglasses, they could see rebel soldiers near White's Tavern.

"There they are. I count perhaps six. Armed, but don't appear particularly alert. They do not seem to expect trouble today," Baker said.

"Most are standing around and chatting amongst themselves. Doesn't surprise me. Most Americans are indolent."

Baker bristled. "There are probably more in the stable, and perhaps in the house or the orchard. My men saw a half-dozen, but, of course, it was dark. There might be more of them."

Tarleton pulled a leather notebook from his saddlebag and spent a few minutes sketching the area around the house, noting the buildings and the positions of the rebel soldiers. After finishing, he placed the book back in the saddlebag and mounted.

Tarleton smiled at Baker knowingly. "Always good to have a map, Baker, even a homemade one. When one engages an armed foe, it is a distinct advantage to know and understand the terrain. Now, let's get some of the lads and take this Mister X of yours."

* * *

The clock over the mantel chimed ten. Lee had finished the last of his correspondence. He just decided to don his uniform while he waited for his visitors. As he stood in front of the dressing mirror in his night robe, he thought over the situation. He was growing impatient. If the "distinguished" gentlemen did not arrive soon, the game might be up.

The *crack* of musket fire shouted commands, and the thundering of hooves suddenly broke into Lee's thoughts. Twenty-five troopers in red jackets, led by Tarleton, raced up the road from the south and spread out into the woods and orchard around the tavern.

Several of Lee's guards let loose a few rounds at the attackers, but their lead was wasted. Lee watched with disbelief from his upstairs window as two of his escorts quickly went down to the British fire. One screamed for his mother as a carbine musket ball shattered his breastbone, spraying blood over his tunic. The other took a belly shot from another carbine and rolled on the ground, grunting as he tried to staunch the ooze of blood and gore from the hole below his navel.

A squad of six dragoons, sabers glinting in the morning sun, stormed the compound and quickly subdued the remaining guards in a flash of steel on steel. One defender, whose cries for quarter fell on deaf ears, had his arm severed by two blows from a burly dragoon corporal.

"Try raising your weapon now, rebel scum!" the corporal responded coldly to the man's desperate plea.

A few guards and some of Lee's officers locked themselves inside the house, and soon musket barrels appeared at the windows.

Tarleton jumped from his saddle, drew his pistol and saber, and shouted like a hellion, "Dismount! Surround the building and fire at the windows! Kill all who resist!"

The *pop, pop* of the short, light dragoon carbines filled the air. The tepid return fire did not disturb the troopers. They knew their quarry was in the bag.

The front door suddenly flew open, and the widow White emerged, wringing her hands and crying for mercy. "Please, sir, I am a loyal subject of His Majesty, spare me and my home, 'tis all I have."

"Where is your guest, madame?" Tarleton demanded.

"The man you want, that rebel General Lee, is inside. He's upstairs in a nightgown!"

Tarleton gazed at the upper window. "There is no escape for rebels this day! Surrender at once, or I shall fire the house and enjoy watching your damned hides roast!"

At first, Lee was confused, but now he was convinced the distinguished gentlemen had decided on capturing him as a cover for their discourse. Deciding appearances had been satisfied, Lee gave his final order to his men. "It is all right, boys, honor is served. We must now submit."

Lee stormed down the stairs and stepped out onto the porch, his night robe blowing in the breeze. "I am Major General Charles Lee of the Continental Army, formerly of His Majesty's Royal Army. I submit to your gallant arms and trust I will be treated as a proper gentleman. I merely request mercy for my staff and time to change into a proper uniform."

Tarleton scoffed, "You are no general, and there is no such army, and thus you have no need for a uniform. Take him!"

The troopers hesitated for a moment.

Tarleton grew red-faced. He snarled, then roared in a rage. "He is a bloody rebel! Take him!"

The dragoon corporal sheathed his blood-soaked saber and seized Lee with his big, leather-gloved hands.

Lee's eyes widened. "I must protest. This is most…"

Quaif and Brent stepped forward to assist the corporal. One of them grabbed the reins of a black mare standing saddled by the house — Wilkinson's horse. The three lifted Lee onto the horse like a sack of flour.

Lee sputtered in surprise when he saw Digby in uniform. "Why, why, Mister Norton, you humbugged me! I expected you this morning, but not with this many distinguished gentlemen!"

Digby shot an evil grin. "It's Digby now, sir. Sergeant Digby, of his majesty's dragoons. But I expect you will get to meet plenty of distinguished gentlemen right soon enough, sir."

Tarleton slipped his boots into their spurs and waved a gloved fist. "Let's return with our game, lads!"

More troopers emerged from the woods and galloped down the lane. One, a young trumpeter, brought his bugle to his lips and sounded the recall. The thundering of hooves once again filled the air, now mixed with cheers as the column moved south like a crimson snake.

In less than fifteen minutes, the second-in-command of the rebellious American forces returned to the embrace of his former masters.

* * *

With his feet heavy in his riding boots, Wilkinson trudged north along the road from Basking Ridge. When the British dragoons first burst upon Lee's party, Wilkinson slipped out the back door of White's Tavern. He didn't go through all the trouble of politicking his way into a position as one of the general's aides just to spend the rest of the war rotting on a British prison ship. He had plans, and they depended on his safety and survival above all else.

Wilkinson reached a slight hilltop a mile from town when he saw two horsemen galloping toward him. In the sunlight, he could tell right away they wore blue coats. He let out a heavy sigh of relief.

The riders stopped in the middle of the road. Wilkinson recognized the officer right away. "Mister Creed, I'm glad to see you."

Creed's response was harsh. "What happened to you? Where is your horse? Your saber?"

Wilkinson suddenly realized he had no idea what had happened because he had abandoned his general and his comrades so quickly. But he improvised a story. "A large force of British cavalry swept into the town. We put up a brave fight for the general but…"

"But what? We heard a scattering of shots, not the sound of a fight."

"Well, yes, General Lee did not want the effusion of blood and ordered us to submit. I, of course, wanted no part of the submission and made my way here."

"So, you fled from your place of duty without a weapon?"

Wilkinson's face turned red and his eyes shifted from side to side. "Well, you see – my pistol I discharged into a British trooper who blocked my way and left the blade of my saber buried in the breast of another."

"Very convenient. Well, we shall see what lies up ahead."

Wilkinson looked at Beall. "There are still many British in the area, I am sure. I had best ride back and warn General Sullivan. Please have your soldier render me his horse, sir."

Creed's face reddened. "My soldier is riding forward with me. We have orders to report to General Lee and hasten his reunion with his army. I shall not turn back from that task until I ascertain his condition. Enjoy your walk, sir."

"You can't just leave me like this, Creed. You must give me a horse."

He stomped helplessly as the two riders galloped off. "Creed!"

***

Creed ignored the demands from the cowardly liar and spurred Finn forward with a grateful Beall right behind him.

They circled their way around Basking Ridge. As they cleared the low ridgeline south of the town, they saw a brown smear tracing across the horizon. Even in the cold weather, the pounding of so many hooves at the gallop stirred up a dust cloud, ever so faint.

Creed turned Finn towards the cloud of dust. "Riders heading south."

By the afternoon, they had caught up with the column, which had halted before crossing the Raritan River near Stone Brook. There were a few sentinels out, but otherwise, it looked like a picnic, with tea boiling and all. Creed and Beall lay flat on their bellies in a stand of pine trees no more than 120 yards away.

Creed snapped open his spyglass. "I count more than forty horses, at least two troops. From the look of it, there's a Tory officer in a green jacket. 'Tis odd. Ah, I see the good general himself in his sleeping gown. He could not have presented much of a fight, I would say."

"That is if he wanted a fight, sir."

Creed looked at Beall and smiled. "Very good, Jonathan."

He continued to scan. "There's a major of dragoons in a red jacket. He's wearing buff breeches—looks strangely familiar. He appears to be chatting and sharing tea with General Lee. A shot from my Jaeger rifle could split the officer in half. We could hurt some of them with our rifles, but there's no way to rescue Lee."

"If that strange officer even deserved, or for that matter desired, rescue, sir."

Creed folded the spyglass back in its case.

"Sir, the green-jacketed officer just pointed in our direction."

They heard cries from the camp, and Creed realized his mistake. "The midday sun reflected off my glass. They've spotted us!"

Six troopers grabbed their carbines and ran toward them on foot, shouting and cursing. Leading the charge was the green-jacket captain, who sprinted straight at Creed and Beall's position.

Creed got up on one knee and turned to Beall. "Leave me your rifle and get the horses!"

"Yes, sir!" Beall tossed him the rifle and ran back.

Creed focused on the officer leading the charge. A sudden doubt hit him. Killing this man would be easy, almost like murder. After a moment of hesitation, Creed steadied his rifle and aimed at the officer. He hesitated again.

Carbine shots rang out, and a few stray musket balls whistled through the pine limbs overhead. Creed's hesitation vanished as quickly as it had appeared. He took a half-breath and squeezed the trigger, sending the hammer forward with the snap and crack of the flint, igniting the powder pan. The instant bang as the round fired and the stock slammed against his shoulder ended with the green-jacket falling to the ground. The British troopers frantically dove for cover.

In the time it took Creed to sight and fire, the burly dragoon corporal had crawled forward to within fifty yards of him. He spotted the flash and smoke from Creed's shot and stood up to try a return shot. His carbine had an effective range of around forty yards against formed troops. Hitting a solitary figure in the shadow of trees was a tough shot for an expert, and the corporal was no expert. He jerked the trigger, a mistake that sent the carbine round careening harmlessly into a tree more than ten yards from Creed.

The dragoon's blood was up, however. He tossed aside the useless firearm and drew his saber. Despite the cavalry boots, the corporal showed surprising speed for a big man and quickly closed on Creed. But not quickly enough. At twenty yards out, Creed fired a round from Beall's rifle through the man's forehead. While Sidney Baker had suffered only a grazed arm from Creed's first shot, the corporal, who had shown so little mercy at White's Tavern, died instantly.

Creed turned and ran back through the copse with the two rifles at the trail. Moments later, he and Beall were mounted and ready to ride hard toward Basking Ridge.

As Creed and Beall began down the steep slope, they saw the crimson of three mounted dragoons and their fiery officer charging straight toward them. The pounding of hooves brought them together in a clash of steel. Metal clashed as their blades clashed in a whirl of sparks and curses.

Fortunately for Creed, the dragoons had followed Tarleton in single file. Creed employed a tactic he had learned in France and rode straight past Tarleton and the dragoon directly behind him. By the time Tarleton recovered and turned his horse around, Creed had run through the first trooper while Beall sheared off the second trooper's right arm with his tomahawk. The redcoat stared in horror as his saber fell to the ground with his fist still grasping the hilt.

As soon as he finished his slash, Creed yanked Finn aside—only to crash directly into Tarleton. Tarleton's horse circled Finn in a tight pattern learned on the drill field. The movement pushed Finn back, despite Creed's efforts to control him.

Tarleton struck with the speed of an adder, but Creed anticipated the blow, and it glanced off his hilt and struck the pommel of the saddle. To Creed's good fortune, the blade was embedded in the wood of the pommel, and before Tarleton could twist it free, Creed smacked his hand with the flat of his blade, causing Tarleton to scream in pain.

But before Creed could finish him off, Tarleton pulled back and turned his horse in a mad gallop toward the British formation. The third dragoon had spurred his horse at

Beall, but upon seeing Tarleton in flight, he quickly spun his mount around and hurried to safety.

Chapter 24

Princeton, New Jersey, December 17th, 1776

The sergeant's red coat and shiny buttons stood out sharply against the white frost that covered the land and buildings. A British line of about six privates stomped their feet and blew on their chalk-white hands to warm up from the freezing cold. They're just as bored and cold as anyone, Creed thought.

After spending nearly two hours watching the sentries, Creed knew enough about their routine. He had ridden miles, avoiding patrols, guards, and supply wagons to evaluate the town's defenses. But now he ached from the numbing cold. His first winter in America was truly bitter, in more than one way. Neither Ireland nor France had been as cold. But at least the wind had lessened, and the sunshine made the frosty landscape shimmer with a beauty he had never seen before.

***

They had left Lee's division for Princeton a few days earlier. After their failed pursuit of General Lee, they returned to the column where they met Parker, who had just returned with Fitzgerald's new instructions.

Creed read the message. He put the paper down and closed his eyes.

"What is it, sir?" Parker asked.

"The good colonel is ever seeking ways to challenge us, lads. But I think we're up to it. I pray we are. We ride at once. But I must report to General Sullivan first."

Creed found Sullivan just as the general was climbing into the saddle. Sullivan slipped his boot from the stirrup and faced Creed.

"General Sullivan, I have the curious pleasure to inform you that you are now in command of this division of the Continental Army."

"What do you mean?"

Our good General Lee is in the hands of the redcoats. Abducted in his nightshirt. His lads put up a fight, but not a very sturdy one, I'd say. I followed the dragoons, but they were too numerous to stop.

"Where did they take him?"

"He's probably in Brunswick by now. After that, New York, perhaps."

Creed continued with a more detailed account of Lee's abduction. Sullivan listened with a mixture of despair and relief.

"You know, Mister Creed, I never trusted or liked Lee. For a former British regular officer, he was not very impressive. And his efforts to undermine General Washington were obvious. Yet…"

"Yet what, sir?"

"The fact that the British would so nefariously kidnap a senior officer shows the ruthlessness of their nature."

"Weren't they ruthless on Long Island, sir?"

Sullivan darkened. New York was his sore point. "That was different. Open combat begets ruthlessness. But the depths to which they have now sunk to shock and subdue the patriot cause bode ill for the future of this struggle."

"We must be prepared for them, then. This is now a different kind of war, sir."

Sullivan nodded. "Yes, it is."

"At the end of the day, they seem driven by tyranny and oppression, not by making a point of law."

Sullivan smiled. "Well put, Mister Creed, well put. The fact is, I had already learned of the British raid on Basking Ridge from some of its survivors. Each had his unique take on the event. None of them quite matched yours. Now I would welcome your opinion as to what is behind all this."

Creed lowered his eyes. "If the general will allow, I'd rather keep my opinion to myself."

"Very well, Creed. I am sure your other duties are pressing."

Creed turned to leave.

"One last thing, Mister Creed."

"Sir?"

"I received a detailed account from Mister Wilkinson."

"Well, I suppose he managed to turn his cowardly flight from the British into a near-heroic tale worthy of the High Kings of Ireland."

Sullivan chortled. "He tried his best. But I wasn't convinced. He arrived, after all, unarmed. Your comment confirms my suspicions."

***

Their eyes merely slits against a biting wind, Creed's small band leaned forward in the saddle, urging their tired horses to go faster. Their journey took them south past Middle Brook and then along Millstone Creek to Somerset Court House. Creed had time to consider his mission: to determine the disposition of the British forces and, if possible, their plans and intentions. He knew he could gather some information from the local militia. But its usefulness? Fitzgerald's message reported that the militias had begun a series of localized hit-and-run attacks, ambushing couriers, sentries, and small patrols. However, accurate intelligence was something these roving bands could not reliably produce.

They stopped to question some locals at Somerset Court House. His men fought the bitter cold with hot cider provided by a local merchant with patriotic leanings. From him, Creed learned that the British had substantial forces near Princeton, and so he made that his first target.

Creed downed his cider in a gulp and effortlessly swung his leg over Finn to mount. The horse's breath began to steam, like bellows blowing air. "Time to ride, lads. We still have daylight."

He reined Finn around to the south. After an hour, he raised his hand, and their horses slowed to a stop. "Thomas, you'll set up a camp in those woods and look after the pack horses. If we don't return by tomorrow evening, assume the worst and head to General Washington's headquarters."

"Where's that, sir?" Thomas's displeasure at leaving the group was obvious.

"Somewhere near a town called Yardley. Crossing the river will be your greatest challenge. Can you swim?"

The young man's eyes widened. "Why, no, sir, I can't!"

Creed's eyes twinkled. "Most people, including many sailors, can't swim a stroke. But 'tis just as well then, for you are sure to freeze to death before you drown."

Thomas's eyes widened. Beall and Parker doubled over laughing.

"Well, with any luck, old Root Hog and company will be back in no time. And as you well know, Thomas, luck trumps almost all our best plans…"

* * *

The sergeant was seen dressing down his men. Their uniforms were spit-and-polish, but their demeanor was slack. Their morale was waning, too.

"We've watched these lads long enough. Time to pay a visit." Creed and his band dismounted, their boots crunching through the fresh snow. They led their horses up the road to the crossroads where a red-faced sergeant of the guard was posting sentries.

A cold and weary-looking fusilier in a red jacket and small miter cap extended his musket and challenged them. "Who goes there?"

"The name is Root Hog, Root Hog Burns. But call me Root Hog. Most folks do. "

The sergeant of the guard turned from his inspection to size them up. "State your business, sir, or I shall have to arrest you."

"Me 'n the boys been traveling for three days now. Sure would like some warm food. They got anything like a tavern here? We could sure use a beer, or a hot toddy or two, or even three."

Parker and Beall guffawed on cue, Parker bending over laughing. Neither were they good actors, Creed thought, but they were getting better. Their escapades in New York had steeled their nerves. They now almost seemed to embrace the danger.

Creed tugged at his beaver-skin hat. "Now see here, soldier, we done worked for General Cornwallis before. He may not know it, but we sure do."

They all laughed again. This time, Creed showed particular amusement with his comment, twisting his mouth in a playful grimace.

The redcoat's face turned a deeper red. "The title is sergeant, and I can tell you, mate, his lordship is not in command of the battalions here. Lord Cornwallis is up north and heading to—nah—I've said enough. For the last time, what's your business?"

Creed's face suddenly turned serious. "Information is my business, sergeant. Now take me to whoever does that line of work for your army."

The sergeant eyed their weapons suspiciously. "Alright then, come with me."

"Where we goin'?"

The sergeant stamped his foot, making a dull thud in the snow. "You wanted to meet the gentleman who buys information. I'm taking you to him."

"Who's that?"

"One Lieutenant Swindells. Mind you, he was relieved of command of a good infantry company for drunkenness, back in New York. Now he collects information from patrols and sentries. Some locals. You'll do."

"He must have been drunk. I hear tell your officers like their wine and such."

The sergeant gave Creed an annoyed look. "It's what he did when drunk. Come along."

***

The staff officer assigned to intelligence for Brigadier General Alexander Leslie was unimpressed with the tall ruffian the sergeant presented. Captain Louis Swindells sat in a folding chair near a small, pot-bellied stove. Despite benefiting from nature's insulation, Swindells always felt cold. More ambitious than industrious, Swindells lacked a steady flow of information. General Leslie had pushed him to find local spies and informants to cut down on patrols and outposts. Yet, despite a surplus of British sympathizers in the area, he had little intelligence to show for it. That's why he was meeting with the ruffian who called himself Root Hog Burns.

After some complicated discussion, Swindells accepted the stranger's story. He only half believed his claim of working for the British. But the man showed such a complete knowledge of events during late summer and early fall that Swindells decided to try using him. Although he disliked this rough American and his companions, he decided they might be useful to him.

"So, Mister Root Hog, if that is indeed your real name, what can you tell me about Mister Lee's column? How are they getting along without their master?"

Creed smiled. "I think pretty good there, Captain Swine-dells. Old Chas Lee didn't have many friends, so far as I could tell."

Swindells frowned, and his forehead furrowed at the obvious mispronunciation of his name. "That is Swindells, to you, Root Hog! Now, just how do you know of all this?"

"Apologize for that, cap'n. Why, we entered their camp as itinerants, you know, selling firewood. Them rebels don't like the cold neither. We overheard officers and men cussin' him, 'cept when he got lassoed by your horse soldiers, then they wuz pretty happy, or so it seemed."

Swindells nodded numbly. "No doubt. Go on."

Creed's eyes widened, and he pointed a finger into the air. "Well, looked to me like they might have headed north and back to where they came, 'cause that was the road they took. But I suspect they finally turned west. Headin' north being just a trick to fool British spies."

Swindells scratched his earlobe and pondered this conflicting information. As he did, Creed looked around and saw what appeared to be a map rolled up and lying against the small folding table.

"Could explain better if I had a map, Cap'n."

Swindells nodded wearily, stood up, and walked to the small folding table. He unrolled the map onto the table. "Now show me where they were when you entered their camp. Then the road they took, and the one you believe they took."

Creed pointed to the junction near Basking Ridge, then traced his finger along a route that led to Morristown. "I expect they turned west here and made a bee-line for the Delaware. 'Course they say, General Sullivan, he's the commander now, is hot-blooded and riled from his time being a captive of you boys. So, he could strike in any direction, maybe east." Creed placed his finger on Brunswick.

Swindells shook his head. "Impossible, General Grant has several battalions garrisoned there, plus artillery and cavalry."

Creed sniffed. "Well, maybe General Sullivan don't know that. All I am saying is a man like Sullivan could strike anywhere, most 'specially if he thinks you're weak."

Swindells shook his head impatiently, his pink jowls flapping. "Not a chance in this abhorrent weather. General Howe has already ordered us to winter quarters. Significant forces are covering the Delaware from Trenton to Bordentown. If Sullivan proceeds in any of those directions, he will be checked."

Creed shook his head. "I suppose I've got a lot to learn 'bout your army, Cap'n. I prefer moving in the cold. Ground's hard and firm. Game's easier to shoot—less bush to hide in. Now, just what is it I need to do for you, Cap'n Swindells?"

Swindells smiled, pleased Creed had pronounced his name correctly. He had heard that mispronounced all too often in and around the mess, and not as a term of affection. Of course, at school and in the mess, cruel schoolmates and messmates dubbed Swindells the unflattering nickname 'Swiney'.

He pointed at the map. "It would be useful to know where Sullivan has gone. If indeed he headed north, that signals the end of the campaign for certain. If he is, as you say, considering an attack against us here in winter quarters, his location might provide some insight into his objective. Better yet, see if you can ascertain that objective. If you do, there will be a couple of guineas in it for you, Mister Root Hog."

Creed's mouth widened in a broad smile. "Why, I lose that much in a poor poker game, Cap'n. For twenty, I'll find out where he is, for twenty-five I'll find out where he is going."

Swindells sneered and then chuckled. "Would you rather I pay you in worthless continental money?"

Creed smiled sheepishly. "Ten guineas then."

"Five is all I can give you, Root Hog. Unless you prefer the gaol."

"You strike a rough bargain there, Cap'n, but as a loyal subject of the king, I am glad to take your money and do my duty. Anything extra in it if I bring back a rebel scalp or two?"

Swindells pursed his lips and squinted with porcine eyes. "If I wanted to engage savages, I expect I would engage those of the red variety."

Creed nodded. "Now I got one last request there, Cap'n. I need a note from you to get me through the lines. My smooth talkin' saved us once, but that might not always work. The backwoods charm wears out from time to time."

Swindells smiled wickedly. "Do tell. Oh, very well."

Swindells rifled through his desk, retrieved his inkpot and quill, and set them on his desk. He spread a blank piece of parchment on the desk. He carefully licked the tip and dipped the point of the nib into the inkpot, and then slowly and fastidiously wrote out a note of passage.

December 17th/1776/Princeton

To Whom It May Concern,

The bearer of this Missive, Mister Root Hog Burns, is on His Majesty's business under the exclusive command and direction of Brigadier General Leslie. All British, Allied, and Loyalist Forces, as well as all loyal Subjects of the Crown, are hereby enjoined to provide him every Assistance and expedite him in carrying out his Duties.

For the Brigadier Commanding,
Captain L. Swindells
Assistant to the Adjutant

Swindells watched impatiently as Root Hog read the note, deliberately pointing to each word with his index finger. *As I expected, this backwoods bumpkin is nearly, if not completely, illiterate.*

When he finished, Creed nodded and grunted, signaling that he understood the words. Swindells took the heavy paper and folded it over twice, then placed it in a white envelope and handed it to Creed, who tucked it in his pocket.

"Gimme three or four days, Cap'n. But before we go, we need some vittles for the road and something warm to get us through the cold nights ahead. I like the cold, but only when I have the means to stay warm if ya know what I mean."

"Sergeant Ogilvy will find you suitable food and drink, but if you piss away this mission, there will be a reckoning of grave significance."

"Now why would you need to say that, Cap'n?"

Swindells ignored the retort and turned away. He wanted no further discussion with the rogue cowboy, Root Hog Burns.

* * *

They galloped from Princeton, riding up the cold, snow-swept road, oddly empty.

"You never said, how did it go with the British officer, sir?" Parker asked.

"Tricked the slothful fellow into showing me their map. It was flush with information he had no business exposing—even to Root Hog."

Parker laughed.

Creed turned serious. "I saw markings near the Delaware towns of Trenton and Bordentown. They must be British positions, as I saw numbers next to each location, probably signifying the regiments. I saw no more than a couple of battalions at each location, though."

Parker shifted his weight in the saddle. "What's that mean, sir?"

"Unless I'm mistaken, the British have dispersed their forces!"

The winter sky was pitch dark when they reached their camp. They found Thomas struggling to keep a small fire burning. He had built a three-sided shelter from canvas draped over fallen tree limbs. Parker attended to the horses while Beall prepared a simple supper from one of the two chickens they had obtained from their British benefactors. The irony of the crown paying for and supplying their efforts against them was not lost on Creed. How lucky he was to stumble upon a novice intelligence officer as lazy as he was corrupt.

Although Creed had been particularly persuasive with his story, no competent officer would have hired, paid, or provided information to them without first checking out their claims. A round-trip to Hackensack would have taken two days at most.

A cold whistled through the shelter as the four planned their next few days' activities while eating a bland but highly satisfying chicken stew.

"Sure am glad you got us a resupply of provisions courtesy of the Royal Army," Thomas said.

"More important than even food, drink, or powder, however, we managed to talk Sergeant Ogilvy into finding two large sacks of oats for the horses and some badly needed horseshoes," Creed said.

"Many horses die in winter. Not enough fodder. But in the cold, they need more food, and there's no grass for grazing," Thomas said.

"Almost as urgent, many horses became lame when shoes wore out or fell off because of the colder, harder road surfaces," Beall observed. "Simon was always busiest in the blacksmith shop in winter."

Creed smiled as he listened. His men's concern for the horses was a good sign. The would-be horse breeder was determined to have their animals survive and even thrive while others went down from mistreatment.

Creed devoured his portion in his usual quick fashion. While the others savored their stew, he munched on a piece of dry bread and spoke over the concerto of noises produced by the howling night wind. "We'll move out one hour after sunrise and visit Bordentown and then Trenton. However, we will not enter either town just yet. Our work, for now, is confined to observing the British from outside their perimeter defenses."

Parker thought carefully for a moment. "Wouldn't it be better to enter the town as cowboys and try to count the number of men and guns?"

Beall chimed in. "Yes, and perhaps we can listen in on some of the men stationed there, or talk to some local innkeepers?"

"'Twould be better indeed. But Root Hog and his cowboys still have a mission to perform for our good Captain Swindells, and I aim to earn the king's gold fairly."

Beall leaned towards Creed. "So, sir, please tell us what you plan then."

Creed pulled out a piece of paper with some notes. "Based on what I observed from the good captain's map, the British have but two small batteries and no more than two or three battalions at Trenton. About the same at Bordentown, give or take a few. However, at Princeton, it looks like several batteries and as many battalions. I'm assuming the markings were battalions or regiments."

"Then don't we need to enter these towns to be sure?" Parker asked.

"Impressive, Elias. Normally, yes. However, I don't want to risk the entire enterprise to confirm what I believe is at least seventy percent accurate. The British don't plan to attack our army. General Howe is content to keep his men in winter quarters. So instead, we'll ascertain the extent of the defenses at Bordentown and Trenton and then proceed north along the Delaware to find our good General Sullivan, whose 'location' we shall 'expeditiously' report to General Leslie himself. That should satisfy our obligation to Swindells."

"Deliberately place our men in danger?" Beall asked.

"Of course not! By the time we report it, General Sullivan will be long gone."

Thomas put down his cup. "Sir, I could enter the town for you. Nobody would pay no mind to me. Could hang around the stables and meet folks. Stable hands generally get wind of things, you know?"

Touched, Creed looked at the boy, not quite a man but with more heart than most men. "Not this time, Thomas, but I do like the way you think. You'll yet have your chance."

They all laughed, each knowing that Thomas, eager to step out of the role of caretaker and horse handler, had become one of them.

* * *

The Bordentown leg of their journey was short. Parker and Beall rode off to reconnoiter the approaches to the Delaware crossings while he and Thomas surveyed the town itself.

The British had few defenses and seemed almost indifferent to the comings and goings of the locals. The dark-blue uniforms worn by the garrison indicated these were German regiments. He estimated they numbered about seven hundred. There were no defenses, but the Germans—he wasn't sure if they were Hessians—had started to build a blockhouse near the road leading to the river.

By midafternoon, Creed's band had reunited and was riding north along the main road from Bordentown to Trenton.

The wind had quieted, and a strong afternoon sun raised the temperature to a crisp, but not frigid, chill. To their left, the woods stretched along a gentle rise, marking the high-water line for the Delaware that followed the river's course. The lightly wooded ridge sloped about a quarter to half a mile before leveling out at the river's edge. To their right lay scattered woods and pastures, including those classic New Jersey farms with homes that had a traditional English look, a mix of brick and wooden clapboard.

But many were charred remnants of once-proud farmsteads. The sight of so many torched by vengeful Tories scarred the tranquil winter landscape. About two miles south of Trenton, they came upon a small establishment called The Whig. Creed saw the name as an unusual coincidence and decided to stop to rest the horses and engage the locals in gossip.

He slid from the saddle and handed Thomas the reins. "Take Finn and his friends around back. Keep a good watch on the horses. Jonathan, you enter this place from the back. Act like you're looking to purchase some vittles. Elias will cover the front. Should be interesting to learn whether the name of this establishment has any meaning, politically."

Creed strolled into the tavern with a swagger that caught everyone's attention, heads snapping toward him. He counted six patrons. Four looked like local watermen. He approached the bar and ordered a rum toddy to chase away the chill. A plate of cold mutton sandwiches sat on a nearby tray, and without asking, he helped himself to one. The tavern keeper glared at him until he slammed a bright silver coin on the bar.

Swiping the coin into his apron, the short, stocky keeper crossed his arms and eyed Creed carefully. "What's your business here, mister?"

Creed gave him a jocular wink. "Ya mean, besides food and drink? Well, ya see pardner, in case ya didn't notice, there's a rebellion going on. Came down here from the hills to get some work. You know, under contract. Where there's an army, there's always a good contract to be had. Suspect it'll be a cold winter here, and I figured the garrison will pay well for firewood."

Both armies engaged woodcutters, but only the British could afford to pay hired contractors in cash. The Continental Army found few local patriots willing to take their worthless paper. So, they engaged fewer woodcutters and relied instead on soldiers to do the work.

The remark got the attention of the patrons, one of whom, a tall, bony waterman of around thirty, slid down the bar and stood next to Creed. "Now, see here, Mister. Do you have a contract to cut wood? We been lookin' for one ourselves and could not get anything from them Dutchmen. How'd you do it?"

Creed grinned wickedly. "Well, pardner, ya gotta give a little to get a little. *Comprendre*?"

The tavern keeper piped in like an old hen. "That sounded French, mister. Say, you one of them Canadians?"

"No, but I did some lumbering, trapping too, in upper New York. Traded with the Frenchies. Picked up some of the lingo, I suppose."

The waterman nodded. "The Dutchmen in town told us they needed a couple of hundred cords just to get through Christmas. Figured they'd be desperate right 'bout now, but so far no luck. Say, can you give us some paid work, mister?"

Creed felt a strange sensation in his stomach and throat. These were not real Tories, certainly not Loyalists. They, like so many of his countrymen, had been caught in the middle of this struggle. Not happy with the old order, yet too fearful to commit to the new. Moreover, both patriots and Loyalists preyed upon them. They likely had families to feed as well.

He drew four coins from his pocket and placed one in each hand. "Use this to make your deal with those Dutchies. I'm heading to Trenton to make another."

The watermen gasped.

"Now, we can't take your charity, stranger," an older man said.

He did not sound like he meant it. Creed knew they were desperate.

"Not charity, pardner. When I come through these parts, I'll ask for the money back with interest. Let's say one percent of whatever you make."

The older man glanced at the others. "Fair enough."

The tavern keeper grinned. "Looks like Root Hog has offered you a pretty good deal, boys. I always like customers with money!"

The coins slipped into ready pockets while Creed ordered another round of drinks from the bar. As they toasted his health, Creed began a round of seemingly innocent questions about the road ahead and the Trenton area. The men appeared disgruntled with the rebel cause for many reasons, but not the least of which was Washington's confiscation of the Delaware boats and barges and elimination of what little employment they had. In the course of half an hour, he learned that the garrison's strength was over 1,000. And they continued a relentless routine of patrols and sentries despite the weather and militia.

One gave him a stern warning. "Now you'd better be careful of the local militia, Root Hog. They are all about the area. They'd likely skin a man helping the British."

"I ain't 'fraid of no militias."

The older man put down his tankard. "Well, maybe you're not, but they've already affected the Hessians. The militias are causing the garrison to react to their raids and ambushes. Just a few militias can keep them up all night hollering commands in Dutch."

"Do tell." Creed wiped his mouth with his sleeve.

Another local chimed in. "Why, I overheard the commander, a colonel named Rall, has boasted that Charles Lee, taken by the British, was the final blow to America's hopes."

He held a copy of the *New Jersey Gazette*. "Why, here's a quote from General Howe that says almost the same thing. And the gazette has one writer claiming Washington's forces will wither away during the winter. He says by spring the rebellion will collapse like a termite-infested table."

The man folded the paper and waved it at Creed. "Maybe then we can all go back to our lives."

Creed nodded. "But I suspect the army will stay awhile an' keep the peace. Plenty o' work for all of us then."

Creed had gleaned enough. More discussion might arouse suspicion. When he made his farewell, the men thanked him for the loan, but he knew each of them hoped never to see him again.

He tossed a few coins at the barkeep and waltzed out with a small bundle of freshly smoked fish, a loaf of bread, and a bottle of corn whisky.

* * *

They made camp in a wooded area about a mile south of Trenton. The four men sat near the horses and feasted on the fish and washed it down with the whisky—they would save the bread for the morning. To stay warm, they huddled close, using their body heat, canvas shelters, cloaks, and the whisky to break the cold. Creed would not risk a fire in case a courier or patrol was about.

"American fish is far better than any I have tasted in Europe, even in France," he remarked.

Beall looked at him. "Sir, I think perhaps you have spent too much time with the Continental Army."

Creed smiled. "Perhaps we all have. However, I fear that, if we are to win this war, it will, by necessity, be a long one. We should all accustom ourselves to that fact and the failings of the commissariat."

Parker raised his knife. "Indeed, sir. I must admit that when Major Gist assigned me to your unit, I had hoped to escape the gruel of the commissariat. When I sailed the Chesapeake, we had no lack of good eating: fish of all kinds, crabs, and my personal favorite, oysters." Parker had struck a chord, and all four licked their lips as he discoursed on the treasures of Maryland's Chesapeake bounty.

Creed finally cut the banter off with words on the next day's work. "Tomorrow, as with today, caution is the key to our success. We'll circle the town to sketch the key terrain and roads. And assess the routine of the German garrison there, as we did at Bordentown."

"Is that all, sir?" Parker asked slyly.

"No. We must locate and mark the defenses around Trenton. Gun emplacements, then outworks such as blockhouses. Then, if we learn where they send patrols to place their pickets, we're done."

Thomas interrupted him in a respectful but emphatic tone. "No disrespect, sir, but we still must get this information back to the army before we are done."

A round of guffaws cut the air, then the men grew silent, all eyes turning on Creed.

"Why, Thomas, your precociousness impresses. You have indeed blossomed into a spy!"

Chapter 25

Trenton, New Jersey, December 19th, 1776

From their vantage point on an overlook south of Trenton, the town did not look like much, just a few score buildings at most. But its position along the main road from Philadelphia to New York and its location on the Delaware River made it a prosperous, if unimpressive, place of commerce.

The Hessian patrols left Trenton twice each day, one at dawn and one before dusk. Their task was to keep track of the pattern. Beall spotted a file of figures in dark blue. He nudged the younger man. "Look, Thomas, there are only six."

Thomas's eyes scanned the scene below. "I don't know anything about Hessians or patrolling, but they seem casual to me."

"You're right. They march slovenly for professionals. No flankers to guard them against a surprise ambush. And no advance man or rear guard."

"Maybe they think they're in Germany, not America," Thomas quipped.

Beall nudged him again and grasped his spyglass firmly. "Look, Thomas, they're turning down towards the river."

Thomas took the spyglass from Beall, who began scribbling down the time, numbers, location, and direction.

They could not make out the unit, so he wrote simply:

Hssn. 6Inf. Fle, ptrl, Brdntn Rd, SW, 7am.

Loosely transcribed, it became: 7 am, Six Hessian Infantry moving southwest on the Bordentown Road.

He knew his lieutenant wanted intelligence documented, and the sooner, the better. Creed once admonished them. "If you do not record it in writing, 'tis as if it had never happened. An accurate record is essential." Beall once thought it an exaggeration but soon came to believe it.

The patrol made its way down the road and soon disappeared into the woods. Beall took the spyglass from Thomas and turned his attention back to the town.

 "Thomas, I'm confused as to why there aren't any patrols heading in the other direction. Surely, they must patrol to the northwest as well as the southeast?"

Thomas pondered a moment. "Maybe they have no reason to patrol in that direction."

Beall removed the spyglass from his eye and smiled. "Why, you just might be right, Thomas!"

***

When Creed and Parker returned, Beall provided a detailed report on everything they had observed, and more importantly, on what they had not observed.

Creed was impressed with the report. His men were improving in their skills. "Thomas may well be right. We must proceed with even more caution when we move to the northwest of the town. Pack up the horses. We'll travel in pairs."

The broken woods along the north side of the River Road provided just enough cover as they urged the horses north toward McConkey's Ferry, a major crossing on the Delaware River. Creed and Beall rode ahead. Beall's years of hunting and ranging the Catoctin Mountains near Frederick, Maryland, made him adept at seeing deep into woods and glens, so Creed posted him at the front. Parker and Thomas followed about forty yards behind, with the pack horses.

Before they left, Creed gave firm instructions, "If we are killed or taken, abandon us and get our report to Colonel Fitzgerald by any means possible."

"I understand," Parker said. "What are your plans now, sir?"

"To find General Sullivan and Lee's division before they cross the Delaware. We'll report what we observed around Trenton and Bordentown, but we'll bring back some useful information to keep Root Hog in the trust of our good Captain Swindells."

The men took turns riding and walking their horses along the lightly wooded hillside beside the main road. It had grown dark, but the sky was clear, and the moonlight gave enough visibility for them to keep a good pace.

"How much farther, sir?" Beall asked.

"I hope to pass McConkey's Ferry before the moon sets. About seven more miles to get there. But the land here is rough."

A few miles further, Beall turned and signaled Creed.

Both dismounted and drew their Jaeger rifles, quietly attaching their sword bayonets to the muzzles. When Parker and Thomas caught up, Creed gathered them around.

"Private Beall spotted something up ahead, about a hundred yards in that direction. We'll reconnoiter. Stay here with the horses until we return."

Creed and Beall stepped quietly through the dark woods, this time with Creed in the lead. They moved from tree to tree Indian-style, one covering the other as they zigzagged toward the silhouette.

At fifty yards, the woods thinned into a clearing with scattered trees surrounding a small two-story log cabin. The lower windows were sealed with mortar and stone. In the fading moonlight, they could see holes bored through the mortar—loopholes for the defenders to shoot from. There were sounds of angry German banter—Hessian soldiers inside.

Creed looked at the upper story. They had closed the shutters tightly against the wind, but Creed was sure he saw a hole about the size of an apple punched through each shutter. The cabin, sitting on a connector trail that runs from the River Road to Pennington Road, had been turned into a blockhouse.

They threw themselves prone on either side of a large elm tree. Creed peered around the trunk at Beall. "This blockhouse must cover the River Road to our left and the Pennington Road to our right. I thought those roads were farther apart, but it seems they are not. The Hessians must be communicating with the blockhouse from the Pennington

Road. That's why you didn't see patrols on the River Road. It may seem odd, but I have learned that German efficiency has a logic all its own."

"Surely they have a sentry posted somewhere, sir."

"Normally, they would. However, they're in winter quarters. Even the best soldiers make mistakes."

A shutter from the second floor swung open, and despite the darkened room, they sensed a face gazing in their direction. They froze like deer, hoping the tree's shadow covered them enough. The cabin door squeaked open, and two figures stepped out. They wore flannel sleep shirts buttoned high against the cold. They also wore curious felt slippers and knee-high stockings. Both held bayonets ready and were heading straight for Creed and Beall. As they drew closer, they chattered away in a thick German dialect Creed had trouble understanding.

Beall raised his rifle, but Creed reached for the barrel.

"I think they are out for their toilet. The bayonets are to shovel over their work. If they get too close, we must take them before they can warn the others. But no firing."

Beall nodded. They had done this bloody work many times before. Creed reversed his weapon. He decided he could not run the unsuspecting men through. A broken jaw or skull from a butt stroke would silence them just as effectively as tearing a belly or jugular.

The Germans moved casually toward the trees, turned left, and quickly dropped into a crouch over what looked like a hole. The mix of pigs' knuckles, beer, and sauerkraut produced a noxious odor that Creed and Beall could smell from fifteen yards away. The grunts and guttural banter continued, as did the stench from the two men.

I think we can safely leave them to this. Creed tapped lightly on the tree trunk, and the two men turned and slithered back into the woods.

***

They kept riding north in search of Sullivan and Lee's division. The cabin blockhouse just north of Trenton was the first of two enemy outposts they saw. They spotted a second blockhouse at the other end of the connector trail, which covered Pennington Road. "This one, too, appears to have a company-sized garrison. We have their strong points. Now we need to move on."

Under the cover of darkness, Creed and his White Knights sped north to find Sullivan and convey this intelligence.

* * *

They caught sight of smoke rising from the dark woods to the north, just visible against the blue-gray morning sky. Creed pulled up on Finn's reins. He took a moment to reflect on his next move and pointed toward the shadowy plumes. "No more than three miles off. I wager General Sullivan's men are preparing breakfast. With any luck, we shall join them in their morning meal."

They trotted up the trail but were stopped by a sentry. His uniform was ragged, his face full of growth, but he stood determined in the cold dawn. "Who goes?"

"Scouts with a report for General Sullivan," Creed replied.

The sentry looked both ways and then signaled them to go on. When they arrived at the American camp, Creed had his men build a fire to cook their victuals. "We have more than we need thanks to our good Captain Swindells. When you have eaten, turn over the remainder to General Sullivan's commissary officer. I'll seek out the general."

Creed and Sullivan shared a meager breakfast of some oatcakes and butter. Creed had carefully written out a report and made some crudely sketched maps. Sullivan seemed pleased.

When the last crumb was gone, Sullivan poured each of them a mug of bitter coffee. The general lit up a pipe made of rough corncob with an ivory tip. "So, they are committed to winter quarters, Lieutenant Creed? I should think Howe would want to finish the work now and spend next year with his mistress, the delightful Betsy Loring."

Creed rubbed his chin. "One would think so, sir. Everything we observed and heard points in that direction. Yet complacency has not quite set in. They periodically send out patrols. And of course, they engaged us to spy on you."

Sullivan took a long drag on his corncob pipe. He paused a moment to watch the smoke spiral upward and dissipate. "Well, it buys His Excellency time to restore his command to a semblance of a fighting force and organize his defenses. Still, the arrogance of it annoys the devil out of me."

"I must report back to our good Captain Swindells. I'll try to verify the situation. But for now, my report stands. They have divided their advanced guard into brigades of between one and two thousand each at Bordentown and Trenton. And, they have slightly more men at Princeton."

"Are they actively patrolling?"

Creed nodded. "Sporadically. They make scant use of the local Tories—quite different from Hackensack."

"How do the people go?" Sullivan took another suck from his pipe.

"The populace is split, but there appear to be more neutrals here than up north. Yet, unabated looting has begun to change some neutral minds in our favor. But there are many of those who, seeing our cause as lost, have taken the oath."

Sullivan slipped the pipe from his mouth. "What of our local militia?"

"Some of the locals reported actions by the militia against these isolated outposts, but to what effect I know not."

Sullivan smiled grimly. "His Excellency will enjoy your report and your map. You have some talent there."

"I should rather lead a company in battle than skulk and spy, but I have committed to this enterprise as His Excellency places great store in it."

"What next?"

"I shall return to Princeton."

"What on earth for? You'll get hung."

"I must present Swindells the 'intelligence' he demands, collect my pay, and then seek further orders. It will be accurate enough to believe, but false enough to confound him. A rare chance to shape their thinking."

Sullivan blew a stream of smoke across the tent and watched as the wind pushing through the flaps erased it. "What if Root Hog's masters provide no further orders, now that they are in… winter quarters?"

"In that event, sir, I shall concoct some subterfuge to leave their camp and report back to headquarters. If Swindells and Howe have no orders for me, I can assure you, His Excellency will!"

Sullivan went into peals of laughter at the wry comment. "True enough!"

* * *

Washington's Headquarters, Buckingham, Pennsylvania, December 19th, 1776

The early winter winds had picked up again, sending a chill through the room. Lieutenant General George Washington stood up from his desk and threw first one, then a second log onto the fire. Sparks and white-hot ash sprayed the general's fine buff breeches, but he hardly noticed. His mind was elsewhere and everywhere. A few days earlier, he had moved his headquarters up-river to Buckingham, where the ragged remnants of his dwindling army were encamped. Although he had sent Elias Parker with instructions for Creed, he still had not received any reply from the young intelligence officer.

Washington had called together his main commanders, Nathanael Greene, Lord Stirling, and Henry Knox, for a meeting. He expected them at any moment. He had sent his aide, Tench Tilghman, to fetch Fitzgerald, who arrived early.

Fitzgerald stood staring into the fire. He almost dared not say what was on his mind, but he did. "Your Excellency, the capture of Lee is not without its advantages."

Washington crossed his arms and stared into the fire. "Such as?"

"For once, you command this army without the drag of the obnoxious General Lee impeaching your every move. This may afford you some freedom of action."

Washington nodded in agreement. "However, we still need Lee's division if we want any chance of facing the British. Recently, we've received vague and conflicting reports about British plans. Meanwhile, the British, now that they have Lee in their grasp, surely understand the dire situation we face. I fear they will risk everything to destroy Lee's division before it can join with us."

He turned from the fire. "I can only hope Sullivan has taken command and is hastening this way."

"We are awaiting an update from Mister Creed. But I think we can assume Sullivan has taken command."

Washington wiped a spark from his breeches. "I do hope you are correct, Robert. If so, the burning question is where Sullivan might be heading. Will he go north to the safety of the Jersey highlands or back to New York?"

Fitzgerald ignored the stray ember on his boot. "Perhaps the British have already attacked him, and even now the luckless Sullivan is marching to a British prison for the second time in a year."

Washington shook his head. "I deem it improbable. Exchanged once, it would not go well for Sullivan to land in British hands a second time. If Lee had shared anything with

Sullivan, he would have known he must march with his command to join us at all hazards. At least that is my hope."

An orderly entered the room with a bottle of claret and poured each of them a glass. They eyed the dark red liquid, swirled it just a bit, and sipped at it quietly.

"If Lieutenant Creed succeeded, he should soon return with intelligence on the British," Fitzgerald said.

Washington placed his glass down. "In many ways, the very survival of this army and the cause depend on him. He cannot fail. He must not fail."

Fitzgerald stared ruefully into the fire. "Sir, did it ever occur to you that he and his fine young men might be killed or worse, be captives of the British?"

Washington looked askance at his intelligence advisor. "Why, Robert, many possibilities occur to me, but I dwell only on what I can influence, coerce, or ascertain. If they are indeed, as you suggest, in distress, then I pray he managed to find a way to send us a report. I tell you in the strictest confidence, this cause may well be lost if we do not make a bold strike against the British."

Fitzgerald's eyes widened. "My God, sir, I thought it unlikely we could defend Philadelphia from a British thrust now. But I nevertheless assumed you would have the army prepare fortifications to make ready for an attack by the British."

Washington hung his head and shook it slowly—as if each move pained him. "We have not the time, Robert. Officers and men are leaving the army in droves. Congress has fled to Baltimore. The morale of the people is ebbing. With each passing day, once fervent patriots become neutral and take Howe's oath. Or worse, take up arms for the Loyalist cause and against their countrymen. Since the summer, I have lost battle after battle, fleeing now to my third state. No, I must make a bold thrust, either against the British landing force when they cross over to Pennsylvania or…"

"Or what, sir?"

Washington stared into the fire, then suddenly his voice grew bolder, and his eyes lit with excitement. "Or strike the British in New Jersey. Strike them hard! Make them feel the sting of defeat just when they believed they were at the moment of victory."

Fitzgerald realized this was not the bluster of an angry warrior but the determination of a man who had carefully and coolly sifted through his options. Fitzgerald concealed his excitement. "Then let's hope Jeremiah Creed comes through with intelligence on the enemy's defenses, for I am sure our good Howe and his generals are not expecting such a thrust."

The tread of heavy boots brought Abner Scovel into the drawing-room. Washington had just transferred Scovel from his staff and given him command of a platoon of his personal Life Guard.

This was quite a coup for the ambitious New Englander. For other than Maryland's Jeremiah Creed and Massachusetts' Captain Caleb Gibbs— the Life Guard officers and men were from the commander-in-chief's home state of Virginia.

Scovel looked almost bear-like with two layers of outer clothing over his frayed blue uniform, a homespun bleached brown woolen tunic, and an oilskin greatcoat of dark gray. In place of his black cocked hat, he had donned a fox-skin cap with earflaps. Scovel removed his cap, revealing a high forehead with a shock of sandy hair tied back in a loose cue.

"Anything of note to report, Lieutenant Scovel?" Fitzgerald asked.

Scovel shook his head. "Your Excellency, two more scouting parties just returned from Jersey."

"And?"

"Neither patrol learned anything of significance, sir"

Fitzgerald looked uneasily at Washington.

"How so, Lieutenant Scovel?" Washington asked.

"Loyalist militia drove one of them back before they could get close enough to the British. The other got lost and made a hasty return to the warmth of the army's campfires."

"Then we need to hear from Mister Creed," Fitzgerald said.

Scovel looked at Washington, who nodded. "Information from him is now crucial."

When Scovel departed, Fitzgerald looked apologetically at Washington. "They did little but confirm what we knew. If Mister Creed fails to provide, your next move will be akin to a blind man in a tavern full of angry revelers."

The door opened once more. An orderly ushered in Major General Nathanael Greene, Lord Stirling, and Colonel Henry Knox. Greene was Washington's most trusted and gifted subordinate, and Knox was a steady and dependable commander of artillery.

The three stood by the fireplace, rubbing themselves to drive the chill away.

Fitzgerald poured them some wine while Washington spoke, "Gentlemen, the capture of the unfortunate General Lee, combined with other factors, has led me to a decision." Washington paused as they took in his words, "I intend to take action to foil our pursuers, and sooner rather than later."

A smile stretched Henry Knox's heavy jowls into a full moon. "That is exceptionally good news indeed, sir! Are we to fall back and prepare a rigorous defense of Philadelphia? It is too cold to dig proper entrenchments, but we can move boulders and surface dirt to position our batteries and then link them with abatis."

Washington cut him off tersely. "There will be no defense of Philadelphia, Henry."

The portly commander of artillery grew agitated, his florid face turned redder than usual, and his jowls quivered. "No defense? Are we abandoning the nation's capital to the enemy? To abandon New York was a bitter enough pill, sir, but now this?"

Greene attempted to deflect the sting of Knox's insinuation with sarcasm. "Well, the politicians have abandoned the capital, Henry? Could we do no less?"

Washington cut him off with a wave of his large hand. "Enough, gentlemen! It is we in the army who serve the people and their elected representatives, not they, us. Where Congress decides to place itself is no concern of mine. Defeating the enemy is."

Aghast, the generals looked at each other-then at Washington.

"What do you mean, sir?" Lord Stirling asked.

"I mean, I accepted this burden to build a republic, not a dictatorship." Washington retrieved a paper from his desk and waved it, almost in anger. "I recently received a letter from the Congress's President. They have granted me full authority over all military and civilian matters for the duration of this crisis. Full authority... do you understand the implication?"

They all looked at each other. Fitzgerald could see this news excited them, as Washington leading the entire country might mean the army finally gets everything it needs, resolving its dire situation.

"But this is good news, sir," Lord Stirling whispered. "Why, you could levy taxes, issue laws, confiscate... "

Washington rose from his chair and walked to the fireplace, throwing the letter into the flames. "No! I will be no dictator. This nation shall have no dictator. I reject, I resent the suggestion of it!"

The officers murmured among themselves. Finally, Greene spoke, "Your Excellency, we concur and what's more, the army would agree. Suffer as our men do, they would rather serve a republican general while starving in rags than a dictator with their bellies full wearing the finest uniforms."

Washington's face softened. "Rest assured, gentlemen, I will use what authority is reasonable to care for this army. But nothing further."

Fitzgerald relinquished his role as a polite observer. "Gentlemen, let us return to the matter at hand. Do you not suppose the enemy is wondering what our next move is? The capture of our good General Lee perhaps gives them reason to think us already beaten. Perhaps causing him to lower his guard."

Greene smiled knowingly. "So, Colonel, you are saying you know the British intentions towards us?"

"No, we do not, Nathanael," Washington said. "However, even as we speak, we have good men trying to ascertain as much as they can. Depending on the conditions and activities of the British, and the reinforcement of this army, we may yet strike a blow."

Lord Stirling had stood silent, but now his eyes brightened, and his face slowly broke into the smile of a child learning he is about to get a treat. "Strike a blow? Sir, do you mean...?"

With the pressures and doubts of many days and nights agonizing over decisions suddenly lifted from his chest, Washington smiled for the first time in a long while. "Yes, Milord, I am considering a strike against the British – in your very own New Jersey."

* * *

The next day began with a light snowfall that gradually grew heavier, falling like cotton balls. A strong wind had begun to turn the snowfall into a minor snowstorm. Unfazed by the threatening storm outside, Washington was at his desk writing yet another plea to Congress for more supplies, more men, and more funds. He had sent his commanders back to their units under strict secrecy orders. He knew his camp was the target of British spies.

The door to his office opened, and Tench Tilghman stepped in, covered in white from head to toe. His face was ashen, and he was short of breath. The young aide removed his hat and beat it against his thigh to shed the heavy dusting of snow that had settled on it.

Washington placed his quill aside and stood up from his desk. "What is it, Tench?"

Tilghman smiled at the general. "A messenger just informed me…General Sullivan has arrived with Lee's division! They have lost many stragglers, are starving for food, and running low on supplies. But they are here, sir. God be praised! They are here!"

Washington suppressed the joy swelling inside. "Almighty Providence has blessed us. I shall ride to them at once. Notify the Quartermaster, Colonel Moylan. We must look after their well-being. Make sure they have firewood, food, and, if possible, blankets."

The young man's face turned serious. "I shall do my best, sir."

Tilghman bowed and hurried off. They both knew Washington's best intentions towards Sullivan's hard-pressed troops would be frustrated by the grievous lack of supplies faced by the Continental Army.

By three that afternoon, Washington had finished his inspection of Sullivan's command. He met with each regimental commander, gathering information about the number, morale, and physical condition of the men. Sullivan arrived with just over 1,500 effectives. Washington had anticipated more than 3,000.

Yet if these men could undertake such a march along the flank of a stronger enemy with limited supplies and worsening weather, they might still fight for him. He knew the men remaining were among his best. They needed to be if he were to deliver a blow to the British. It was time to meet with Sullivan.

A sturdy Life Guard corporal held open the tent flap, and Washington bent his tall frame to enter. Scovel waited outside Sullivan's command tent with the escort. Sullivan had used the time Washington spent inspecting the troops to prepare the division's encampment and to organize the distribution of supplies from the quartermaster. The small warmth in the tent came from a large candle that flickered as the wind whipped through the tent flaps. Washington kept his great coat on but sat on a wooden crate and removed his hat.

Sullivan looked gaunt, with several days' beard and hollow eyes. "Well, sir, with the help of God, we made it. Depleted in numbers, for certain, but not depleted in spirit."

Washington managed a slight smile, hiding his disappointment. "I hoped for almost double the number. But then, the ones who made it here appear as fit as can be expected. The question is, how quickly will they be ready to return?"

Sullivan winced, but then slowly began to smile as the meaning of his commander-in-chief's words sank in. "Why indeed they are, or they will— nay, they shall be, Your Excellency. Only if…"

"If what, general?"

"If I can only get them a few days' rest and some supplies, Your Excellency. Shoes and stockings, for instance, would help much."

Washington gave him an intense look. "The country needs a signal. Howe's supply line extends over one hundred miles. I plan a strike against the British before the

Delaware freezes over. However, I lack, among other things, intelligence on the enemy. Did you send out scouts or hear reports from local sympathizers?"

Sullivan's eyes met Washington's. He shook his head. "Sir, there was little time for such forays, and with the increasingly bad weather, few locals reached out to us."

"An army in retreat has precious few friends," Washington said.

"I assume most remain neutral, at least until they know how the struggle goes. We did hear of some militia units attempting to strike at the Hessian and British outposts, but to what effect I cannot say."

"Anything else?"

Sullivan lowered his eyes sheepishly. "Your Excellency, I was remiss in not informing you immediately that a certain Lieutenant Jeremiah Creed managed to rendezvous with us just before we crossed the river…"

Washington gasped, "Lieutenant Creed! I feared him dead or captured. We have been awaiting word from him. Did he provide us with anything on the British?"

Sullivan managed another sheepish grin. He fumbled in his saddlebag and pulled out an envelope. "He prepared a report, sir. I should have sent it forward sooner. But in the struggle to move the column, I simply forgot. I'm sorry."

Washington reached across the makeshift desk and grasped Sullivan's wrist. "General Sullivan, you have accomplished a noble feat. You saved your men and the entire army. In no small way, your efforts provide us the opportunity to reverse our fortunes here and now. You have no reason to apologize."

Washington tore open the envelope, taking extra care not to damage the contents. It contained two sheets of written notes and a sketch with British forces on a makeshift map. His face grew more intent as he pondered the words and symbols. A plan was slowly forming in the general's mind. When he finished, Washington folded the contents and returned them to the envelope, which he carefully placed in his vest.

He looked up at Sullivan. "What can you tell me of General Lee's capture? In his written notes, Mister Creed only writes that he failed to retrieve the hapless officer from the hands of the British."

Sullivan told him what little he knew of Lee, then answered questions about the route of march, road conditions, and, most importantly, the flow of ice on the Delaware. When they finished, Washington rose and pulled his gloves back on his large hands.

Sullivan's gaze grew anxious. "Your Excellency, since returning from British hands, my position with General Lee's Division was based solely on my seniority, not on any formal authority. Both you and Congress are justified in denying my future command. After all, I am accountable for losing the passes at the battle on Long Island, for the loss of many brave men, and for my capture. Certainly, General Lee never affirmed my status."

Washington lifted back the tent flap and looked back at Sullivan. "Attend your new command, general. You will have two days to rest and refit as best you can. We are in want of all kinds of supplies. If what you say is correct, the ice flow on the Delaware will, in great part, dictate events. So, I must hazard a thrust before it gets too heavy. I will summon you to join the war council when I have refined my plans. Until then, tell nobody of our conversation. The camp may well have spies."

Chapter 26

Princeton, New Jersey, December 21st, 1776

The door creaked, and the portly figure of Swindells entered the drafty room. A strong fire burned hot, casting a faint red glow on the potbellied stove. His manservant took care of that. Swindells shivered. He found the American weather far more bothersome than the rebels.

A rough-looking man sat by the stove savoring a mug of tea laced with rum. Swindells pursed his lips as he spoke to the man, almost as if his words tasted bitter. And indeed, they did. He disliked Americans in general but most especially the rougher sort such as this Root Hog Burns.

Swindells shuffled beside the stove and extended his hands. "Don't bother getting up, Mister Root Hog. I prefer to stand near the stove. It's warmer. I hate your blasted Yankee winters."

Creed took a loud gulp of strongly spiked tea and wiped his mouth with the back of his hand. "Americans are just more hot-blooded than you Englishmen. Winters don't bother us as much. Makes us quick with the gun, knife, or tommy-hawk, too."

Swindells sniffed, "I have sent your report to Leslie and Grant. I trust for your sake they will be pleased." Generals Alexander Leslie and James Grant were the two British generals commanding in New Jersey under Lord Cornwallis.

Root Hog had arrived at Princeton that morning, waving his letter of passage and demanding to see "Captain Swine-dells." Root Hog's lack of manners disgusted Swindells. However, he promised himself he would control his revulsion toward the man as long as the man provided helpful information about the Americans. And this he did, at least this time.

So, Swindells, now eager to report something, anything, to his superiors, agreed and saw him immediately. The report was brief but contained vital information about Sullivan's force. Swindells suspected the report was not entirely accurate. After all, this Root Hog fellow was a bumpkin. However, the report had just enough truth and enough falsehood for him to submit to his superiors, who would never notice the difference, he reasoned. He would build up his new informant's credibility to make himself look good.

Swindells pursed his lips. "The rebel column is heading north. Are you certain?"

"Why, as certain as I could be, Captain."

Swindells pondered the news. "Hmm… most likely going back to join Heath in New York or repair to winter quarters somewhere in northern New Jersey."

Swindells moved his hands over the stove. "I may need you to go back out again, Mister Root Hog."

"Again?"

"But that can wait until I receive further guidance from Grant. A rider just left for Brunswick. With luck, we'll have a response by tomorrow morning."

"How's the response matter? You English can whip 'em wherever they go."

Swindells stared at the glowing hot stove. "Since General Howe has ordered us into winter quarters, I for one do not think it matters a whit."

Creed swirled his tea and gulped down the last few ounces. "Winter quarters? So your generals ain't planning to attack till the spring?"

"Indeed not. General Howe's objective was, and is, to crush the rebellion and bring the rebel leaders to justice. His timetable is no concern of yours."

"Oh, that's right. So long as I make my money."

Creed rose and Swindells led him by the elbow to the door. "I shall send for you when I receive word back. And try not to get too besotted! I paid a handsome sum in guineas for what you have delivered me so far; I want your services — sober."

* * *

Princeton, New Jersey, December 22nd, 1776

Creed decided Root Hog Burns needed some fresh air and grog. A visit to a few of the town's watering holes might sniff out more information.

Creed had indeed provided Swindells with the information he wanted, not to say the information he needed. He thought back on the efforts his men had made to bring it to him. They had ridden hard and suffered much to deliver the information the captain demanded. Information he carefully spun.

Creed gathered his band around him. "All right, lads, Root Hog has been confined to these stables long enough. The dung and animals keep it warm enough, but the heat gives a man a terrible thirst."

They broke into laughter.

"You might need some assistance, Root Hog," Parker said.

Creed's face turned serious. "I'll manage on my own. Two of us might arouse suspicion. In the meantime, clean and load your weapons. Be ready to depart Princeton at a minute's notice. I hope to eavesdrop on some of the garrisons and then force a decision from Swindells. Either way, we're leaving this fair town." Creed tucked two pistols and a tomahawk into his belt and slipped out the door.

He heard the loud noises of men as he turned off the King's Post Road and approached Greenland's Tavern. The tavern was filled with sergeants and corporals eating their midday meals at the sturdy oak plank tables that lined the great room from one end to the other. *Here's one tavern keeper who plans to squeeze in as many customers as possible, especially British regulars with hard cash.*

He scanned the crowd for likely companions and settled on a small group of civilians standing along the far corner of the bar. *Yes – more discreet than directly approaching the men in uniform.* He pushed his way over and smiled broadly at the barkeep. "Mister, pour me a tankard and bring one for each of my friends."

The stranger's largesse surprised the men at the bar. One of them, a middle-aged man in a brown corduroy suit, gave him a pleasant smile. "That is extremely good of you, sir.

Is there an occasion, or do you always bestow drinks upon strangers with such obvious ease?"

Creed pushed back his hat, wiped his nose with his sleeve, and looked at the man with one eye closed and his head cocked. "Now see here, pardner, Root Hog Burns will share when he is on the rise and borrow when he is in decline. Right now, I'm on the rise. Just made some real money on a firewood deal. These lobsterbacks pay real good. But Lord only knows for how long."

"I am sorry, sir. My name is Lyman Stockton, and I certainly meant no offense. However, if you are selling wood to the British, I would say your business here is secure for at least the next four months."

Lyman Stockman! Creed recognized the name. Stockton hailed from one of the original Quaker families that had settled Princeton in the last century. He was a lecturer at Nassau Hall, the College of New Jersey. As a professor at the College of New Jersey, Stockton kept his political affiliation discreet.

Stockton raised his tankard in a toast. The others joined him, and a murmur of chatter arose about the British garrison staying here in winter quarters and its effect on the citizenry.

"What's it like now for the locals?"

"Most of the rebels and Whigs have either left of their own volition or been driven out of their homes. In any case, they have all been dispossessed of their property," Stockton replied.

"Well, now a few have taken Howe's oath. So far, they haven't been discommoded," one of the drinkers said.

"So, this here General Howe seems to be winning folk over?"

"Not quite," Stockton replied. "Withal, Howe's plan to win over the American citizenry from under the rebel leaders' noses has gone flat. So much for winning the population's heart and mind for king and country."

Creed continued his probing. "Well, that's right good to hear. When I asked them their numbers and how long they would need firewood you'd think I asked 'em what their strength wuz, an' how long they would defend this place. Why, they threatened to shoot me as a spy!"

"Well, such questions could be seen as of some value to the rebels. Did they answer you?"

"No. But in the end, I got paid." Creed slapped his knee, and the men joined him in laughter. Creed could see the idea of such a bumpkin getting over on the British amused them.

Stockton took another swallow of the brew, then casually glanced over at the soldiers eating and drinking loudly. "You only get paid if you are a Tory or you take the oath, Mister Burns, so Tory you must be."

"Call me Root Hog, not Tory. However, some accuse me of being a cowboy. What do I know of cows?"

The men laughed, again unsure of the strange man's meaning or his political leanings.

Creed continued bantering, "Well, I do admit I done some work for the lobsterbacks. They are the law in most places. But I got no head for poli-ticks, if ya know what I mean."

One of the other men said, "So you are neutral, Mister Burns? That is, Root Hog."

The men exchanged smirks.

Creed cocked his head mischievously. "Didn't say that, pardner. I take the side of whoever is paying me. Seems simpler these days."

"Indeed," Stockton retorted.

Several muttered, avoiding eye contact with Stockton, almost ashamed. Despite their Whig leanings, these men chose to take the oath and enjoy hearth and home with their families during the winter. Many justified their decision by convincing themselves they would become patriots in the spring if things improved for the cause.

Another round of ale gave Creed all the information he needed. He confirmed his estimate of the British at Princeton and Trenton. He verified that the forces at Trenton and Bordentown were indeed Hessians. He learned that Colonel Johann Rall commanded the brigade at Trenton, while a Hessian named von Donop was in charge at Bordentown.

One of the men, a lawyer, waved a copy of *Rivington's Gazette*, the notorious Tory newspaper in New York. "See here, the British have captured Charles Lee, Washington's number two. He is reputably the most capable of the rebel military commanders. The paper quotes Howe proclaiming that Lee's capture—effectively ended any hope of resistance by the rebels."

One of the men muttered, "Howe's statement underscores the widely-held belief that when his army turns out of winter quarters in the spring, they will march unopposed to Philadelphia."

"That so?" Creed asked.

The lawyer nodded. "Exactly so, and there he will accept the rebels' unconditional surrender."

Creed had learned enough to forgo any other forays that afternoon. He decided, instead, to pay a surprise visit to Swindells.

* * *

When Creed walked in, Swindells had his face in a piece of cold mutton with ale and bread. Swindells wiped the grease from his cheeks and stood to face Creed, waving his fork at the upstart. "How did you get in here, Mister Burns?"

Creed smiled impishly. "Ain't many locks or guards can keep me away from something I want, Captain Swine-dells."

"Burns, I thought I made it clear to you I would send for you when your services were needed." Swindell's voice was icier than the New Jersey roads.

Creed grinned. "Call me Root Hog, Captain Swine-dells…"

Swindells stammered with barely suppressed rage, "You… American scum! I should call for your arrest."

A red-jacketed private stormed into the room and pointed his bayonet menacingly at Creed. "I'll skewer him for you, sir!"

I still need this man. Swindells regained his composure. "It's quite all right, Private. You may leave us. His eyes narrowed. "Very well, Root Hog, what is the meaning of this intrusion?"

Creed stabbed his finger in the air. "Me and my men are tired of sitting in that stinking stable waiting for your next order. Especially when that order might never come."

"What do you want?"

"Either you give us some work or let us go. Maybe your friends in Brunswick or Perth Amboy have work for us. I hear tell that the cowboys and skinners up north are near waging war with each other. Ya know, there are lots of cowboys runnin' around your army, but damned few that produce results like Root Hog does."

Swindells felt his heart turn cold with fear. He did not want to lose this man's services, at least not just yet. He had come to despise him, but if his intelligence, false as it might prove, received approval from his superiors, it would make him look good with little effort. If the intelligence was found to be questionable, he could have Root Hog Burns and his associates arrested as spies and hanged after a perfunctory trial. That would set an example for the citizens and earn him accolades as a master counterspy, if not a full-fledged spymaster. Swindells just needed to stall.

A rider from Grant had arrived that morning with word that the information from Root Hog Burns had been sent to Howe's chief of intelligence, Major Sandy Drummond. A response from Drummond was expected within twenty-four hours.

***

"What do you propose I have you do, Mister Root Hog?"

The question at first stumped Creed. Strangely enough, he did not anticipate Swindells throwing the problem back at him. *Could this be a test, or worse, a trap?* Whatever he proposed might lead Swindells to demand the opposite. If he suspected a subterfuge, he might put impossible conditions on the proposal.

Creed scratched his whiskered chin thoughtfully. "Why, I figure them rebels might be just as cold as we be 'bout now. Expect they need firewood and vittles. Supposin' I take some samples across the river and try to barter with them. Maybe meet some officers and such. Might be able to learn a thing or two about 'em."

Swindells rubbed his hands together reflexively and thought for a second. "Cross the Delaware? An interesting proposition. How long will you be gone?"

"Not too long, 'less the weather turns nastier. That river will be getting full of ice floes 'bout now. Maybe a week, no more."

"You shall have four days. And you shall leave no earlier than tomorrow noon. Meanwhile, use the good king's silver I gave you to purchase your goods. What you do with the worthless rebel script is your problem. When we meet again, I will provide you with my shopping list."

Swindell's glare turned into a grin at the last remark. Creed cursed him to himself. The scoundrel was making them finance his espionage with their pay. Both knew the rebel script, continental dollars, were near worthless in many places, but most especially on the ground the king's troops held. *What contempt these English have for their American cousins.*

* * *

Creed wore down his boots, knocking on shop door after shop door. It took most of the day, but he finally managed to buy two dozen sacks of cornmeal from a warehouse on Maidenhead Road. It was old grain, almost stale, and the British refused to buy it from the granary, so he got a good price.

Still, Creed knew the starving patriots in Pennsylvania would make good use of it. His men had eaten, cared for their horses, and packed all their gear. Beall had fashioned a sled from a damaged boat that was abandoned near the stable. They would use it to haul the grain, extra vittles, and clothing. Parker had rigged the boat to make it a decent vessel to cross the river.

Earlier, Creed had visited Greenland's Tavern again, where he had an "accidental" encounter with Lyman Stockton. He bought Stockton another tankard of ale and told him stories about Indian fighting near the Canadian border, all complete nonsense.

Stockton mentioned that General Cornwallis was rumored to be planning a long leave back to England to care for his sick wife, another sign of Howe's confidence in his victory. Creed noted all of this for his next report, but what caught his interest even more was a small group of green-jacketed soldiers quietly eating in the corner of the tavern. A New Jersey volunteer unit. *Provincials!*

When Creed reported back to Swindells, the large iron stove hissed constantly. The captain sat at his small table, wearing a scarf, ear mufflers, and gloves. Next to him sat a man of indistinct age and plain features. Creed immediately recognized him as the stranger who had met Charles Lee at the Blue House in Ridley. However, this time he was dressed in the uniform of a British dragoon sergeant.

"Take a seat over here, Root Hog, and meet Sergeant Digby of His Majesty's 17th Light Dragoons," Swindells said, accentuating the word, dragoons.

The polite tone surprised Creed.

Numbly, Creed did as he was told. His entire being was now gripped by the fear that this sergeant and erstwhile secret agent might recognize him. Despite the room's stifling heat, a chill went through him. As he sat, he muttered a silent "Jesus, Mary, and Joseph," praying the trooper did not connect him to the Blue House.

Because of his devotion to his mother and the upbringing she gave him, Creed remained committed to his religion, though he practiced it sporadically. His dedication paid off.

The sergeant did not recognize him. Curiously, he appeared anxious, almost fearful. One of the ironies of the espionage trade is that men who can face a rain of bullets or cold steel in battle often melt when the dark shadow of espionage casts a pall of fear over them.

Swindells poured a measure of dark rum for each of them. Digby downed his dram without a word. Creed waited for Swindells to tip his glass, and then both men did the same. The portly captain opened the discussion, "Sergeant Digby has requested our support in a special mission."

"Actually, sir, it's my master's request."

Digby's tone patronized Swindells, who nodded like a schoolboy. Creed thought it odd that such a pompous and rank-conscious officer would defer to a sergeant. *Something unusual is afoot.*

Yet the exchange enabled Creed to regain his composure and return to being Root Hog. "Now I don't know 'bout that. This sounds serious. Why me 'n my boys…"

Swindells abruptly cut him off. "Now see here, Root Hog, you came to me looking for a mission. If it is the king's silver you want, now you shall have your fill of it. Sergeant Digby has a mission that, if you succeed, shall pay double what we earlier agreed. And in British sterling."

Creed's face did not betray his surprise. He had learned over time that the king parted with his gold and silver with the greatest reluctance, especially when it came to paying spies.

Creed rubbed his hands together. "Well now, you are talkin' my language, Captain Swine-dells. Just what have ya got in mind?"

Digby laughed out loud at the butchering of the officer's name. When he regained his composure, he looked intently at Creed. "Mister Root Hog, you must find someone whom we have reason to believe is in the vicinity of the rebel army."

Creed stifled his shock. "And do what with this, someone?"

"That depends, Mister, ahhh, Root Hog. We expected communication from him quite some time ago. We sent this person to New York in September. We hoped to hear from him thereafter. But the rapid defeat of the rebels and their cowardly flight through the Jersey hinterlands likely precluded him from getting word to us."

"Just how wuz that supposed to happen?" Creed chided. He wanted more information. Digby took the bait.

"We provided him a contact, but a good part of the city was burned the night he visited our contact. We assumed he died in the fire, so many did. However, we recently obtained control of someone who…" Digby cleared his throat with a gravelly "Harrumph."

"What do you mean, someone?" Creed asked.

Digby paused, then licked his lips. "Well, if you read the papers, you know we recently obtained an important prisoner."

"Root Hog cannot read, Sergeant Digby," Swindells said.

"Neither can I, sir. Bastard sergeants can only do the company rolls," Digby said. "We had hoped our prisoner would know something of our person."

"Does he?" Creed asked.

"It is not your place to ask questions, Root Hog," Swindells said.

"That's quite all right, sir. Mister Root Hog is a savvy gentleman. We like that. My master likes that."

"So, he does, huh?" Creed asked brazenly.

Digby shook his head. "My master, Major Drummond, has decided to force communication. When our good Captain Swine-dells, excuse me, sir, Swindells, reported on your efforts, we…"

Drummond? Now that's useful information. Creed asked boldly, "What is it ya major wants, pardner?"

"Well, we thought to use your good offices to try to locate him. And to establish a channel for the flow of information."

Creed's mind raced in a hundred directions. A bumper at Whist or Royal Flush in poker was nothing compared to this incredible stroke of luck. His Irish luck had returned after weeks of miserable riding and skulking across New Jersey. *Could this be a trap?* The sheer chance of the British coming to him seemed unlikely. He needed to be cautious, but he calculated that the potential gain outweighed the risk. "So, you want me to, to spy?"

Digby gave him a curious look, at once solicitous and demanding. "No, Mister Root Hog. Our friend is the spy. You'll merely be a humble courier. A go-between. Your apparent facility at traversing our armies proves most useful, that's all."

* * *

McConkey's Ferry

The White Knights were packed and ready. Creed swung effortlessly into the saddle and patted Finn's withers. He looked up. Snowflakes drifted through the cold December air. "Already, the weather's changing for the worse, so we'll make straight for the river."

"Where do we cross, Root Hog?" an anxious Parker asked.

"Near McConkey's Ferry. I think with a little work on your part, our sled will handle us one at a time."

"Beats swimming, sir," Thomas said.

They all laughed.

"I'll take the lead." Beall spurred his horse down the street towards the Post Road.

They arrived at the river as the crown of the winter sun dipped to the east. Creed still had his letter, which helped them get past the British sentries and patrols.

A few minutes later, Parker was digging his boots into the frozen embankment and sliding the boat into the icy Delaware waters.

As the boat eased across choppy waters, Creed looked back at the far bank. "Row faster!" A dozen men with firelocks on the Jersey shore!"

Strong arms worked paddles and poles against the current.

Pop! Crack!

"The British are on to us!" Parker drew his musket from the sling.

A ball zipped past Creed and hit a nearby tree with a splat. "No, lads, we are exposed here."

More lead whizzed just over their heads.

"Getting closer," Parker exclaimed.

"What'll we do?" Thomas gasped as he struggled to control the pack horses.

"Keep rowing," said Creed. "We can't return fire."

"How did they find us?" asked Jonathan.

"They trailed us most of the way. Either cowboys or skinners out for plunder."

Creed was worried but didn't show it. But as their craft lurched toward the far shore, in the twilight shadows, the freebooters' shots splashed harmlessly into the dark waters and eventually stopped.

Chapter 27

Washington's Headquarters, New Town, Pennsylvania, December 24th, 1776

Fitzgerald played pensively with his quill, occasionally jotting down a thought or two on the paper. Creed had done remarkable work, he thought. The young man had returned from Princeton with a wealth of information about the British and Hessian garrisons just across the river.

The British ploy to use him as a courier between their spymaster and what could only be their once and future spy, Golden Apple, confirmed they were still unaware of their agent's demise in New York. More importantly, Creed's last trip to New York successfully convinced the British that Golden Apple had established himself near Washington's headquarters.

Creed has brought us a great coup indeed. Fitzgerald now knew about the British spymaster, a major named Drummond, and at least one of his associates, a sergeant named Digby. Fitzgerald had started to piece together a picture of the intelligence network arrayed against him.

An hour later, Fitzgerald was in Washington's room to report on what he knew and to plan their next move. When he finally finished his report, Washington's reply caught him by surprise.

"The news you bring is good, Robert. However, I have little time to develop it. I'll leave that to your capable hands."

"But the strategic implications are enormous, Your Excellency."

"There will be no implications If I don't focus on the next few days. Please bear with me."

Fitzgerald felt a tinge of guilt. The man had much on his shoulders. "I will keep you apprised of our progress. Have you decided yet on the army's situation?"

"As you know, for days I have had the idea to attempt a bold move to restore the morale of the army and our new nation. The information young Creed provided Sullivan earlier led me in that direction. But now, the latest report from Creed himself removes any doubts I might have had earlier."

Fitzgerald was pleased. "It's good to see our espionage efforts are proving useful. Will you move soon?"

"Preparations are underway as we speak. Orders have already gone out to prepare the troops. Rations for three days were cooked and issued. Fresh flints and such powder as could be found have been distributed throughout the army. The time for planning is over. The time for action is now!"

"How will you cross?"

Washington took a deep breath. "I have once more called on the services of Colonel John Glover and his Marblehead sailors. They saved the Continental Army from the jaws of destruction on Long Island. By God, I need them once more."

Fitzgerald's mouth tightened. "But now Glover will face a more daunting task. Transporting an army across the Delaware River amid ice floes during the dark of a cold winter night."

***

Washington called Creed to a war council that afternoon. Creed arrived early, and a Life Guardsman took him straight to Washington's study. Fitzgerald was already there, waiting with the commander-in-chief.

Washington rose from his desk and extended his arms, taking both of Creed's hands in his own. "My heartfelt thanks to you and your men, Jeremiah! Because of your efforts, I now comprehend the nature of the enemy's defenses and the character of its leadership. Enough to risk a strike—and so we shall do."

"Thank you for your words of confidence, Your Excellency. Only would that I brought more..."

"You have brought enough for me to risk a strike at their posts, and we shall do so on Christmas! Come and take a seat. Let us discuss our intelligence needs once more…" Washington led Creed to a seat by the small fire burning in the corner fireplace.

Fitzgerald leaned forward in his chair and raised his spectacles. "We have further need of your services, Jeremiah. But, this time, in a more conventional setting."

"Conventional, sir?"

"Yes, in uniform."

Creed's eyes brightened at the comment.

Washington chimed in, "There will be several columns involved in the attack. Brigadier General John Cadwalader will move on Bordentown with his division of nineteen hundred men. They are mostly locals, militia from Pennsylvania and New Jersey. Brigadier General James Ewing will strike directly across from here and seize the bridge across the Assenpunk River, just south of Trenton. His force is smaller, only around seven hundred men, against the local militia. The rest of the army will move north to McConkey's Ferry and cross north of Trenton."

Fitzgerald leaned forward. "That is where you come in, young man."

Creed gave a puzzled look.

Washington nodded. "I shall split the command into two wings. One wing will take the River Road, the other the Pennington Road. Each wing will be about a thousand strong. From there, we will advance on Trenton, where I hope to drive this Colonel Rall and his Germans into the waiting arms of General Ewing."

Creed pulled nervously at his ear. "And my role, sir?"

Washington did not answer.

Fitzgerald briefly closed his eyes before opening them again. He looked at Creed with notable intensity. "Your role, Jeremiah, and that of your White Knights, is to move ahead of the two wings by one hour and secure the Hessian outposts without disrupting the

Christmas celebrations in Trenton. Once that's done, you will position yourselves to watch over the town and warn us if they become aware of our presence."

Fitzgerald opened his valise and spread a map across Washington's desk. "Does this look familiar?"

"Of course, sir, 'tis the sketch map I made while observing Trenton."

Fitzgerald pointed to the markings at Pennington and River Roads. "But what are they?"

"They are the two strong points we encountered on our way to find General Sullivan. At this one, we were nearly discovered by some Hessians relieving themselves in the dark."

"And this one?" Fitzgerald asked.

"'Tis the strong point along the Pennington Road."

"You must secure these in advance of the attacking columns, Jeremiah," Washington said.

Creed eyed the map carefully and replied slowly and with hesitance, "Your Excellency, the outposts are one mile apart and a little more than half that distance from town. If we take them, it must be with cold steel."

"Precisely," replied Washington.

Creed smiled sardonically. "I suppose when this work is done, I should just slip into Trenton and seize this Hessian Colonel Rall in his very nightgown."

Fitzgerald shot back. "My dear lad, have you been spying on us? We had that very conversation before you arrived."

"Young man, it is Colonel Rall's brigade I want, not him," Washington said. "I need not tell you these are desperate hours for this army, this nation. Many of our troops' enlistments expire in early January. I must strike a blow now if I am to save the rebellion from collapse. That is why I risk you and your men on this venture."

"Long term, your role as a courier between the late Braaf and his spymaster, this Major Drummond, poses unique opportunities," Fitzgerald said.

"But the reality is if we do not achieve a victory here and now, there will be no tomorrow for this nation," Washington said. "So your role, and the risks involved in it, are a calculation I take reluctantly, but with a certainty of conviction."

Creed had no reply to the eloquence and passion of America's most respected man. He simply nodded as the fire crackled and hissed in the background.

Fitzgerald broke the mood. "You shall have some help in this enterprise, Jeremiah. General Sullivan has graciously offered a file from the remnant of the ranger battalion that served with you at Haarlem. They number only eight, but he speaks highly of them, as he does of you."

Creed raised his chin. "So long as they know how to use cold steel, sir. I need men who can use the bayonet, tomahawk, and knife."

Fitzgerald smiled. The young officer's tone and look showed he embraced this new mission regardless of the danger. "Yes, and you shall need some of our good Irish luck. Let us hope it holds out for you, and all of us."

But Fitzgerald's humorous riposte met with silence.

* * *

The Blue House, Ridley, New Jersey, December 25th, 1776

The clock struck four. In the Blue House's large room, more than twenty Christmas revelers lay in various states of drunkenness. Eruptions of snoring, moaning, and flatulence sporadically broke the early morning quiet. The only light came from a dying fire in the stone fireplace that once lit the vast room with a blaze. Now it emitted a dull red glow and spat the occasional ember across the floor.

The Blue House's Christmas Eve celebration was a swamp tradition. While most of the Jerseys attended church and celebrated at home, Ridley gathered a rough crowd of peddlers, tradesmen, backwoodsmen, and criminals who soaked themselves in ale and rum, washed down with cheap frontier whisky. No prayers. No songs to God's son for these revelers. The drinking was tough, the songs bawdy, and the women quick.

Jannetje gazed across the dark chamber like a general surveying the day after a great battle. For Jannetje, the Christmas event was all business, no pleasure. She and her servants catered to nearly one hundred celebrants, freely serving joints of beef, mutton, or pork along with fowl and venison washed down with large quantities of drink. She wondered each year why she did it and promised herself that this year would be the last. Jannetje would never admit it, but the revel was a favorite of her late husband, and its continuation was her only memory of him.

Satisfied that all the revelers were gone, Jannetje shrugged and climbed the stairs to her room, exhausted. She entered the room and threw her apron on her chair. She was too tired to light a candle, so she began changing in the dark. As she slipped out of her stockings and petticoat, a pair of strong arms wrapped around her waist, and a whiskered face buried itself into the nape of her neck. From the touch, feel, and smell, she knew who it was.

Rather than fight the intruder, she succumbed to his caresses. After what seemed an eternity, she moaned, "What kept you, Harry?"

He murmured, almost inaudibly. "Everything— nothing."

* * *

Harry awoke with Jannetje asleep beside him. He peered at her face in the early winter morning light. He wondered how someone so pretty and kind could become so easily involved with men, especially men of questionable character like him. He knew of her connection to Lee. He understood the allure a powerful general might hold for the daughter of an impoverished backwoods farmer.

Then there was— the door handle turned. The *click* woke Jannetje from her sleep. Harry reached reflexively for his pistol—too late. The shot rang out with a *woosh* and then a deafening *bang* that seemed to envelop the room in smoke. Harry leaped from the bed just as the pistol's hammer struck the firing pan.

In the split second it took to launch the lead ball, Harry rolled to the floor and lunged at the shadowy figure in a half-crouch. The ball whizzed past his cheek, and like a swamp cougar, Harry was on the intruder.

A shadowy figure swung the smoking pistol at Harry's head like a club, but Harry grabbed his wrist and twisted it to the side. A fist crashed into the side of Harry's head. But the punch was slow and clumsy, making it sound worse than it was. Harry stepped back to catch his breath.

The intruder raised the pistol with both hands in another attempt to club his naked opponent. Harry slipped under his arms and delivered a hammer blow to the taller man's chin. The head snapped back, and Harry followed with a left jab to the man's rib cage. The cracking of ribs enraged the man.

"Damn you, Roy Harry, I'll slit your balls off," croaked the attacker.

He reached for his belt and drew a long dagger. His long arm rose as the wicked blade slashed at Harry. But in the darkness, he caught the bedstead with the blade.

"*Verdammt!*" he raged.

Harry pounced on the knife-wielder, kicked him in the side of the knee, and wrestled the knife from his grasp. But still, the intruder towered over Harry and once again waved the heavy pistol over him.

"I'll scatter your rebel brains, Harry!"

The intruder's eyes and mouth widened as Harry stabbed the dagger into his stomach. His large frame stiffened, then collapsed to the floor. Harry stood over his body for a few seconds, panting to catch his breath. He suddenly realized he was completely naked.

Harry struck a flint and lit a candle. He went over to the bed to grab a blanket and his boots. A sudden smirk crossed his face *She slept through it all, the vixen!* "You may come out now, Jannetje. Our intruder can't harm us now. What sort of Christmas were you celebrating here anyway?"

She did not respond. He snatched the candle and held it over the bed. Even in the faint flickering candlelight, he could see Jannetje's body sprawled across the blankets in a pool of blood. Her lips were pursed as if to say something, and her eyes stared blankly up at the canopy.

"My God... Jannetje... oh my God... damn...." Harry fought the urge to cry.

Shaking with fear and despair, he closed her eyes and covered her body with a quilt. He slipped into his buckskins and then went to examine his assailant, Jannetje's killer. The dim candlelight revealed a tall man in a green uniform—Dierk Van Buskirk. The body suddenly convulsed. *He's still alive!* Harry pulled his saber from its scabbard and placed the point against Van Buskirk's throat.

"Go on, Harry, and make it quick. I'm a dead man anyway."

Van Buskirk's comment was followed by a rush of bloody sputum that dribbled down his chin.

"Your jealousy cost you the object of your twisted lust, Dierk. I won't kill you, but I will watch you die. For Jannetje's sake."

"Jannetje?" Van Buskirk's eyes blazed for a moment.

"She's dead. You killed her, you Dutch scum. The ball meant for me found her breast. Was your jealousy worth that?"

"Jealousy? You think this is about my jealousy. You are a fool, Harry." Van Buskirk's breathing became halting. Harry knew he was almost done.

"You've moments left, Van Buskirk. Rid yourself of what demons you have. You came to kill me for being with Jannetje, but you killed her, and through that, yourself."

Van Buskirk smiled grimly. "That's not true. Jannetje—lured you here. We hoped... to recruit you ...or kill you. Either way, the English pay in gold." He spat and coughed more blood.

"Go on."

"Jannetje... came over to our side. She wanted me, Harry, not you... But more...she wanted... the king's gold even more... to keep her in the Blue House. Worthless rebel paper would not. "

It dawned on Harry that this was likely true. Jannetje was as avaricious as her late husband. It was a quality Harry had found most attractive.

"Well, now she's on the dark side. Thanks to you—she picked the wrong side. Do you know why I went over to the cause, Van Buskirk? Because the side that aims best wins. Patriots are gonna win, Dierk. Not because our cause is righteous or liberty triumphs over tyranny. The patriots will win because they shoot straight. Your one shot missed me, Dierk."

Van Buskirk's eyes widened into a blank stare. Harry cursed himself for his lapse in judgment. *You can have each other and the king's gold—in hell.*

* * *

McConkey's Ferry, December 25th, 1776

Nearly 2,400 anxious men trudged along winding roads covered with a layer of snow. They moved quietly under strict secrecy, slipping behind low-lying hills along the Delaware to avoid the eyes of Loyalist spies watching from the opposite shore. Once they reached their assembly areas west of McConkey's Ferry, regimental adjutants began issuing the order of march for the crossing.

Washington galloped up to the ferry, eager to meet with Glover, whose Gloucester regiment was vital to their success. He found him at the edge of the riverbank.

"How goes it, Colonel Glover?"

Glover's face looked grim. "A bold and risky plan, sir, but I think we can do it. We'll use locally available boats, mostly those Durham Boats."

"Durham boats?"

Glover pointed at several long, dark barges. "Durham boats, Your Excellency. That's what they call them here. Barges specially designed to ferry heavy freight, mostly lumber and pig iron. They shuttle across the Delaware between New Jersey and Pennsylvania, or downstream to Philadelphia."

"They're impressive looking. How do they differ from normal long boats and barges?"

"Oh, sir, these sturdy boats are large, some as large as eight feet wide and sixty in length. But they have a draft of only a few feet when properly loaded. "

Washington crossed his arms over his chest. "I'm no sailor, but how will your men row amidst the ice floes if they come?"

"Oh, they shall come, Your Excellency. Oaring will be difficult, but most of the boats have poles and extra-long steering sweep." He smiled sheepishly. "That's a rudder to you, sir."

Washington nodded patiently. "Go on."

The long sweeps help us navigate the swirling currents of the upper Delaware. Most of our crews will use poles to push the boats ahead. Four to six men walk toward the stern on a narrow plank along the gunwale. Each man pushes off, driving the iron-tipped setting poles into the riverbed and moving the boat forward.

Washington was impressed. "The danger, the hazard, this night would try the nerves and strength of even your experienced seafarers, Colonel Glover."

"They are the best, Your Excellency, and take pride in doing what no others can do."

* * *

Creed and his small command had arrived at the ferry landing earlier that day. It would be several hours before the main party arrived, and only the Gloucester sailors and some local militiamen standing watch occupied the ferry landing. Creed used the time to get to know the new men, present and rehearse his plan. He also chose the Durham boat for his crossing. They would cross before the rest of the army. Washington himself would give the order to depart, expected to be some time after dark.

They took shelter in a small nearby boathouse, where Creed decided to review the mission plan. "We'll stay here while I walk us through it," Creed said. "I know you Rangers are familiar with the planning process."

"That we are," said their leader, Lieutenant Evander Mason.

Most of the Rangers had heard about Creed's exploits at Haarlem, even though none had served in his company. They also knew he was the first officer to visit their revered Lieutenant Colonel Knowlton after a British musket ball struck him down at the height of the battle. This meant a lot to them.

The Rangers wore tattered homespun uniforms. A few had brown or grey blankets used as ponchos to shield them from the cold and rain. Despite their fatigue and obvious undernourishment, they appeared and were as tough as deer hide. Creed and his men dressed in their continental dark blue uniforms but wore the darkened belts and leggings he had devised for night operations on Long Island. He traded his regulation cocked hat for a warmer, more practical beaver skin hat.

"Now, lads, our mission is simple. Cross the river while avoiding the crush of the ice floes. Navigate through the dark woods. Find the enemy sentries and strong points. Eliminate them with cold steel. Last but certainly not least, establish a position to watch over the advance of the main body on Trenton. There will be a spot of hot tea with rum for our efforts when we enter the town."

The men stared at him blankly, not knowing how to take his last comment.

Finally, Lieutenant Mason spoke, "Lieutenant Creed, most of this army's enlistments end in a few days. Rumor has it that His Excellency himself is offering hard currency to anyone who extends for the duration of this campaign. Many have extended, but most plan to leave regardless. And who can blame them? There has been little food, shelter, or clothing, not to mention suitable weapons and powder. If the enemy doesn't get them, they still face starvation, disease, and freezing from exposure."

Mason walked slowly by each of his men, wagging a finger. "Many of my boys have families and farms, some of which are suffering from the ravages of the British and Hessians, not to mention the damned Tories. Despite this, they have already taken the oath. The boys signed for the duration, and they didn't do it for money, but for the cause. A spot of tea with rum is always appreciated, but my Rangers have stayed on to fight."

Creed's face reddened. He was impressed by Mason's eloquence and not a little ashamed of his unintended slight to these fine men. "Yes, of course, Lieutenant Mason. Your Rangers, all the Rangers, serve with dignity and courage. However, my men have also sacrificed much with little break since New York. They have, in fact, agreed to stay for the duration of the war, not merely the campaign. If I may speak for them, you may rest assured that we are honored to serve alongside you."

Creed then went through his plan. "We'll split into two six-man teams and proceed along the Pennington and River Roads, identify any *vedettes*, that is, pickets, and quietly dispatch them."

"Have they any defenses?" Mason asked.

Creed nodded. "Yes, each road has a strong point approximately one mile distant from Trenton. The cabin near the River Road is of particular concern. We came upon it when trying to link up with General Sullivan. It has been fortified into a blockhouse."

Mason spat a piece of something onto the ground. "How many defend it?"

"Maybe thirty men. Not more than fifty."

"Hessians?" The American fear of Hessians came through in Mason's voice.

"Yes. It's Hessians we'll face throughout this night."

"And the other strongpoint, on the Pennington Road. How many are there?"

"Cannot be certain, so assume the same."

"Why not go around them?"

"These strong points could delay or even stop our two main columns."

Mason nodded. "I get it. That in turn could change the timing of the attack or give warning to the main Hessian force in Trenton. Anything else for us to take?"

"As best we could tell, these are the only attempts at fortifying the approaches to Trenton from upriver. "

Creed sketched a rough map on the frozen ground. "Now, to take them, we need to split into two groups and move along these parallel roads. Each group will press inward once the roads and woods are cleared of pickets."

Mason eyed him. "Who will be in these groups?"

Creed swept his sword blade along each of the roads. "Your men and one or two of mine. Each group will lead a company of Virginia riflemen. But we will assault the strong points and cut them off from Trenton."

Mason turned to his men. "A little complicated, I'd say, boys, but doable."

Creed nodded. "The challenge is ensuring nobody escapes and warns the garrison at Trenton."

"How far is that?"

"Less than a mile away. So, we can't risk firearms."

Mason's men began whispering.

"Lieutenant Creed, how in the name of heaven can we take these blockhouses without using firearms? Can cold steel be enough if the buildings are as well defended as you describe?"

Creed grimaced. "With great difficulty and much luck, of course. Also, I count on the weather and the festive nature of this holiday for the Germans. Besides, they will be tired and on edge from chasing down militia patrols, real or imagined."

Mason looked incredulous. "Surely a sentry or two will stand watch…"

Creed cut him off. "Perhaps. Or perhaps not, even professionals make mistakes. We observed them making that mistake some days ago. That, plus the fatigue, the weather, and the strain of a long, arduous campaign, will help our situation. These are mortal men after all. Mortals make mistakes."

Mason's face showed his skepticism. "So how do we link up with these Virginians, these riflemen?"

Creed smiled weakly. "A good question. They'll follow our tracks along the road, leaving one-quarter hour behind us. That will give us time to clear out any sentries and do a final check of the strong points. You'll take one file along the River Road. Private Parker will guide you. I'll lead the rest along Pennington Road. Once that strong point is cleared, I'll link up with Colonel Knox and his artillery and guide them to their positions just north of Trenton."

Mason remained relentless in his skepticism. "All well and good, Lieutenant Creed, but my objective is a locked, two-story building. How do we take it?"

Private Elias Parker stepped forward. "By seizing the high ground, sir."

Mason gave a confused look. Parker lifted an anchor he had purloined from one of the Durham boats and held it up for all to see. The small iron anchor had three sharp prongs, giving it the appearance and the utility of a grappling hook.

Parker tossed the anchor into the dark sky like it was a feather. "The second story is about twelve feet off the ground. I have two of these anchors with twenty feet of sturdy rope. We'll sneak up on the cabin quietly and use these to pull a few of us onto the roof, enter the house from a gable, and work our way down with cold steel. The riflemen will surround the house, disarm the defenders, and cut off the retreat of anyone who tries to escape."

Creed chimed in, "You see, 'tis a natural instinct for soldiers defending a building to flee threats from above. In sea battles, they place snipers on the masts to rain bullets down on the enemy's deck. And when besieging fortifications, siege towers have a morale-boosting effect on the defenders that far exceeds the tower's actual usefulness."

"The noise will alarm the sentry or the watch."

"You don't know Elias. Moves like a cat. He'll take care of things."

Mason now grew excited. "This makes things interesting. Why, a couple of my good Rangers at the roof with tomahawks and knives can drive them out of the building — into the arms of the Virginians."

Creed nodded. "Exactly, although I pray they'll be ready to hoist the white flag by then."

The door to the boathouse suddenly opened, and Scovel joined the band of determined warriors.

Creed stood and smiled. "Let's pray the good Lieutenant Scovel is here to arrest us and save us from our trouble this bitter night."

Scovel did not smile. Instead, the normally loud New Englander spoke in a soft, sympathetic voice, "Pardon my interruption, gentlemen. I know you are about important business, but I have a concern to address with you."

The Rangers looked askance at Scovel, dressed in an officer's uniform from Washington's Life Guard and, more notably, the aigrette of the Provost. Since the Continental Army lacked a proper military police unit, they used some of the commander-in-chief's Life Guard as a makeshift police force. Scovel appeared weary and cold, but his weariness was unusual, the expression of someone carrying a heavy burden.

Creed suddenly became ill at ease. "Of course, Lieutenant Scovel, please go on."

"His Excellency insists on crossing with the first regiment. I understand your boat is ahead of them in the queue. My duty is to keep His Excellency alive, yet Colonel Glover tells me His Excellency's boat is full. I ask you to consider a way to place me on your vessel so that I may fulfill my duty."

"I agree. His Excellency's welfare comes first," Creed replied.

"But all the seats are accounted for, sir," Beall said.

Creed grabbed Thomas Jeffries by the shoulder. "Thomas, you will remain behind, and Lieutenant Scovel will take your seat. I had hoped to leave our horses in the hands of the gunners. The cannons cross last, it seems. But withal, I prefer to have a trusted man of me own with them."

Thomas began to anger at the affront, and his face showed it. "Now, Lieutenant, I expected to be crossin' with you. I am a White Knight too."

Creed wagged his finger in Thomas's face. "See here, young man. You are a critical and valued member of this enterprise. We must take the road to Trenton on foot, but once there, we shall need Finn and all our horses for the challenges ahead. There is no greater charge than caring for them."

***

Early in the evening, they left the boathouse and shuffled down to the quay. Creed went straight to the vessel chosen for his mission and was surprised when the helmsman greeted him with a firm grip on his forearm.

"Lieutenant Jeremiah Creed! Not surprised to see you here on this mission. I see His Excellency is still intent on killing you off, eh?"

Creed startled, then grinned and returned the handshake with both hands. "Well now, if 'tisn't Ezekial Hazard himself! Why, with you in command of this ship, captain, there is no telling what mischief we might yet cause the bloody lobsterbacks."

Sergeant Ezekial Hazard, a member of the Gloucester Regiment, had served with Jeremiah Creed and his men in New York. He and his crew transported them on a secret mission across the East River, leading to the capture of the British spy, Braaf. They grew to respect each other through the trials of an eventful night. The bonds forged by men in combat proved lasting and rarely broken.

Creed waved his hand at the long, black craft along the riverbank. "So tell me, captain, have ye had much experience with these, Durham vessels, are they?"

Hazard pulled his pipe from his mouth. "None whatsoever, but crossing should be little problem. They are good vessels, for sure. Sturdy and rugged enough for our work."

Creed glanced across the dark water. "Assuming this lovely weather stays as good."

Scovel stood there aghast. "I'd say the weather is anything but good. The temperature hovers just over freezing, visibility is poor, and the snow continues to fall. Worse, the icy water moves in fearful agitation. Look at it swirling around the rocks and islands in the channel."

A pair of figures rode slowly toward the quay. Even in the inky darkness, Creed could distinguish the silhouette of General Washington and his stocky companion, Colonel Henry Knox.

Behind them, a third figure struggled to keep his horse—Colonel Fitzgerald. Creed and Scovel moved to assist the officers from their mounts. Washington jumped out of the saddle before they could reach him, while Fitzgerald remained mounted. Knox slowly dismounted.

Washington addressed them, "The time has come, gentlemen. The army is moving up now. I will cross when the first regiment goes over, but your men must depart first. Make sure no sentries warn the British. I should say, the Hessians. As for the strong points, especially the blockhouses, I am not convinced you have enough men to force them to surrender. Not without firing, and we cannot afford firing so close to Trenton."

Creed nodded. "I assure you, sir, our firelocks are mere transport for our bayonets, augmented by the occasional tomahawk and saber. We have done such work before. Besides, with your good Virginia riflemen backing us, 'tis the Hessians I feel sorry for."

Washington grunted, "Indeed, you have two of our best companies, and they will rely on you to guide them. This night offers us the chance to strike a blow for liberty and show all that the cause is not lost. Your action is the key to our success at Trenton. Remember the watchword, Jeremiah, 'Victory, or Death'."

There was a strange finality in Washington's tone. All the weeks of failure and frustration weighed heavily on him. The army and the nation now relied on his success. He knew better than anyone that for the cause, it was truly victory or death.

Suddenly, his mood shifted, and his voice grew firmer while his face lit up. "In a few hours, we shall give the enemy a thrashing like he never has had."

Fitzgerald had dismounted, slowly and uncertainly. He pulled a map out of his valise and used his great coat to shield it from the snowflakes. "Jeremiah, show Colonel Knox a good spot to place the artillery so it commands the town and covers the river approach."

Creed placed a finger on the map near a hillock north of the town. "Here's your place, Colonel. It dominates the town and has a gentle slope with fields of fire suitable for a battery of guns."

"After you clear the strong points, secure that location and wait for us there with your men," Washington said. "Send someone back to guide us. Colonel Knox will have the guns in tow."

Creed's face darkened. "Sir, there will be no time to send someone back for you. With the weather and the darkness as 'tis, there are too many ways he could miss your column or be delayed. And if we fail, there may be no one to send back."

Washington's mouth tightened at this questioning of his order.

Fitzgerald looked nervously at Creed, then tried to ease the tension. "Now just what have you in mind, Jeremiah?"

"Yes, what do you propose?" Knox asked.

Creed pointed to Thomas. "You have your guide, sir. Private Thomas Jeffries of my unit is staying with the artillery and is charged with the care of our horses, noble steeds that they are. He shall guide your guns to the place."

Thomas stepped forward. "I can do it!"

Washington seemed to frown, but then glanced over at Billy Lee, his manservant. Lee nodded at his master.

Washington turned to Creed. "If you vouch for him, Lieutenant Creed, I am satisfied with the decision."

Billy broke into a grin as white as snow. His manservant, Billy Lee, was one of his slaves but also his close confidant and friend. He well knew the plight of Black Americans was now made even worse by the rebellion. Those who were slaves had become pawns for both sides: some fighting for the rebellion in hopes of eventual freedom, others fighting for the king with the promise of immediate freedom.

Creed put his hand on Thomas's shoulder. "He is an able scout. He knows the road and the place and is the best rider I have ever seen."

Fitzgerald harrumphed, eyes widening at his protégé.

Creed recovered quickly from his gaffe. "Except for Your Excellency, of course."

* * *

Trenton, New Jersey, December 26th, 1776

The clock above the Trenton Tavern's fireplace chimed twelve times. *Oberst* (Colonel) Johann Gottlieb Rall looked up at it and grunted. First Christmas had ended and the second day of Christmas had begun. His mood during this holiday didn't quite mirror the peace and love brought by the birth of Jesus.

Rall, in command of the three Hessian regiments at the Trenton garrison, had spent two days celebrating this, a German's most important holiday of the year, mostly drinking and playing cards. Several of his officers expressed concern that Rall had overlooked the level of readiness.

Hauptman (Captain) Wilhelm Germer raised the sensitive issue once more, "*Herr Oberst*, the militia probes grow worse with each day. We must fortify better."

Rall scoffed, "Germer, I assure you there is little threat of attack. And, what could be the effect of an attack? We have patrols and continue to man the sentry posts, do we not?"

"*Ja*, but the men are…"

Rall cut him off with a wave of the hand. "*Die Rebellen* are finished, their militia patrols a mere nuisance. They are mere *Fliegen*, flies to be swatted away."

Rall was unaware that the New Jersey militias were rallying and were increasing their efforts in response to the devastation caused by the invading troops. General Howe's attempt to win over the Americans was thwarted by his soldiers, whose anti-rebel fervor exacted special vengeance on the Jerseys. A state that was once open to reconciliation instead became the testing ground of resistance.

Rall had decided, after all, to turn in early. Some of his officers gathered around the fireplace and kept drinking the American ale they had come to accept instead of their more popular German pilsners. Rall got up and waved at his aide, *Leutnant* Decker, who went to the cabinet and retrieved a valuable bottle of blood-warming Asbach brandy.

The stubborn Germer trailed the colonel into his room. While Decker removed Rall's boots, Germer and Rall shared a brief nightcap.

Germer gazed at the warm brown liquid. "*Herr Oberst*, I will see that at least one *Zug* (platoon) is fit for duty. At dawn, I shall check the sentries."

Rall flushed with a mixture of anger and amusement. "Mist! (Crap) This has been a long campaign. Since landing in New York, our soldiers have fought five pitched battles and dozens of skirmishes. They marched across two colonies in weather ranging from hot as Africa to cold as Siberia, covered in dust and mud. Many are sick. Some of our best are dead from horrific wounds or a score of illnesses. No, Germer, this day our men will rest. We must rest. Our officers have suffered, too: General Mirbach and Colonel von Bose, sick in New York; Colonels Scheffer and Bretthauer also sick; Dechow and Borke wounded."

Germer nodded. "*Ja*, but surely one *Zug*, how do the English say, a platoon, to check the sentries and patrol the main roads?"

Rall waved his hand dismissively. "If I thought there was anything to fear from this scum, I would have allowed Donop's chief engineer, that annoying *Hauptmann* Pauli, to build his redoubt at the saddle of the Pennington and Princeton Roads."

Germer responded, the drink now dulling his usual reserve. "But that might have given us some protection. This command is scattered. There aren't enough troops to cover the entire town. Our brigades in Princeton and Bordentown are too far apart to support each other. And the attacks by these rebel patrols over the past few days and nights have worn the men down."

Rall's head was spinning and his mouth dry, the effect of too much drink. "We are professionals, Germer. They are scum, a rabble, a mob. And if they do come? *Umso besser*—so much the better. Easier to destroy them in one honorable battle than a hundred skirmishes, eh? Get some sleep, Germer. You are fatigued, that is all."

He raised his last glass of brandy in salute, downed it in a gulp, and collapsed into his featherbed.

***

Germer looked at his sleeping colonel and shook his head. Rall was the best regimental commander among the Hessians and was well respected by everyone, but his contempt for the Americans was unsettling. Germer entered the drawing-room where a few officers still played cards.

Germer approached Rall's adjutant, *Leutnant* Jakob Piel, and put a large, fleshy finger into the officer's chest. "Piel, have an orderly wake me before dawn with some coffee. Alert the *Feldwebel* of *Erste Zug*, *Zwote Kompanie* — First Platoon, Second Company, *Regiment* von Knyphausen. Tell him his men must retire now, so they can be up and ready to march by dawn."

Piel's jaw dropped. "But *Herr Hauptman*, Colonel Rall has expressly forbidden this. By regulation, disregarding a superior's orders is a court-martial offense, and the sentence is death."

Germer poked a finger into the man's chest. "Do as I say, Piel, or I will gut you like a sow! Let me deal with Rall."

Germer would be true to his word. The anger in the captain's face accentuated the dueling scar on his face and chin. Among the Hessian officers, he was known as a man of integrity but also of great acts of impulsive rage and violence.

Piel stiffened like a board and clicked his heels. "*Jawohl, Herr Hauptman.*"

Chapter 28

McConkey's Ferry, December 26th, 1776

The unfolding operation was filled with urgency and hope. Creed looked at the commander-in-chief. From his expression, Washington understood that it was time.

The commander-in-chief turned to Glover. "I have waited long enough for the guns, Colonel Glover. Launch the first boats, if you please. If we must take Trenton with knuckles and bayonets, by God, we shall."

"Aye, Your Excellency." Glover's eyes remained fixed intently on the Delaware's current, the gathering ice, and the roiling waters. "Any longer and we risk it all."

Glover walked over to the line of boats lining the shallow riverbank. In the darkness, they looked like long, black sea serpents. "Mister Hazard, your lads can go now."

Hazard stood at the tiller. His voice burst with authority, "Alright, boys! Runners out. Oars up."

Each crewman worked with an efficiency that only comes from years of experience. Half of them pushed their staves into the water, feeling the muddy bottom give way a few inches. The other half raised their oars to prepare. Creed's men and the Rangers leaped to the side and grasped the cold, wet top of the gunwales. Feet slipped in the ice-cold mud along the bank. Some men sank into frozen mud that rose above their ankles.

"Heave and push— out!" Hazard commanded.

Grunts and low cries erupted as the men lifted and pushed the craft out into the choppy, frigid water.

"God, it's cold," a Ranger exclaimed.

"Save your breath," Mason chimed. "Now push, damn it!"

The boats moved forward with sucking sounds and splashes as they entered the water.

"Everyone into the boats!" Hazard exclaimed. "Pole men pole, rail men push!"

The polemen dug their poles into the shallow, murky water and, straining and groaning, drove hard. The boats shivered out into the current where the battle against nature began in earnest. Cold, sweeping winds made it hard for the men on the sideboards to avoid slipping on the wet decking and plunging into the treacherous river currents.

Parker wiped the rain-snow mixture from his eyes. "Never faced weather like this on the Chesapeake."

"Ah, you'll be the better seaman for it," Creed replied.

"My hands are raw already, sir," Beall said.

"Think of the lads at the poles and oars, Jonathan."

"Thought you'd been in those cold western mountains, farm boy," Parker chided.

"This is different cold," Beall replied.

Parker craned his neck. "Wish I were at the oars and being useful. We're drifting downriver!"

"You'll be useful, soon enough." Creed conned the dark shadows of the opposite bank while cold, dark waters mixed with slices of ice slapped at the boat's hull.

Hazard cupped a hand around his mouth. "Steer upriver, boys! We can't stop the current's drift, but we can slow it."

Patient strokes from powerful arms drove poles into the water, while more skillful arms pulled hard on the oars and steadied the tillers. Like a well-oiled clock, the sturdy Gloucester men worked in unison, and one by one, the boats nudged up tide as they moved slowly toward the Jersey bank. None had noticed the ice and snow mix growing in intensity.

"Keep it up, boys! We're halfway there," Gloucester announced. His calm voice had a steady effect.

Then, a large piece of ice slammed into one of the Durham boats with a sickening *crunch*. Not thick enough to cause damage, but large enough to surround the boat and start spinning it downriver. The craft was struck upriver from Creed's, but it quickly began to slip past them, gaining unwanted speed while heading in the wrong direction.

The crew fought desperately to break apart the thick, scum-like ice floe that threatened to capsize it. The struggle seemed nearly lost.

Parker was the first to notice. "Lieutenant, that boat is out of control. If it gets any further downriver, she'll be lost for this mission. "

Creed turned to Hazard. "Can we save her, captain?"

"We could, but it would put the rest at risk."

Suddenly, the dark silhouette of Elias Parker obscured the prow of the boat. "Turn right at her, sir. When I give the word, steer upriver and have the crew push and row as hard as they can. Jonathan, lend a hand. And wear your gloves."

Creed realized what Parker was up to. "Do as he says."

The other boat began to spin like a pinwheel.

"But she's out of control. If she hits us, our hull might split and send us into these currents," said Abner Scovel. "Have I bargained my way onto this boat only to sink to the bottom of this damn'd river?"

Parker had his grappling hook and line out poised to strike like a New England whaler. Hazard only then realized what Parker had in mind. "Heave in on her, boys!"

The Durham boat sharply turned to the port, the left side, and as the helpless vessel passed by, Parker released one, then two, grappling hooks. One bounced off the boat's gunwale into the cold water, but the second sank in and held. Its hooks caught firmly on the inside of the gunwale, and the line snapped tight.

Hazard's men rowed and pushed as hard as they could as the rope stretched tight and both boats hovered in the current for a split second. Then, the skilled strokes of Hazard's men and the frantic efforts of the other crew combined against the forces of nature. Slowly, the men began to gradually gain a slight advantage in the struggle against the unyielding current.

Hazard exhorted them, almost pleading, "Pull hard, boys, thrust hard."

Creed, Scovel, and Beall moved forward to help Parker with the line.

"Hold tight, and pull when I say," Parker said. "Now!"

They pulled with every ounce of strength as Parker took in the slack rope and wrapped it tightly around the forward bench. In seconds, a knot that would make any sailor proud secured the fate of the two boats. To Creed's surprise and relief, both boats had broken through the ice and were moving slowly but steadily toward the bank.

Hazard rose in the thwarts. "We'll hit the shore in moments, boys. Mister Creed, be on the lookout for enemy lookouts. Oarsmen, secure the lines. Polemen, hold fast—now!"

The vessels slid onto the bank, crunching through the scum-like mixture of mud and ice covering the shore. The White Knights and Rangers scrambled up the icy bank and into the woods. By the time Creed looked back toward the water, Hazard and his crew were poling back to start what would be a long night of work. He gave his friend a silent wave in thanks.

* * *

Washington stood impassively watching the first boats slip out onto the dark river.

"Don't worry, sir," said Gloucester. "Ezekial Hazard is the best. He'll deliver your lads and be back for more in no time."

Thoughts raced through Washington's mind. Dark thoughts. *Have I made the right decision? Am I sending men to their deaths for naught? Will my plan succeed in these conditions?*

Suddenly, Washington spotted faint movement on the dark river. *An ice floe?* Moments later, he got his answer. The first Durham boats appeared from the shadowy waters and reached the ferry shore.

Hazard climbed out of his boat and hurried across the narrow wharf to where Washington was standing in his dark greatcoat.

Gloucester stood beside him. Behind them, a few of his aides waited. In the shadows, he stood at the head of the infantry columns, patiently waiting to cross. "How goes it, Ezekial?"

"Lieutenant Creed and his men are on the other side, sir. And from what I see here, all look impatient to get on with this mission."

"I know that, Ezekial. How are conditions?" Gloucester demanded. "The other crews are anxious to know."

"Difficult as a winter sail to Newfoundland, Colonel Glover. Tide's up, current's strong, and ice's forming."

"Just the brisk conditions the boys like, Your Excellency," Gloucester said to Washington.

"The spirit of these men gives me hope."

Washington turned toward the men behind him. The snow and rain dampened their impatient faces. They showed no fear, only anxious impatience to do their duty. He looked up at the dark sky and the icy spray hitting the water. He stared hard across to the other side. He paused for a moment. *The destiny of the nation is in the hands of providence and a few brave lads. We must succeed.*

Washington pulled his timepiece from his waistcoat. "It is nearly eight o'clock. Have General Greene move the first regiment forward to the boats. I am crossing with them."

Then he stretched out his arm and pointed at the columns of infantry standing in the not-so-distant shadows. "Colonel Gloucester, if your men can get the best of this weather and the river, those men will take care of the enemy. Providence will take care of the rest."

Soon, scores of half-frozen men scrambled along the riverbank and onto the quay. Hushed voices issued orders. Washington felt relief. The first six companies were in the boats. Washington eased his large frame into Hazard's Durham boat.

He made his way to the prow, taking a moment to talk to the crew and the anxious soldiers. "This isn't our first such crossing, boys. But it is our first crossing *towards* the foe. Each of you should take comfort in the fact that you are the lead column in our first attack on the enemy. Stay close to your officers — and heed your sergeants' words. If you do your duty, Providence will reward your faith and perseverance."

The boats pushed against the current. The wind seemed to pick up just as the first wave launched from the ferry. Washington watched across the river toward the New Jersey side. To the east, everything appeared black. Only the increasing flecks of wind-driven ice and snow broke up the dark sky. The water was a swirling torrent of black, broken only by the sheets of ice moving downstream. The Durham boat pushed through, but it yawed uneasily.

Washington wiped a flake of snow from his eye. "How long to cross, Mister Hazard?"

"Not long, sir. Another ten minutes, maybe, Your Excellency."

"If we make it," an aide muttered under his breath just before he heaved his last meal over the side.

"Thanks for lightening the load, captain," one of the oarsmen said. The crew broke into a laugh.

"The current quickens here, boys! Steer upstream! Have your pole men push hard on the starboard," Hazard called out to the crews on his left and right.

The Gloucester sailors approached their task with the precision and speed Washington had learned to rely on.

"How fortunate this army is to have such men as you, Gloucester lads. Marble Head indeed produces our finest sailors," Washington said.

"I agree, Your Excellency. Although there are boys from Rhode Island and Connecticut who might argue differently," Hazard replied. "And Mister Creed's man from Maryland saved one of my boats right about this spot."

As if on cue, the Durham boat began to pitch and started drifting downstream.

"Hard to the port! Drive those poles, damn you!" Hazard called out with his hands cupped over his mouth.

Washington disregarded the foul language. He needed men like these.

The boat's prow was soon turned back toward the eastern bank of the Delaware. New Jersey was only fifty yards away. Washington could now make out the outline of the bank. He looked around and saw that the Durham boats were nearly in formation as they approached their target. He smiled and thought for the first time that he might just succeed.

Minutes later, they reached the shore. Washington once again pulled his watch from inside his waistcoat. It showed just a quarter past eight. "We have arrived. Thank you, Mister Hazard."

"We are almost a quarter-mile downstream, sir. But that's only because my boys work hard. Most crews would have drifted halfway to Philadelphia under these conditions."

"A good effort, withal. But we are behind schedule already. Please enjoin Colonel Gloucester to move things along."

Washington climbed over the gunwale without any help and moved up a small hill near the riverbank. As the men scrambled out of the boats with their gear, he noticed that many had little clothing suited for the conditions. Some had almost no clothing at all. He looked up at the sleet flakes falling from the sky. He couldn't have known that the chaos on the other side had worsened.

He heard a familiar voice in the darkness. "Your Excellency, I have found a suitable spot where you can observe the landings."

"Mister Scovel? What are you doing here?"

"By your leave, sir, I crossed with Mister Creed. I am your personal guard until Captain Gibbs arrives."

Washington was not pleased with the action but satisfied with the outcome. "Very well, Mister Scovel."

Washington was particularly eager to get his cannons across the Delaware. The guns were crucial to his plan. Although Creed reported that the Hessians had neglected to fortify Trenton, the stone barracks and other buildings could offer shelter from fire, helping the defenders keep their muskets dry and firing in heavy rain. The Continental Army lacked this advantage; they would be exposed to the weather during both the march and the battle. Cannon, however, could be kept dry, ensuring they could provide firepower when needed. In another setback for Washington, a note from Henry Knox indicated the cannon would cross last. The increasing snow and sleet raised doubts about their arrival.

Scovel took Washington to a small overhang by the river. From there, they observed the crossing as regiment after regiment reached the New Jersey side. The commander-in-chief noticed that the tattered uniforms and shabby equipment did not seem to affect their morale. They appeared to have shifted from anxious to ebullient.

The regiments jostled and men pushed and shoved as they queued up to board the boats. Several boats capsized, and many of the raggedly dressed men froze to the bone while waiting. Still, Gloucester moved his boats back and forth methodically. Each

Durham boat picked up a new group of men as soon as they returned from the far shore. There was no rest for the Marblehead sailors that night.

Washington spoke in a voice grown hoarse from the wind and weather, "Mister Scovel, I fear our well-planned schedule is for naught. I had hoped to be on the march by midnight. I can see now that it will not happen."

"Your Excellency, Mister Creed says the march to Trenton should take little more than two hours by road. There's yet sufficient time to surprise them."

Hands tucked into his greatcoat, Washington stared into the river's cold darkness. "You don't understand. This is not the only force crossing the river. I planned three attacks for this evening."

"I don't understand, sir."

Ewing and Cadwalader are crossing separately downriver. Cadwalader has orders to cross near Bordentown and seize it swiftly. Ewing has orders to land between Trenton and Bordentown and support the attack on Trenton from the southeast. If they attack on time while we are delayed, the Hessians at Trenton will have plenty of warning and either escape our trap or rally a proper defense.

"Perhaps, sir, they will also meet with delay."

Washington nodded grimly. "Strangely, that may well be our only hope of achieving the surprise needed to assure a victory. I am counting on those men to take Bordentown. But we must take Trenton. If only the weather cooperated, we could…"

A messenger appeared and handed him a note from Glover. The river had begun to freeze over even faster. The crossing slowed as the Gloucester sailors and the troops stopped to break up the sheets of ice forming around their craft.

Washington placed a hand on the young soldier's shoulder. He looked no more than twenty. "Cross over and tell General Greene to make up for the lost time anyway that he can. The success of this night depends on it. Tell Colonel Knox that we must have his guns. No matter what the cost, we must have those guns!"

* * *

Creed's men trudged slowly along the wooded ridge and halted when Creed raised his hand..

"We divide up here," said Creed.

"Your man Parker can take the lead for me. I'll be sticking right behind him, though," said Mason.

Creed grabbed his forearm. "Godspeed."

Parker motioned his head toward the River Road approach. "This way, sir."

In the moonlight, the fallen snow illuminated the otherwise dark and gloomy landscape of broken woods and hills. They spent nearly an hour carefully edging their way along both sides of the road. They reached a mound of snow concealed within a small stand of trees about ten yards off the road. It didn't look quite natural.

Parker decided it was better to move further into the woods and take the position from the other side. He unsheathed his twelve-inch fishing knife and checked the blade, rubbing it twice along a leather strap hanging from his pack. He slung his musket over his back diagonally with the muzzle pointing down. He then pulled his tomahawk from his belt and advanced quickly in a half-crouch.

Two of the Rangers followed behind him with bayonets fixed to their light infantry fusils, which they held ready. The short muskets had less range and power but were more convenient in the bush and easier to carry on patrols. After struggling through bare trees, they discovered the mound was a pile of snow fashioned into a makeshift bunker, a hasty V-shaped earthwork known as a fleche.

"Sir, this wasn't here when we came through before," Parker said

Mason grunted. "Check it out."

Parker saw no movement inside. Flanked by Rangers with bayonets ready, he inched closer. He spotted a dark spot against the snow. *A tunnel?* Then he heard a very familiar sound to soldiers—snoring. The snoring was coming from a bunker in the fleche. *Too risky to use a torch.*

Parker dropped to his knees and crawled across the ice and snow into the dark den. He moved slowly in the dark, his outstretched arm feeling ahead. Then he felt something—a boot! His hands groped blindly, sensing a second object. Only one sentry was in position, and he was deeply asleep. *The Hessians are as tired as we are.*

Parker slowly pulled back, dragging the sleeping Hessian by his feet. The Rangers bound and gagged him. He offered no resistance and appeared content to be left alone. Parker spotted the main Hessian stronghold. He pointed at it and slowly approached the blockhouse with his Rangers right behind him. Now, all they could do was wait for the riflemen from Virginia.

***

Creed and Beall led the rest of the Rangers and the second company of Virginia riflemen along Pennington Road. They reached their objective hours after midnight. A light shone from one of the windows on the ground floor of the fortified house. Creed immediately realized they faced a more complicated problem. The Hessians were awake and alert—at least some of them.

Beall carefully made his way to the house from the shadow of the woods. The Hessian defenders had shuttered the upper windows tightly and cut loopholes for firing on both floors. A dirt rampart mixed with snow was built around the lower floor to protect against cannon fire. Creed signaled for one Ranger to check the barn for enemy troops. He wanted to avoid surprises when they moved.

The Ranger returned a short while later. "The barn's clear. Just a milk cow left. From the look of it, the cow's mates made a proper holiday meal for the Hessians. Blood and entrails are piled up outside the barn, and a few slabs of frozen beef are hanging off a meat hook."

"Let's hope they are sleeping off their Christmas feast," Creed said.

Working his way along the side of the building, Beall reached the window and peeked inside. A pot was boiling on an iron stove, and two solid-looking Hessian grenadiers sat at a table drinking coffee. Between them was what appeared to be a bottle of rum.

Beall circled back to Creed. "There's at least two of them. They're enjoying some coffee and grog."

"They suspect nothing. Very good." Creed pointed to a line of silhouettes fanning out from the woods like a pack of wolves. "The riflemen are encircling the strongpoint to nab anyone who tries to give the alarm in Trenton, and to stop anyone coming to its relief."

"Should we then wait them out or call on them to surrender?" Beall asked.

Creed gazed at the blockhouse lamplight, beckoning in the night. "No, we'll storm it! The Rangers are finding an appropriate piece of fallen timber. Once they batter the door, we'll charge through and rush the Hessians and then clear the house."

The Ranger sergeant in charge looked at Creed and nodded. "The boys are ready for this."

The wind had picked up again, and the snow started blowing sideways.

"We must make a show of force great enough to cause their capitulation," Creed said. "Let's hope they're dazed and confused enough to submit. It must be nearly three o'clock. The column could be here within the hour."

The Rangers returned with a long-dead tree trunk. "This should do as a battering ram," the sergeant said. "Trim it down, boys. But quietly!"

Creed met with the rifle company commander. Captain Jared Rydell was a second-generation German immigrant whose family had settled south of Winchester, Virginia. Creed and Rydell agreed on where to position his men and how to cover the blockhouse's doors and windows.

When everything was ready, Creed nodded, and Rydell raised a gloved hand and quickly snapped it down.

Four Rangers lowered their heads and charged at the door, slamming the ram into it with a chorus of grunts and curses. With a sharp *crack*, the wooden planks split apart on impact. The hinges snapped back, and the heavy wooden deadbolt rolled harmlessly across the floor.

Creed and Beall burst through the jagged wooden planks.

At the crash of the timber, the two startled sentries sprang into action. One, a burly man, reached for his musket, but it was just out of reach. Creed slashed his arm and then ran him through. He fell to his knees, choking on his blood. The second, an older and angular corporal, pulled a pistol from his belt and pointed it at Beall. But Beall brought his tomahawk down on his skull, splitting it down to the eyebrows.

A series of shouts and commands echoed in the back room and the upper staircase as more than a dozen irritable grenadiers were stirred from their sleep like hibernating bears. The lieutenant in charge of the outpost had ordered all the muskets cleaned, oiled, and stacked in the outer room, now occupied by the rebels. Now desperate to seize their firearms, the lieutenant led his unarmed men in a frantic charge, marked by screams and curses in the Hessian dialect.

The officer and three large grenadiers charged madly at Creed, knocking over tables and chairs. With no time to react, Creed could only slash his blade from side to side.

Likewise, Beall, who was outmatched, stood beside him, holding back two other Hessians who had rushed down the stairs.

One of Creed's slashes caught the neck of the officer with a neat slice of the blade. Then, with a reverse blow, he slashed the grenadier next to him. Blood seemed to be spurting in all directions. But the powerful arms of the third desperate grenadier pinned Creed's shoulders, making his blade useless. The Hessian's strong grip quickly squeezed the air from Creed's lungs, and his head began to spin.

In the tight quarters, Beall was able to use his tomahawk more effectively. He cut down the two Hessians with a single swing above the knees, sending them tumbling down the stairs and causing the men behind them to trip and fall.

He turned to his left just as Creed slumped into the arms of the powerful grenadier. The grenadier let him fall, grabbed Creed's sword-bayonet, and raised it to deliver a fatal blow. But Beall's tomahawk struck first, sinking deep into his shoulder blades.

The Rangers burst into the room, wielding tomahawks and hunting knives. Like the riflemen, Rangers seldom carried bayonets, as their hunting rifles were not suitable for that purpose. The cabin echoed with screams and curses in a mix of English and German. In the dim lamplight, men moved instinctively.

When Creed recovered, Beall was standing by him and announced, "The Hessian force within the blockhouse has surrendered to Captain Rydell, sir. As planned."

* * *

On a night when success depended on timing, darkness and weather challenged the Americans at every turn. The swirling snow and fierce wind reduced visibility, making their trek through the woods not just tough but dangerous. The men's hands and feet felt like frozen cement, and their ears and noses like icicles. Yet, the excitement and urgency of the night's mission kept them energized and alert.

Parker saw a dark outline ahead and quickly dropped to a knee.

The strong hand of Mason grasped his shoulder. "What is it? I don't see a thing."

Parker pointed at the outline. "Look closer. There's the other strong point."

Like hungry wolverines, eager eyes gleamed in the dark as Mason delivered his final instructions, "The building is dark, and I suspect they're all fast asleep. Private Parker and I will climb up and enter through one of the windows. Make sure both doors are covered and round them up as they exit. We've no time to waste. Anyone who refuses to surrender must be dealt with quickly, but quietly."

Parker crept closer to the cabin and rose, throwing both anchor hooks, now muffled by wrappings from a torn woolen scarf. With a barely audible grunt, the prongs sank into the shingles, holding firmly to the roof. He and Mason pulled hand over hand up the ice-encrusted wall, their feet pushing off each of the cabin's horizontal timbers.

Suddenly, Mason lost his grip, and Parker helplessly watched him tumble into the snow below. *This could end things here and now.*

Numb but unflustered, Mason dusted himself off and slung his rifle across his back. He then reached into his pack and grabbed his mittens. The deerskin leather gave him the grip on the rope he needed, and a few minutes later, Parker's strong arms pulled him up onto the roof.

The two made their way across a roof covered with ice and snow. At the window, they found that the carefully closed shutters had not been locked. Parker pried the hinge with his knife and quietly pulled the shutter free. He then loosened the other shutter and opened the window. Mason clambered over the sill into the dark room. Parker handed him their weapons and climbed in.

Parker could not believe their luck. The room was empty. Mason pulled out his hanger, a short officer's sword. Parker very quietly fixed his bayonet. Mason nodded, and the pair pushed through the door into the other room.

A half-dozen Hessians lay asleep in various states of dress. The hardships of the weather and the constant probing by the local militia had left them physically and mentally drained. But one was awake, and hearing noise from the other room, lit a lantern. When he saw the silhouette of the intruders at the doorway, he shouted.

"Alarm! Achtung! Die Rebellen! Herein schon! Alarm! Die Rebellen sind da!"

Mason slammed the butt of a rifle into his broad face, knocking him out with a broken jaw. But now the others stirred like a pit of snakes responding to the sudden warmth of the morning sun. The Hessians struggled to move quickly, but as each tried to rise, Mason and Parker slammed them with the rifle butts. Within seconds, all of them were on the floor with various fractures to their skulls, jaws, and arms.

But the alarm had sounded, and the Hessians on the ground floor were springing quickly into action. The sergeant in charge clutched his pistol and lit a lantern while two of his men, wearing only pants and shirts, grabbed their muskets and followed.

Mason charged down the stairs shouting. "Surrender at once! The night is ours!"

The sergeant grunted something inaudible and squeezed the trigger. It flashed and spat out smoke, but his weapon failed to fire. Mason ran his sword cleanly through his thigh. The sergeant's eyes widened, and he slumped forward, desperately trying to stop the blood pooling down his leg. The two soldiers hesitated—Parker hurled his tomahawk into one and plunged his knife into the other.

Mason planted his foot on the wounded sergeant's leg and pulled out his blade. A blow to the face muffled the sergeant's agonized screams.

Mason called out, "Hands high! Submit now, or we shall show no quarter. The building is surrounded."

Almost a dozen exhausted and confused Hessians hurried to the door and rushed out into the bitter cold. Disoriented and unarmed, they waved their hands wildly. Mason's Rangers and a platoon of Virginia riflemen quickly surrounded them, putting an end to any thoughts of resistance or escape.

"We did it," said Mason. "But we couldn't have done it without you, Private Parker." He was quaking from nerves and utter fatigue.

Parker nodded as he wiped the blade of his knife. "They made a mistake. Just as Lieutenant Creed said they might."

* * *

Creed estimated it had to be nearly four. He knew he had a critical decision to make and turned to Beall. "The attack is already behind schedule. We need to push off shortly. However, I am not comfortable leaving here without confirmation that the other strong point is taken. What think ye?"

"Sir, we will need all the men when we arrive at the artillery point. I suggest we wait for Elias to join us. I'm sure he'll get here."

Creed struggled with it. "Something has gone wrong with the crossing, or the column would be arriving now. His Excellency wanted to have Trenton in hand before dawn. We can wait a bit longer for Private Parker, but then we must follow through on our orders and get to Trenton."

"I pray to the good Lord that the army has crossed in time, sir."

Chapter 29

The Landing, December 26th, 1776

Scovel shuffled his feet and clapped his hands to stay warm. The motion brought sensation back to his fingers and toes, but only briefly. There was little he could do to prevent the cold from stinging his nose, ears, and eyes. He looked up at the dark sky. *Still a few hours before dawn.*

The night had been cold, but the morning was proving colder. At times, the wind and snow were so intense it appeared as if a white shroud covered the entire world. Scovel strained his eyes against a curtain of white that seemed to surround him. He could make out the figure of the commander-in-chief, now in a heated debate with his chief of artillery. A file of the Life Guard had finally crossed over and stood patiently by their charge.

With the arrival of the protective detail, Scovel could now focus on other matters, especially how to control prisoners when they took Trenton. He had teamed up with Colonel Fitzgerald, who wanted to select key prisoners for detailed questioning. Scovel and his small Provost guard would assist him.

Washington approached almost casually. Despite the freezing weather and terrible conditions, the commander-in-chief seemed calm and steady. "Well, Abner, all is ready. Colonel Knox informs me that our artillery has crossed and is being limbered. With any luck, we may still catch the enemy sleeping. Although even if everything goes well, we will not reach Trenton before sunup as I originally planned."

Scovel caught sight of the first guns moving off toward the Pennington Road. He could make out Thomas Jeffries leading the vanguard. "Perhaps I should ride with Creed's young man and help him lead the guns, sir."

Washington shook his head. "Jeremiah Creed vouched for him, so he is man enough for the job. Knox tells me he likes him, too, and that counts for something. No, you should stay with me. When we take the town, you will have your pick of the prisoners to bring back to Colonel Fitzgerald."

Scovel was surprised by the news. "He's not here?"

"Colonel Fitzgerald will remain at camp. He has had some trouble riding, and the cold, damp weather is affecting him."

Scovel pondered this. *Should we take prisoners, I guess I'm in charge of the whole lot.* "Very well, sir. We shall move up once the last caisson passes the intersection."

Scovel swung into the saddle and rode out to check on his small group of Provosts, six carefully chosen sergeants from different states. Washington wanted his Provosts, unlike his Life Guard, to represent the new nation, not just a single region.

The Cavalier Spy

Horses struggled against the icy ground as the Provosts moved toward the intersections of the connecting road between River Road and Pennington Road. Each man wore a lanyard, a symbol of authority, and carried two horse pistols instead of a carbine. They also wore infantry officer swords, indicating they held a special authority. Each also had a brace of manacles and a length of rope in their saddlebags, the basic tools of their trade, needed for incarcerating deserters, miscreants, and felons.

***

Washington's charger trotted past Scovel and pulled up beside Nathanael Greene, who was leading the column struggling along the icy stretch of Pennington Road.

Greene nodded in recognition. "Any word on the other column, Your Excellency?"

"General Sullivan has cleared the intersection and is closing in on Trenton along River Road."

Greene smiled. "So, Your Excellency, our forces are within striking distance despite this abominable weather."

"I thought you New Englanders thrived on this?"

Greene's belly shook with laughter. "Purely a myth, sir. We New Englanders like sitting beside a warm hearth in the winter as much as anyone else."

Washington pursed his lips. "If your column can maintain this pace, we shall arrive just as Sullivan closes. But many things can yet go wrong, Nathanael."

"So far, they have gone as well as we could expect, sir."

"Any word on the strong points?"

Greene broke into a wide grin. "Yes, sir. The advance guard has made contact with them. A rider just informed me the Rangers and Virginians have secured their objectives."

Washington took a deep breath. "And what of Mister Creed?"

"It seems Creed and his men have moved on to reconnoiter the artillery position."

Washington did not reply. Instead, he turned his head toward a passing formation and called out in a low, but authoritative voice, "Keep moving, boys, keep moving. Victory is ours if we can keep moving."

He stayed at this position for nearly an hour, exhorting and pushing the men as they struggled over icy rocks and snow, even as more snow and then light hail fell on them. They moved their frozen feet as though each step added even more to their miseries. Many had tatters for clothing, and not a few walked barefoot. Their bloodstains in the snow marked the trail for those who followed.

When he saw the units thinning as men drifted off the road or fell behind, Washington exhorted them more, "Keep by your officers, boys... for God's sake keep by your officers!"

Knox finally had the vanguard of the artillery rolling, with Thomas leading.

Washington nodded at him.

His face was barely visible under the old woolen scarf wrapped around his neck in a serpentine pattern. His large eyes seemed obscured beneath his hat, but Washington could sense the determination in them. Washington mused: it will take efforts from men like him, willing to face hardship and confront the British if the cause is to succeed.

It was nearly seven when Greene's column of 1200 men and ten guns approached the strongpoint. There, his three brigades separated and formed into regimental-sized units for the final assault on Trenton.

Knox rode part of the way with Washington. "Your plan is complex, Your Excellency."

"Not so much complex as multi-faceted, Henry. Sullivan and Mercer will lead their brigades towards Trenton. Mercer will attack the center of the town, pinning the enemy."

"And what of Sullivan?"

"He is to link with General Ewing southeast of town."

"Ewing?"

Washington nodded. "He is supposed to land south of Trenton and cut it off from Bordentown. I pray he arrives."

"And if not? The weather…"

"I plan for Lord Stirling's Brigade to descend on Trenton from the north, where hopefully Mister Creed has secured a suitable position for your guns."

Knox grunted. "If he finds the right position, my guns will blast the enemy into the Delaware."

Knox's bold remark bolstered Washington. "If not, Greene and Fermoy are now moving their brigades around the north side of town. They'll descend on it from the northeast."

"That should discommode the garrison. We'll soon have them on the run, regardless, sir."

Washington took Knox by the arm. "I don't want them on the run, Henry. We must stop them from escaping over the stone bridge across Assenpunk Creek."

"Assenpunk Creek?"

"Yes, a narrow but deep body of water that runs southwest into the Delaware. I intend to capture the entire Hessian force—but we must cut that escape line. For that, I need Ewing."

* * *

Down River

General James Ewing halted his horse at the riverbank and looked over the rumbling waters in front of him. The boats were ready, and his men waited anxiously at their camp a mile upstream. But he decided to take one last look at the river before giving the order. Even in the darkness and snow, he could see large floes of ice dancing on the water as they moved downstream.

A despondent-looking captain approached him. Captain Ralph Glynn was a tough, no-nonsense sailor who had spent most of his life sailing the Delaware. He barely noticed when Glynn placed his bare, nearly frostbitten hands on the steaming sides of the horse, desperately searching for warmth in the bitter cold.

"Are the boats ready, Captain Glynn?" Ewing asked.

"Ready, sir? The boats have been ready since noon. So have the crews. But the elements aren't ready," Glynn said.

Ewing's jaw tightened and his face flushed. "What do you mean?"

"I mean, the ice-floes and the surge of the river make it impossible to cross here. At least right now."

Ewing reined back his horse in anger. "Get those boats ready, and I'll have my men on board in thirty minutes. We are already behind schedule!"

Glynn shook his head. "You know I've been on this water for over twenty years. I command the crossing. And it's my decision whether those boats cross, and I say venturing now is certain destruction."

"I can't let His Excellency down, Captain Glynn. We must cut off the Hessian retreat across the Assenpunk Creek."

"I'll take the blame, sir. They may court-martial me. But by God, I've seen boats crushed by smaller floes in calmer waters. It's just not meant to be this night."

Ewing, realizing Glynn was right, nodded. "Very well. Likely His Excellency didn't cross as well."

"I am not so sure about that, sir. Delaware is more forgiving upriver. But downriver, I doubt if the others will make it either."

"You mean Cadwallader?"

Glynn nodded grimly. "I'm afraid I do, sir."

Ewing turned his horse around. "Very well, captain. I wouldn't hazard such a trip just to have my men trapped alone on the enemy's shore. If he did cross, then God help His Excellency. Hide your craft from prying eyes and get your men back to camp."

"Aye, sir."

Ewing turned his horse around with a pull on the reins and spurred down the ice-covered road.

* * *

Trenton, New Jersey, December 26th, 1776

The band of exhausted, frost-covered men in uniforms encrusted with ice reached the northern end of the town just after dawn. Creed looked south. In the early morning light, they could see the outlines of the homes along the edge of town on King and Queen Streets. These were wide roads running parallel north and south. The weather felt warmer. Light snow was falling, but the icy mix and chilling wind had stopped, and Creed saw a soft streak of light on the eastern horizon. *A good sign.*

The young officer raised his spyglass and surveyed the town and its surroundings. He scanned from left to right. "This will do it, lads. From this low ridge, a few well-placed guns can dominate most of the town with plunging, enfilade, or ricocheting fire. Now, let's pray Thomas can find us." The movement of gray figures in the distance caught his eye. "Oh, but wait. We may have something brewing and 'tis not tea."

* * *

Hauptman Wilhelm Germer marched proudly, head high and shoulders straight, with a parade-like bearing. Behind him, nearly twenty men followed in a clockwise arc around the town. He hoped to lure out some of the local militia, who had been harassing couriers and supply wagons over the past several days. However, he did not go out to check on the strong points, deciding instead to patrol only as far as the wood line, a quarter-mile from the town.

At the first post, Germer heard snoring, with a sentry sleeping with his head resting on his chest. Two musketeers dragged the hapless private back to face certain and severe punishment. With sixteen men remaining, he moved on to the next sentry point. There, he found two more sentries cowering together under their greatcoats, trying to stave off the cold and damp.

Germer exploded in frustration and rage. "*Verdamte Schweine*! Damned pigs! Such behavior in the face of the enemy! Have we not one professional left among us?"

Germer's sergeant delivered a harsh kick to the sides of the pair, causing them to scramble to their feet desperately. Years of strict discipline had trained these men to react instinctively to orders and to expect severe punishment for even minor infractions. They would be disappointed.

When the first musketeer got to his feet, Germer's robust fist struck his stomach, doubling him over. Germer's sergeant then brought the second man down with a sharp crack of his cane on the shin.

"Sergeant, take four men and ensure these two spend the morning together, in the gaol. They, too, will face swift justice when I return."

The sergeant and four of the strongest men lowered their long bayonets and prodded the two back to town amid a chorus of shouts, curses, and blows. Germer knew the men were worn out and tired from the constant alarms caused by small militia bands. The bitterly cold weather did not help either.

From the hillock, Creed watched these events with great amusement until the patrol began resolutely marching in their direction. He folded the spyglass, tucked it away, and drew his sword bayonet. "That enemy patrol is following the wood line in a path leading here. Prepare your firelocks, lads. But we shall only use them as a last resort lest we spoil His Excellency's surprise."

Creed spotted a small cluster of boulders and shrubs about fifty yards to the north, at the point where King Street crossed Princeton Road. "Discretion is indeed the better part of valor, lads. The steel in the hands of those Hessians is even colder than the snow. Keep low and follow me!"

Creed slung his rifle over his shoulder and started crawling toward the rocks with his men right behind him. Once they reached the shelter of the boulders, Creed risked a glance back. He stayed low to the ground and looked south.

"What do you see?" Parker asked. He saw the Hessian officer standing not far from their position, making a notation in a book. "Looks like the officer is making notes for his report. Very professional."

The officer gave an order, and his men marched along the connector road to Queen Street, where they turned south and back to the center of town.

"Looks like they are heading back, lads."

"Sir, two men are running toward the Hessians," Parker gasped. "They must be Loyalists. They'll warn the Germans. Got to stop them!"

Parker and Beall dashed from their cover and sprinted across the snow-covered field to intercept the men. Before the Loyalists could get within earshot of the Hessian patrol, Creed's men had cut them off and stood with bayonets flashing in the morning sun.

"Surrender!" Parker demanded.

The Loyalists dropped their muskets and tiringly raised their hands. Instead of being heroes who saved Trenton, these proud subjects of the king would soon face Colonel Fitzgerald's questioning.

Then, out of the early morning shadows, a band of infantry streamed from the wood line behind the Loyalists. The small company of Virginia riflemen was the lead unit of Nathanael Greene's division

They had accidentally flushed out two local Loyalists, who ran from the woods to warn the Hessian patrol of the approaching rebel column.

Creed challenged the advancing troops. "Victory!"

The officer leading the file responded without hesitation. "Or Death!"

Creed lowered his weapon. "Who are you?"

"I'm Lieutenant James Monroe, under the command of Captain William Washington, cousin of the commander-in-chief, himself. We have orders to link up, but it looks like we spooked some Loyalists, too.

As Monroe finished speaking, the captain arrived panting heavily despite the morning chill. "Move those Loyalists back and turn them over to the provosts," Washington ordered one of his sergeants. "Lieutenant Monroe, take the company and put a skirmish line out in front of those rocks."

Monroe motioned toward the boulders, and the riflemen fanned out in a V.

The sergeant motioned at the prisoners. "Come on, you lucky bastards. No hot Yankee lead for you now."

Creed greeted Washington. "Lieutenant Jeremiah Creed is at your service, sir. Hopefully, you are the first of many Continentals we shall greet this foin morning."

The Virginian, who was from Stafford County, was the same age as Creed and about the same height at six feet, but his slightly plump build and round face made him look older.

"My compliments, Mister Creed. With all the delays at the crossing, we feared the enemy might have bagged you before our arrival. Lieutenant Monroe and I had wagered against finding you here with all the bad luck the army of late has experienced."

Creed smiled. "Why, Captain, 'tis nothing but luck that keeps me thrivin'. What unit is this now?"

"The Third Virginia Continental Line. But truth be told, I was never advised as to your unit's appellation."

Creed decided to improvise on the truth. "Truth be told, then, my men and I joined the cause to serve on the First Maryland Continental Line."

Washington frowned. A puff of steam escaped his lips. "First Maryland? Mercer's brigade. Well, I reckoned you fought and died valiantly on Long Island."

Monroe rejoined them. "Sir, the men are in position along the ridgeline. It is good ground for guns. As soon as the batteries begin to arrive, we can advance."

Washington pulled a timepiece from his waistcoat. It was a simple white metal watch, but useful and sturdy in the field. "Past seven-thirty. The guns should be up shortly."

Creed gazed at the sky. The temperature was rising, and the snow began to turn to cold rain, drenching and chilling everything further. "If this rain stays with us, those guns will be decisive."

Just then, Parker, who was lying atop one of the boulders, called out, "Horses, sir!"

As if on cue, a rider, who they soon realized was Thomas, leading a line of horses, trotted down the Pennington Road. Behind him rolled the column of guns. Creed also saw files of infantry slipping their way to the left of the guns. They moved around to the north and headed through the light woods and orchards between the Pennington and Princeton Roads.

"This must be the first regiment of General Greene's division. His Excellency intends it to block any Hessians from withdrawing east of town," Creed said.

Washington nodded. "If General Ewing has blocked the stone bridge over the Assunpink Creek and Sullivan pinches off the ferry south of Trenton, my dear cousin will yet have them all."

Thomas trotted up and jumped from the saddle.

Creed patted his shoulder. "Good work, Thomas. The success of His Excellency's plan is secure, and in large part, it's thanks to your efforts. But now, we need to join these Virginians in the final push."

Creed took Finn's reins and gently patted his neck. "Stay with the horses, Thomas. They'll be safer behind these boulders. We'll need them soon enough. Once this town is taken, find a stable that hasn't been looted of oats. These lads deserve some real nourishment after the night's ordeal."

Beall saw the look of disappointment on Thomas's face and looked askance at Creed. Creed realized his mistake. *Thomas is now a warrior, not a stable hand.*

Creed shook his head gently and smiled. "Very well, Thomas, secure the horses. Then join the gunners on the ridgeline. I am certain they will welcome your help."

Thomas broke into a grin. "Never fired anything bigger than a pistol, lieutenant. But I do believe I would enjoy throwing some cannonballs at the Hessians."

"After your performance this night, I would say that is the least Colonel Knox can do for you."

Just then, the batteries of Pennsylvanian Captain Thomas Forrest and New Yorkers Sebastian Bauman and Alexander Hamilton began moving into position. It looked like orchestrated chaos: sergeants rushing to pick firing spots; corporals unlimbering the guns; gunners straining their legs and shoulders as they rolled each piece into firing position.

Arranged in a slight arc along the low ridgeline, their brazen gun barrels now pointed at the still-sleeping town. And at its Hessian garrison.

Chapter 30

Trenton, New Jersey, December 26th, 1776

Captain Washington's saber flashed in the dim morning light, and over twenty riflemen stepped out silently. Faces grim with determination, their boots and moccasins crunched through the icy snow covering the slope. Creed and his men sprang into action, joining the Virginians just as the last of the guns was being set into position.

The line gradually bent back into a loose V formation. Creed signaled his men forward into the apex of the V, leading it toward the houses at the north end of King and Queen Streets. They tread quickly but warily, eyes watchful for any sign of the enemy.

Creed glanced furtively towards the wood line. Somewhere behind the dark trees, the main body of the continental infantry was forming battle lines with Stirling's brigade to their rear, Mercer's to their right, and Fermoy's on their left.

Washington's company was closing on King Street when two Hessians emerged from a small wood-frame house. They halted a moment, gazing in disbelief at the line of grim-looking riflemen descending on them. Then they turned, and with feet sliding in the snow, ran into the town, bellowing the alarm. *Achtung! Alarm! Die Amerikaner!*

"Let's go, lads!" Creed and his men bolted after them.

As he began to run, Creed saw a dark line of men, half a mile away, silently moving toward Trenton from the western woods. A single cannon shot echoed from the ridgeline behind them. The circle of tired but determined Americans closing in on Trenton recognized the signal to attack. The Hessian garrison was about to be caught in a trap that nearly, but not quite, enclosed them.

One of the Hessians went into a small tavern at the end of the street.

"One of them's in that tavern." Beall pointed at the building.

"Let's get him," Parker said.

As they reached the tavern's entrance, Hessians started to stumble out in various states of readiness. Two of them carried muskets, which they immediately lowered at Creed. But shots rang out from all around, knocking down both soldiers before they could fire.

Now, the Virginians swarmed through the streets like a pack of hounds and started emptying their rifles at nearly point-blank range. With cries of *Angreifen* – attack! Six more Hessians dashed from a building and charged with bayonets lowered.

The cold morning air was now filled with gun smoke and curses as the Hessians and Virginians clashed in a close-quarters fight with gunfire, bayonets, tomahawks, and knives. The fight was over within minutes.

Two more Hessians fell—clutching desperately at their wounds. The rest looked around, confused. With faces showing disgust and anger but no fear, they began throwing their muskets onto the snow.

Some of Washington's men secured the prisoners while the rest of the company began searching the buildings along the edge of the town. Creed and his men pushed past the gaggle of prisoners and ran deeper into town, followed by one squad of Virginians. The attack was on.

All ears were now filled with the slow, deliberate pounding of the cannon as the American artillery opened fire. The crack and pop of rifles and muskets also erupted to the south and west. Sullivan's column had begun its attack.

Creed stopped his men behind a low garden wall. "Take a few gulps of water and reload your weapons, lads."

The squad of Virginians looked around and realized the rest of Washington's company had not followed them.

"Where are we going, Lieutenant?" Beall asked.

Creed pointed southeast. "To the stone bridge that crosses over the creek. General Ewing should be moving there to block any Hessians who try to escape to Bordentown. I plan to link up with him and guide him into position."

Parker and Beall exchanged a look of disbelief. Even including the Virginians, they were fewer than a dozen.

"Sir, how are we to make our way through a town full of Hessians and block the retreat of more than a thousand regulars?" Parker asked.

Before Creed could respond, the Hessian commander, Johann Rall, rushed out of his headquarters at the Potts House.

Rall shouted a mix of commands and curses in German. By now, Hessians had started leaving their billets in groups. Like a machine, officers gathered their units, and the drummers sounded commands. Regimental flags were raised, and soon a disciplined, if somewhat chaotic, formation blocked the American advance.

"Now's our chance, lads. Follow me!" Creed led his men, and the Virginians followed. As the cannons roared and muskets cracked, they loped to the southeast, panting and perspiring despite the cold. Creed pointed towards some trees. "Take cover there."

Legs pumping like pistons, the men sprinted. A few slipped in the snow but quickly staggered to their feet and trudged their way to the safety of the apple orchard east of the town. Behind them, the sounds of musket and artillery fire ebbed and flowed like a summer thunderstorm.

* * *

Captain Wilhelm Germer turned his patrol around as soon as he heard gunfire coming from the northern end of King Street. He drew his saber and led his men toward the sound of battle, rallying stray musketeers in search of a leader.

"*Herr Hauptman*, there are two unmanned field pieces nearby," one of the sergeants reminded him.

Germer gazed north, where he saw dark figures descending on the town. "This is a full-scale attack! We must hold the rebels until our battalions can form. Take some grenadiers and position the guns to stop the rebel advance. I will take what infantry I can muster and form a battle line."

***

A series of sharp orders filled the air, and soon the cannons were rolled north to block the Americans. Hessian grenadiers worked like seasoned artillerymen, and they quickly fired a few aimless shots at the Americans.

But before the guns could be effectively used, Captain Washington and Lieutenant Monroe led a charge of Virginia riflemen straight down the center of King Street. They were joined at the last moment by a gun crew led by a sergeant named Joseph White.

White's gun was damaged during the movement on Trenton, and White was ordered to leave it and help with another gun. However, he believed his gun was needed and refused to abandon it.

Despite the harsh weather, he and his crew managed to drag the gun along behind the rest of the column. Shortly after they arrived, the carriage finally broke, making the weapon useless. So, when the Virginians rushed the Hessian battery, Knox ordered White to join them.

The Hessian grenadier sergeant coolly directed his men through the drill of loading powder, ramming grapeshot, and aiming the field piece at the advancing tide of Virginians. But Washington's men were upon them before they could light the touchhole, and the two groups of brave men clashed like a pair of rutting stags.

The grenadier sergeant swung his short sword at Washington, slicing gashes into both his hands. A sturdy Virginian farmer from Berryville brought down the Hessian sergeant with a single blow of his musket.

Lieutenant Monroe led the detachment forward until a well-aimed musket ball struck his leg with a sickening crunch and cut an artery.

Sergeant White's crew seized the Hessian gun and turned it, unleashing a deadly spray of grapeshot on its former owners, killing several and forcing the survivors to scatter for cover.

The remaining Hessians began to retreat down the street, with some soldiers turning back to fire on the rebels. But they had lost their valuable weapon. Amidst the stray bullets flying through the air, the Virginians carried their prize back up to the head of King Street.

***

Along the high ground north of the town, Thomas approached a small officer dressed in blue. "Sir, I'd like to volunteer my help."

The officer, Lieutenant Alexander Hamilton, eyed him with interest. "I don't see too many youths like you with the artillery. Do you know anything about cannons?"

"No, sir, just horses. But I can learn. Learn quickly."

The Cavalier Spy

Hamilton glanced at the men working to position the New York battery to fire. "The second gun is undermanned. Report there. Tell Sergeant Nicholson I said you'd make a fine matross."

"A what?"

"Assistant gunner. Now go, before I have you sent to the infantry."

Thomas joined the crew of a six-pounder, not the heaviest caliber, but a formidable field piece. The six-pound iron ball could reach up to six hundred yards, and in the hands of experienced gunners, ricochet another two hundred or so. The ball's velocity and weight could tear limbs, crush bones, and cut men and horses in half. The combined blast of a battery of guns could destroy the morale of even the best troops. And at close range, tightly packed bags of musket balls called grapeshot could rip formations apart like a shotgun tearing into a flock of birds geese.

"If Mister Hamilton says you're up to it, I've got plenty of work for you," said Nicholson.

Thomas quickly learned to assist in manual handling the gun back into its firing position after it recoiled from firing. His youthful strength was a welcome addition to the exhausted crew.

Hamilton calmly paced behind the line of guns, checking the positioning of each and inspecting the men's gear. Waiting for Colonel Knox's signal, Hamilton stood behind the battery, giving final instructions to the commanders. "Each of you will mark a target. Priority fire is to enemy formations. No fire into buildings without my express permission. We are here to liberate this town, not destroy it."

"Target marked! Target marked!" each gunner announced.

Hamilton nodded at Knox.

Knox raised a powerful fist into the air and quickly brought it down in an arc while bellowing across the line of guns. "Fire!"

Hamilton repeated the order. "Fire!"

Each gun was fired, unleashing devastation and shrouding the ridgeline in smoke. Thomas covered his ears, but they started ringing from the first gunshot. The blast echoed loudly. The gun recoiled more than six feet.

Thomas and the other assistant gunners pushed and pivoted the gun back into its firing position. One assistant loaded a powder bag into the barrel, then another rammed in the six-pound ball. Some loose powder was poured into the vent. The gun was now ready and primed.

Nicholson carefully checked their work and adjusted the sighting. A gunner stepped forward and handed him the burning match.

Hamilton's voice rose above the din. "Sergeant Nicholson, let the lad have the honors."

Nicholson placed the burning cord in Thomas's hand. "Touch the hole, lad. That's all there is to it."

Thomas felt nervous. *What if something goes wrong? They'll blame me, the outsider.*

"We trust you, young man," Hamilton said. "Do as your crew chief commands."

Thomas inhaled and carefully pressed the burning ember to the touch hole. It sparked, then exploded, releasing flames, smoke, and shot forward before rolling back.

"Good shot," Nicholson said.

Before Thomas could take it in, he was back with the crew and beginning the drill once more.

***

Knox's artillery now unleashed a full barrage. Rounds careened through the town, knocking down anyone foolish enough to gather on King and Queen Streets. Some of the Hessians tried to duck for cover into the buildings, but now American troops from the north and west were pushing through the side streets, taking over house after house, from which they poured effective musket fire into the Hessian formations, now struggling to retreat south and east.

General Washington watched his plan unfold from a small saddle on the high ground north of Trenton. He patted his white charger, calming it against the blasts from the nearby battery. Tench Tilghman sat astride his horse nearby.

"Look at that Mister Tilghman! General Greene's division is making its way south and around the eastern side of the town, while Sullivan's men continue to press along the southern extreme of King and Queen Streets. I pray that one of these pincers will link up with Ewing."

"But as yet we have had no word from General Ewing, sir."

Washington grimaced and looked to the southeast. Hopefully, he has landed. He should be somewhere between Trenton and Bordentown by now. "

But Washington had no idea Ewing, and his men had already gone back to camp in Pennsylvania, and the stone bridge over Assunpink Creek, Rall's only way out of Washington's well-laid trap, was still open.

* * *

They trudged south along the eastern edge of the town, careful to avoid the constantly assembling Hessian formations. Anxious men sprinted across a road, running past a Presbyterian church, where they paused to catch their breath. Creed took out his spyglass and observed the way ahead. He saw a group of red-coated dragoons galloping across the Stone Bridge toward Bordentown. The column of scarlet quickly vanished behind the hills.

Creed shut the spyglass. "Lads, a troop of dragoons just rode through the ground General Ewing was to occupy. Yet not one musket shot. Something has held him up."

"Meaning what, sir?" Parker asked.

"Meaning we'll be on our own when we arrive at the bridge. I'm unsurprised that his division has not arrived. The weather conditions made His Excellency's move to Trenton a near miracle. It would be cheating fortune to repeat such a feat more than once in an evening."

"What do you propose to do, sir?" Beall asked.

"We must take the ground over the bridge or His Excellency's plan, and all our efforts will be for naught. Are ye game, lads?"

Heads nodded as the men took a few more deep breaths.

"Good! Let's be off."

They tramped behind him at a slow trot, with the Virginian riflemen following in a tight, single file. Each man grimly believed this would be his last fight. They could hear battle from Trenton: the anxious shouts of men in English and German, the staccato *pop* of muskets and rifles, and the nearly continuous *boom* of cannon. Creed realized that if the Hessians held their ground and pushed the Americans back, they would be trapped behind enemy lines just like they were in Brooklyn that past summer.

He looked back and saw the Hessians had now abandoned Trenton and were forming a new line along the apple orchard east of town. An officer, whom he assumed was the Hessian commander Rall, sat stiffly on a horse, waving a saber over his head. Lines of deep blue were forming. The Hessians were now desperately trying to rally and return volley fire on the Americans storming from the town.

Americans dressed in blue and buckskin began taking cover in the houses along Trenton's western edge. The mixture of rain and snow hampered the Hessians' ability to fire effectively. Muskets misfired. Shouts of "*Verdammte Pulver*! Damned powder!" Belched from wavering voices. Soon, they began falling to the well-aimed fire of the Americans sheltered in the houses.

Creed watched from afar, mesmerized by the clash. He winced when the mounted officer suddenly clutched his side, struck by some American marksman. But Rall did not go down. He kept rallying his men until he saw an American force had enveloped the town from the east. The Hessians were now surrounded on three sides.

Creed's eyes narrowed. "It appears His Excellency and our guys have things under control. Now we need to do our part."

They nearly slid down the slope toward the creek and slipped past the Barnes house on the north side of the bridge.

Parker pointed to a mill on the other side. "Sir, that's the best place from which to cover this bridge."

Creed instead pointed to a knoll overlooking the bridge and forming an outcropping that dominated the south side of the creek. "The Hessians will certainly have posted men at the mill, and if we take it, they could trap us there and pass us by. I'll settle instead for the high ground above it. Up we go, lads."

They sprinted across the bridge and reached the high ground before the surprised and nervous sentries in the mill could stop them. Luckily for Creed, they were not Hessians but a Loyalist militia unit planning its escape from Trenton.

Creed carefully positioned each man so that every musket or rifle covered a range of just under eighty yards to the bridge. The trees and bushes had shed their leaves, but the bare limbs and branches were dense enough to hide them from view. Each man took a position behind the large boulders scattered across the knoll. *We have a pretty good kill zone if they cooperate.* Creed knew they could delay and disrupt a determined thrust by the Hessians, but they could not stop it.

He summoned Parker, Beall, and the senior Virginian, a sergeant named Sam Debbs. With graying brown hair tied back in a loose queue, Debbs was just over five feet tall but had broad shoulders. At thirty-five, Debbs was older than most of the men. He was a hard-lived laborer whose family had been slaughtered during a French-led Indian raid on their Shenandoah cabin. Hardened by life on the frontier, Debbs had joined the rebellion because he believed it was the right thing to do, and given his circumstances, the only option.

They each took a knee around Creed. "Sergeant Debbs, there is a house fifty yards behind us. Take your best man and position him there."

"Might need him here," Debbs said.

Creed shook his head. "The man you post must warn us of a return of those dragoons, or the enemy garrison from Bordentown."

"And if they come?"

"Have him fire once and then fall in on us."

"Suppose they cut us off?"

"Then we work our way to the river. A trail runs along it— that may be our only escape route."

The taciturn Debbs nodded and stood up. "I'll fetch Private Dean. He'd be our best shot—after me, that is."

Creed grinned.

But Debbs had not intended his remark as humor and looked blankly at him. "I'll get him there right away."

He scurried around the rocks to position Dean near what the locals called the Douglass house.

Creed pulled out his spyglass and zoomed in on Trenton.

* * *

Rall was now desperately trying to position his men where they could fight the rebels on terms that gave them some advantage. He needed to engage the attackers and drive them from Trenton. Despite the initial surprise, he was convinced the Hessian discipline would carry the day.

Ignoring the pain from his wound and the blood staining his tunic, Rall waved his saber towards Trenton and signaled his adjutant, Piel. "We shall take *Die Rebellen* with the bayonet. One good rush and they will break and run. They always do, the scum. Form column of companies and advance!"

Piel, who had seen men cut down by grapeshot from the American guns in the town, was not so confident. "*Herr Oberst*, perhaps we should fight our way to the Assunpink and try to get to the garrison at Bordentown."

Rall's wound and exhaustion affected his judgment, but not his courage. He ignored Piel's plea. "*Vorwaerts! Advance!*"

With years of tradition demanding unquestioning obedience to orders, the Hessian formation began to push forward into the sights of several hundred Continental Line under Hugh Mercer's command. They occupied nearly every building in Trenton and filled the alleys with overlapping fire. The Hessian counterattack would face a barrage of musket balls from the front and grapeshot blasts from the side.

***

Germer also received the order to move to Trenton. But he saw the rebel guns to his right and immediately understood the town was lost. He looked around and saw columns in dark blue with brass miters, and dark green with slouched hats. *These are our best. I won't let them die uselessly.* He rallied a few companies of grenadiers and Jaegers, mustering to join the attack.

Waving his saber, Germer bellowed a countermand to Rall's order. "Grenadiers! Jaegers! Hold fast! Turnabout!"

Moments later, nearly three hundred of Rall's best troops, including his grenadiers and jaegers, were marching quickly toward the Assunpink. Rall and the rest of the brigade would face the rebels' fire without the elite members of his command. However, still wounded and caught up in the fervor of the attack, Rall did not notice.

***

Creed shut his spyglass. "There's a column moving southwest toward the bridge. It will soon present us with a problem, Sergeant Debbs."

"Should we try to warn General Washington?"

Creed shook his head. "No time. And I don't think either General Greene or Sullivan can push forward quickly enough to block the escape route."

"What do we do?"

"We're the only ones between that column and safety." Creed cupped his hands to his mouth. "Listen well, lads. An enemy column fast approaches the bridge — double load. Fire onto the bridge at my command. Repeat fire on your own. Keep your ammo boxes open, you'll need to use every cartridge you can, quickly!"

The dark mass of the Hessian column slithered onto the bridge, the iron nails of their boots striking an eerie rhythm as row after row moved forward.

Marched right into the kill zone. Creed's command broke the cold morning air. "Fire!"

Well-aimed rounds struck the front ranks, taking out half a dozen grenadiers. Unfazed by the volley, the Hessians paused to straighten their ranks and then picked up their pace. Bluecoats and brass miter hats now formed a clear outline against the snowy winter landscape.

The Americans grabbed fresh cartridges from the boxes and, desperately, rammed them home.

Germer bellowed, "*Die Jaeger vorwaerts!* Jaegers forward!"

A pack of Jaegers, expert marksmen in dark green coats and black cocked hats, raced to the head of the formation, plunging through the thin ice crust into the frozen, chest-deep creek.

Parker was the first to spot the new threat. "Lieutenant! Skirmishers! Skirmishers coming at us from the creek!"

"Ignore them! Keep your firelocks on the formation. Fire into the bridge!" Creed's response was tinted with resignation. "If we can't prevent their escape, we shall make them pay dearly to cross the creek!"

The tightly packed column on the narrow bridge became an easy target as Creed's men poured deadly fire into them, sending more Hessians tumbling off the side into the cold creek.

But now, the Jaeger skirmish was in the scrub brush and among the boulders along the near side of the creek. Some of the world's best infantry began peppering Creed's men. Lead balls whistled overhead, snapping tree branches and slapping against the boulders that were providing the Americans with cover. And the column began moving forward again.

Debbs called to Creed over the crack of the muskets, "Mister Creed, more than half the Hessians are across the bridge. We can't stop the rest!"

Creed cupped his hands again and called out over the fire. "All right, lads, one more volley at the bridge, then have at these skirmishers!"

Dean scrambled back from his position and joined in. On Debbs's signal, he rose from behind a boulder to aim at the Hessian officer.

Another volley struck the column. Debb's shot hit Germer in the shoulder. The captain staggered and spun around, holding his wound. One of the musketeers broke ranks and rushed to his aid.

Germer's heavy-gloved fist struck him in the stomach. "Get back into formation, you fool! Your indiscipline will cost you fifty lashes at Bordentown."

Stunned by the blow, the soldier bent over. Gasping for air, he staggered back to the column, which had just cleared the bridge and was now marching toward Bordentown as if on parade.

Germer's feet wobbled, but he gathered his last reserves of strength and discipline. With one hand gripping the bridge's handrail, he waved his saber in the air. "*Die Jaeger zurueck*! "Jaegers fall back!"

Still clutching the handrail desperately, Germer held his position until the last Jaeger cleared the road and rejoined the column as its rearguard. Then, without making a sound, he collapsed with a soft thud onto the frost-covered planking.

Creed thought about sneaking behind the enemy to snipe from the woods. But the sudden loud burst of musket fire from Trenton grabbed his attention. He scrambled onto a boulder high on the knoll to get a better look at the town. He took out his spyglass again and gasped at what he saw.

The main body of Hessians was attempting to charge the Americans. But the Continentals now had the orchard and its occupants nearly surrounded.

Rall, clearly struggling with his wound, was leading the charge. He twisted wildly. Another bullet struck him! Creed saw him clutch his side again and fall out of his saddle. Watching their commander fall before their eyes, company after company of Hessians began to lay down their weapons in surrender.

Creed swung the spyglass south and saw that Sullivan's column had completely cut off the town from the south. "Huzzahing" at the top of their lungs, a company of Sullivan's Continentals was coming toward the bridge at a run. Trenton was now firmly in Washington's hands.

Creed lowered his spyglass, and his tired face gradually broke into a smile. "Sergeant Debbs, call the lads in."

Beall was the first to reach Creed. "What happened, sir?"

Creed felt a surge of joy and relief throughout his body like he'd never experienced before. "It can't be much past nine, yet Jonathan, I believe—His Excellency has just won a miraculous victory."

* * *

With the bridge now secured, Creed and his men went back to Knox's artillery to find Thomas and get their horses.

"How'd it go, Thomas?" Beall asked.

Thomas's mouth creased his face with a wide grin. "I think good. I sure liked pounding those Hessians with those cannonballs."

Sergeant Nicholson strode up. "Thomas performed so well serving with my gun crew that Mister Hamilton plans to enlist him in the battery."

"I don't want to go. But I'm not sure I can say no," Thomas said.

Creed was indignant. "You're not chattel, to be taken." He stormed off to see Hamilton.

The two had words that became so severe it seemed to some who saw it that it would become a matter of honor and end in a duel.

"Your insolence is telling, Mister Creed. If it were not for His Excellency's strict rules, I'd call you out right now."

Creed's eyes narrowed. "Sir, I hope you don't. I've carved better men than you to pieces, and I've shot down more than I dare admit. But this army needs all the artillerymen it can get. So, this will have to wait for another day."

After withstanding a good deal of pressure from the pushy Hamilton, Creed quickly gathered his White Knights and left to report to Washington.

***

As the four trotted off, Hamilton complained to Knox about the Irish officer's cavalier, almost pugnacious manner. Knox grasped his large belly and laughed. "Now, Alexander, I know for a fact that man has done as much to secure this victory as anyone. He's obstinate and determined, but not for himself, for the cause. In any case, he reminds me of a certain artillery officer. Don't you agree?"

Knox laughed so hard his belly shook like a bowl of jelly. The bantam-like Hamilton saw little of the humor and, with a silent scowl, stomped off.

Chapter 31

The Harris House, Newtown, Pennsylvania, December 27th, 1776

Fitzgerald handed Creed the first hot drink he had had in days. Even the stalest coffee tasted great when served steaming hot on a cold December evening. Fitzgerald picked up his meerschaum pipe, packed a small wad of poor-quality tobacco, and lit it with a spark from the fireplace.

"I am sorry, my boy. I have been busy with the prisoners. Well over one thousand we now have counted. Over eighty Germans were killed, and just two of our officers were wounded."

Creed slowly nodded. "I saw Captain Washington and Lieutenant Monroe wounded. They fought well and gave worse to the enemy."

Let's focus on our real business, shall we? I've already spoken with several captured officers. Their colonel, Rall, unfortunately, is on death's door. Interestingly, his pocket had a note from the British General Grant, warning him of a potential rebel attack.

"Thank the Lord his overconfidence worked in our favor."

"This portends something else."

Creed pursed his lips. "You mean…?"

Fitzgerald nodded grimly. "Yes, a spy in our midst. A secret Tory, no doubt."

Creed sipped at this mug again. The taste was bitter, but not as bitter as the thought of a traitor in their midst. "I suppose we shall never know."

The door opened, and General Washington crossed the threshold. Creed and Fitzgerald came to their feet.

"Please, remain seated, gentlemen. I have appointed Lieutenant Scovel to lead the search for our spy, although I suspect he is long gone."

"If the spy is still with the army, sir, Scovel will find him."

Washington ignored the remark. "I need you two to help me determine General Howe's next move."

Fitzgerald pulled the pipe from his mouth. "Most of the officers we interrogated seem to think that Howe will not stir from winter quarters. In that sense, we are safe in our defense of Philadelphia."

Washington removed his cloak and heavy winter gloves and collapsed exhausted into a chair near the fire. He tilted his head back and closed his eyes. "If I could only ascertain that. Our men have achieved a great victory. The numbers involved are small, but the message we sent to our people is grand. At the very moment of its death, this army struck back at the enemy, and in doing so, will revive America's spirits and the cause. Already, the word is spreading throughout the Jerseys, and many are rallying in support of their local militias. When word travels across the land, the people will be heartened.

"Indeed, had Ewing and Cadwalader our same fortune with the crossing, you could have taken Bordentown, even Princeton. Perhaps more," Fitzgerald said.

Washington shook his head ruefully. "But they, alas, did not. Providence's hidden hand."

"Perhaps in the spring, we can try again."

I am convening a war council to decide our next move. Some of our best troops have extended their enlistments until the first of the year. But now I must once again ask for their patience on behalf of the cause. A task I do not take joy in. Until then, I will need your patience as well, Jeremiah. I'm afraid we must ask you and your brave men to brave the elements once more."

Creed politely bowed his head. "Ah, Your Excellency, 'tis forbearance I have enough of. I learned that, as well as sufferance, in the seminary."

Washington and Fitzgerald exchanged knowing looks. Creed raised two fingers to his temple in a small salute. "So, I remain, as always, your humble and obedient servant and delighted to be of service to the cause."

Washington smiled grimly. "Indeed, you shall be, Jeremiah, indeed, you shall. This time you must do so as Root Hog, or should I say Golden Apple?"

Creed looked stunned. Before he could respond, Fitzgerald removed his meerschaum pipe from his mouth and held it up like a teacher's pointer. "I was just getting to that point, Jeremiah."

"What point was that, sir?" Creed swallowed the dregs of the coffee, the bitter grains grinding his tongue.

"Now that your friend, this Sergeant Digby, or rather his Major Drummond, wants you, or should I say, Root Hog, to act as a go-between for Golden Apple, the time to oblige him may have arrived."

Creed appeared upset, as he indeed was. "Sir, I am not so sure I see what we will gain by playing this game of cat and mouse. With Roy Harry's Swamp Rangers, I have established a solid network across New Jersey. They will keep watch on the enemy through the winter. Isn't that enough?"

"The flow of the campaign and the season precludes sensible communications with them, and besides, all they can do is observe from afar and report." Fitzgerald's tone seemed indifferent.

Creed bristled. "You do these men a disservice, sir! Harry's men run great risk spying behind British lines in a land swarming with Tory informants and Loyalist cowboys."

"Valuable enough, but for later. And only if we can truly trust Roy Harry. Do you trust him, Mister Creed?" Washington looked into Creed's eyes.

"I do have trust in him, sir. 'Tis confidence I lack. That can only come with time. But I believe he will prove invaluable."

Fitzgerald puffed on his pipe. "I am glad to hear you say that, young man. We received a packet from General Heath late yesterday. It contained our first report from

Mister Harry. The information is a week old, and much has changed since then, but the papers in the Hackensack Valley report that Howe intends on staying in New York through the winter and is busy making plans for the social season."

Creed beamed. His pride in Harry was evident in his face. "So, the Swamp Rangers have already made some progress in their intelligence gathering."

Fitzgerald looked blankly at him.

Creed did not like the look. "Is there something else, sir?"

Drawing a deep breath, Fitzgerald intertwined his fingers. "It appears several senior officers are returning to Britain for the winter. Suspicions are that Cornwallis may be one of them. Or so Harry's purloined copy of *Rivington's Gazette* indicated. The New Jersey Volunteers are still aggressively recruiting, Harry also reports."

"I see, sir. Well, 'tis no surprise, really. I heard as much myself."

Fitzgerald shifted slightly. "I have other concerns, Jeremiah. What was the true nature of Jannetje's connection to the odious General Lee? And was his capture a mistake by an overly scheming knave, or the start of a deeper British plot?"

Creed paused to reflect. "Her connection to Lee was born of a previous assignation, which the British and Tories learned of and exploited. Lee craved attention more than gold. Surely, he chafed at his subordinate role in the army. But his arrogance led to most of his scheming. As to whether he is or was a spy, I'm not even sure Lee knows the answer to that."

"At this juncture, it may make no difference," Fitzgerald said.

Washington nodded. "I respected Charles Lee's expertise on things military. But I was more than vexed by his self-serving ways. Spy or no, his removal from the scene has proven a boon to the cause, and that is all that matters right now."

Washington's eyes seemed to drift far away. "You see, what this army accomplished here is only the beginning. Not necessarily the beginning of our victory over the British, but the beginning of our hope for victory. However, I intend to give this nation much more than hope."

Fitzgerald forced a wry smile at Creed. "Meanwhile, Jeremiah, you and your men have a full day to rest and enjoy the pleasures of Newtown."

Washington shifted from a business-like demeanor to casual banter, "Speaking of hope, I understand one of Henry Knox's officers tried to wrest that young Black man from your services."

"He tried."

"A compliment indeed! Alexander Hamilton is no easy taskmaster. Nor is he easy to defeat in matters of internecine warfare. Yet Knox says you did not back down to the young blood. Bravo, my boy."

Creed's face turned crimson. "Your Excellency, I assure you the altercation, such as it was, was brief and pointed, but…"

"But what?" Fitzgerald chided.

"I know His Excellency's order proscribes it, but I would have taken it as far as a duel if need be. Thomas will remain a White Knight as long as I am breathing."

"Now really, Jeremiah, dueling with a captain?" Washington smiled.

Creed was thunderstruck. "Captain Hamilton, sir? I would not have been so blunt with a superior officer. Determined, yes, but blunt, no. I thought he was a lieutenant, you know, like me."

"Henry repeated some of your blunt words to me, Jeremiah, and yes, he was a lieutenant, but he has just been named to the captain's list and will, in short, join my staff as an aide-de-camp."

Creeds rolled his eyes, then smiled. "Well, 'tis a good thing my words did not lead to anything more serious, as the army needs all the good captains it can get."

Washington and Fitzgerald laughed. Creed tried to excuse himself. He stood and was about to leave.

Fitzgerald stopped him. "One last thing, Jeremiah. I had almost forgotten. There was a second letter Harry sent in the packet. It was addressed to Mister Root Hog Burns, Hackensack, New Jersey. It has no return address."

Creed took the envelope from Fitzgerald and carefully opened it, then closed it quickly. "I shall read this later, sir, thank you."

"What is it, Jeremiah?" Fitzgerald asked. "Or should I say Root Hog?"

"Minor details on the Swamp Rangers. Harry has some questions, that's all." Creed bowed and left, quickly closing the door behind him.

***

"It soon will be necessary to send the White Knights out again, Your Excellency," Fitzgerald said.

Washington's lips tightened. It was time to unfold things. "As you know, it appears our victory bagged a Hessian brigade at the cost of a handful of casualties. There will be much cursing in London and in Kassel when the news arrives."

"Indeed, sir. A bargain…"

"A bargain, yes, but not quite what I am willing to settle for. Mister Creed and his men did well for us tactically, but I need them to play a bigger role strategically."

"Exactly how, sir?"

"Exactly how, only time will tell."

Fitzgerald pulled the pipe from his mouth and gazed pensively. "I shall prepare the plan. Once you approve it, I'll issue his instructions. I shall try to include the necessity for some of his famed luck, to boot."

Washington grinned. Despite the fortitude and stamina shown by all his men and officers, he knew very well the role fortune played in their success. "Indeed, Robert, perhaps now it is time to make some luck. But perhaps this time, some Yankee luck."

* * *

Creed strolled through the town until he spotted a small coffeehouse with a light glowing inside. He settled into a quiet corner and nervously tore open the envelope. By the flickering candlelight, he read and re-read the letter. It wasn't from Harry at all.

S.W. O'Connell

The Stanley House
New York
December 12th, 1776

My Dear Root Hog,

I wanted to take a small risk and thank you and your men for all the help you provided me in New York. I honor your commitment to your Cause – the King needs more good Cowboys like you if we are ever to stamp out this horrible Rebellion. Things in the City are awful right now. The Fire caused by the
Rebels destroyed so much and left so many people Refugees in their own City. Fortunately, Mister Cunningham's good Provosts are cracking down hard on anyone suspected of rebellion.
Father is home, now that our good Gen. Howe has returned and begun the process of establishing Winter Quarters. I shall be very busy until Springtime. It seems our House will have its fill of officer Boarders while the Army winters here. There will be at least a Brigade garrisoning the City and the rest of the Army quartered on Stn Isl, the Brnswcks, etc. They might well need of your good Services in trade goods and especially wood.
Mister Root Hog, I want you to know that my Esteem for you and all you do is unabated and will ever endure no matter how long this War. No man has more bravely served a more noble Cause. I hope so much that we achieve Victory very soon, so that good Britons can lead their lives again in peace. Would that bring you back to this forlorn City would make Victory all the sweeter!
And never forget… no matter where or how far you travel in your duties, sleep comfortably knowing that I look forward to such a Peace that brings us once more into an intimate acquaintance. I hold my dearest Friend in the fondest Esteem and regard him with the most fervent Affection.

With my warmest Thoughts,
I remain fervently, fondly, and eternally yours
E. Stanley

Creed's steady gaze lingered over the letter multiple times, each reading revealing a new nuance in her words. Emily took a bold and unexpected, if not unwelcome, risk by sending him a message, disguised as a business letter to a loyal British subject. He couldn't reply in writing, and there was no way to know if he would return to the city before the war ended. *Why did she send it? To affirm their feelings?*

He downed the coffee dregs from the cup. It tasted cold and sour, ironically reflecting his mood. Usually, he would be happy to receive any missive from a beautiful woman, especially one he… Creed would not let himself even think the words. *Times are too dangerous.* His duties, if they did not outright result in his death, still precluded romantic entanglements.

Creed read the letter a fifth time, and suddenly a thought struck him. Yes, Emily used the letter to express her feelings indirectly, but she did more than that. The report on events in New York might prove useful, and indeed, the passage about the officers at the house offered... *offered what?*

Creed looked up from the paper and smiled. If the war lasted through the winter, Emily was giving him an opportunity. He folded the letter into a loose roll and carefully placed it over the flame of a nearby candle. He memorized her words as he watched the parchment quickly catch fire and consume itself in a small plume of smoke that seemed to engulf him with her presence.

* * *

British Headquarters, New Brunswick, New Jersey, December 27th, 1776
Major General James Grant, commander of the British forces occupying central New Jersey, was awakened from a midday nap. The news enraged him, turning the fat officer's bull-like face bright red and causing his drooping jowls to shake like pieces of fresh liver. His initial disbelief and anxiety were quickly replaced by Grant's practical side, which got to work. Orders were sent to the other posts at Princeton, Burlington, and Bordentown, as well as to the numerous small detachments scattered in a wide arc from central to south Jersey. After that, Grant sat quietly to a sullen midday meal with his staff.

One of his aides, a subaltern, broke the silence. "Do you think the rebel attack on Trenton portends a renewed vigor by a beaten foe, sir?"

Grant shook his head. "The surprise inflicted by the Americans was caused not so much by their enterprise and daring as by the unimaginative defense of the Hessians. Rall failed to act on the intelligence I provided him with. I indicated as much in my dispatch to General Howe."

"Has General Howe responded, sir?" a light infantry major asked.

"No, but he knows of the defeat and likely new orders are on the way."

"What are your plans in the meantime, sir?"

"I'll spend the afternoon inspecting the defenses around Brunswick. You must ensure the supply columns and messengers have adequate security. We need to fend off the rebel militia activity, which is increasing by the day."

A doleful look crossed the subaltern's face. "I suppose now the prospect of a peaceful and comfortable season in winter quarters seems more and more out of reach."

Grant merely grunted.

* * *

The afternoon was busy as Grant made his rounds, checking men and weapons past dusk. He finally dismounted at eight in the evening. Handing his horse to an orderly, he strutted into his headquarters to read the dispatch he expected from Howe. Instead of the dispatch, he found Major Sandy Drummond sitting at a small table near the fire. Drummond, writing hurriedly on a piece of notepaper, saw the general out of the corner of his eye but kept writing.

Grant just stood there, staring dumbfounded at Drummond.

His page finished, he methodically cleaned the nib and placed it in its case with the ink well. Only then did Drummond stand to greet the general.

When the major came to his feet, Grant affected a thick burr to his fellow Scot, "I didna expect ye here, Sandy. Did Howe send ye? Did he take the news of Trenton badly? 'Tis the fault of those damned Germans, I ken."

Drummond paused thoughtfully before responding to his senior officer. The two shared bonds of nationality and loyalty. Both were Lowland Scots, loyal to the king and the army. Additionally, Drummond's father served with Grant in the French and Indian War. Grant was by his side when the elder Drummond fell in combat. Still, both knew this defeat at Trenton put the army, their careers, and the colonies at risk.

"When I received word of the German defeat at Trenton, I rode straightway from Amboy, sir. I dinna ken what General Howe's reaction might be. But I can imagine. He was quite proud of driving the rebels from the Jerseys. Expected to pick up thousands of new Loyalists and finish Washington and his cronies in the spring."

Grant rolled his eyes as he took off his riding gloves and sank into an overstuffed chair near the fire. "I see. Well, I can tell ye this, Sandy. Coddling rebels and traitors is no policy. They all need a swift kick— then give them the scaffold! And I'm just the man to do it. I was hoping orders would already be here, releasing me for action."

Despite their long-standing relationship, Drummond thought little of Grant as an officer or a general. He was unimaginative, arrogant, and conceited. He stared coldly at Grant, who sat before him like some troll king on a throne.

"General Grant, there is no evading yer responsibility as commander of this division and the outposts. Your longevity in command may now be in question. I rode down here out of respect and concern for you and our long-standing connection. However, unless you heed me, you may well become William Howe's scapegoat for this affair."

Grant choked, and his small eyes widened in agitation. "Na way! Why I…" He lifted his stocky frame from the chair and wiggled over to a small cabinet near his desk. With fingers trembling, he extracted a bottle of Scotch whisky. He poured each of them a glass, three fingers deep, of the soft brown liquid.

The two men stood silently as they sipped the sweet, peat-flavored beverage.

Grant's droopy eyes narrowed, accentuating his bulldog look. "What exactly do ye propose, Sandy?"

"Louis Swindells must take the blame for this defeat. He failed to produce intelligence to warn us of the possibility of attack."

Grant exploded. "But we had a member of the rebel camp provide us with a warning, which I expressly sent to Rall!"

Drummond's mouth widened, and he pensively ran his index finger around the rim of his glass. "Seems Rall ignored it, sir, or came to believe the information was false."

Grant's evident anger was now turning into despair. "We may never know for certain, Sandy. They say he fell mortally wounded at Trenton. The bastard will never face a court-martial. And now that colonial, Washington, may find our spy."

"Not necessarily, sir. Besides, I've recruited more than one spy. One is well placed, I believe, among the rebels. The problem has been communication. Despite his obvious incompetence, Swindells somehow stumbled on a cowboy, those rascals who plunder in the name of the crown, who have had some success moving across the lines."

"What use have ye for a-a cowboy?"

"He shall be our conduit. We need to find out what Washington will do next."

Grant poured a second glass, this time just for himself. He eased back into his chair and smiled. "Frankly, Sandy, I am more interested in what our commander will do next."

"Regardless, I propose you take action to reprimand Swindells and Rall, too — posthumously, of course. Swindells must be removed. And, whatever officer you select to oversee your intelligence must take direction from me. No questions asked."

Grant startled. "Well, this is highly irregular, Sandy, and..."

Drummond's voice hardened. "Sir, I should say it is a small price to pay to deflect what I believe will be some harsh criticism against you."

Grant nodded. "Ahh... very well. Ye may be right, Sandy. I will send a dispatch to General Leslie."

Drummond began rubbing his knee. "And I will send one to General Howe, confirming that Rall was forewarned. Do you know the name of the agent who brought you the warning?"

Grant stared blankly. "No. And I have na way of contacting him. I think he was a low-placed staff officer who decided to come over with the rebel plans. Just a deserter, ye know — an opportunist."

"All spies are opportunists, General."

"All Americans are opportunists... He left a note. A dragoon patrol found it. Likely, he has returned to his home, as I doubt anyone so cowardly would return to the rebels after that."

Drummond stiffened. "Well, sir, if he had worked for me, he would. If ye get an inkling, sir, as to who he is or where he is, please let me know. I need to build a network of informants so we can box the rebels in the spring."

"I don't care much for the spy business, Sandy. I'm a simple soldier."

Drummond held back a smile. "That, ye are, sir. You'll have little enough to do. I have a good man I want to appoint as an intelligence officer in this region."

"And the catch, Sandy? I know there is one."

"He shall support the garrisons but work for me."

Grant raised his glass and stared into it. "I see. Who is he? Another dragoon officer?"

"No. He is an American, sir. A Loyalist captain by the name of Sidney Baker."

"Are ye daft, man? The army cannot have a colonial in such a post."

Drummond's eyes narrowed. "Can and shall, sir. He is efficient, experienced, and has shed some blood for the king. He knows the rebels, and he knows this land and..."

Grant's eyes glared at him. "And what, Sandy?"

He returned the glare. "He is loyal to me. It is both our interests that the intelligence officer here in the Jerseys be loyal to me."

Grant shrugged. "Very well, Sandy. God knows I have little interest in such matters."

Epilogue

Newtown, Pennsylvania, December 28th, 1776

Colonel Robert Fitzgerald fought the fatigue that wracked his body. The recent victory energized him as it did the entire Continental Army. Most of the men and officers thought they were done for the year. But he knew his work had just begun. He stretched his achy fingers and began to dip the nib of his quill into the icy black ink.

Summary of Intelligence Activities and Concerns

Your Excellency,

Despite our perseverance against the best efforts of Mother Nature and our recent Success with regard to the Grmns at Trenton, the campaign season may not yet be over. Militia along the Del. R. have reprtd no sign as yet of a Cntr-stroke. In addition, only a few stray sightings of Tory Scouts. Yet, withal, I cannot fathom that our other Frnds in Brdentwn and points east have completely gone to ground.

Concerning the White Knights, the Success of their activities underscores the need to expand our horizons, and as you have indicated on more than one occasion, use them in a more Strtgc fashion. Having said that, there yet may be times when they can more usefully obtain more local intelligence than our usual line crossers, Sntrs, Miltias, and Scts.

Of immediate concern is the Enemy reaction to your recent Vctry. I assure you that every Effort shall be taken to ascertain this.

More Strtgiclly, we shall make strenuous Effrts to ascertain Loyalt vs. Patrt Strength in the Jerseys, with particular attention in those Areas extending from the Highlands to the Sandy Hook. To that end, the Whte Knghts must, at some point this winter, recnnect with the Swmp.Rngs'.

Lastly, we must commence efforts to determine Howe's spring intentions, should he indeed remain in winter quarters.

As no public display of Approbation can be extended these Gentlemen, I want to take this opportunity to commend the Whte Knghts to Your Excellency and enter their recent success into our Scrt Rcrd.

I Remain as Always,
Your Most Humble and Obedient Servant -

R. Fitzgerald

* * *

Johnson's Livery & Stable, Newtown, Pennsylvania, December 27th, 1776

The door swung open, and Creed led Finn in by the halter. The large whitewashed wooden building housed the Continental Army's couriers. These express riders carried messages between Washington and General William Heath in New York, to the Congress (now in Baltimore), and to several key militia leaders and state capitals.

Thomas, during his wandering around headquarters, shrewdly realized that the express riders always had the best supply of feed for their horses. Feed, as well as shoes, nails, and tack—things hard to find in an army where men had little food and even less clothing and shelter.

Of course, it helped that most of the grooms and stable hands were Black, many of whom were around Thomas's age. Before long, he had made the acquaintance of several and, through them, found everything needed for Finn and the other mounts, as well as provisions for the White Knights.

Creed's men were about to start on a simple broth with buckwheat dumplings washed down with rum. Joining them, Creed took off his gloves, mantle, and boots and sat on Finn's saddle, digging into his tin bowl with relish. They ate silently, huddling from the cold wind gusting through the gaps in the wooden plank walls.

When they finished, Beall cast a quick glance at his officer. "Lieutenant, do you think we'll get any rest if the British stay in winter quarters? I'd like a furlough home to check on my cousin Simon. With some fast riding, I could make it to Frederick and back in less than two weeks."

Creed took a sip of the rum and tilted his head back in thought, trying to figure out a way to soften the impact of refusing such a simple request. His men had fought with great bravery and dedication, while thousands returned home after their enlistments ended, and many even before their enlistments expired.

"Well, the fact of it is, Jonathan, should leave be granted, it would go first to Elias, as he has a family. That is, a wife and baby await him."

"Let Jonathan go, sir," Parker said. "If I went home to them I…"

"What?" Creed knew the answer full well.

"I might not find it in me to return, sir."

"And who could blame you? No, I believe you would do your duty on that account. But the point is moot."

"How do you mean moot, sir?" Parker asked.

"Well, for one thing, I suspect the British will not go into winter quarters quite yet."

"Why not, sir?" Beall asked.

Creed sipped at the rum. "I reckon His Excellency has awakened their ire."

"But, sir, we caught them in winter quarters at Trenton," Parker insisted. "Now they're sure to hunker down and try to wait out the winter."

Creed shook his head. "That, my dear Elias, is speculation. And the White Knights, I'm afraid, might be the only thing standing between His Excellency and such speculation."

Parker swallowed his rum and tossed the cup. "What do you mean, sir?"

Beall stared blankly into his cup. "I think I know."

Creed threw back his head and finished his rum, then leaned forward. "Another mission, lads. We are the White Knights now. Cavaliers, of a sort. While others rest and refurbish or return to their hearths and homes, we must seek information for His Excellency. Get some rest while you can, for soon — we ride."

- The End -

Author's Notes

General George Washington's autumn of defeat and retreat concluded with a surprise attack and victory as winter approached. Although the victory involved few men, it carried great symbolic significance for both sides. It made the British and Loyalists hesitate and offered hope to a patriot cause that was nearly defeated and in financial ruin during its darkest hour.

More importantly, it provided the stimulus for some of his best men to remain beyond their term, at least for a few precious weeks. As it turned out, it was a precious few weeks that became the razor's edge of survival or defeat for the cause.

Although Washington's use of his intelligence resources was critical to his success, he needed to make it even better if he were to win the war. When Congress approved the establishment of several new continental regiments, two of which would be dragoon regiments, Washington decided he would carve a new operational intelligence unit out of one.

Washington foresaw this critical need and placed it on par with his need for munitions, supplies, and even combat troops. He knew this special troop of dragoons would play a special role in waging the kind of war he saw unfolding. In that troop, each dragoon would become a cavalier spy.

Jeremiah Creed and his comrades are fictional characters, as is Colonel Fitzgerald. A Lieutenant Colonel John Fitzgerald did serve with Washington's staff—I'll let the reader decide if there is a connection. Of course, Nathanael Greene, Henry Knox, Lord Stirling, and Sullivan all played important roles in the campaign. The story of Captain Nathan Hale is well known.

Few casual observers of the Revolutionary War era realize the destruction inflicted on New York by the great and mysterious fire that consumed one-third of the city. Its origin remains a subject of speculation, although Washington's conflicting views on a scorched earth policy are well documented. In any case, most have consigned it to the dustbin of history, but it was arguably the city's greatest wartime disaster until September 11th, 2001.

The events described here—Washington's defeat in New York, followed by his defeat and subsequent victory in New Jersey—are all historical events, with some artistic embellishments to enhance the story. For example, there were no Scorpions in the British Navy (to the author's knowledge).

The residents of the fictional hamlet of Ridley and the Hackensack Valley are entirely fictional. However, some characters may resemble real people from the area. The internecine fight among the Dutch factions in the valley is well documented and reflects the larger conflict between Tories and Whigs-Loyalists and Patriots. Abraham van Buskirk was a real person and did command the 4th New Jersey Volunteers in His Majesty's service. The other characters are fictional, although I used authentic Dutch names from that period.

Cowboys and skinners roamed the no man's land between the armies, engaging in marauding, skirmishing, and plunder to support their masters and pursue their own goals. Roy Harry and his Swamp Rangers offer a fictional look at this phenomenon, as do Root Hog Burns and his cowboys.

General Howe, Lord Cornwallis, Grant, and Leslie all played vital roles in the campaign, as did Johann Rall of the Hessians. Colonel Harcourt of the 16th Light Dragoons and Lieutenant Banastre Tarleton successfully carried out the raid at Basking Ridge, which led to the surprise capture of Major General Charles Lee. However, Sandy Drummond and his crew are fictional.

Finally, the irascible Charles Lee and his unruly pack of hounds, unfortunately for the American cause, did exist. He competed with Washington for high command and power and certainly aimed to replace Washington at the earliest chance. Why he left his command on that cold December only to fall easily into British hands remains a subject of historical speculation. I choose to imagine an ulterior motive.

About the Author

S W. O'Connell holds degrees in History (Fordham University) and International Relations (University of Southern California). He is a retired US Army intelligence officer who spent most of his service in the field of counterintelligence. Most of his time was spent overseas in US Army Europe and Allied Command Europe, but he does admit to a tour in the Pentagon and a stint at the John F. Kennedy Center for Special Warfare at Fort Bragg.

A native New Yorker, S. W. O'Connell settled in northern Virginia when he returned from his last overseas tour with the US Army. His long-held love of history made it only natural that he would turn to the historical novel when he finally succumbed to a decades-long urge to craft fiction.

The Cavalier Spy is book two in his acclaimed Yankee Doodle Spies series.

www.ingramcontent.com/pod-product-compliance
Lightning Source LLC
Chambersburg PA
CBHW031103260626
47172CB00001B/199